BURN
THIS
NIGHT

Also available by Alex Kenna

What Meets the Eye

BURN THIS NIGHT

A NOVEL

ALEX KENNA

CROOKED
LANE

NEW YORK

Copyright © 2024 by Alix McKenna

Published in the United States by Crooked Lane Books, an imprint of The Quick Brown Fox & Company LLC.

Crooked Lane Books and its logo are trademarks of The Quick Brown Fox & Company LLC.

Library of Congress Catalog-in-Publication data available upon request.

ISBN (hardcover): 978-1-63910-937-1
ISBN (ebook): 978-1-63910-938-8

Cover design by Heather VenHuizen

Printed in the United States.

www.crookedlanebooks.com

Crooked Lane Books
34 West 27th St., 10th Floor
New York, NY 10001

First Edition: November 2024

10 9 8 7 6 5 4 3 2 1

To DW,
for continuing to put up with so much

PROLOGUE

Eight months ago—Grace

MY EYES SHOT open when I heard the yelping. Barney was going to wake the baby. I dove toward the old dog, grabbed his snout, and held it closed with both hands. "Shh," I pleaded.

I lowered one hand and rubbed Barney's back, trying to calm him. He let out a whine, and like clockwork, Liam started to cry. I closed my eyes, sucked in a deep breath, and braced myself for another late-night nursing session. My body felt heavy with milk and stress and exhaustion.

Carefully, I scooped up the howling baby, carried him over to the rocking chair, and lifted my T-shirt to feed him. Liam quieted down and nestled against me. I sniffed his hair and stroked his cheek as we rocked back and forth. Part of me wanted to stay like this all night. But a bigger part of me longed to be under the covers, passed out in a warm oblivion.

I heard the shower turn on down the hall. Ted must be back from serving his warrant. A few months ago, he'd gotten smart with a lieutenant, who then started feeding him late-night assignments. These frequent absences were brutal now that I was back from maternity leave and needed sleep to function at work.

Barney whined again and clawed at the bedroom door. Clutching Liam, I rose to let the dog out of the room.

I looked down at the baby, who was asleep and making little cat-like snores. With slow, deliberate steps, I made my way toward the crib and lowered him until his back rested against the fabric. But the change in angle caused his eyes to open and his lungs to inflate. Then came the cry—and Barney ran back to the bedroom, joining Liam in a horrible wailing duet. I reached out toward the dog and felt wet fur. *Damn it*—Barney must have peed in the house. Hot tears ran down my cheeks. What I wouldn't give for *one night's sleep*.

The door opened and Ted walked in with a towel around his waist. "I need help," I snapped.

"What?" asked Ted, surprised by my tone.

My eyes were closed, and I was crying. But Ted couldn't see that in the dark. He just sensed the anger in my voice. I knew it wasn't his fault that the baby wouldn't sleep, that the dog couldn't hold it, and that his boss was a jerk. But I'd reached my limit, and Ted was the only living being in earshot who understood human language.

"Barney peed in the house. Take Liam so I can let the dog out before he does it again. Just try to get him back to sleep." I placed the screaming, wriggling infant in Ted's arms before either of them could protest.

Flipping on the hall light, I made my way to the kitchen. Barney scampered ahead of me, spinning in circles. I threw on Ted's faded hoodie. It reeked of old sweat, but I was too tired to care. I hooked Barney's leash to his collar and, bracing myself for the cold, I unlocked the back door and stepped outside.

The Santa Anas blew hard, and I shivered as cold air soaked through the hoodie's weave. I could hear the Jeffrey pines rustle in the wind. Thrusting my hands into the central pocket, I rubbed them together for warmth.

A smoky odor hung in the air—maybe the residue of a neighbor's barbecue dinner. But the wind should have blown away the scent by now.

Barney tugged at his leash. I let him drag me toward the street. Now that we were outside, he wouldn't be satisfied without a walk, and it might clear my head as well.

The sky was lighter than I'd expected. Idlewood doesn't have streetlights. It's a conscious decision to preserve the log-cabins-in-the-woods feel of the place. Darkness adds to the storybook charm, and it can be hard to find your way on moonless nights. But the sky had an orange-gray glow that reminded me of LA smog. Maybe it was later than I thought, almost morning.

Barney tugged on his leash again, half-dragging me up the road toward the intersection. He seemed agitated, and I wondered what had gotten into him. As we passed the Hernandez's place, our footsteps activated the motion sensor, and the automatic light above their garage snapped on with an electric hum.

I noticed something floating in the air. Tiny particles, like gray snow or dryer lint. The flecks danced in the air, and Barney snapped at one as it fluttered toward his jaws. The smell of smoke was growing stronger.

Oh my God.

Clutching Barney's leash, I ran the rest of the way to the cross street, which cut straight to the mountain. High in the pines, I saw an orange glow—luminous against the dark sky. My vision tunneled, and all I could see was the fire on the hillside. The light was near Abby's cabin. But I couldn't tell how near.

I grabbed my phone and scanned my recent calls, but it had been weeks since I'd spoken to my sister, and her name didn't pop up. I pulled up my contact list and clicked on her name. After four rings, a cheerful recording prompted me to leave a message. *Maybe she's already fled.* No, Abby would've called if she were awake. She might hate me, but she'd warn me about a wildfire.

I called back, praying that her cell wasn't on silent. *Come on Abby, answer the phone.* When I heard the prerecorded message again, I started to panic. I left a voicemail: "Abby, it's Grace. There's a fire by your cabin—you need to leave *now!*"

The orange glow was getting bigger as the Santa Anas blew the flames toward Idlewood. It was how I'd always imagined an erupting volcano would look, with lava flowing down its sides. I called Abby a third time, cursing under my breath. Across the street, a door opened, and an old man stepped outside, holding a little white dog. "There's a fire!" he shouted.

I looked at him and then back at the mountain, ringing phone pressed against my ear. *Dammit, Abby, pick up!* "My son works at the fire station," said the man. "They're about to put out an alert. We have to evacuate. The whole town could burn."

"My sister's cabin is on the hillside, and she's not answering," I shouted. "Can you call your son and tell him someone's up there?"

I heard a chime and looked down at my phone. It was a text from the fire department, ordering us to leave Idlewood. But my feet stayed planted. My sister was on that mountain, with nothing but a narrow dirt road leading down to safety. If the fire overtook the path, she'd be trapped.

"Jeffrey, it's Pop," I heard the old man say. "There's a lady here whose sister has a cabin near the fire."

Hearing those words unleashed a fresh wave of panic. Abby's cheerful answering machine message sounded for a fifth time in my ear. "Abby, get out of there!" I screamed into the phone.

"We have to go," said the neighbor. "This thing could spread faster than they can contain it."

My phone chimed and I looked down at the screen, hoping to see Abby's name, but it was a voicemail from Ted. Before I could call him back, a text flashed across my screen: *FIRE—COME HOME NOW*

I looked back and forth from my screen to the mountain. My sister was up there. But my husband and son were at the house. I couldn't wait any longer. I tugged at Barney's leash and ran home.

1

Present—Kate

I WAS IN MY ninth week of sleeping on an air mattress in my childhood bedroom when I learned that my dad wasn't my biological father.

The plan was to live with my mom until I could afford a custody fight with my ex-husband. I'd rented out my dinky LA tear-down on Airbnb and was saving every penny for a lawyer. It's amazing what people will pay to stay in what's essentially a dump in a trendy location. Hopefully after six months, I'd have enough money to take my ex to court and get my kid back. Amelia, my daughter, lives with her father, and I'm relegated to every other weekend—never mind how that all came about. It's been this way for two years, and now I was in a different place, a different state of mind, and ready to fight to change the arrangement. But living at home and opening my house to a parade of strangers was turning into a nightmare.

My mom and I don't have a ton in common. She's a neat freak who collects ceramic clowns and binge watches Hallmark Christmas movies. I'm a pathologically messy ex-cop-turned-private-eye with flaming ADHD. Funny, while growing up, I used to wonder if I was adopted, because I've always been the quirky one with a dark sense of humor, who none of my relatives could relate to. So when I learned by accident that I'm genetically different from half my family, it was literally finding the answer to a question I'd never had the words to ask.

How it made me feel was something I don't think I could describe if my life depended on it. I couldn't eat. I couldn't sleep. I'd be doing something routine, like emptying the dishwasher, and it would suddenly hit me. I'd have to brace myself as my vision blurred and my heart pounded like I'd just run a marathon.

It started with a hunt for a coffee maker, of all things. My mom swears by this instant stuff that tastes like muddy water with bits of gravel mixed in. I'd bought her a real percolator for Christmas, which she never took out of the box. But after two months of drinking rehydrated sludge from an ancient plastic mug, I decided to search the garage for the coffee machine.

I waited until she was distracted watching *The Voice*. My mom doesn't like it when I poke around in her things. But I knew she'd take offense if I brought up the subpar caffeine issue. And there was no point starting a fight over something so trivial. As a trio of insanely good-looking siblings performed a folk rendition of "Seven Bridges Road," I snuck out the kitchen door to the garage.

Both side walls were covered in floor-to-ceiling shelving that my dad had built about a year before he died. Each row was deep and double-stacked with boxes, and you often had to move things around to find what you wanted. I started with the boxes closest to the washing machine, and pulled out a set of family albums. Behind them, I noticed a plastic bin labeled "Doctor Metcalf." I knew the physicians who treated my dad when he was sick, and the name Metcalf didn't sound familiar. Maybe it had to do with my mom's health. She never shares anything bad that's going on in her life. In the back of my head, there's always a nagging worry that she could get sick and hide it from me. It would be just like her.

I pulled the box forward and opened it. Resting on top was a yellowing brochure from a fertility clinic. *A fertility clinic?* Curious, I lifted it, having no idea that I'd just opened Pandora's box. Underneath the brochure was a pile of documents, stained and crinkled with age. I picked up a set of records and saw, with a chill, that they were dated the year before I was born.

The door to the garage opened, and I turned around to see my mother. "What are you doing out here?" she asked. "I thought you were folding clothes."

"I was looking for the coffee machine," I said, my voice sounding funny even to me. "The one I got you. Mom, why do you have this? From a fertility clinic?"

Her eyes locked on the box in front of me. "You should have asked me if you needed something. I don't want you mixing everything up." My mother stared at the paper in my hand for several agonizing seconds and then let out a long sigh. "You'd better come inside."

I followed her into the kitchen, where she poured me a cup of sludge and proceeded to blow my mind. It wasn't an unusual story. My parents wanted kids. After years of trying, they decided to get a little help. The only remarkable thing about it was that I'd been kept in the dark for almost four decades. I had many, many questions, but once my mom had said her piece, she had no interest in discussing it further. For her, the subject was closed.

For me, my world had just turned upside down.

The next day, I tried to confront her again, but she wouldn't go there. As a family, we've always been on the repressed side. Poignant heart-to-hearts are not our style. But this revelation wasn't something I could stuff in a box. Part of my core had been ripped away. *My dad was not my dad—and I had no idea whose blood was coursing through my veins.* And this meant that the family history I'd grown up with was basically a lie. Pieces of my character were now clues that I'd never really belonged. No one in my family shared my sloppiness or my focus problems. Both my parents were deeply religious, but I've always been agnostic. Even little things, like my love of antiques and spicy food, seemed to have come out of nowhere.

Now I knew why.

After a couple more attempts to talk about it with my mother, I stopped pushing. I was starting to feel like a bully. But I had nowhere to stuff my anger and sense of betrayal. I couldn't scream at her—an older woman who kept mum about something that was taboo in her day. Something she probably viewed as a sin. I couldn't talk to my dad about it, ask him if I was the daughter he'd wanted, tell him I couldn't have loved him more if I'd been his genetic child. And why *didn't* he tell me? Had he been worried that I'd pull away if I knew the truth? That it would have ruined our relationship? I didn't know, but the fact that I'd never get a chance to reassure him broke my heart.

Who could I tell this to? I thought about my friends—Jenny and Rachel. But I couldn't just call them up and say, *"By the way, I just found out my dad isn't my dad."* It's not a topic for casual conversation, and not one I could have over the phone.

Instead, I let it fester. The tension between my mother and me magnified all her little nags about laundry or putting the peanut butter back on the wrong shelf, until I wanted to tear my hair out.

My daughter came over that weekend, which forced us to play nice. We made cookies and steamed vegetables smothered in melted cheese and watched thirty-year-old Disney VHS tapes. But when not in a heated board game, Nana and I barely spoke.

When Monday rolled around, Amelia went back to her father's house, and I felt totally alone. The tension with my mother was only part of it. Growing up, my dad's personality had filled the house. He'd been dead for two and a half years, but I still felt like he might walk through the door, kiss my mom on the cheek, and flop down on the couch. I felt his presence when I sat at the kitchen table. I saw him when my eyes traveled across the yellowing lawn he once took pride in maintaining. I thought of him when I cleaned out the gutters. My dad used to have me hold the ladder while he pulled out handfuls of sticks and dried leaves. Climbing the ladder as an adult, I understood that my seven-year-old strength had made no difference. My dad was just trying to make me feel like a good helper. That realization made my chest tighten. I wanted to cry and scream all at the same time, and I didn't know what to do with this feeling.

Now, a formerly joyful home housed two sad, silent women. And that was where I had to process the news that my dad and I shared no genetic link. Not to mention the fact that he had lied to me for decades. I couldn't be mad at him: he was dead. So all my anger fell on my mother. I wanted so badly to yell and say things I knew I'd regret. Instead, I retreated to my childhood room, which my dad had painted pink when I was five years old; closed the door; and buried myself in work.

I was a private investigator, and had been for a year and a half, since leaving my job as a police detective for various reasons I don't like to go into—a car crash, some painkillers, spinal fusion, all of which are linked to the reason my ex has primary custody of our daughter.

I finished up a report about an employee committing workers' comp fraud. My clients were a married couple who owned a three-restaurant chain. They were teetering on the edge of bankruptcy and couldn't afford to have their insurance rates skyrocket. Luckily for them, their suspicion that a disgruntled assistant manager was faking his leg injury had panned out. According to his doctor—who happened to be his wife's cousin—the guy had cracked his kneecap during a fall on the job. But I'd driven behind him for miles as he rode his bicycle to a bowling tournament. The pictures of him throwing a strike should help my client avoid a lawsuit.

As I hit "Send," another email popped onto my screen, one of the occasional messages I get from the website GeneExploder. Four years ago, my former mother-in-law got John, my ex-husband, and me genetic test kits as an awkward Christmas present. I wasn't particularly interested in genealogy, but to appease her, I filled the test tube with spit and sent it back to the company.

Talk about timing—a genetics email after I'd learned that half of my genetic makeup wasn't what I thought it was. When I first got my test results years ago, they'd been confusing. I had French and Italian blood from my mother, but hardly any of my dad's German ancestry. Now I knew why. At the time, I hadn't given it much thought because who knew how accurate these things were. According to the results, I also had way more Neanderthal in me than the average girl, which supposedly makes me prone to depression. *No great shocker there.*

Since then, I'd gotten occasional update emails, which I hadn't bothered to open. But a month ago I'd thought I knew who my father was, and now I didn't have a clue.

I logged into the website and started to reexamine my results. It had been years since I'd looked at them, and I found myself wondering what surprises I might find. What if my biological father was on here? Or a half-sibling? My mother is the only adult relative I'm still in contact with. As an only child and a single mom, I warmed to the idea of connecting with a long-lost sister. Maybe she'd have kids, and my daughter would have brand-new cousins to play with.

I clicked on "Relatives" and held my breath as the screen loaded. There were only two hits in Southern California: a woman named Myra Davies, and a man who went by Jay W. Both were distant cousins. I was surprised by the depth of my disappointment.

On impulse, I clicked on Myra's profile and typed out a message. *Hi there, just beginning to explore genealogy, and I'd love to chat.* I sent an identical note to Jay W. Maybe one of them would write back and educate me about the time Cousin Fred donated sperm to the baby clinic. But as soon as I hit "Send" on the second message, I regretted it. What was I doing, contacting random third cousins on the internet? These people had families and lives and didn't need a stranger prying into their business.

I closed out of the website and tried to work, but I couldn't focus. I'd been in a daze since learning about my dad. My mind was foggy, like after a hangover, and I felt an overwhelming sense of dread. On top of that, my temples throbbed with the beginning of a caffeine headache. I decided to make an emergency Starbucks run. Hopefully, coffee and a change of scenery would help me shake off this funk.

Driving down my mother's cul-de-sac, I passed rows of the identical ranch houses I'd grown up with—beige mid-century boxes with Spanish tile roofs. A couple of neighborhood boys were playing basketball in what used to be my friend Jenny's driveway. Now Jenny and our other friends were off living their lives, and I was back here. I had a weird feeling of being trapped in amber while the world moved on without me.

My phone beeped as I drove down the street, alerting me to a new email. After a few blocks, I hit a red light and pulled up a message from Jay W: *Hi Kate M. I'd love to chat. Are you free tomorrow?*

That was faster than I'd expected. *Sure,* I wrote back.

The light changed, and I continued on my caffeine quest. I pulled into a Starbucks drive-through behind a minivan full of kids. The driver was trying to get them to calm down long enough to convey a Frappuccino order. I pulled out my phone and checked my email. There was another message from Jay W. *How about 10 a.m.? What's your number?* Okay, wait a minute here. This eagerness was off-putting. This guy was acting like a recent divorcé with a brand-new Tinder account—not someone connecting with a distant relative on a genealogy site.

I thought about not responding. But then my eyes drifted back toward the minivan. A curly-haired tween, sitting shotgun, was leaning over and noogying her brother in the back seat. He tried to squirm free while a third kid looked on, delighted. I'd always wanted a big family, but I doubted I'd ever marry again. And realistically, my daughter, Amelia, was all I could handle on my own. Maybe Jay was just a friendly, family-oriented guy who liked to connect with people, I told myself. If I got serial killer vibes, I could thank him for a nice chat, and that would be the end of it. I sent him my number.

The minivan finally moved up. I rolled forward and placed my order.

My phone rang with a blocked number, which usually meant a cop or a telemarketer. "Myles here," I answered.

"Myles?" said a laughing baritone. "Kate M *is* you. I can't believe my luck!"

I recognized the voice from somewhere. "I'm sorry, who is this?"

"Harry Castile from Sheriff's Homicide—aka Jay W." The two parts of that statement had no business being connected. I'd worked with Harry on a gruesome murder when I was still with LAPD. A couple of lost hikers had stumbled on a toothless, fingerless corpse out in the desert. Harry had been assigned to the case and was struggling to identify the victim. I was a gang detective at the time, and Harry reached out because the body was covered in Rollin' 60s tattoos. Eventually, we'd identified him as a major player turned snitch, who'd been tortured, killed, and left for the Mojave coyotes to gnaw on.

Now Harry was retired and working cold cases for the sheriff on a contract basis. But that didn't explain why he was contacting me under a fake name through a genetics website. What was going on here?

"I was gonna wait 'til tomorrow to call you," said Harry. "But then you sent your number, and my phone showed I already had it stored. What a crazy coincidence!" He laughed again, like we were sharing some joke. But I was still totally in the dark.

"Harry, it's great to hear from you, but I'm really confused. Are we cousins or something?"

"It's not my DNA, Kate—it's a killer we haven't identified yet." My stomach lurched. "He murdered a seventeen-year-old girl twenty years ago. No one's been able to crack the case, but I've been working with GeneExploder to upload his DNA and identify relatives. I was crossing my fingers that I'd find a brother or something, but the closest hit I got was a distant cousin. She lives near the victim's last address, in Idlewood."

"Myra Davies," I muttered.

"Exactly!" said Harry. "I was gonna contact the next closest match—a user named Kate M., when you sent me a message."

The waiting barista cleared her throat. I smiled apologetically and handed her my credit card. "Well, Harry, I wish I could match your enthusiasm, but I'm kind of in shock. You're saying I have a cousin who murdered a teenager. I'm assuming you're calling because you think I can help?" The barista gave me a look that was halfway between horror and intrigue.

"Yes," said Harry. "You could be the key to this whole thing."

His tone said I should join in the excitement. But finding out I'm the missing clue in a homicide case really hadn't been on my bucket list. Then again, neither was learning I have a different birth father. One thing I had discovered: genealogy wasn't my thing.

2

Two years ago—Kate

I DON'T KNOW HOW long I stayed parked in front of my parents' house, staring at their front door. I'd turned the engine off, and my car was an airless sauna. I felt dusty and gross from speed packing, and the heat wasn't helping. My back ached, and my shirt was damp with sweat. I could smell myself—and it wasn't pretty.

Rather than getting out, I turned the key in the ignition and felt cold air start to blow again. Just then, my parents' door opened, and my mother came outside. I should have been prepared to see her, but I wasn't. My stomach clenched into a hard ball. I turned off the ignition and stepped out of the car. "Hi, Mom," I said. I was trying for calm, but my voice was on the verge of breaking.

"Kate, what's wrong?" She glanced over at the back seat of my car, which was filled with boxes and suitcases. "Why do you have all that stuff?"

The words caught in my throat. How could I explain to my devout Catholic mother, who'd spent years nursing my father though cancer treatments, that my husband had left me—and that it was my fault? I tried to blink back tears, but it didn't work. My mother hates scenes, and here I was breaking down in the middle of the street.

Before I knew it, she'd put an arm around my shoulders and was leading me inside. My body felt limp, like all of my muscles had turned to jelly. She closed the door and spun me around to face her. "What's wrong, honey? What happened? Is it John?"

I nodded. "He wants a divorce."

"What?" demanded my mother. "I don't understand. You guys were doing fine. And think of Amelia."

Hearing my daughter's name made the tears start afresh. "Oh, honey—have a seat," said my mother. She led me to the kitchen table, pulled a Mike's Hard Lemonade out of the fridge, and placed it in front of me. This caught me off guard. My mother lives alone and doesn't drink. "Beverly Fincher left it here after book club," she told me. "Now what happened? Did you guys have a fight? I'm sure you can work this out."

I took a long pull of the sweetly sour drink. She'd set out a cup, but I went straight for the bottle. "It's more than that. There's no fixing this."

"Is it another woman?" she asked. "You know marriages have ups and down. Your father had a flirtation when you were little. I chalked it up to human weakness, and we moved past it."

Jesus Christ, was that supposed to make me feel better? What the hell was a flirtation? No—I couldn't go there. Contemplating my dead father's infidelity was not something I could handle at that moment. "No, it isn't that," I said. Although honestly, I had no idea if John had been faithful. I just knew things had been bad for a long time, and his lack of empathy when he walked out the door had raised a lot of questions in my mind. "We should never have gotten married. We're not compatible. If I hadn't gotten pregnant, we'd have broken up years ago."

I had never been open with her about my relationship struggles. My parents preferred to bury their problems, to spare their loved ones. I only found out about my mother's hysterectomy after the fact, when my dad sent me a text asking me to call and cheer her up. We'd ended up chatting awkwardly about everything but the surgery.

It wasn't until my late twenties that I'd started to question the healthiness of this pattern. But by then, old habits were too hard to break. And learning to compartmentalize had helped me deal with a lot of bad shit I saw on the police force. Unfortunately, it had also prolonged my ill-fated marriage.

At any rate, I'd clearly done a solid job hiding my marital problems. So much so that my mother was completely blindsided. She sat down across from me and reached for my hand. "Honey, of course you're compatible. You're both smart, reasonable people. I don't think I've ever seen you argue."

I withdrew my hand and rested my face in my palms, rubbing my forehead with my fingers in frustration. "We're discreet, mom. We don't argue in public."

"But what about Amelia? How can he leave his daughter?"

This was the part of the conversation I'd been dreading the most. I couldn't look at her. To my mother, marriage and raising a child were the defining achievements of her life, and I'd failed at both. I had no idea how I was going to come to terms with what happened. But talking to her could only make me feel worse. I got up from the table and steadied myself against the kitchen counter. "Amelia is going to stay with John," I said quietly.

"What are you talking about? That little girl needs her mother." She paused waiting for me to say something, but I just stood there with my back turned. "Kate," she said, her voice sharp now. "You can't do this."

My hands clenched around the counter, and I bit down hard on the inside of my cheek, tasting blood. "I don't have a choice." My cheeks were wet with tears, but my voice was calm, almost robotic. "After the car accident, they put me on these pain pills—"

"You told me you were doing okay," she cut in.

I gripped the counter harder and felt the tips of my nails buckle under the pressure. "I lied, Mom. I didn't want to worry you. I have serious spinal damage, and I'm in pain all the time. They gave me pills and I got hooked."

"So, stop taking them!" she said.

I wanted to scream at her. To shake her into understanding. "I'm trying, but it's not that simple."

"Of course, it is!" she said. "Focus on your daughter, and do what's necessary."

"Mom," I said quietly. "Please, just let me finish. This isn't easy."

"Of course it isn't easy, but you do what you have to do."

I walked back to the kitchen table and took a swig of the hard lemonade. Alcohol and opiates aren't supposed to mix, but I had to get through this conversation. "The doctor's weaning me off the pills." She started to say something, but I cut her off. "John has lots of evidence about my problem. It got pretty bad." I didn't tell her that I'd fallen asleep and hit a parked car—with Amelia in the passenger seat. I couldn't do it. She'd never look at me the same way again. "If I take this to court, I could lose her altogether."

"You don't know that!" she cut in.

"Yes, Mom. I do. John's willing to give me two weekends a month. I talked to a lawyer. He thinks I should take it."

"This is absurd!" she said. "Kate, it's unnatural. A child has to be with her mother. You have to do everything you can to fix things with John. You could damage her for life." I already felt like someone had sliced open my belly, and now my mother was salting my insides. "Kate, are you listening to me?" she demanded. "Honey, this is madness!"

I'd been hoping to stay with her for a month while we sold the condo. Until I could pick up the pieces of my life and mold them into something tolerable. But that clearly wouldn't work. I already had a voice in my head howling that I'd failed as a wife. That I was a horrible parent. I needed to mute that scream to start functioning again, and I couldn't do it here.

"I should go," I said. "I can't talk about this anymore."

"Why don't you stay here in your room tonight? Maybe tomorrow you can go back and talk things out with John."

I had to get out of there. I kissed her on the cheek and left the kitchen. She called after me, but I didn't turn around. I opened the front door and walked to my car. She stood in the doorway, shielding her eyes from the sun. I forced a smile and waved before driving off.

3

Present—Kate

I MET HARRY AT the Sheriff's Homicide Bureau the day after learning about my killer relative. He was joined by his partner, Phil, another retiree working on a contract basis. Phil exuded a quieter version of Harry's enthusiasm and had a less than charming tendency to call me "Hon."

The merry duo brought me into the windowless conference room and placed an ancient accordion folder in the middle of the table. The aging cardboard was marked by an old coffee spill and a large rip that had been repaired with Scotch Tape. Apparently, it hadn't occurred to either of them to create a digital file or at least hole-punch the evidence and stick it in a binder.

Phil pulled out pictures and yellowed reports and laid them in front of me. They shouldn't be showing me this stuff—I knew it and they knew it. I wasn't law enforcement now, and this material wasn't public. But these guys were from a time when the concept of protocol didn't exist.

Harry slid a dog-eared picture of a smiling teenage girl across the table. I picked it up and studied her face. "I assume she's your victim?"

"Lisa Forester," said Harry. "She was a straight A student with a passion for science."

Lisa looked like a nice, nerdy girl. She wore her brown hair cropped at the shoulders and crimped in a style that was popular back when I was in high school. Lisa would have been about my age if she had lived. Looking at her picture, I could see myself two decades ago and my daughter ten years from now.

Harry slid over a second picture of Lisa holding a violin, next to a girl with a guitar and smudgy eyeliner. Lisa wore a pleated black skirt with raw edges and combat boots—I'd had an identical outfit back in high school. I could have passed those girls at the mall when I was a freshman, scouring the clothing racks at Hot Topic for edgy miniskirts. She should be alive now, approaching middle age, maybe raising a kid or two. "Here she is with her best friend, Regina. Lisa was a talented musician."

Harry was doing his best to pull on my heartstrings, and it was working. They must really need my help.

"All right, Harry," I said with a sigh. "What happened to Lisa?"

"They found her buried under a woodpile at a Christian summer camp in Idlewood," he told me. "The coroner thinks she was strangled."

I felt sick. My parents had taken me to Idlewood several times when I was a kid, a picturesque mountain town with cool summers and white winters, just an hour and a half outside LA. Sometimes we went up with other cop families. My friend Jenny, whose dad worked at the same patrol station as mine, joined us one year. We'd spent long afternoons roaming around town, gossiping, and stuffing ourselves with fudge from the candy shop. Once or twice, we'd ducked under a chain blocking the driveway to Camp Idlewood—snuck in and smoked cigarettes. If our timing had been different, that could have been us buried under the woodpile.

I was getting distracted. I shook my head to bring myself back to the present. "You think Lisa was strangled, but you're not sure?"

Harry winced and I knew I was in for something awful. "The body was in bad shape when they found it, and we can't tell much of anything." He took a third picture out of the folder and handed it to me. The smiling pink-cheeked teen was now a gray, mummified corpse, barely recognizable as human. My jaw clenched. That poor girl.

"They didn't look for her right away," said Harry. "Lisa sent her parents a message that she needed a break from school and was leaving for a while. The police thought she was just another runaway." His words set my teeth on edge. As if a teenage girl on her own in the world wasn't reason enough for concern. But Harry was a dinosaur, and lecturing him wouldn't get us anywhere. "They found her body after the snow thawed," he continued. "Some parishioners on a retreat noticed a smell coming from the woodpile and thought it was a dead raccoon."

"Any idea who killed Lisa?" I asked. "Or why?"

"None. We think she tried to hitchhike and got picked up by the wrong guy. It's not a perfect theory, but it's the only one we have."

I winced. Hitchhiking murders tend to be brutal, sadistic crimes by monsters who kill for the sport of it. "Was she raped?"

"We don't know," said Harry. "They didn't find semen, but he could've used a condom. All we have are a couple strands of the perp's hair recovered from her hands. They found bits of scalp material at the buds, with your cousin's DNA."

"Don't call him that," I said automatically, although it was technically accurate. How could I share blood with someone who had murdered a young girl and left her to rot? Genetically, I had more in common with this freak than the man who raised me. I felt nauseous.

Harry and Phil were looking at me, and I realized that I'd zoned out for a moment. I smiled awkwardly and jumped back in. "Hey, if the body was found in San Bernardino, why is this case with the LA sheriffs?"

"They found Lisa's sweater on a hiking trail in LA. The jurisdiction line runs right through there. We think the perp killed her offsite and dumped her body in San Bernardino. The case could have gone either way, but Lisa's dad worked for the San Bernardino sheriffs, and the brass wanted to avoid allegations of bias."

"Anyone's DNA besides Lisa's on the sweater?"

Harry shook his head.

"So, all we have are a couple hairs. Is that enough for a DNA comparison?"

"It wasn't twenty years ago," said Harry. "But these days, they can do amazing things with forensics."

After months of catching cheaters and insurance frauds, I was dying to work on something juicy—and of course I wanted Lisa's killer brought to justice. But I didn't understand why two homicide detectives with a combined fifty years of experience needed my help. "All of this is horrific," I said. "But guys, why am I here? If you need a DNA sample, I'm happy to help. But I don't think you brought me down here to spit in a tube."

Harry started in with their pitch. They wanted me to go to Idlewood, insinuate myself into Myra's family, and casually ask whether any of her relatives might have strangled a teenager. They clearly hadn't thought this through.

"Harry, I'd have to be embedded in Myra's family for months to find out anything. Do you know if she even has relatives in Idlewood?"

They glanced at each other awkwardly. "We just loaded your cousin's DNA a week ago. We're still working out the details."

"Stop calling him my cousin," I said. "Did Myra live in Idlewood when the murder happened?"

Harry looked down at the table and rubbed his stubby chin. "She's been there for ten years. Before that, she was in Fontana."

I shook my head. These guys were grasping at straws. "Okay, so Myra wasn't living in town when Lisa was killed. I doubt she has any more of a connection to the perp than I do. And what are the chances your sergeant wants to pay my hourly rate?"

Harry hemmed and hawed and offered to get me the few-hundred-dollar informant fee. That made me laugh. "Guys, I'm staying with my mother in La Verne and commuting all over creation to make ends meet. Now you want me to schlep to San Bernardino to solve a twenty-year-old case—for free?"

Harry frowned and rubbed the back of his neck. "I wish I could pay you more. We just don't have the resources."

"Why don't you just get a deputy to pose as me?"

There was a long silence. "We don't have the manpower, Kate," said Harry. "Recruitment is at a multi-decade low, and we can't spare a body for a long-term investigation on a cold case."

I opened my mouth to end the conversation, but Harry cut me off. "Wait a minute—what if you had other work in Idlewood? A deputy I know called me last week, looking for a PI recommendation. His crazy brother-in-law killed his wife's sister. Lit her place on fire and ended up burning down a chunk of the town. The family's standing by him."

This sounded familiar. Had the case gotten press attention? "What was his name?"

"It was all over the news. Jacob Coburn's the arsonist. Abby Coburn was his sister. The deputy, Ted Vera, is looking into things for his wife, but he has to do it on the down-low. San Bernardino sheriffs did the investigation, and it can't get out that he's helping the defendant."

This was a horse of a different color. Work had been slow and boring. A chance to get paid to solve a murder again would be amazing. And ever since I'd learned about my dad, I'd felt like I was sleepwalking through my days. Maybe a high-stakes case where someone's life was on the line would get me out of my own head.

"Okay, I'm interested."

Harry grinned like a man reeling in a large fish. He leaned forward and rested his elbows on the table. "It gets better. The wife's family owns a ski resort and a bunch of short-term rental cabins. The family's offering to put up whoever takes the job. They want an out-of-towner, since the local PIs know the sheriffs up there."

I had wonderful memories of being in Idlewood as a kid. Now I had a chance to go back and bring my daughter. For months, she'd spent her biweekly visits sleeping next to me on an air mattress at her grandmother's place. Now I could take her on a mini vacation.

"If your friend hires me, I'll do what I can to help with Lisa's case."

A broad grin stretched across Harry's face. "But if I take the job, my daughter will be coming up and staying with me on weekends, and I won't be working those days. Do you think that'll be a problem?"

"I doubt it," said Harry, grinning. "By the time I'm done singing your praises, they won't want to hire anyone else."

4

Eighteen months ago—Abby

"CAN YOU SHARE a happy memory of him, from before the drugs?" I was just supposed to help her fill out paperwork—I wasn't a social worker yet. But I could tell she needed someone to talk to. The old woman took a deep breath and closed her eyes. For a second, I thought she was going to break down.

Instead, she launched into a beautiful story about her son, now a forty-year-old meth addict living on the streets, from back when he was studying to be a pastry chef. She told me about the time he came over for her birthday and taught her how to make chocolate soufflé. When it was ready, they ate the whole thing in one sitting, scorching their tongues on molten chocolate and washing it down with dessert wine. By the end of her tale, I was the one close to tears, and I knew I'd made the right decision.

I'd enrolled in social work school after a decade of trying to make it as an actress. It was a chance encounter that changed my life. I'd just gotten a devastating rejection. After several rounds of auditions, I was one of three finalists for a role in an edgy Western. The character was a resourceful prostitute who doubled as a midwife and carried a knife tucked into her garter. I read the script and fell in love with her. She was funny and brave, and used a spittoon while rocking a corset.

Above all, it was an opportunity to do some real acting. I love playing quirky parts. But I'm a generically pretty blonde with big boobs and a button nose. Actresses who look like me get cast as cheerleaders until we're put out to pasture. Or as my ex-agent once put it, *"sent to the glue factory."* So, when they almost offered me the role of a lifetime at age thirty, I was ecstatic.

In the end, the director thought my face looked too "modern." As if people's bone structures had somehow changed since the 1880s. The part went to a friend of mine from USC with a more interesting look and a personal connection to the producer. She threw a party to celebrate at a bar in Los Feliz. I showed up, to be a good sport, and did my best not to seem devasted.

After one too many Moscow mules, I ended up puking in an alley behind the bar. When I looked up from retching, there was a man next to me, asking if I was okay and handing me a glass of water. It was Ben, the social worker husband of a screenwriter friend. He was handsome in a hipster kind of way, with a dark beard, shaved head, and a sleeve of intricate tattoos.

I ended up pouring my heart out to him. The years of hope and despair, pride, and self-doubt all flowed out of me, like a dam had broken. Then I found myself telling him about my brother. I don't talk about Jacob much. It's hard to explain what happened. How my brilliant, creative sibling, who could make me laugh until my stomach hurt, had morphed into a lost soul running from a shadow cabal that only existed in his brain.

Ben just listened. I knew his wife was waiting for him inside the bar, but he didn't make me feel like I was imposing. When I'd finally let it all out—and was left spent, with tears and vomit staining my shirt—he asked me to share a good memory of Jacob.

The question caught me off guard. But then it came to me.

Two winters earlier. Jacob was supposed to drive me home after Sunday dinner at my parents' house in Idlewood. Instead, he had turned toward the ski resort. "What are you doing?" I'd asked.

He grinned mischievously, pulled a flask out of his pocket and handed it to me. "We're going sledding."

I laughed. My brother was like that. He made crazy, impulsive decisions that usually ended in disaster. "It's freezing and we're not dressed for it," I pointed out.

He nodded toward the flask. "That'll warm us up. I grabbed Mom's parka for you. It's in the trunk."

I've never been able to say no to Jacob, and it sounded like fun. I took a swig from the flask and felt brandy warm my insides.

When we pulled up, the ski slopes were already closed, and the parking lot was empty. The lights were out, but a full moon lit up the night. The fresh snow glowed a soft cornflower blue under the black sky. In the darkness, with the cold stinging our eyes, it was hard to make out the placement of the Jeffrey pines. My depth perception felt off as I squinted against the freezing wind. If we took a wrong turn, we could end up crashing into a tree at twenty miles per hour. "Maybe this is a bad idea, Jake," I said.

He waved his hand, dismissing my concern. "We'll be fine."

I took another swig and followed him out of the car. We didn't have a sled, but Jacob found a plastic garbage can lid for him and an unfolded cardboard box for me. Together, we sipped brandy and laughed and tumbled down the hillside. When the dark line of trees came into focus, I rolled to the side, breaking my momentum. I felt the shock of cold as my face hit the snow, which slid under my collar. When I sat up again, I saw Jacob hurtling toward the pines. "Jake!" I called. "Abort, you're too close!" But he kept going. I screamed again, but he ignored me.

He never knew when to stop.

My brother was almost at the tree line. I put a hand to my mouth in terror and screamed. At the last second, he flipped over, rolled onto his side, and tumbled through the snow. The trash-can lid kept flying toward the woods.

Furious, I ran down the hill and caught up with him. He was laughing like an idiot. "You should have heard yourself!" he cackled.

I smashed a snowball in his face and ran back up the hillside. A shock of cold hit me on the neck. Slush rolled down my back, and I shivered. When I turned around to face Jacob, a flashlight beam criss-crossed the pines. "Security!" I shouted.

"We gotta go!" said Jacob, with mock urgency. He grabbed my hand, and we ran back to the car, laughing and panting as the wind burned our faces.

When I was done telling the story, a weight had been lifted from my chest. In that moment, I knew that a chapter in my life had closed, but somehow that was okay. I'd been kidding myself for years. I was never going to make it as an actress. But maybe there was something else I could do—help other people get to this same place of peace.

"How did you become a social worker?" I asked.

5

Present—Kate

IDLEWOOD SEEMED TO appear out of nowhere. After a hot dusty drive through the desert and a fifteen-minute climb up the mountain, I was in the Swarthout Valley. It was exactly as I remembered it. The town was built on a flat break in the San Gabriel Mountains. A glance north or south gave you beautiful views of evergreen peaks. Century-old cabins painted deep red or forest green lined quiet roads with no streetlights.

Rolling down my window, I felt the late September air smack against my face. I'd climbed six thousand feet, and the temperature had dropped from ninety degrees in the LA suburbs to a crisp seventy. I stuck my hand out the window, letting the wind flow through my fingers like water.

It was the smell of pine and sage that transported me back in time twenty-five years. I remembered coming here with my parents as a kid. My dad had tried to teach me to ski before realizing that I was hopelessly uncoordinated. The first time we hit the bunny hill, my legs slid out in front of me, and I fell backward, smacking my head against the ground. Once the world stopped spinning, we went back to the cabin, drank hot chocolate, and played board games by the fire. Skiing was one of my dad's many talents that I didn't share. Now I understood why.

I hadn't been prepared for the visceral way that coming here would affect me. I couldn't separate Idlewood from the memories of my father. *Grilling hamburgers when we came up in the summer or walking around and looking at Christmas lights in the winter.* Now I was here, my dad was dead, and I'd just learned that another old man, maybe one in Idlewood, was my biological father. Part of me was dying to meet the guy. Another part of me felt guilty for being curious, like I was betraying the man who had raised me.

I pulled into the driveway of the little cottage where I'd be staying. It was painted a cheery red with white trim, and surrounded on two sides by a wooden porch. Evergreens shaded the front yard, which was carpeted in pine needles.

The front door was unlocked, as my new employer, Ted Vera, had promised. Inside, the small living area was centered around a giant stone fireplace. My eyes traveled to built-in shelving filled with mysteries, kids' books, and games. The place looked a lot like a cabin we'd stayed in one winter when I was little. The smell was familiar too—a mix of mildew, damp stone, and smoke from a century of soot in the old fireplace.

I dropped my bag in the main bedroom and climbed a rickety staircase to the attic. Short, wood-paneled walls met the steep planes of a triangular ceiling. A tiny kid-sized bed was tucked to one side. There were several bins of vintage toys on the other side—Jenga, My Little Ponies, even a rain stick.

As I sat on the narrow bed, part of me felt like a small girl getting ready for a family vacation. Then I caught my reflection in a cloudy old mirror on the wall. I couldn't recognize myself. I looked old, and my features were alien to me. I ran a finger down the bridge of my nose, feeling the slight bump that no one in my family shared. I'd always wondered where it came from. I looked down at my hands. Narrow with long fingers. Nothing like my dad's warm, thick hands or my mom's small, pudgy ones.

A lump formed in my throat, and I swallowed hard. The walls seemed to tip inward, and the odor of mildew and old smoke became unbearable. I rested my back against the wall and closed my eyes, trying to steady myself. My breath came short and fast, and my throat felt like it was closing up.

Is this what a panic attack felt like? I'd watched my marriage fall apart, had guns pointed at me, and survived a serious car wreck, without ever experiencing one. But through everything, I'd always retained a sense of who I was—even my mistakes felt like mine. Now I found myself questioning everything. I'd become a cop to emulate my dad. I'd always thought of myself as a good investigator and assumed that I took after him that way. I still listen to the old-time country music he used to blast in the car. We never had much in common, but I idolized my father for his warmth and charisma. In many ways, I'd modeled my life and personality on him. Now I felt like an imposter.

I needed to see my daughter. Hug her, smell her hair. She was the only thing I still felt connected to. But she wasn't here, and that was my fault. I took out my phone and flipped through pictures of Amelia, trying to regain my grip on reality.

The doorbell rang and my stomach clenched. I had to calm down before meeting my clients. I took several deep breaths and exhaled, trying to slow my heart rate. The doorbell rang again. Time was up. Holding tightly to the railing, I climbed down the attic stairs. I jogged over to the front door and opened it.

A thin, brunette woman in her thirties, with granny eyeglasses and a baby strapped to her chest, extended a hand. "You must be Kate," she said. "I'm Grace Coburn, Ted's wife. This is our son, Liam."

"Nice to meet you." I was still breathing faster than normal and wondered if she could tell. *Snap out of it,* I ordered myself. This woman was here to tell me about her family's unspeakable tragedy. My baggage wasn't her problem—I needed to get my act together.

The baby flashed a bright smile, exposing new front teeth. "Hi, Liam!" I said. "He's beautiful. How old is he?"

"Ten months." I waved at the little boy, who spun his face around and buried his eyes in his mother's shirt. "You have a daughter, right?" asked Grace. "Did you want to bring her with us? She can play in the other room while we talk."

I flinched but quickly recovered. "She's with her dad this week, but she'll come up for the weekend."

Grace opened her mouth and started to ask a follow-up question but thought better of it. Other people's custody situations don't make for easy small talk.

"Will your whole family be at the house?" I asked, turning the conversation away from my personal life. "I'd like to meet everyone." She bristled and I realized my mistake. *Grace's brother is in jail for killing her sister.* Her family hadn't been whole in a long time. I needed to choose my words more carefully.

"Do you need a few minutes," asked Grace, ignoring my blunder, "or are you ready to walk over?"

"Let's go," I said, hoping the fresh air would help shake off my feeling of unease.

Grace handed me a key, and I locked the door behind us. She looked tense as we walked down the driveway. "I want to make sure you understand what you're dealing with. My mom's in denial about what my brother did, and my dad basically shut down after it happened."

Interesting—Harry had told me that the Coburns were on Jacob's side. But apparently Grace thought he was good for it.

"Ted and I were against bringing you on," she admitted. "It's not personal—you have a great reputation. But the evidence against my brother is overwhelming. I don't think it's healthy to pretend otherwise."

"You're worried about creating false hope for your parents?" I asked gently.

She nodded. "The uncertainty is making this even more painful for them. You never really get closure after something like this, but my parents need peace. And my dad has a bad heart. He's had a couple heart attacks, and the last one was right after he learned about Abby. The emotional roller coaster of my brother's case isn't helping." Her voice was strained, and I could tell she was fighting to control her emotions. "I hope you won't drag this out."

I took a breath. "I'm not here to waste people's time and money. If this investigation hits a dead end, I'll say so." Grace seemed satisfied by my answer. I wanted to know why she was so sure Jacob was the killer. If I was here on a fool's errand, I needed to know. "So, you think your brother's guilty?"

Her eyes were focused on the road. "There's no doubt in my mind. I've been a prosecutor for a long time. I know how to evaluate evidence."

"What can you tell me about Jacob?"

"Think of all the fifty-one fifties you've seen in court," said Grace, using the code section for involuntary commitment. "Jacob is as far gone as any of them. He used to be a bit off, but functional. Then he discovered meth, and it triggered a schizophrenic break. We're talking . . . my brother thinks he's a god. He thinks he communicates through telepathy. For a while, he was convinced there was a conspiracy of people trying to kill him. I mean—crazy stuff."

"Does he have a history of violence?" I asked. Most people with mental illnesses are harmless. What Grace was describing was tragic, but it didn't mean he'd hurt anyone.

"He has a record," she told me. "Mostly misdemeanors, but there's also battery on a peace officer, and assault. I think he broke the guy's nose."

Next I asked if he had ever been violent with the family.

Grace hesitated and stroked the top of her son's head. "I've never seen him hit anyone. He screams a lot, though, and smashes things."

"Tell me about his relationship with Abby."

She worked a strand of her long brown hair out of the baby's curled fingers. "Before Jacob went off the deep end, he and Abby were close. They were very similar. Smart, reckless, immature, but amazingly creative. My sister acted, and my brother liked to write. He even won an award for a short story in high school. Jacob was like a more concentrated version of Abby. The big difference between them was that Abby knew when to stop. She had a self-preservation instinct and empathy. Jacob is selfish and likes living on the edge. Things were never going to end well for him."

"What do you mean when you say he went off the deep end?" I asked. "Are you speaking generally, or did something happen?"

She paused for a minute and thought. The little boy was staring up at the swaying pines—transfixed by the pattern of green needles and blue sky. "Jacob got hostile and paranoid around the time he discovered meth. He withdrew from us and ended up living in some gross motel. It happened really fast, and his decline was hard on Abby. She did what she could to help him—bailed him out from jail, gave him money. If I had to guess, I'd say she finally denied him a handout, and he killed her in a rage."

Her theory made sense. People murder their relatives for drug money all the time. It didn't explain why he would light the house on fire, but Jacob wasn't exactly in his right mind.

"We're over here," said Grace, gesturing toward a dark-wood-shingled mansion.

I followed her up the driveway. As we got closer to the house, I could see my distorted reflection in the antique glass windows. The place was spectacular, if a little creepy.

"Let's go inside," said Grace. "I'll introduce you to my folks."

6

Thirty months ago—Abby

"READY TO CELEBRATE?" asked Jacob, with a mischievous gleam in his eye.

I smacked his arm. My sister was making an effort, and I didn't feel like mocking her. "Grace means well."

I'd been hired for a steady voice-over gig, which would give me a small income. The plan was to save up, so I could move out of my parents' spare cabin and rent a studio in LA. With any luck, my days of commuting for auditions would soon be over. Grace had insisted on taking me out to celebrate, which was kind of her. But even when she tries to be nice, there's a patronizing edge to her voice that drives me up the wall.

"Don't tell her about the play," I warned Jacob. On top of the voice-over job, I'd landed the lead role in an amazing two-person play at a small theater in Glendale. The play was gory and experimental— nothing my more conventional sister could relate to. But the venue was struggling. I didn't want her driving to Glendale only to hate the show *and* comment on the empty seats.

"Why not?" asked Jacob. He was sprawled across an old wicker chair on my front porch, a hint of a smile on his face.

I shouldn't have said anything. Jacob loves to make trouble, and I'd just planted a seed. I ignored his question and glanced at my watch. "We should go. I don't want to keep her waiting."

Jacob was quiet on the walk over. I tried to make conversation, but he responded in monosyllables. After a few minutes, I gave up.

"I know you're gonna leave," he said finally. "I can't stay in this town without you."

"You have Mom and Dad and Grace," I reminded him.

Jacob laughed darkly. "Oh yeah, living with my parents and occasionally seeing my bitch sister for Sunday dinners. Lucky me."

I winced, "Don't call her that." Jacob's expression was blank, but I sensed his anger brewing. Jacob had asked to stay in one of the rental cabins, and Mom had refused. I think she wanted to keep an eye on him. My brother has a self-destructive streak. When you mix it with alcohol and isolation, things get ugly.

"I need to be on my own. I'm a grown-ass man." He was almost shouting now, and I sensed his desperation. I felt for him. He wanted so badly to be independent—who wouldn't at nearly thirty? But he couldn't quite pull himself together. "This town is like a graveyard. Even the dive bars are lights out at eleven."

Maybe you shouldn't be at a bar after eleven, I wanted to say. But I kept that to myself. "Where would you go?"

"My buddy teaches waterskiing in Arrowhead. He thinks they'll hire me. His dad runs a motel out there. We can share a room."

"You've only waterskied, like, twice in your life, and you can't drive a boat."

Jacob stiffened. "He'll show me how to work the boat. And I don't have to waterski. I just have to yell instructions at tourists."

You can't reason with my brother. If you point out problems, he digs in more. I usually try to provide support from the sidelines. And pick up the pieces when he implodes. "Just be careful."

"Don't start, Abby," snapped Jacob. We lapsed into silence.

After a few minutes, the Bighorn Grill came into view, and I spotted our sister. She looked out of place on the picnic bench, with her black cashmere sweater and matching slacks. You'd think she was a tourist if you didn't know she was born here.

"Hey, guys!" said Grace. I slid in next to her on the bench. Her enthusiasm pricked something inside me. I wish I liked her more. Maybe getting out of town would make me appreciate her finer qualities.

The waiter came over to take our order. Cute, with shaggy hair and blue eyes. I picked up the sticky plastic menu, more out of reflex than curiosity.

"I'll have the chicken Caesar, and a glass of white," said my sister. Jacob ordered a drink and three appetizers, since he knew Grace would pick up the tab.

I smiled at the waiter. "Bacon cheeseburger and an IPA."

"You got it," he said, grinning and meeting my eye.

A minute later our drinks were in front of us, and I sipped mine to take the edge off.

"Tell us about the new job," said Grace. She was leaning forward and putting on her listening face. It made me want to change the subject.

"It's not that big a deal," I told her. "My friend Hannah suggested I try voice-over, and it turns out I'm good at it."

"Is it like commercials and stuff?" asked Grace. Jacob had already stopped paying attention. His legs were fidgeting, which caused the whole table to vibrate.

"It's a gig for a major toy company," I explained. "They have a collection of noise toys that need voicing. There's a Disney Princess-y voice I do, and they like it."

Jacob suddenly looked interested. "Let's hear the voice."

I cleared my throat and raised my pitch by an octave. *Your hugs make me feel so special!*

My brother laughed so hard that beer streamed out his nose. The people one table over stopped talking and stared at us. "Can you keep it down?" snapped Grace. As if we were the first people to get a little loud at the Bighorn Grill.

"You actually have to say that?" asked Jacob, ignoring her. "What else?"

I smiled at my brother. "I have a song about a magical unicorn. You wanna hear it?"

"I think we get the idea," said Grace.

Jacob pounded his fist on the table. "Un-i-corn!"

My sister was starting to get agitated. I knew I should rein it in, but I have a hard time saying no to Jacob, and it was nice to have someone interested in what I was doing. *"There's a magic unicorn. With a happy, golden horn. Who flies, so high up in the air!"* A little girl in a Dora the Explorer T-shirt pointed at me, her mouth hanging open. I winked at her.

"I think we get it, Abby," hissed Grace. Her arms were folded in front of her, and she seemed to be shrinking into herself. I took pity on her and stopped. After all, she had invited us here.

"That's the big job," I said quietly. I looked over at the mountains, golden in the soft evening light. It wasn't lost on me that after ten years of auditions, my biggest paycheck was for shout-singing jingles for the under-three crowd. This was just a slightly better version of the meaningless gigs I'd been juggling for years. And who knew how long voice-over work would even be available? A friend of mine had discovered a cloned version of his voice on some website. Turns out he'd given up the rights to his voice a decade ago, when he was too naive and desperate to study the contract language. Heck, AI technology didn't even exist back then. It was only a matter of time before the robots replaced us.

That thought was depressing. I spotted the waiter and held up my glass. "One more please."

"She's in a play too," said Jacob, grinning at me out of the corner of his eye." I winced and sipped my beer.

"What's it about?" asked Grace.

"It tracks a relationship between two dysfunctional friends over thirty years."

"That sounds interesting," said Grace.

"Jacob has news too," I announced, to change the subject. "He's leaving Idlewood."

The smile evaporated from Jacob's face, and I instantly regretted bringing up his departure. Although a part of me foolishly hoped Grace could talk him out of it.

She stared at him. "Where are you going?" Jacob took out a cigarette and lit it.

"He's gonna drive rich water-skiers around on a boat in Arrowhead."

Grace leaned forward. Her forehead scrunched up, and a deep frown line formed between her brows. "You don't know how to drive a boat."

"I'll learn," he mumbled, inhaling deeply from his cigarette.

"Have you thought about my offer to pay for EMT school?" asked Grace. She'd been on the EMT kick for months. It was a good idea: a high-stakes, high-energy job where your work really matters. Jacob was intelligent, fearless, good with his hands. A job like that could harness his strengths and shake him out of his angst and restlessness. But because Grace had suggested it, it was a nonstarter.

Jacob's phone beeped, and he disappeared into a long text exchange. His cigarette had burned down to a hot stub, and he tossed it onto the sidewalk.

"You can always quit if you don't like it," pressed Grace, who sucks at picking up signals.

Jacob stood up, pushing the whole bench backward. "I'm gonna go for a walk." He lit another cigarette, hopped the railing, and wandered down the street.

Grace and I sat there in silence. The waiter came over and brought me another beer along with a second glass of wine for my sister.

"You think he's meeting a dealer?" asked Grace.

I rolled my eyes. "He leaves when he gets overstimulated, which happens when you nag him."

"I didn't nag him!" she protested. "I'm worried about him. He's just drifting along. He's always seemed haunted, but it's getting worse."

I'd noticed the same change in Jacob, but I get stupidly defensive of my brother when other people criticize him—even family. "I bet you say the same thing about me. Flittering from job to job. Still hoping for that big break." I instantly wanted to take the words back, but they lay there between us.

Grace blinked in surprise. "I've always tried to be supportive."

"But am I wrong?" I asked. I looked down and sipped my beer, willing her to let it go, which of course she didn't.

Grace crossed her arms over her chest. "You really want to know what I think, Abby?"

I definitely didn't. But my sister needed to say it, and maybe I needed to hear it. "Why don't you enlighten me?" *How had this dinner gone so quickly off the rails?*

"Fine," she said. "You're talented. But there are a million talented actresses in LA. You're a beautiful woman. But Hollywood is full of pretty girls. You've been at this for a while now, and I think you can do more with your life than sing about unicorns."

My eyes started welling up, but there was no way I was going to break down in front of Grace. "I need to go to the bathroom," I said. I got up, entered the restaurant, and spotted the hot waiter. *Screw it,* I thought. I needed something to make me feel better, and fast. I scribbled my number on a cocktail napkin and handed it to him. He looked up at me, surprised. "Call me if you want to hang out."

I walked back outside to our table, chugged my beer, and dropped twenty dollars on the table. "Grace, somehow I don't feel like celebrating. Have a good night."

7

Present—Kate

THE INSIDE OF the mansion was straight out of an old Hollywood movie. Wide beams supported high vaulted ceilings. A taxidermied moose head adorned a stone chimney that rose above a grand fireplace. I tried not to gawk at the oriental rugs and beautiful Mission furniture as Grace led me through the house onto a redwood deck surrounded by pines.

Three people were seated at a rustic table. A small, elegant woman of about seventy stood to greet me. I heard the jangle of her charm bracelet as she extended a long, thin hand to shake mine. "It's nice to meet you, I'm Nancy, Jacob's mother," she said.

Next to her was a short, well-groomed man in a three-piece suit. "Hi, Kate, I'm Richard Evans, Jacob's lawyer." Richard gripped my hand with too much force. A few of my ex-husband's attorney friends came to mind as he pulverized my fingers.

"Hello, there," said an older man seated at the far side of the table. I noticed a cane hooked onto the railing behind him.

"That's Carl, Jacob's father," Richard told me.

I reached across the table to shake Carl's hand. "Nice to meet you, Mr. Coburn."

"Go ahead and start without me," said Grace. "Liam needs a diaper change." She walked back toward the house, putting a little bounce in her step to soothe the baby.

Richard cleared his throat. "I was thinking we could have an introductory conversation first. And then, Nancy, if we can use your deck, I'll discuss the details of the case with Kate." Richard turned to look at me. My face must have registered surprise, because he added, "Carl and Nancy don't need to be retraumatized. I can fill you in on the facts."

A little alarm went off in my head. This was not how I like to operate. If I was going to help this family, I needed an open line of communication, even about the ugly stuff. I wondered if this was coming from Richard or my clients.

I turned to Nancy. "I can't imagine how horrible this must be for you, but it's important that I talk to everyone in the family. It doesn't have to be today, just whenever you're ready."

Richard looked taken aback. His cheeks reddened and his eyes narrowed. I noticed that his forehead stayed perfectly smooth, and I wondered if he'd been hitting the Botox. "Kate, Nancy and Carl have already gone through every detail with me. There's no need for them to repeat everything."

I waited a beat to see if Nancy or Carl contradicted him. They didn't, so I had to assume he spoke for them. If that was their attitude, I faced an uphill battle. Jacob's parents—at least in some ways—would know their children better than anyone and were a vital source of information. "Of course, I understand," I said before turning back to Nancy. "We don't have to walk through the details of the tragedy. Only what you personally saw or heard."

"I'll let you know if that becomes necessary," said Richard. His tone was sharp, signaling the end of the conversation. *This guy doesn't know what he's doing,* I thought. Every decent defense lawyer wants their investigator to talk to witnesses. Richard was probably a small-town attorney in over his head on a murder case. And a control freak to boot. I don't do well with micromanagers, and I had a bad feeling about how this would go.

But I didn't want to antagonize Jacob's lawyer on my first day in Idlewood. I could circle back to my clients at a later point. In the meantime, maybe I could glean some background information about Abby and Jacob. "Mrs. Coburn, can you tell me about your daughter?"

Nancy's eyes lit up at the prompt. "Abby was a wonderful person."

I nodded and pulled a notebook out of my bag. I reached for a pen and instead pulled out one of Amelia's red crayons. Feeling my cheeks turn red, I shoved the crayon back into my purse and dug for a pen. Richard handed me an expensive-looking one from across the table, and I noticed a hint of disapproval on his face. So much for first impressions.

"What did Abby do for a living?" I asked.

"She spent years trying to be an actress, but she never managed to break in," said Nancy. "After a while, Abby went back to school for social work at UC Riverside. She was in her second year when she died."

Grace returned and slid Liam into a blue walker. He immediately raced around the deck while his mother trotted behind him, offering a course correction when he bumped into the table. I smiled, remembering Amelia when she was first learning to walk.

"Did Abby work while she was in school?" I asked.

"She was a barista at the Bean and Grape," said Grace. "It's kind of an artsy coffee shop. They also sell wine and do tastings."

I made a mental note to swing by and talk to Abby's coworkers. "Did she get along with her boss?" I glanced over at Richard, who was responding to emails on his phone. After his strong reaction earlier, I wasn't really sure what questions were off-limits.

"She got along with everyone," said Nancy.

Grace stopped to reposition the baby, who'd driven into the railing. I caught her rolling her eyes. "Mom, that's not true. Abby could rub people the wrong way."

Nancy stared at her daughter. "Who did she rub the wrong way?" Grace shot me a look, which said she'd fill me in later.

"What about boyfriends?" I asked.

Nancy shook her head. "Not recently. She was focused on her studies."

Grace nodded again and mouthed, "Call me." There was a story here. And if Grace was still hiding it from her parents, it almost certainly was a doozy.

I hesitated before bringing up Jacob. Richard had basically ordered me to stay away from the crime. But surely, I could ask for background information on their son—they'd hired me to help him. "I understand that Abby and Jacob were close. Do you know if they talked a lot in the weeks before she died?"

Carl got up from the table. It was a slow process, and I could see why he hadn't stood to greet me. "Excuse me," he said, clearing his throat. "I need to use the bathroom." He grabbed his cane and carefully made his way inside.

Nancy smiled sadly. "This is hard for him."

The man was so traumatized, he could barely stand to hear his son's name. Maybe I'd been too quick to judge Richard for his protective instincts.

"Yes, maybe we should pause here," said Richard. "You and I can go over the details, and we can schedule a follow-up meeting with Mr. and Mrs. Coburn."

"Kate, it was so nice to meet you," said Nancy before rising from the table and disappearing into the house.

I'd hoped that Grace would stay and participate, but Liam was starting to fuss. She scooped him up from the walker and held him against her chest. "I'm sorry—he really needs a nap. Kate, we can catch up later."

After she left, I turned to Richard. "Tell me about the case." We'd started off on the wrong foot, and I got a weird, controlling vibe from him. But as Jacob's lawyer, he was responsible for setting the defense strategy. The Coburns had hired me, but I'd be answering to him. I had to make this work.

Richard looked toward the house to see if anyone was within earshot. "Listen, I know you mean to help, but the case against Jacob is airtight. I'd love to think my client is innocent, but I'm a realist."

I appreciated his candor, but the defeatist attitude bothered me. The Coburns had hired me to help defend Jacob, and his lawyer was basically saying, *"Don't bother."*

"I've only seen what I read in the paper."

Richard handed me a folder with copies of police reports. "There's security footage of Jacob walking toward Abby's cabin on the night of the fire. In court I'll argue that it's not him. But I'm going to lose. And they found his phone on the street outside Abby's cabin, with a smear of her blood on it."

"Could he have dropped the phone at some earlier point?" I asked. "Maybe Jacob visited Abby the day before?" There wasn't a ton of foot traffic in Idlewood, and a phone might have gone unnoticed for a while. Of course, that wouldn't explain the bloodstain.

Richard shook his head. "Jacob sent her text messages that night, saying he was coming over."

"I'm assuming they tested the phone for DNA?"

Richard nodded. "It's a match for Jacob. And a witness remembered seeing him with a similar phone case. It's turquoise and very distinctive."

Another bad fact for the defense. "How do they know this was a murder and not just a terrible accident?" I asked. "Bodies are usually in bad shape after a fire." I'd worked one arson murder before. The corpse was just a charred skeleton, and most of the bones had snapped or shattered from the heat.

Richard glanced toward the house, making sure his clients were still inside. "This is why I wanted to talk to you alone," he said, lowering his voice. "I'm not sure if Nancy and Carl know the forensic details. Abby had a skull fracture consistent with blunt force trauma. There was also a large rock next to her body, which the investigators think he used to knock her out."

The words *knock her out* caught my attention. "The blow didn't kill her?"

He shook his head. "The coroner found soot in her lungs."

My hand flew to my mouth. "So Abby burned alive?"

"It looks that way. They think Jacob hit her with the rock, poured an accelerant around the cabin, and started the blaze. The forensics are the weakest part of the prosecution's case. But I don't see a jury letting him off. The facts are too awful. They're also going to hear about Abby's neighbor, a ninety-year-old woman, who burned alive in her bed. They'll be ready to convict him by the time the prosecutor is done with the opening statement."

There was a long silence while I contemplated the horror of what Richard was describing. It seemed I'd been too quick to judge him. He wanted to sanitize the information that reached the Coburns, and I couldn't blame him for sparing them the grisly details. Particularly if Carl had a weak heart.

"The awfulness is partly why I took the case," continued Richard. "Only a madman would do this. And Abby was childhood friends with my sister. I felt like I owed it to her to get involved."

"I don't understand. You're defending Jacob as a favor to *Abby*?"

He smiled, sadly. "Abby loved her brother. The best way to honor her is to get him placed in a mental health facility instead of prison. He'll get treatment, and his mother will be able to visit him in a nicer setting."

So this was why he'd separated me from my clients. Richard thought their strategy was pointless. But I still had an ethical obligation to look into Jacob's innocence if that's what they wanted. I'd have to find time to help build an insanity defense while also trying to exonerate him.

Richard handed me a folded piece of paper. I opened it and saw a few names and phone numbers. "These are some of Jacob's friends. People who've witnessed his decline. Talk to them. You might want to start with Chris Taylor."

"I'm on it." I refolded the paper and stuck it in my pocket. "I also want to talk to Jacob."

"He's in tuberculosis quarantine," said Richard. "But we can schedule a meeting when the jail gives us the all-clear."

I winced. Talking to Jacob would normally be my first step. But if he was in isolation, there was nothing I could do.

"Grace mentioned that you're looking into another Idlewood murder," said Richard. "I was surprised to hear that because I've been practicing law out here for a decade, and I haven't heard of any unsolved cases."

I told him about Lisa Forrester and my weird genetic connection to the killer. I made a point of mentioning Myra Davies, but he didn't seem to recognize her name or Lisa's.

Richard whistled as I wrapped up my story. "That's tough, a twenty-year-old case. You'll have your work cut out for you."

That was putting it mildly.

8

Two years ago—Jacob

R ON ALWAYS REEKED of sweat and cigarettes. Sometimes I thought about shoving him in the water to get rid of the stink. My stomach churned as he came toward me. I was already feeling nauseous. A whiff of him could make me throw up last night's whiskey and ramen.

"Jake, I need someone to take this family for a spin around the lake," said Ron, motioning toward a couple and their kid. "Can you do it?"

I nodded. The movement made my head throb like gremlins were jackhammering my temples.

Last night, Chris had brought these girls back to our room. At first they just stood by the door, eyeing the rumpled laundry and fast-food wrappers on the floor, and wanting to get out of there. Then Chris pulled out some ice and asked if they wanted to party.

Pretty soon we were laughing, turning the music up. We did cannonballs off the motel roof into the pool. I landed head-first and plunged into the water. When I reached the bottom, I pushed against the concrete with my legs and erupted into the night air. The stars were brighter than I'd ever seen. I howled at the moon, feeling alive and electric. An old lady in the room next door barked at us to quiet down. Chris yelled at her to shut the fuck up. His dad owns the place, so he can do what he wants.

Chris and one of the girls went inside together. When I got close to the door, I could hear her moaning—that loud, fake kind that some girls do. Me and her friend walked down to the lake to share a bottle of whiskey and watch the sunrise. I felt like I was drowning in color.

Now Ron snapped his fingers right in front of my eyes. "Earth to Jake," he said. If he did that again, I thought, I'd bend those fingers back until they popped. "Don't keep these folks waiting. They're over there by Katya, getting fitted for skis."

I walked over to the family. The dad gave off major douche vibes. Katya was trying to explain gear options while he talked over her—just another alpha dick who thinks he's better than everyone. He looked familiar, and I wondered where I'd seen him before.

"It's our policy. Everyone has to wear a life jacket," said Katya.

"I appreciate that, but I was an All-American swimmer in college," said Alpha Dick. "I don't need a life jacket, and I don't like wearing used ones." His voice was loud.

"The rule applies to everybody," Katya told him. "Even strong swimmers. It's in case the boat capsizes, or you fall and hit your—"

Alpha Dick cut her off, "I'll take my chances."

I laughed once. Just a short burst of air, but it was enough to get his attention. He spun around and glared at me. "You got a problem, pal?"

"Not if you wear your life jacket," I said. "But I'm the driver, and I'm not going anywhere until you put it on."

"If the boat police catch us, they'll give us a ticket," Katya explained.

His eyes narrowed. "You know what, pal? I don't like your attitude. I want someone else to take us out." He turned to Katya. "Can you drive our boat?"

"No, she can't," I said. "She's about to go on break, and we're short a person today." Katya wasn't going on break. But fuck this guy. And Katya was nice. She didn't deserve to get bullied.

Alpha Dick turned to his wife, with a face that said *"Can you believe this guy?"*

She forced a smile, and I figured she was used to him treating people this way. "Honey, it's fine. I'm sure this young man can show us a good time. What's your name?"

"Jacob," I said.

"It's nice to meet you, Jacob. I'm Harper, this is Bill, and this is our son, Winslow." Of course his name was Winslow.

"We should get going," I told her. "The hour goes pretty fast."

They followed me down the dock. I hopped on the boat and then extended my hand to Harper and the kid as they climbed aboard. Bill got in and sat down on the bench. He was wearing his vest open and unlatched. Normally I'd let it go, but I wasn't in the mood. "You need to buckle it," I said.

"What?" asked Bill.

"You need to buckle your vest," I repeated.

Bill laughed. "Give me a break. The boat police can't tell from fifty yards away." My fists curled into balls. I don't like being laughed at, and I was running out of patience.

Harper read my energy and intervened. "Honey, don't turn this into a thing." She leaned over, buckled it for him, and gave his arm a quick little pat.

I flashed on where I recognized them from. I had a second job washing dishes at a Mexican restaurant in Lake Arrowhead Village, and last week I'd seen Bill yelling at the waitress for forgetting to float Grand Marnier on his Cadillac margarita. Harper had made that same soothing gesture. "Honey, it's okay—I'll drink it," she'd said, touching his arm. "Just order another one."

"It smells," he muttered to her now. "They probably never wash these things. It's unsanitary."

Their kid was staring down at his skis. He'd put on his vest without complaining.

I hopped in the driver's seat. The sun reflected off the water and hurt my eyes. I could barely see, but I managed to pull us toward the middle of the lake. The sound of the engine caused my head to pound harder. The boat rolled through someone's wake, and the jerking motion made me nauseous. I tried to concentrate on the cold wet wind slapping my face.

"Are you from Arrowhead, Jacob?" asked Harper, still trying to make a fun outing out of this disaster. But they weren't paying me for small talk.

"No," I said. We lapsed back into silence. I looked over my shoulder. The kid was playing a game on his mom's phone, and Bill was pouting.

"What brought you to Arrowhead?" she asked.

"Change of scenery," I said.

"You like it?" she asked.

"No."

Bill laughed to himself. "Surprise, surprise. He doesn't like it."

I slowed the boat, almost to a stop. "What was that, Bill? I didn't hear you."

Harper squeezed her husband's thigh.

"Nothing, pal. Why don't you like Arrowhead?" Bill spoke in that singsong, pretend-nice tone you use when you think someone's unreasonable.

"You know the lake is fully privatized," I told him. "Most of the kids around here can't swim in it because their parents don't own waterfront property."

"We know," said Bill. "We like that it's not too crowded. You probably think that makes me an asshole."

"You said it," I replied under my breath, but I knew he could hear me—I didn't care at this point.

"Both of you—stop it," said Harper through gritted teeth. She clapped her hands together to change the subject. "I want to waterski. Who's first?"

"I'll go," said Bill. I started to give him my spiel about what to do, but he cut me off. "I've done this before. Don't go easy on me." Bill lowered himself into the water and got into the starting position. "All right, pal—let's go."

I started the engine. The boat jumped forward, and Bill managed to pull himself to standing. Seconds later, the momentum was too much for him, and he faceplanted in the water. I pulled the boat around to pick him up.

"You gotta keep it steady," he whined. "You pulled me off-kilter." Of course, I was responsible for his shitty water-skiing skills. He grabbed the rope again and crouched down. This time Bill stayed up for a bit longer, but the boat cut through someone's wake, and the waves knocked him off balance.

"What are you doing?" he yelled. "You pulled me right through that wake."

"Honey, why don't you just try it again?" called Harper.

By now I was seething. If Bill wanted a ride, he was going to get one. I turned on the motor full blast. "Slow down!" cried Harper. I glanced over my shoulder. Bill was horizontal, and for a moment his body lifted above the water. Bill finally let go of the rope and dropped into the lake. I slowed down and circled back to get him.

"What the hell was that?" demanded Bill as he climbed onto the boat. He charged up to where I was sitting. "What was that?" he asked again, pushing my arm.

"Don't touch me," I said, shoving his hand away.

"Were you trying to mess me up? In front of my kid? Look at me!" he demanded. "Look at me!" He grabbed my shoulder and spun me around. I'd had enough.

I lunged forward and crashed into him, flattening him against the deck. Harper screamed, but I could barely hear her over the sound of the blood pounding in my ears and the thud of my fist connecting with Bill's face. I punched him over and over. He turned his face to escape the blows, and my hand collided with the deck. Something snapped in my knuckle, and the pain jolted me back to reality. Bill just lay there. Blood streamed from his nose, which was now off center. I looked up and saw Harper, who was huddling against the back of the boat, with her hand over her son's eyes.

I'd really fucked up this time.

What was I supposed to do now? I couldn't drive them back and hang around while my passengers called the police. I jumped into the lake and swam toward the shore. Besides Chris, no one knew I was staying at the motel. I needed to hide out and then disappear.

CHAPTER

9

Present—Kate

RICHARD HAD GIVEN me contact information for Jacob's friends, but I couldn't reach any of them. One had a number that had been reassigned, and the new owner hung up after declaring that she didn't know Jaden and wouldn't sell me drugs. The second number didn't work at all. Chris Taylor had an active voicemail, but his inbox was full. Instead, I sent him a text introducing myself and asking him to ring me back. He didn't.

I'd followed Richard's instructions. He would probably have other tasks for me, but in the meantime, I needed to see the crime scene. Bryce Chen, the arson investigator, had graciously agreed to walk me through it and was meeting me at the ruins of Abby's cabin. I headed over on foot. It was a bit of a schlep, but I wanted to get a feel for my surroundings and keep an eye out for surveillance cameras.

I could hear the trees swaying in the wind as I walked. Many of the cabins were already decked out in Halloween swag, with plastic headstones, pumpkins, and homemade scarecrows. Others were covered in flowers and kitschy, year-round decorations. Every block had at least one house sporting weirdly hostile "No Trespassing" signs, several alluding to death by dog or gun. How many trespassers could they possibly get in a town in the middle of nowhere with four thousand people? But paranoia aside, those were the houses most likely to have camera footage.

One thing linking the "Home Sweet Home" folks to their "pissed-off-grandpa-with-a-shotgun" neighbors was a collection of sculptures carved out of tree trunks or into the side of living pines. Every fifth house seemed to have one. There were bears, Steller's jays, owls—even a bighorn sheep. The pieces varied in skill level, from crude to almost beautiful. I wondered if they were made by a group of people or a single artist who'd gotten better over time.

Eventually, I came to a narrow road marked "Private." I followed it up toward the mountain, past a clearing covered in yellow wildflowers. The fire damage appeared suddenly. Swaying pines were replaced by blackened spires that tapered to menacing points. Burned trunks were dotted with stubby little protrusions that used to be branches. I saw the ruins of four houses, now reduced to rubble. Everything was gone except the foundations and four stone chimneys sprouting from the ground like weeds.

It was a miracle that the fire changed course before destroying more homes. But the bald patch on the hillside was a stark reminder to locals that their town could be destroyed overnight.

I stepped onto the foundation of Abby's cabin. The outside edges were rimmed with crumbling stone that had likely served a decorative purpose. The actual house had been built on a concrete slab, now cracked from heat damage. It was easy to identify the kitchen, as a few blackened linoleum tiles still clung to the floor.

I reached into my tote bag and pulled out the arson investigator's report, which had a diagram of the scene. Moving into what had been the living room, I stood in the spot where Abby had died. The picture showed a large rock by her body, supposedly the murder weapon. But I'd checked the weather report. The Santa Anas blew hard on the night of the fire. One of the decorative rocks lining the edges of the foundation could have easily dislodged and rolled toward her body.

The sound of car wheels on the narrow, dusty road caught my attention. I looked up as a red Jeep pulled into the driveway. "Kate Myles?" called the driver as he strode over to where I was standing. He was a fit man in his mid-forties, wearing a "Baker to Vegas" T-shirt and snug jeans. "I'm Bryce Chen."

I grabbed his outstretched hand. "Thanks for meeting me— especially on your day off." I wondered if he was always this generous with his time. And whether his fire chief knew he was meeting with the arsonist's private investigator.

"No problem. I've never had an issue talking to the defense. And Ted and I go way back." *Okay, that explained it*—this guy was pals with Jacob's brother-in-law. "Anyway, I'm glad you found this place. Idlewood feels like a grid until you realize it's not. Newcomers get lost a lot."

"It's so beautiful here, I don't think I'd mind getting lost." The afternoon sun crept into the corner of my vision. I brought an arm across my brow, to shield my eyes.

Bryce laughed good-naturedly. "I can't argue there. Anyway, I don't have a ton of time before I'm due back home, but let me show you around the scene." He pointed to the ground by my feet. "This was where it started. We think he used an accelerant, which is why the cabin went up so quickly."

"What kind of accelerant?" I asked.

"We don't know; it all burned away. Possibly alcohol—friends said Abby kept a few bottles of liquor in the kitchen. He could have poured them around the room and then lit a match. Or gasoline—a lot of folks around here have golf carts and off-road vehicles and store a bit of gasoline at home."

"Why do you think he used an accelerant?"

Bryce pointed toward the corner of the room. "You see how there are still bits of flooring left in the corners?" I nodded. "That means the fire burned hottest in the middle—where the floor's totally gone. It tells me this wasn't an electrical fire, which would've started by an outlet in the wall." I couldn't fault his logic.

He went on. "Then there's the position of the body. What are the chances that an electrical fire would start right after the victim was knocked unconscious on the floor?"

"Assuming she was knocked unconscious," I countered.

"Fair," said Bryce, considering this for a moment. "But look where they found her. She wasn't in her bedroom, even though the fire happened late at night. She was in the middle of the living room floor. It's not a place where most people choose to sleep."

I pushed a lock of hair out of my face. "Do you know where the TV was?" Bryce looked confused. "My dad used to fall asleep by the TV," I told him. "In the middle of the living room."

Bryce laughed, "Okay, I see where you're going with that. My gramps does that too. But if I'm remembering right, I don't think she had a television."

"There's another thing I wanted to ask you," I said. "The first investigator on the scene wrote that the cause was undetermined." Bryce winced and looked down at the ground. His face told me I was on to something. "It sounds like he wasn't convinced this was arson?"

Bryce rubbed his forehead. "God, Nick Fieldstone . . . look, off the record, he didn't do the most thorough job. Nick lives in Idle-wood. I think he was so worried about his town that he didn't bring his A game. I mean the guy had just shoved his stuff into a van and watched his family drive off to a motel because of the fire."

I had a feeling that Bryce was holding something back. I opened my mouth to ask a follow-up question, but he cut me off before I had the chance.

"Let me take you through the rest of the scene," he said, glancing at his watch. "My church is having a potluck, and I'll be in the dog-house with my wife if I miss it."

Bryce walked me over to what used to be the house next door. Ninety-year-old Lydia Birch had probably been asleep when the wind blew an ember from Abby's cabin onto her roof. I thought about the dry pine needles that blanketed Idlewood. Lydia's home had basically been covered in kindling. The poor woman never stood a chance. The neighbors in the other burned cabins had been comparatively lucky: they'd woken up, smelled smoke, and escaped with their lives.

After the tour, Bryce shook my hand again and sped off to his potluck. I started walking back toward my cabin. On the way down, I saw a shabby wooden house with five "No Trespassing" signs stuck to a rusty metal fence. In case potential intruders failed to get the message, the owner had added a sixth plaque, reading "Closed circuit television and Audio Monitoring on Premises." I studied the roof line and spotted two cameras pointing at me. My eyes traveled down the wall, and I noticed that the blinds in one of the windows were crooked.

"Can I help you?" asked a reedy male voice over a loudspeaker.

The unexpected greeting caught me off guard. I wasn't going to talk to a disembodied voice, so I walked up to the front door. The house was decked out with wind chimes and several species of ceramic lawn ornaments. Maybe Mrs. Doomsday Prepper was friendlier than her husband.

An old man opened the door just wide enough to peer out at me. A slight vinegary smell of dirty clothes and unwashed bodies wafted out from the house. I took a step back, worried that I might gag if I moved closer. I started to explain why I was there. But before I could finish my pitch, he interrupted to say that he'd given his video to the police, and closed the door in my face.

As I stood in the doorway, stunned by his rudeness, I remembered that somewhere out there was an old man who shared half my genetics. For all I knew, it was the smelly surveillance freak or another paranoid shut-in. Weirdly, the thought made me laugh. *Being here is doing a number on my head.*

Since the cops had already collected footage, I decided to see what they had before going door to door. I could always come back if there were gaps in coverage. I walked another few blocks and saw a man with earmuffs and goggles shaving pieces off the side of a pine tree with a chainsaw. He must have sensed my eyes on him, because he switched off his machine, turned around, and met my gaze.

"Sorry, I didn't mean to interrupt," I said.

He pulled down his mask and smiled. My pulse quickened. He was startlingly handsome, with shaggy brown hair and blue eyes. "That's okay—I was about ready to stop for the day," he said.

"Are you responsible for all the carvings around here?" I heard myself ask.

"Yeah—that's me. Sam Fabian, also known as the crazy guy with the chainsaw."

"That's what a girl likes to hear when she's in a new place, talking to a stranger."

Sam laughed, and I liked the sound of it. Friendly and open. "So, you're new around here. What brings you to Idlewood?"

"Work," I said. "I'll be staying here for at least a week, maybe more. Any recommendations?"

"Sure. Come to my bar. The Bighorn Grill—on Park Drive."

He was casually leaning against the tree trunk, with the sleeves of his plaid shirt rolled up. I was very aware of the outline of his body under his clothing.

"I'll check it out," I told him. *After all, a girl's gotta eat.* "Glad to know you're more than just a chainsaw weirdo. What are you making, by the way?" My heart pounded. He was distractingly good-looking. The kind where it's hard to focus on a conversation because you're worried he can read your attraction on your face.

"It's a coat of arms. But I think I may have bitten off more than I can chew," said Sam, running a hand through his hair.

"How so?"

"Well—they liked the crest I did for the Fitzgerald family. But that was easy, it's just a red X on a white shield. I agreed to do this one before seeing the Grady coat of arms—it's three identical lions. As you may have noticed—my skills are a bit more rustic than Irish heraldry calls for."

I laughed. He was funny too. Gotta love a man who can be self-deprecating.

"Anyway," said Sam, "hopefully I'll see you at the bar. But I should warn you, everything starts and ends early in Idlewood. People are usually good and merry by seven, tipsy by eight, and by ten or eleven I'm giving them rides home."

"Duly noted," I said. "Good luck with the lions. I'll see you around."

My cheeks burned as I turned and started down the street. I never stop and flirt with strangers. On the rare occasions when men talk with me, I'm usually too oblivious to notice or too insecure to offer much in response.

But I felt less inhibited here. Maybe because I knew I'd be gone in a couple of weeks. I was a stranger in Idlewood. I could pretend to be a blank slate with no baggage. And since learning about my father, I'd been numb. It was like I was floating above my body, watching myself go through the motions of my day. The magnetic pull feeling of meeting someone that attractive had taken me out of my head for a minute. I wanted more of it. I should probably be hitting up the local spots and talking to people, anyway. If I happened to spend more time chatting with Sam in the process, was that so terrible?

10

Two years ago—Jacob

"Dude, you're a fucking psycho!" said Chris as he burst through the door.

Ignoring him, I picked through a heap of crushed cans, dirty clothes, and cigarette butts, throwing anything worth saving into a duffel bag. I had to get out of here—fast.

"And why didn't you answer your phone?" he demanded. "I've been calling you for half an hour."

I shrugged and heaved the bag over my shoulder. "I don't have a phone anymore. It got wet when I jumped in the lake."

Chris's eyes shifted to the bag, noticing it for the first time. "C'mon, man, where you gonna go? You broke that guy's nose—the police are gonna be looking for you."

"My parents' house," I said, walking past him. "I can't stay in Arrowhead." I opened the door, but Chris reached around me and pulled it closed again. "Listen to me—stop! You can't go home. It's only an hour away, and that's the first place the cops are gonna check."

I felt trapped in the dark, filthy room. The air was thick with the smell of feet, stale clothes, and old carpet. Every inch of me was bursting to get out. I started breathing heavily and glared at Chris, who was blocking the exit. My hands balled up. He was too close. I felt like punching him. "Get out of my way!"

He moved to the side, startled by my anger. I left the motel, squinting in the noonday sun, and walked to my car.

"Just listen to me for two minutes," pleaded Chris as I threw my bag in the back seat. "No one knows you're here. Your name isn't listed in the hotel register. As far as my dad's concerned, I'm staying in a room with a buddy, but he doesn't even know who you are. It's a perfect place to lay low. And in another month, no one will care about the tourist who got his nose busted."

He had a point. If the sheriffs ran my RAP sheet, they'd see three misdemeanor arrests out of Idlewood, with my parents' address on the booking sheets. For all I knew, a couple of deputies were already driving there to look for me.

But that didn't mean I had to hide in this rotting dump like a caged animal. I could leave and just keep driving—find someplace new. The problem was, I was dead broke and couldn't work with a busted hand. Dishwashing was my usual go-to, but I wasn't sure I could push through the pain—rubbing soap on ceramic for eight hours and ignoring the throb in my knuckle. I had a crumpled twenty in my wallet and a quarter tank of gas. I wouldn't get far on that.

I opened the driver's door and sat behind the wheel, trying to think. Chris slid in next to me. "I don't know what to do," I said. "I blew all my cash on booze and weed. I can't work, and there's probably a warrant out for me." Forgetting about my injured hand, I punched the steering wheel in frustration. Lightning coursed up my finger and down my wrist.

"Get a grip," said Chris, shaking his head. "We'll figure this out."

I glared at him. I hate it when people pretend things are fine when they're obviously not. And this was Chris's fault. He'd dragged me out here, promising we'd work together on the lake. Instead, he'd told me he got some other job and left me there alone, making minimum wage and taking orders from an aging frat boy who smelled like sweated-out beer. "Easy for you to say. You still have a job, and the cops aren't looking for you."

Chris took a deep breath and exhaled slowly. "What if I can bring you in?"

I turned and looked at him. "What are you talking about?"

"My work. Look, I know I've been shifty on the details. That's 'cause it's not exactly legal. But I think they could use another guy. And the heavy—he kind of looks for people down on their luck, you know? Out of options."

That was me all right. "What kind of work?" I asked. Chris never talked about his job, but he always had more cash than he could have made from waiting tables, plus a never-ending supply of drugs.

"It's this guy—he goes by Byron. It's not his real name. He comes up with these scams but has other people do them for him. That way he's protected if someone gets caught."

"What kind of scams?" I asked.

Chris shrugged. "Small- to medium-level stuff—nothing that could draw serious heat. But he's always got something going on; I'm only in on a fraction of it. The guy's making bank. And I can vouch for you. You're strong, you have a work ethic. And your parents are fancy, so you can talk smooth if you need to."

I rolled down the window, lit a cigarette, and inhaled deeply. The nicotine felt good. What did I have to lose? I'd already have to eat a felony assault charge if the police caught me. Some two-bit scheme was a drop in the bucket. "Okay," I said. "Give him a call."

CHAPTER

11

Present—Kate

GRACE HAD STAYED quiet during my meeting with the Coburns. But she'd thrown me a couple of looks that I wanted to follow up on. I called her the next day after five o'clock, when her workday was done.

"Hey," she said. "What's up?" Her voice sounded muffled, like she'd been crying.

Grace was a direct person, so I didn't beat around the bush. "Yesterday I sensed there was something you wanted to tell me."

She inhaled deeply and let it out slow. "I'm going to walk the dog in about fifteen minutes. Can I call you then?"

I hate phone interviews. I need to look at a person's face when they're talking to me. "Why don't I join you on your walk? I can meet you at your place."

Grace's house was a few blocks south of the small downtown. When I got there, she was waiting for me on the front porch, holding the leash of an aging German shepherd.

"He's beautiful. Can I pet him?" I asked, reaching toward the animal.

She shook her head. "Bad idea, he's a retired police dog, and he gets territorial." I pulled my hand back. "Let's walk downtown. I'll show you where Abby worked."

We headed toward the strip of bars and restaurants. Grace jumped in before I could ask a question. "My sister didn't make the best choices—either personally or professionally. Men liked her and she liked them. But she didn't get that she could be picky."

I nodded in understanding. One of my friends had that problem. Sometimes I wished I had a superpower where I could clap my hands and make her break up with her latest creep. Then again, she'd probably felt that way when I was married to John.

"A few months before Abby died, I stopped by with a gallon of ice cream. We'd had a fight, and I was coming by to make peace. I found her sobbing on her porch, with a bottle of vodka. She asked me to leave, but I refused to go until she talked to me. Eventually, she told me she was in love with a married man."

This was huge. A married lover would've had a motive to kill Abby. If Richard could point a finger at another suspect, Jacob might have a chance at an acquittal. "Did she give you a name?"

The baby squinted against the late afternoon sun, and Grace put up a hand to shield his eyes. "I tried to get it out of her. But Abby just kept shaking her head. She said it was one more reason for me to be disappointed in her." Grace looked over at me, her eyes shining. "We didn't have the easiest relationship. The truth is, we didn't really understand each other."

Grace was harboring a ton of guilt, and I sensed that she didn't have a lot of people to talk to. I felt for her, but I needed to keep this conversation on track. "Did Abby tell you anything else about her lover?"

Her brow furrowed as she tried to remember. "No. I tried to pry, but I didn't get much out of her."

"Could you tell if he was a local?"

Grace considered this. "At the time, I thought so, but I guess it could have been someone from her graduate program. You might want to talk to her thesis advisor—Dr. Luna. I think they were pretty close."

I made a mental note to follow up on that. *Pretty close* could mean a lot of things. Abby wouldn't be the first person to start an ill-advised romance with a teacher. "Is there anyone else she might have confided in?"

Grace paused to give the old dog a chance to do his business. "There's a girl named Carrie who works at the Bean and Grape—kind of an artsy type. I went in a few times and saw them laughing together. It's right there, actually." She pointed to a coffee shop with a wide deck under a tan awning.

She pulled her phone out of a pocket in her black stretchy pants and checked the time. "They close at six," said Grace. "You'll have to come back tomorrow. Also, it's getting late. I have to get back and pick up Liam from my mother-in-law's house."

"Before you go," I said, "Richard wants me to interview a friend of your brother's named Chris Taylor—any idea how to reach him?"

Grace laughed darkly and shook her head. "My brother's friends were a bunch of degenerates. I know Richard's harping on this insanity defense, but talking to them isn't gonna get you there. I remember Chris, though. He's kind of a drifter. But not dumb. He can turn on the charm when it suits him."

"How did he know Jacob?"

"They both worked in the café at my parents' ski resort. Chris was silver-tongued when he spoke to my folks. They wanted to promote him to manager. Instead, they ended up firing him for stealing cash at the end of his shifts."

Great, a conniving thief. Richard was out of his mind if he wanted to call this guy to the stand. "Any idea where I can find him?"

"Actually, you know what?" said Grace. "A while back, Jacob moved in with a friend whose dad owned a motel near Arrowhead. I don't know if that was Chris, but I wouldn't be surprised. They were close."

I thanked Grace and we parted ways. The sky was starting to darken, and I noticed a rumble in my stomach. I didn't have any food back at my cabin, so I decided to pick up a burger in town. Turning onto Park Avenue, I spotted the Bighorn Grill and remembered the handsome woodcarver. Maybe he was working tonight. I smiled at the thought of seeing him again.

The restaurant was nothing fancy—just a log cabin painted red and a patio with six hunter-green picnic tables out front. A wooden sign hung over the doorway, bearing the name of the place and the carved head of a bighorn sheep. I had a pretty good idea who the artist was.

It was a chilly night, but the cold felt refreshing. I sat down at one of the picnic tables and picked up a plastic menu in front of me, left by the last customer. I studied the offerings. Standard bar fare with decadent touches. Burgers with gruyere, chicken Caesar salad with avocado, sweet potato fries with garlic aioli.

Sam came outside, caught my eye, and walked over to my table. My cheeks warmed at the sight of him. He was as gorgeous as I'd remembered. "Hey, didn't I see you earlier?" he asked.

"Yeah. You were working on a Celtic crest, I believe." I tried to sound casual, but my breathing had sped up. I turn very red when I'm blushing. Hopefully, he couldn't tell in the evening light.

Sam grinned, displaying a set of straight white teeth and sending a current of electricity through my body. "It's been slow tonight, so I've been practicing my lions. I think I'm in trouble." He pulled a little notebook out of his pocket and showed me a lopsided cat whose knees bent in the wrong direction. I laughed and Sam put a hand to his heart in mock grievance. "It's a little goofy, but laughter's kinda harsh," he protested.

"It looks like a My Little Pony that fell off a cliff."

Sam was laughing now. "What makes you the expert on My Little Ponies?"

I touched my phone screen, which lit up with my background picture of Amelia. "I have a seven-year-old girl. I could testify in court as a pony expert."

"Fair enough," said Sam. "She's a cutie. Can I get you a drink?" I hesitated for a second. The thought of a gin and tonic made my mouth water. And my stomach had been a ball of knots for days now. But if I had one, I'd want another. It wasn't a good idea. "Club soda with lime," I said. "And a cheeseburger."

"You got it."

My mood deflated as Sam disappeared inside. Bringing up Amelia had shortened the conversation. I make a point of mentioning my daughter in my rare flirtations with men. If someone's going to be scared away by the fact that I have a kid, I want to know up front. They basically always are, but I'm used to it.

I heard a loud cackle from a few picnic tables over. Two gruff-looking women sat across from a skinny, bearded man in a dark beanie. The noise came from the older of the two, who had stringy bleached-blond hair. The other woman, whose dark hair was tucked under a baseball cap, put her phone on speaker and started shouting at a friend on the other end of the line. "Bitch, get over here!" she said. "Before I beat your ass!" Her tone was playful, and the two of them had clearly been drinking. I looked at my watch. It was six thirty.

A young and reasonably attractive yuppie couple with a toddler was sitting at a table between us. "Boy or a girl?" asked Blondie.

"Boy," the woman replied with a tight smile.

"Boys suck!" shouted Blondie. "I have three of them."

The yuppie woman nodded awkwardly and looked down at her plate.

Blondie started to say something else but then noticed a trio of people across the street. She stood up and walked over to the retaining wall surrounding the small patio, and called out a greeting from thirty feet away.

Sam came back and placed my drink in front of me, along with a little white bowl with limes in it.

"How many does it take to get like that?" I asked, nodding toward Blondie.

"She's been going strong since about four o'clock. Which is actually late for her—sometimes she comes in at noon." Sam fumbled with his phone and pulled up a picture. "If your kid's here, you should take her to the cat arcade."

Cat arcade? "The what?" I asked, thinking I'd heard wrong.

He handed me the phone, showing a picture of him in an old school arcade with a girl Amelia's age and a beautiful young woman of about twenty, his much-younger girlfriend, I guessed. A shabby white cat was standing by the little girl's feet, and another had climbed on top of the *Pac-Man* machine.

"Right on Evergreen. It's called Purrfection, and my kid loves it." I noticed his hands for the first time. No ring.

"I'm slightly allergic, so that might be my personal version of hell," I told him. "But I'll try it. My daughter's in a Hello Kitty phase, so it's probably right up her alley."

Sam laughed. "The things you do for your kids."

The people Blondie had seen across the street were now approaching her table. She squealed as she jumped up to hug them.

"Regulars?" I asked.

Sam nodded. "The louder one—she's had a rough go of it, so I tend to let a lot of things slide, but I have a feeling it's gonna be a bad night." One of the newcomers was holding a cigarette, and the wind was blowing smoke in our direction. Sam tapped on my table once with a closed fist, as if to say, *"I'll be back."* I watched as he went over to the newcomers. "Excuse me," he said discreetly. "There's a toddler right over there. Do you mind smoking by the side of the building?"

The woman turned and glared at the yuppie couple. "I'm not going to stunt your kid's growth," she said. But she did get up and move. The young mom mouthed, *"Thank you"* to Sam, who nodded and went back inside the restaurant.

Blondie and one of her friends were now locked in a weird embrace. Blondie reached her hands underneath her friend's hoodie, exposing several inches of stomach fat. "I'm gonna share your warmth!" she slurred.

"Bitch, your hands are freezing!" complained her friend, and pulled away, taking a seat on the bench.

Blondie laughed and sat down across from her. "It's not my fault, I got bad circulation!" My phone rang. *Amelia.* I'd gotten her a flip cell phone, so she doesn't have to go through her dad when she wants to talk to me. It was a slightly ridiculous gift for a seven-year-old, but I wanted her to feel like she could always call me without getting the other parent involved.

"Hi, sweetie," I said. "How was your day?"

"I went to the principal's office," she told me.

"What happened?" I asked, trying not to sound alarmed. *John never fucking tells me anything.*

"Cameron called me a space cadet, so I kicked her in the shin."

I inhaled deeply. Cameron was a nasty little bully who liked to pick on Amelia for zoning out in class. I hadn't heard about her in a while and had hoped she'd stopped. Apparently not.

"You can't do that, sweetie. Even if someone says something mean, you still can't kick them."

I heard John's voice in the background. "I have to go, Mommy. It's time for my bath." It's like he has a sixth sense for when I'm on the phone. He always finds a reason to make her get off.

"Okay, honey, but you can call me later. I'll sing you a song before bed. She hung up and I felt dejected. I wanted to hug her and remind her of how special she was. Instead, I was here, and she'd have to make do with my rigid ex and her icy twenty-six-year-old stepmother. I sipped my water and wished I'd opted for the gin.

My eyes drifted back to Blondie, who was crying now. "If I didn't drink, I'd kill myself. My husband is dead. My sons are far away. If I didn't drink, I'd have nothing."

Her dark-haired friend rubbed her back. "I'm here for you," she cooed.

I looked away, finding this lonely woman depressing. I wished Sam would bring my burger so I could eat and go home. As if reading my thoughts, he came out of the restaurant and set a plate in front of me. "Colorful place you got here," I said, sounding more judgmental than I'd meant to.

He smiled sadly and slid into the booth across from me. "You came on a bad night." He leaned forward and lowered his voice. "Myra over there," he nodded toward Blondie, "has had a sad life and deteriorates pretty quickly. She comes in three or four times a week. I usually just let her do her thing and make sure she's got a ride home. She has nowhere else to go, and Idlewood nights can be lonely."

"Did you say *Myra*?" I asked. "Please tell me that's not Myra Davies."

Sam looked puzzled. "Um, yeah, I think that is her last name. You know her?"

I put my head in my hands. "Her name popped up on a genealogy site. Apparently, she's a distant relative of mine."

Sam looked at her and then back at me. "I'd say pretty distant. You want me to introduce you?"

I shook my head. "I'd rather wait 'til she's in a better state. You said she comes here regularly. What would be a good time to come if I wanted to catch her before she deteriorates?"

Sam sighed and thought a moment. "Hard to say. A lot of the times she comes in at lunch and holds court for hours. You could try to come by early tomorrow afternoon."

I shook my head. "My kid is visiting this weekend."

"Well," he said, "I keep funny hours in the off season—it's bad for business, but it lets me spend time with my daughter. We're closed Monday and Tuesday, and we're only open 'til seven on Wednesday and Thursday. But you could try her around lunchtime."

I didn't want to wait until Wednesday. "You mentioned making sure she has a ride. Do you know where she lives?"

Sam looked taken aback. That was a weird question since he didn't know me, and I clearly didn't know Myra. I thought about whether to tell him about the investigation. Sam was a stranger, but I was new here, and the local bartender could be useful in filling in some gaps.

"I'm not just a cousin," I said. "I'm also a private investigator here on a murder case, and I really need to talk to her when she's coherent."

His expression changed to interest. "Wow, I thought you guys only existed in books and old movies."

I rolled my eyes. "I promise, we're real and we're far less glamorous than what you see on TV."

"I drive her home a couple times a month," Sam told me. "She's in a dark green cabin on the corner of Jennifer and Pine."

"Thanks," I said.

I felt a pair of eyes on me and looked over my shoulder to see an old man on the other side of the short cinder-block wall surrounding the patio. "Do you know what stinks about getting old?" the man asked. I shook my head. "You start to sway after you've had some drinks."

"Careful, Frank," warned Sam.

The old man tried to continue his journey, but the effort proved too much. He started to lose his balance. Like clockwork, Sam leapt to his feet and managed to catch Frank's head before it collided with the pavement.

"All right, Frank," said Sam. "You know the drill. Give me your keys—we're going back to your place."

A bar owner who regularly drove his drunk patrons home—this was a first for me.

CHAPTER

12

Twenty months ago—Abby

THE FIRST TIME I read the play *Gruesome Playground Injuries*, it made me cry. It told the story of Doug and Kayleen, two platonically in love friends, from childhood through their late thirties. I jumped at the chance to play Kayleen, whose shitty parents set her on a lifelong path of self-destruction. Meanwhile, Doug, her reckless, daredevil friend, adores her from a distance, periodically maiming himself in a series of increasingly stupid and preventable accidents.

The story moves around in time, tracing their lives through different injuries—both mental and physical. In one scene they're eight, chatting in the school nurse's office, him with a head scrape, and her with a tummy ache. Flash forward ten years, and Doug's just been beaten up for defending Kayleen's honor. Meanwhile, she's curled up in bed, in deep denial about a nonconsensual sexual encounter.

What moved me about the story was how much it made me think of my relationship with Jacob—minus the romantic connection. Well into their thirties, Doug and Kayleen talk to each other like kids, never losing the immature kid speech they had when they met. I loved how that immaturity was paired with the intense adult bond they shared. Even though they're both too broken to help each other. It made me think of my brother—how I act like a teen around him. How I feel in my gut that something is really wrong, and he's starting to spiral in a way that I'm powerless to stop.

This was the fifth play I'd done at the Sabertooth, a tiny hole-in-the-wall in Glendale. You'd never find the place if you didn't know it was here—buried in a blink-and-miss-it strip mall, between a late-night kabab joint and a store selling hookahs that's probably a money laundering front. Beau Erwin, the theater director, ran it as a labor of love. The Sabertooth was never going to make any money charging fifteen-dollar tickets in a venue that maxed out at seventy-five people. But Erwin was brilliant and had amazing taste in material.

Performing here fed my soul. It replenished my love of the craft when I felt numb from soulless gig work. The last part I'd landed before this was a sexy storm trooper in a Star Wars–themed burlesque show. I quit after a week of doing the cancan in fishnets while breathing through a plastic mask. *We all have our limits.*

But now I was back at the Sabertooth, bringing a beautiful, flawed, sensitive person to life. My scene partner, Rodney, and I held hands and took our bow. Most of the twenty people in the audience were on their feet, applauding. I caught one woman, a regular, wiping away tears. I knew I'd reached her. The last scene was the one that got me too.

As I was coming out of the changing room, Erwin tapped me on the shoulder. "You up for kabobs?" he asked.

"Sure," I said.

"All right, I'll grab Rodney. Let's meet out front."

Erwin and I have a history. We had a little thing back when I was in acting school. He was fifteen years my senior, and teaching a class on experimental theater. I'd found his passion for the stage irresistible. He'd even gotten me to solicit a donation for the Sabertooth from my parents. In retrospect, our relationship was entirely inappropriate, and he'd used it to extract money from my family. After things ended, I kept my distance for a few years. But eventually, Erwin had reached out and offered me a part I couldn't resist, and we'd patched things up. Professionally at least.

We walked next door, and Erwin bought us delicious plates of shawarma. He ordered us each a Coke and then pulled out a tiny bottle of rum from his messenger bag and a set of lime wedges wrapped in tin foil to make Cuba libres. That made me laugh.

"Wow, Erwin, love the attention to detail. Looks like you planned this!"

Rodney smiled, but Erwin's face stayed serious. "I did," he said. "I need to talk to you both, and I thought the alcohol would help." He took a long pull of his drink. "I'm probably going to be closing the Sabertooth."

"When?" I asked. My heart ached at the news, but I can't say I was surprised. Covid had decimated LA's theater scene, but Erwin had managed to keep this place afloat by hustling donations and renegotiating his rent. Through all of it, he'd kept his faith that LA needed theater and the audience would come back. But even after vaccines came out and pandemic warnings lessened, a portion of the former audience stayed home. Attendance had been meager for this production, and I had a bad feeling that the writing was on the wall.

"I'm gonna do an emergency fundraising pitch, but if that doesn't work, it'll be a matter of months. I need both of your help. If you know anyone who can contribute, please reach out to them."

He stared at me as he was talking, and I realized that this dinner was his way of asking me to hit up my parents again. Rodney was just there as a prop. Last night, Erwin had been talking about putting on *Hedda Gabler*, with me in the lead role. He knew I loved Ibsen. The whole thing had been a ploy to butter me up. But I wasn't a naive, twenty-year-old ingenue anymore, and I didn't like being handled. "If you want to ask me something, Erwin, just ask it," I said coolly.

"I'm fucking asking, Abby," he snapped. "I'm basically begging."

I leaned back in my seat and crossed my arms. "Is *Hedda Gabler* really in the works?"

Rodney looked back and forth between us, confused.

"Not if we close, it's not," said Erwin.

I looked down at my plate and ate in silence. Rodney and Erwin kept the conversation going while I sulked. My phone lit up with a number I didn't recognize. I picked it up, mostly as an excuse to leave the table. "This is Abby," I said.

"Abby, it's Jacob."

"I gotta take this," I told Rodney and Erwin, and quickly moved outside. A couple of days ago, a sheriff had come to my parents' place, looking for my brother, with an arrest warrant. I'd left him half a dozen voicemails, but he'd never called me back.

"What's going on, Jake? Why are the police looking for you?"

He launched into a story about assaulting a guy for disrespecting him on a boat. Now he was in hiding, convinced that all of law enforcement was after him, and that the boat guy had mob connections. His speech came out fast and pressured, almost in shouts. I've been in the acting world long enough to know when someone's on drugs. An old scene partner of mine had a coke problem and sounded just like Jacob when he was using.

"You don't sound like yourself. What are you on?"

"Does it matter?" shouted Jacob.

"Were you on something when you punched that guy?"

"Yeah, I took some ice, but that had nothing to do with it."

My heart sunk. Jacob needed my help, and he needed it fast. "Come home, Jake. I can pick you up."

My brother let out an exasperated sigh. "I can't do that, Abby. They're looking for me."

"Then turn yourself in before this gets worse."

Jacob didn't say anything, but I could hear him breathing heavily into the phone. An ambulance drove by, and I pressed my free ear into my shoulder to block out the sirens.

"Goodbye, Abby," I heard Jacob say. Then the line went dead.

13

Present—Kate

M YRA DAVIES' HOUSE had once been well cared for. The outside
had been painted a pretty forest green with white trim, and her
yard was populated by an impressive collection of lawn ornaments: a
plastic deer, wind chimes, a sun-bleached sign reading "Faith, Family,
Friendship." Now the paint was chipping, and I could see signs of dry
rot on the eaves. Long weeds grew up around the figurines, creating a
weird effect, as if they were peeking out at you.

I knocked and Myra answered the door in plaid pajama pants
and a hole-ridden men's T-shirt. Her straw-colored hair was stuffed
into a messy bun. It wasn't time for the bar yet, and it seemed that
Myra hadn't felt a need to get dressed. "What do you want?" she
demanded.

"Hi, Ms. Davies, my name is Kate Myles. I sent you a message on
GeneExploder." I'd actually sent two—the second one telling her that
I was in Idlewood. Myra hadn't responded, so I'd decided to try my
luck in person. On seeing her expression, I wished I'd waited 'til she
was a drink or two in.

Myra crossed her arms over her ample chest. "Yeah, I got your
messages. What are you doing here, and how do you know where I
live?"

Both fair questions. "I'm sorry to show up like this. I'm a private investigator, and I got your address from a public records search," I lied, not wanting to throw Sam under the bus. "I'm reaching out because it turns out that you and I have a distant relative in common whose DNA is linked to an old murder investigation. The police are trying to identify him. Can I come in and ask you a few questions?"

Her mouth hung open, and she stared at me in shock. "I'm related to a killer? Who'd he kill?"

"A seventeen-year-old girl, twenty years ago. He strangled her and left her body at Camp Idlewood."

Myra shook her head and her eyes welled up. "Jesus, she was just a baby."

She opened the door wider, and I followed her into the living room, which looked like it hadn't been cleaned in years. Myra collapsed into a stained recliner and lit a cigarette. I sat across from her on a creased leather couch with a permanent dent in the middle. "You're working with the police?" she asked.

"Yeah—informally, but that's not why I messaged you." Myra's guard was up. I needed to build rapport and decided to start with my background. "It's a long story—but basically I learned after my dad died that I was conceived through a sperm donor. I reached out because I saw that we're a match, and I wanted to learn more about where I come from. I'm single and an only child, so it can get pretty lonely."

She nodded at this last part. I could tell from seeing her the other night that Myra was no stranger to loneliness. I was making headway. "You got any kids?" she asked.

"Yes, a girl. Anyway, after I sent in my DNA sample, I matched with you and one other person—"

Myra cut me off. "The killer. I know. The police called me about some kind of investigation, but they didn't say nothin' about a seventeen-year-old girl. I told them what I'm telling you—I don't know nothin' about a murder."

"Of course, you don't," I said. "But maybe you know something about our family that can help—or help me meet other relatives."

Myra inhaled deeply from her cigarette. I waited for her to say something, but she stayed quiet.

"Do you have kids?" I asked.

She nodded. "Three boys. My youngest is nineteen. Joined the Marines and knocked up a girl before he left town. Baby's due in March."

"That'll probably keep you busy."

She tapped her cigarette in an already full ashtray. "Yeah, I didn't sign up for none of this. I did my time. Raised my boys. I'm fifty-six and I don't feel like changing diapers."

The age reveal caught me off guard. I would have guessed closer to seventy. "How old is your oldest son?" I asked.

Myra's eyes narrowed. "Thirty-one. He's not a killer if that's what you're after."

"No—of course not," I said quickly. "Genetically, it couldn't be one of your kids."

She seemed to relax. "Elijah—he's a good boy. He works for an energy company in Kern. My babies are all scattered." Myra made a sweeping gesture to illustrate her point. "Enjoy yours while you have her."

Her words stung, but I plastered on a smile. "Like I said, no one's looking at you or your kids. I'm trying to figure out if you have a cousin or a nephew who lived in Idlewood twenty years ago and could have done this. I know it's unpleasant, but you can help bring closure to this poor girl's family."

Myra lit another cigarette. As she puckered her lips around it, the skin by her mouth formed dozens of little grooves. "Don't put that on me," she said. "I get it. I'd like to help, but like I told you, I don't know anything. I came here for my husband's work. He's been dead now for three years. As far as I know, I don't have any family in Idlewood. I had a brother who was a trucker who sometimes came through. But he's dead, so that won't help you."

"Did he have any kids?" I asked. Myra shook her head. "What about relatives in nearby towns? Anyone you can think of?"

"Wish I did. Idlewood's a nice place to raise a family. But if you're by yourself, it's the loneliest place in the world." She shrugged. "A beautiful place to rot."

CHAPTER

14

Twenty-three months ago—Jacob

CHRIS SET UP my first job for Bryon by text message. I didn't meet the boss in person, and Chris wasn't allowed to give me his number. If I proved trustworthy, Byron would reach out.

The scam involved targeting old people with roofing issues. Arrowhead is a paradise for the elderly—some live here all year long; others come up in the summer to lounge by the lake. Thanks to heavy winter snows, they all occasionally need to replace the shingles on their fancy A-frames. Byron had installed somebody at a local roof-repair company, who supplied us with a list of customers with pending service requests. Of those, we'd single out the oldest and most gullible and pay them a visit.

We'd already executed phase one and gotten several hits, including Mrs. Pfeiffer, a widow in her eighties. I stopped by her house with a clipboard and a fake sob story. After a five-minute chat about a made-up animal sanctuary, she handed me a check to help save abused livestock. Mrs. Pfeiffer passed the gullibility test, and we were ready for phase two.

The old lady had an outstanding roofing appointment in two weeks. The plan was to show up at her house and tell her we had an unexpected opening in our schedule. I was supposed to chat her up while two others would march around the roof, making noise, and a fourth would sneak into her bedroom and steal her jewelry. Then we'd collect an inflated check for the repair and disappear before she noticed that anything was missing. When I pointed out that the check would be made to the roofing company, Chris just laughed and showed me how to wash a check with a Q-tip and acetone, which dissolves the ink. Then we could write in whatever we wanted.

I didn't feel great about the plan. But Mrs. Pfeiffer lived in a mansion on a lake and had plenty of money. At the end of the day, she'd be fine, and I needed cash.

No one came to the door when I rang the bell. Inside, I could hear opera music blaring. I knocked harder. Mrs. Pfeiffer was probably too deaf to hear us. I spotted her through a window. She was standing at her kitchen counter, stirring a cup of tea. "Smile and wave—she'll remember you from the other day," said Chris.

I walked over to the window and peered inside. She'd moved over to the kitchen table and was sipping her tea and sorting through a pile of mail. I rapped on the window. Mrs. Pfeiffer jumped at the noise and looked over at me. I waved and gave a big fake smile. She stood up from the table and slowly walked toward the front door.

I wished I weren't sober for this. But Chris said I needed to be able to think and talk smooth. He refused to give me any ice until the job was done. I felt sick to my stomach. I couldn't tell if it was the guilt or the lack of drugs. If I were high right now, I wouldn't care about robbing her. I'd just do what needed to be done.

"Hurry the fuck up," muttered Ivan, one of the two goons we'd been paired with—Ivan and Jonas, but those might not be their real names.

The door swung open, and Mrs. Pfeiffer looked us over, confused. "Hello there," she said. She had stubby yellow teeth, hollow cheeks, and hair so thin I could see liver spots on her scalp. This was messed up.

"Hi, ma'am," I said. "Remember me from the other day? From the farm sanctuary?"

"Of course!" said Mrs. Pfeiffer. "I see you've brought some friends."

"We work for Luigi's Roofing," I told her. "Nice to see you again. I recognized your name when I saw today's agenda."

"But I spoke to Luigi," she protested. "He said he wouldn't have time to fix my roof until after Labor Day. He said he'd be sending over an estimate."

"Ma'am," Chris cut in, "we had an unexpected opening in our schedule, and it's supposed to rain next week. Luigi didn't want it to leak in your house." Chris sported a poker face, but his eyes danced. He was enjoying this.

"How thoughtful of him," said Mrs. Pfeiffer.

"We have our ladder with us," Chris told her. "We could walk around, but it'd be a lot easier if we could cut through the house." Chris had already checked out the place on Google maps and noticed the deck. He's smart—he thinks of these things.

"Of course," she said. "Why don't you come in."

We followed her inside. Ivan, Jonas, and Chris went out on the deck to set up the ladder. It was my job to distract Mrs. Pfeiffer so Chris could sneak back in and steal her jewelry. Meanwhile, Ivan and Jonas would march around making noise, to simulate a repair in process. At the end, we'd tell her the damage was worse than we'd thought, and collect a check for eight grand—Chris had set up a bank account under a fake name specifically for this scam. In a couple days, we'd empty out the money and close the account.

I scanned the room, hoping my eye would land on something that could spark conversation. Everything was soft and pink and floral.

She looked at me funny, probably wondering why I wasn't outside with the others. My heart sped up. Ivan and Jonas gave off a scary vibe, and I didn't know how they'd react if Mrs. Pfeiffer called us out.

"Ma'am, I'm sorry to trouble you. Could I get a glass of water?"

"Sure," she said. "Follow me, dear." We moved through the living room. She walked slowly, and her back had a hunch to it, like Gollum's from *The Lord of the Rings*.

We passed an old-fashioned wooden bookshelf covered in glass, with rows of creepy dolls stacked shoulder to shoulder, like something from a horror movie. Abby would tell me it was a sign I should run. I pretended to admire the dolls. One of them had a broken eyelid that stayed closed, like it was winking at me.

Mrs. Pfeiffer came back and handed me a glass, with a trembly hand. "They're pretty, aren't they?"

"Very nice, ma'am," I said. "My mother collects dolls, so seeing them makes me a bit homesick." I've always been good at lying on the spot. Not a skill I'm proud of, but it's gotten me out of a pinch more than once.

"Oh, it's hard to be away from home," said Mrs. Pfeiffer. "My daughter lives in San Francisco now, and I never get to visit with her. She loved the dolls when she was a little girl."

We both fell silent. I tried to think of something to say, but weird toys aren't exactly my thing.

"I guess I should let you get to it," she told me.

"Your daughter—what does she do?" I asked, stalling for time. I thought I heard the sound of feet upstairs. Chris needed to hurry up.

Mrs. Pfeiffer blinked, surprised and pleased by the question. "Oh. She teaches third grade."

"How nice," I said. "That's a job she can do anywhere—would she ever move back home?"

"Alas, I don't think so. Her husband is a heart surgeon at UC San Francisco. Amy moved for his career. He's very impressive, always saving lives. He even invented a new procedure where they use a robot to operate on your heart. I don't understand how it works, but it's very cutting edge, from what they tell me."

So far, so good. "Wow, your daughter must be so proud. Do you get to visit her in San Francisco?"

Mrs. Pfeiffer said it was hard to travel alone at her age, and her daughter was very busy. She didn't want to be a burden. I listened, nodding and making sympathetic noises. She was nice, and I liked how talking to her seemed to ease her loneliness. But we were here to rob her. I felt like throwing up.

A crunch of wheels on the gravel driveway grabbed my attention. "Who's that?" I asked, swiveling my head toward the front door. "Didn't you say the other day that you live alone?"

"Oh, that's my son, Ethan. He's visiting for the week. I'm so thankful he's here. There are so many errands I can finally get to, and—"

The door handle started to turn. "Let me check on the guys." I turned and sped toward the deck, where Ivan and Jonas had set up the ladder. "Need any help?" I called—hopefully loud enough for Chris to hear. It was our code for "time to go."

Ivan and Jonas climbed down the ladder while I held it steady. "The son is here," I whispered.

"Tell her we forgot a tool," said Ivan, "and we'll come back tomorrow to finish up."

We walked inside just in time to see Ethan confronting Chris. "What were you doing in my mom's bedroom?" he demanded.

"We're here fixing the roof, but we forgot a tool," I said.

Ethan turned to me and then back to his mother. "Mom, Luigi said they couldn't get you for two more weeks."

"We had an unexpected opening," I told him.

"Bullshit," said Ethan. "Luigi said he'd send a written estimate before doing the job."

"There's no need to get upset," said Chris. "Like he said, we had a cancellation and wanted to get your mom's roof done before the rain."

Ethan's eyes narrowed. "I haven't heard anything about rain." He moved toward Chris, gesturing at his work sack. "What's in the bag?" he demanded.

Chris leapt backward, moving the bag away from Ethan. There was the unmistakable rattle of pills in prescription bottles, tucked away inside.

"Give me that," demanded Ethan. He was a big guy—maybe six one and fit. Chris is small and out of shape. I stepped over and grabbed Ethan's arm, but he shook his arm free. "Get off me!" he demanded.

I didn't see Ivan coming until he grabbed Ethan by the neck and shoved him against the wall. Something glinted, and I saw the hunting knife in his left hand. I froze, unable to look away from the blade. Ivan held the tip against Ethan's stomach. Mrs. Pfeiffer screamed and stepped toward her son, but Jonas held her back.

"We're gonna go now," said Ivan, coolly. "You're never going to see us again. But if you call the police, I'll come back and flay your mother alive. Do we understand each other?" A small bloodstain was forming by the edge of the knife.

Ethan nodded. The front of his jeans had darkened, and the smell of urine filled the room.

Wordlessly, Chris, Jonas, and I filed out through the front door. Ivan followed, a beat behind. We jumped into the unmarked van and sped away. "Did you have to hurt him?" I asked Ivan. He didn't answer.

15

Present—Kate

J OHN WAS BUSY preparing for depositions and happily granted me
an extra weekend with my daughter. On Saturday, I woke at the
crack of dawn to drive to pick her up. Amelia ran to the door and
hugged me so hard, I had to step back to keep my balance.

She stayed quiet in the car. When I looked over, she was leaning
against the window, lost in thought. I tried to ask her about school,
but she gave one-word answers. Eventually, I put in a Disney CD, and
we drove without talking.

After about an hour, she finally opened up. Cameron, the bully,
was having a birthday party and hadn't invited Amelia. Her jerk of a
mom had sent the kid to school with invitations, which she handed
out to twelve of the fifteen girls in the class. My daughter was one of
the ones left out.

And as it turned out, her teacher wasn't doing much to make her
feel included either.

"Miss Weaver asked me where I go," she told me.

"What do you mean?" I glanced over at Amelia. Her forehead was
still pressed against the window. There was a little cloud of condensa-
tion where she'd been breathing on the glass.

"I wasn't listening, and Miss Weaver snapped her fingers in front of my face and said, *'Earth to Amelia.'* Everyone laughed."

My blood boiled. I was going to have a word with Miss Weaver.

I hated to see my daughter in pain, and it stung to know that she'd inherited the problem from me. I could never pay attention in school. The teacher would call on me, and I'd have no idea what was going on. It was as if a chunk of the lesson had never happened. I couldn't articulate where I'd gone either—I was just lost in my own mind. After a while, teachers ignored me, assuming that I was lazy or stupid. No one in my family understood because they all had standard-issue brains. In class, I learned to fade into the background, and accepted that my academic skills were nothing special. Even though I always knew on one level that I was smart.

In college, I finally realized that I had ADHD. I'd taken one of my roommate's Adderall pills before a party. It didn't get me high. It made me feel focused and normal in a shocking way. It was like discovering that I needed glasses for the first time and realizing most people had always been able to see clearly. But I was too embarrassed to get a proper diagnosis and a prescription. There was still a ton of stigma around these issues in my college days. Besides, by then I was planning to become a cop, like my dad, where college grades wouldn't matter.

It had been years since I'd thought about any of this. But seeing my daughter suffer brought everything back. She was still young enough that real schoolwork hadn't started. But we needed to do something before her self-esteem was permanently damaged. I just didn't know what.

"Listen to me," I said, reaching over and squeezing her hand. "You're smart and creative, and there's nothing wrong with you. You're just a dreamer, like Mommy. Lots of writers and artists are dreamers, and I bet they had a hard time in school too."

She looked at me skeptically. I didn't know if I was feeding her a line of BS. As much as I disliked John, I wished Amelia was more like him in some ways. It would make life easier for her.

Once we got to our cabin, Amelia ran straight up the rickety stairs to the attic and squealed with delight at the sight of the vintage toys. My stomach rumbled, and I promised her we'd have plenty of time to play with them after breakfast.

I took her to the Bean and Grape for brunch. While Amelia munched her waffle and drank hot cider, I scanned the place for people who looked like regulars. I felt guilty for semi-working during our time together. But being here with a kid gave me a cloak of mom invisibility. No one noticed me, and I watched them come and go. After all, these were Abby's customers. Maybe someone knew something.

My eyes hit on two men in their sixties, playing backgammon. Lately, I'd been scrutinizing the faces of every older guy I came across, trying to find a hint of resemblance to my daughter and me. One of the backgammon players had high cheekbones and a bump on the bridge of his nose, like I do. I had a weird urge to get up and talk to him. But what could I say? *Hi, your nose looks like mine. Did you donate sperm in the eighties?*

His eyes met mine and I looked away, embarrassed.

Amelia was playing with something small and white, rolling it along the table, like a marble. "Sweetie, did you lose a tooth?" I asked. She shook her head. "What's that in your hand?"

"It's Cameron's tooth."

My stomach did a backflip. "Amelia, why do you have Cameron's tooth?" I tried to keep my voice calm.

"She lost it at school, and I took it from her desk so she couldn't get money from the tooth fairy."

I took a breath. "Honey, you can't take people's stuff. Give me that." She handed me the tooth, and I wrapped it in a napkin. I considered telling her to apologize and give it back on Monday, which was probably the right thing to do. But this was the kind of thing a kid never lives down. They'd be calling her Tooth Girl until the day she graduated. "We're gonna throw it away, and we're not going to tell anybody what happened. I know you were mad at what Cameron did, but stealing is very wrong. Promise me you won't do anything like this again?"

Amelia didn't answer. She just stared glumly at her lap.

"Stealing is wrong. You're not gonna do it again, okay?"

"Okay," said Amelia in a sad little voice. She looked so unhappy. My heart ached for her. I needed to do something to cheer her up.

I remembered the cat arcade that Sam had mentioned. While Amelia studied her lap, I googled it on my phone and found Purrfection, just a few blocks away. "Let's go," I said. "I'm taking you somewhere fun."

The arcade was housed in a one-story building with a space-themed mural of comets and shooting stars. The window was filled with velvet-covered feline play structures. Three red-gold tabbies were stretched across the display. I opened the door and braced myself for a sneezeathon.

The cosmic theme continued inside the arcade, with giant murals of cat astronauts. Old-school games lined the walls: *Mortal Kombat*, *Street Fighter*, *Asteroids*. And then there were the cats. At least ten of them. My eyes started to itch.

"This place is awesome!" cried Amelia. At least she was into it.

I dumped a twenty into the token machine and then handed her several gold disks. She ran over to a royal-blue machine emblazoned with *Space Invaders* in neon lettering. Within seconds, she was having a blast shooting aliens.

In the corner by a *Pac-Man*, I spotted Sam laughing with a little curly-haired girl about Amelia's age. I smiled at the sight of him and felt blood rushing to my face. Man, he was gorgeous. Part of me wanted to tap him on the shoulder and say hi, but I kept my distance. We were both here with our kids, and I probably looked like a hot mess.

After several rounds of killing space invaders, I led Amelia over to an air hockey table. "Have you played this before?" I asked. She shook her head. I explained the basics, and we had a go at it. Amelia was a natural and beat me on her second try. She grinned and I remembered the tooth incident, feeling a little guilty that I was basically rewarding her for stealing someone's tooth. But she was having a rough time right now, and it was so good to see her smile.

Something moved against my leg. I glanced down and saw a gray kitty rub against my calf. The cat dander suddenly caught up with me, and I let out five sneezes, much to my daughter's delight. I pulled a tissue out of my tote bag and wiped my watering eyes. "Glad you're so entertained."

I looked up and saw Sam grinning at me. "You weren't kidding about the allergies."

"It's not enough to send me to the hospital, but I definitely checked my dignity at the door."

"Honey," he said to his little girl, "this is my friend Kate." Sam bent down to my daughter's eye level. "And who are you?"

"Amelia."

"I'm Sam and this is Willow," he told her. Sam pointed to the air hockey table. "You guys wanna play a round?"

We each took a side, and the battle began. Sam had a knack for it but held back—probably since his only adult opponent was a serial-sneezing wreck. I stole glances at him as he cheered on his daughter. He was good with her, sweet and engaged.

After losing three times in a row, we moved on to a giant, human-sized game of Connect Four, where Amelia and I redeemed ourselves. After about an hour, my sinuses had reached their limit, and I announced that we had to go.

"Did you guys walk or drive?" asked Sam.

"We walked," Amelia told him. "Mommy took me for waffles."

"Why don't we give you a ride?" he suggested. "We came by golf cart."

I was about to say no, but Amelia clasped her hands together and jumped up and down. "Can we? Please, Mommy!" she begged.

I wouldn't normally accept a ride with my kid from someone who was basically a stranger. But Sam was here was his daughter. The chances of him being a serial killer were pretty slim. *And it was a golf cart.* If anything felt funny, we could always jump off. "Sure. Maybe the wind will air out my sinuses."

"I doubt it," said Sam. "You're gonna be suffering through tomorrow."

Amelia and I climbed into the golf cart's back row. She squealed with delight when it sprang to life. The wind blew our hair into our faces as we flew down the road. I knew I was going to look like Medusa when we came to a stop. But the cool air felt good against my skin. And despite my runny nose, I could smell the pines.

"Where are you staying?" asked Sam.

I shouted our address over the motor. The cart drove over a speed bump, and we bounced in our seats. My daughter shrieked happily.

When we reached our cabin, I quickly smoothed down my hair before thanking Sam for the ride. We waved goodbye as they drove down the road.

I felt giddy as we walked to the cabin. I'd forgotten what it was like—that rush when you click with someone attractive. After my marriage blew up, I'd convinced myself that I could live without romance. It's basically impossible to meet someone in LA in your late thirties—even without a kid. And for the last two years, all my energy had been focused on putting my life back together.

There had been someone a while back—Luke, my former partner from LAPD. We worked on an art-forgery-turned-murder case and both realized that something was there between us. But that case is still pending, and I'll be a witness in the trial, which last I heard got continued for another six months. Luke is the detective, and sleeping with a witness would torpedo the case and ruin his career. I've been keeping my distance from him, to avoid temptation.

Other than Luke, I hadn't felt a flutter about anyone since the first few months with my ex-husband. Now here I was, grinning like an idiot over a man I'd just met. Since learning about my dad, I'd been sad and numb, and I desperately wanted to feel something else. The timing was terrible—with me investigating not just one case, but two, *and* keeping an eye out for someone who could have supplied half my genetics—but maybe I should go for it.

Amelia scrambled up the stairs to play in the attic while I fixed lunch. The cabin had a CD player and a stack of discs on the bookshelf. I was in a good mood and wanted a little music. I put on Johnny

Cash and sang along off-key, still smiling like an idiot while I grilled us cheese sandwiches and heated tomato soup for dipping.

As I was sliding the sandwiches onto plates, I heard a knock. I opened the door and saw Sam, holding Amelia's pink cardigan and looking amused. Behind him, Willow waved from the golf cart, which was parked in the street. "I think you guys forgot this," he said. "Also, I didn't know you liked old-time country."

I was mortified. Had he heard me singing? "Yeah, I do," I said, too embarrassed to think of anything witty. "Thanks for bringing back her sweater."

Sam leaned back like he was about to leave and then hesitated. "Hey," he said in a quieter voice that his daughter couldn't hear, "Would you want to get dinner sometime? The bar closes in the beginning of the week, so maybe Monday?"

Although I'd just been thinking about him, the invitation caught me off guard. It had been a while since a man asked me to dinner. In LA, you're lucky if a guy buys you a drink while reciting his résumé. "Sure," I said, "Monday sounds great." I gave him my number, and he waved and ran back to the golf cart. I watched him from the window as he drove away.

Finally, something was going my way.

CHAPTER

16

Present—Kate

Two days in Idlewood with Amelia left me dreaming about a whole different life. I imagined watching her grow up hiking and breathing fresh air. In the summer, we'd go swimming in a nearby lake. In the winter, we'd play in the snow and have a proper white Christmas. But all of that was a pipe dream, of course.

On Sunday evening, I took her for pizza before driving her back to her dad's house, and tried to enjoy our last few hours together. When you're a weekend parent, separation is always on your mind. I treasure my Sundays with Amelia, but they're hard. I wake up knowing she'll be gone in a matter of hours. Sunday nights, when I'm alone again, are the blackest part of my week.

We finished our meal and got in the car. Amelia looked glum, and I could tell she was upset. "I want to stay with you," she pleaded.

"I know, sweetie, but you have to go back to your dad's and go to school. I'll see you this weekend."

"I don't want to go to school." There was a quiver in her voice, and my heart ached. School was hard for her right now, and I couldn't even be there for support. I wanted to take her back to the cabin, read her a story, and curl up next to her in the little attic bedroom. Instead, I'd have to make do with another week of phone calls. And if John changed his mind about granting me an extra weekend, I wouldn't see her for two weeks.

She stayed quiet for the drive, and we listened to music. Before I knew it, we were parked outside John's house. I took Amelia by the hand and led her over to the front door. I try not to let her see how much it hurts me to leave her. But then I worry about seeming indifferent and making her feel unwanted.

John's wife, Kelsey, opened the door, looking beautiful and young in designer leggings and a tight pink workout tank. John usually stays inside on drop-off nights, to avoid me. "Hi, honey," said Kelsey to my daughter, with exaggerated sweetness. Gross. I want them to bond, of course. But hearing her talk in that practiced, phony mom voice made me want to retch.

I hugged Amelia for a long time and then forced myself to let go of her. My back hurt from the drive, and I'd be in agony after the hour and a half drive back to Idlewood. The town had seemed magical when Amelia was with me. But the thought of returning alone to a cramped cabin full of other people's things was almost unbearable.

By the time I arrived, I was emotionally depleted. It was a moonless night, and everything looked black when I turned off my headlights. As I stepped into the fall air, a gust of wind blew against me, and I shivered.

The cold followed me into the drafty old house. I turned on an ancient space heater, which gave off a funny smell. Amelia and I had made a fire the night before, but making another was too much effort for one person. I didn't want to be here, but I had nowhere to go. I thought about swinging by the liquor store and picking up a bottle of wine. But if I started, I wasn't sure I'd be able to stop. Myra Davies' words rang in my ears. *"If you're alone, Idlewood is the loneliest place in the world."*

As a distraction, I threw myself into my work. Richard had dropped off a flash drive with surveillance video from the police. I pulled out my computer and inserted the drive. Several clips showed a shadowy figure walking toward the dirt road that led to Abby's cabin. The man's face was obscured by a hood, and from one angle it looked like he was wearing a ski mask.

It had been chilly on the night of the fire, but not freezing. A mask would suggest that Abby's murder was planned. A person covers their face because they know they're about to do something bad, and they don't want to be recognized. But the prosecution's theory was that Jacob had killed his sister in a fit of rage. So something wasn't right.

I wondered how they'd settled on Jacob as the person in the footage. I skimmed the reports again and found one where a witness identified the man's hoodie as coming from the restaurant in Arrowhead where Jacob used to wash dishes. But Arrowhead was a popular vacation spot less than an hour from Idlewood. It wasn't a stretch that someone else in town had eaten there and bought a sweatshirt. I took a screenshot of the shadowy figure, to compare it to other possible suspects.

This case just didn't feel like a slam-dunk for the prosecution, which was how Richard and Grace had presented it. A flicker of doubt was forming in my mind. I needed to identify Abby's secret boyfriend and see if he fit the build of the figure in the video. Grace had mentioned that Abby had been tight with a girl named Carrie from the Bean and Grape. Maybe Abby had confided in her about the affair.

But I wanted to get a sense of who Carrie was before ambushing her. I found a Facebook page for the Bean and Grape and scrolled through their photo gallery. It didn't take long to find pictures of Abby. Even in casual snapshots, she oozed charisma. Here she was smiling at the backgammon players I'd seen the other day, wearing a vintage *"Rocky Horror Picture Show"* T-shirt with the sleeves cut off, and white jeans. Her curly hair was bleached to an old-Hollywood blond, but her mousy roots poked through. In one image, Abby was hugging a tall waif with thick mascara and chin-length auburn hair. I hovered my cursor over the redhead, and a name popped up: Carrie Goldberg.

I found a picture from the shop's twenty-year anniversary party. Dozens of people were crammed into the small space. I spotted Abby talking to a dark-haired man in a blue button-down shirt. His face was turned, so I could only see a sliver of his profile. But his body was angled toward hers, and they stood a little too close together. Abby's eyes danced, even more than in other pictures. I zoomed in on the pair of them and took a screenshot. Maybe this was the happy husband Grace had told me about. Tomorrow I'd head over to the Bean and Grape and look for Carrie. Hopefully, she could help me connect a few dots.

Next, I started searching for an address for Chris Taylor. My best bet was to track down his father's motel and hope he still lived there. I'd suggested asking Jacob for the address, but according to Richard, he was still in tuberculosis quarantine and unreachable. Instead, I spent an hour running motels through the secretary of state's website. Most businesses are incorporated for liability reasons, but the owners are usually listed as company officers, at least for smaller mom-and-pop places. I needed a motel near Arrowhead with an owner who shared Chris's surname.

Eventually, I came across the Welcome Inn, run by Douglas Taylor. Judging from the pictures and the sub-two-star reviews, the place was a dump. There was a faded plastic sign with eighties block lettering and a depressing kidney-shaped pool filled with soggy pine needles. More of a hideaway for down-and-out locals than an escape for the wealthy vacation set, for sure. I'd call in the morning and ask if Chris was staying there.

I closed my laptop and headed to the bedroom. My mind pinballed around, and I could tell that sleep wasn't going to happen. I never sleep well after dropping off Amelia. And since learning about my dad, I'd spent a lot of nights lying in bed with a stream of childhood memories playing through my mind like home videos.

At one Thanksgiving dinner from my preteen years, everyone was talking about how my cousin, Sarah, was the spitting image of my grandmother. "Who do I look like?" I'd asked. The table went quiet before my uncle jumped in and said I resembled my mom. *Did they all know?* My dad's parents had always been chilly with me. Kind enough, but they didn't dote on me like they did my cousin. I'd assumed it was because she was pretty and bubbly, while I was awkward and withdrawn. In retrospect, maybe they all knew that my dad wasn't my biological father, and I wasn't genetically their grandchild.

It made me sick to think that my whole family might have known something so personal about me while I was kept in the dark. Did they know about the sperm donor? Or if my dad had stayed quiet, maybe they suspected that I was the product of an affair. I looked nothing like that side of the family. And my mom and my grandmother never got along. What if my grandmother suspected that she'd been unfaithful?

As my mind went off in different directions, I found myself questioning everything, reaching new conclusions, and then second-guessing them. The narrative of who I was, how I fit into my family, had been basically fiction. I desperately wanted to make sense of things, but I didn't know if that was possible. I couldn't know what went on in the minds of people who were dead. All I could do was speculate because I knew my mother wasn't going to tell me any more. But I couldn't let it go. I knew I'd have to face this head-on if I was ever going to get hold of my mind again.

I wasn't going to sleep, so I went to the kitchen, poured a glass of water, and turned my computer back on. Then I pulled up the Ancestry.com account I'd opened the day after learning about my father. I hadn't gotten far—basically I'd put in my name, and my parents had popped up on my fledgling family tree. Ancestry pulls from public records, like birth certificates and census records, and lists possible relatives based on name matches. Then the site suggested parents for my dad and listed my grandparents. That's when it hit me that a whole half of the tree would be wrong. It was like being punched in the stomach. I'd snapped my computer closed and hadn't opened the website since.

But Ancestry.com lets you build family trees for other people and view ones created by different users. If Myra had had enough interest in genealogy to get her DNA mapped, she'd probably explored other websites. I searched for Myra, but it didn't look like she'd ever signed up for Ancestry. There were probably other sites that didn't require a monthly fee. From the looks of her house, Myra didn't seem to have a lot of money. I googled "free genealogy site" and quickly found Family-Tree.com. Sure enough, Myra had started an account and mapped her lineage going back centuries. Unfortunately, everything consisted of direct ancestors and culminated with her. There were no offshoots for cousins or great-aunts and great-uncles. Still, it was a starting place.

I noticed that one of Myra's great-grandfathers, Adrian Dragomir, was from Romania. That had been the big surprise when I got my DNA results: a small percentage of Romanian blood. When I'd mentioned it to my mother, she'd shrugged and said that people move around—maybe a great-great-grandparent had emigrated from Romania to Germany. She hadn't even skipped a beat. I wondered what else she'd lied to me about over the years. My heart started pounding, and I felt dizzy. I closed my eyes and took several deep breaths. *Focus on the work*, I told myself.

Myra had a lot of Italian and Spanish blood, which I didn't share. That allowed me to eliminate a good number of her relatives as potential suspects. Since Myra and I were both slightly Romanian, I decided to start with Adrian Dragomir's descendants. The free site didn't have access to public records, like Ancestry did, so I switched back and created a family tree for him.

Adrian was born in Brasov in the 1880s and died in Phelan, California, in 1947. Using birth and marriage records, I started building out his tree. Adrian's wife, Lavina, had given birth to nine children, many of whom had big families of their own. Tracking all these people down would take time. Luckily, many of his descendants had moved out of state, which narrowed my search.

One second cousin of Myra's, a man named Victor Dupont, had been born in Idlewood, and would have been in his early forties the year Lisa Forester was buried under a woodpile at Camp Idlewood. I googled him and up popped a website for an antique shop in Escarra Hills, about a twenty-minute drive away. He was certainly in the right age and geographic range to be a potential suspect.

My stomach clenched as another thought occurred to me. I've always loved old things—a trait I didn't share with either of my parents. My mom came from a family where every dollar counted. She grew up in a house full of thrift-store and yard-sale finds because that's what they could afford. To her, "making it" meant having your own brand-new stuff. When my dad joined the LAPD, he'd taken pride in buying her what they thought of as cutting-edge modern design. Forty years later, her house is an eighties time capsule, full of big patterns and overstuffed furniture.

When I got older, my mom never understood my interest in making pilgrimages to the Rose Bowl flea market or sifting through estate-sale junk in search of vintage treasures. But here was an antique dealer in the LA area, with Romanian ancestry, who was the right age to have donated sperm in the eighties. I pulled up a Yelp page for his store and started flipping through the photo gallery. That's when I recognized the backgammon player, from the Bean and Grape, with the bump on his nose, and was struck again by how much he looked like me. My heart pounded, and I felt a wave of nausea. Was that Victor Dupont? *And if so, could he possibly be my biological father?*

17

Present—Kate

A ROUND THREE AM, I finally fell asleep, mentally and physically exhausted after hours of sifting through online obituaries and marriage certificates. When my alarm went off four hours later, I was vaguely nauseous from sleep deprivation.

After a quick shower, I headed to the Bean and Grape to see if Carrie was on duty. It was a slow day, and I didn't see any customers on the front patio. When I arrived, the door was locked, but I could hear music playing inside. I hung back, with my arms crossed over my chest for warmth. Walking over, I'd barely noticed the chill. But now that I wasn't moving, I could feel it in my bones.

Carrie finally emerged from the back room, carrying a tray of grab-and-go sandwiches. She had on burgundy lipstick and cat-eye makeup, with a little black eyeliner swoosh elongating each of her dark eyes.

She smiled apologetically and came over to let me in. "Sorry, I needed some stuff from the back, and I don't like to leave the door open if I can't see the front of the store."

"I get it. You don't want some weirdo making off with the cash register," I said.

"Exactly. You know we've had a couple guys in here who gave off a bad vibe. Just enough to make me a little paranoid. Anyway, what can I get you?"

"I actually came to ask you a couple questions." I handed her my card. She stared at it and looked up at me in surprise.

"I'm a private detective working for Abby Coburn's parents. They're trying to find out what happened to their daughter." Carrie had her arms wrapped around her stomach, and she looked like she was going to throw up. "Abby's sister told me you guys were close. I thought maybe you could help me with a few things."

"Oh my God—Abby," muttered Carrie before bursting into tears.

"I'm so sorry, Carrie," I said. I mentally kicked myself—I shouldn't have been so direct and caught her off guard. Carrie seemed young, barely twenty-five. She'd probably looked up to Abby, who'd been in her early thirties. And Carrie still worked in the same place. For all she knew, the killer was someone she waited on every day.

"I know Abby was your friend. I can't imagine how horrible this was for you." I gestured toward one of the tables. "Why don't you sit down?" I walked over to the front door, threw the deadbolt, and flipped over a laminated sign that read "Closed."

"Actually," said Carrie, "do you mind if we go back in the kitchen? I don't want people to see me like this."

"Sure, whatever you need." I followed her to the small industrial kitchen. She slumped down on the floor, leaned against the wall, and crossed her legs in front of her. I sat down next to her and handed her a couple of napkins I'd grabbed from out front. "So, you were close to Abby?" I asked.

Carrie nodded. "She was like the big sister I never had, you know? I grew up in Bakersfield. I had to get away and I came out here 'cause I heard it's more progressive, but still not a city. I'm not a city person. I need room to breathe. Anyway, Abby took me under her wing. She showed me how to do stuff at work. Then a couple times on the weekends, she took me into LA and brought me to these parties full of actors and movie people. She introduced me to my boyfriend."

"She sounds like a great person," I said.

"The best," agreed Carrie. "It was awful what happened to her."

"Yes, it was, and I'm trying to make sure she gets justice. Did Abby ever talk to you about her brother?"

Carrie nodded. "She loved him. She said he was immature but a decent person. Then he started doing drugs, and it screwed up his brain."

"Did she ever say she was afraid of him?"

Carrie shook her head. "She said he yelled and broke things, but never hurt anyone."

"What about her love life?" I asked. "Did she ever talk about that?" Carrie didn't answer, which told me I was onto something. "Did Abby tell you if she was seeing someone?" I pressed. She dropped her gaze to her lap and picked at a hangnail. "Carrie—Abby was murdered. I was a cop for a long time. When a woman is killed, it's often at the hands of a sexual partner."

Carrie started crying again, heavy sobs that made her mascara run down her face. "Abby told me not to tell anyone."

She was leaning forward now, and I reached over and rubbed her back. "I get that," I said. "You're a good friend. But she's dead, and she died in a horrible way. What's important now is making sure we catch who did it—and making sure we don't convict the wrong person."

"She made me swear," said Carrie. "She said it would destroy his family. His wife would leave him, and he'd lose his kid."

Carrie pulled her knees into her chest and wrapped her arms around them. I felt for her. She was harboring the dirty secret of a dead woman she admired. A woman who had burned to death just a mile from her workplace. I needed to try a different approach. "I get all that. But you also told me that Abby loved her brother. He's been arrested for her murder, but what if he's innocent?"

She turned her head to the side and looked at me, searching my face for help with what she clearly felt was a terrible dilemma.

"I'm going to tell you what I think happened," I said. "I think Abby was killed, and the police hurriedly arrested her brother, who has mental health problems. I think they wanted to quickly solve a horrible crime, and didn't put in the time to look for other suspects. Did they even bother to interview you?"

Carrie shook her head.

"That's lazy police work," I told her. "If I were the detective on this case, I would've had this conversation with you within forty-eight hours of her death."

"So, you think they have the wrong person?" asked Carrie. She was nervously scratching at the polish on her thumbnail.

I thought about exaggerating, telling her that I knew Jacob was innocent. But I wanted her to trust me, and that didn't feel like the right move. "I don't know," I said. "And I don't think the cops do either. But if Jacob didn't kill Abby, I know she'd want to clear his name and catch the person who killed her."

Carrie nodded and dabbed at her eyes with the napkin. I took my phone out of my purse and pulled up the picture of Abby laughing with the dark-haired man in the blue shirt. "Is this him?"

Carrie shrugged. "I don't know for sure. But that guy came in a lot, and their body language was always flirty. Sometimes she'd go over to his table, and they'd chat for a few minutes in low voices."

"Who is he?" I asked.

"Nick something—I don't know his last name."

I felt a stir of déjà vu. Had I heard the name Nick while working this case? "What else can you tell me about him?"

She shrugged. "Not much. I'm pretty sure he works at the fire station. He comes in a lot, and I think I've seen him in uniform once or twice."

Her words stopped my breath. *Nick Fieldstone, the arson investigator.* He'd written a report saying the cause of the fire was undetermined, when the other investigators thought it was arson. It could just be a difference of opinion. But deflecting like that would also make sense if he'd lit the blaze himself. It was too early to jump to conclusions, but Nick potentially had the motive and the know-how. The guy had investigated countless fires. He'd certainly be able to start one.

I typed his name into my phone, and a Facebook page popped up for a handsome, dark-haired man who looked like the one in the still. He was on a hike and standing next to a petite blonde while balancing a laughing little girl on his shoulders. I could see the glint of a ring on the woman's hand.

"Is this him? I asked.

Carrie nodded and then buried her face in her hands.

CHAPTER

18

Twenty-three months ago—Jacob

AFTER THE ROOFING job, I threw my things into bags and loaded up my car, hell-bent on getting out of Arrowhead. I'd done my share of shitty things. But conning an old lady and scaring her and sticking a knife into her son in front of her was a new low. I'd started the engine and was about to pull out of the parking lot when Chris climbed in next to me and sweet-talked me into coming back inside. He passed me a bowl and promised we wouldn't steal from regular people again. The next job was targeting companies, he said.

What could I do? I had no money. My hand was still busted, and the cops were looking for me. That night I smoked more than ever before. I wanted to kill whatever brain cells held the memory of Mrs. Pfeiffer, her son, and the bloodstain on his shirt. I kept seeing Ivan's knife against Ethan's belly and that bloom of red. Soon I was seeing men with knives everywhere. Peering in the window. Staring at me from the TV screen, hiding in the background. I went for a walk and called Abby, but she didn't understand. She just kept asking what I was on, like any of that mattered. I gave up and hung up the phone.

Chris wouldn't let me touch more than beer for two days. He said we had to be sharp for the next job. So, we mostly just lay around and watched crap TV. But even after the high faded, I kept seeing things. Chris had the TV set to sports, which I never cared much about. But something was wrong with one of the announcers. He was staring at me when he talked, in this mocking way. Like he was watching me through the screen.

"Turn that off," I demanded.

"What's got into you?" asked Chris.

"Just turn it off!" I didn't feel like explaining.

After two days of waiting, Chris told me about the job, basically stealing lots of goods from chain stores. The boss had set up a bank account in the name of a fake grocery mart. Then he'd created a member account at Sam's Club, using the name of some old guy in a nursing home. For weeks now, the boss had been sending someone into stores to make purchases with the company debit card. The bank account had just enough money in it to cover those buys. If a clerk were to get suspicious about the size of the sale, he'd call the "store owner," who was really just Chris using the old guy's name.

Now that we'd built up a track record with the target businesses, the plan was to load up on goods and pay for them with bad checks. By the time the bank caught on, we'd have made off with a quarter million in liquor, cigarettes, and electronics.

I rolled down the window of the van. I'd rented it for the job, using a fake driver's license they made for me—my picture and someone else's name and birthday. "Why me?" I asked. "Why am I the one doing this?"

Chris didn't answer right away. His window was down, and he leaned one arm on the opening. A lit cigarette rested between his fingers. "What do you mean?" he said finally.

My face grew hot and my hands clenched into fists. He knew exactly what I meant. "Why am I the one taking all the risks? Why can't the guy who made the legit purchases finish the job?"

He brought the cigarette to his mouth and inhaled. "He got picked up on a murder. We needed someone, so I volunteered you. I'm trying to show them we can rely on you for bigger jobs. Trust me, this is a good thing."

Chris's voice was flat, and he kept his eyes on the road. There was something he wasn't telling me. "Why not you?" I pressed. "You're getting a cut for this, right?"

He shrugged. "I have curly red hair, bro. These places have cameras, and I stand out. You're super anonymous-looking. I'm your friend and I could barely pick you out of a lineup. That's why you're going in alone. I'll stay out here and help you load the stuff. And yeah, I'm gonna get a cut. But so will you. Way bigger than last time."

Chris was using me. I was the one sticking my neck out, and he'd probably get most of the money. But this beat robbing old ladies.

Suddenly a guy stepped off the sidewalk directly in front of the van. "Watch out!" I reached past Chris, grabbed the steering wheel, and pulled hard to the right. The car swerved and jolted to a stop as the tire hit the center median.

"What the fuck, man?" shouted Chris.

My heart pounded. "Didn't you see him?"

"See who?" demanded Chris.

I looked around, but the pedestrian was gone. "The guy in the street. He must have jumped out of the way."

Chris gave me a funny look. "You're losing it. There was nobody in the road. Just cool it, okay?"

I'd seen the guy clearly. Skinny with long, white-blond hair and wearing all black. I looked over toward the sidewalk and spotted him. "Right there!" I said, shaking Chris's arm and pointing.

Chris pulled away from my grasp but glanced over at the sidewalk. "There's no one there, Jake. You need to chill. Just do me a favor and be quiet for a bit. Let me concentrate on driving."

Sure enough, the man was gone. Lately, I'd been seeing things in the corner of my vision. Animals and weird figures or sometimes just flashing lights. They were always blurry and disappeared pretty quick. But this guy had been crystal clear. And I wasn't even high—I hadn't touched ice in days. He was definitely real, but maybe he wasn't a man. Maybe he was a spirit and that's why Chris couldn't see him.

We pulled into the Sam's Club parking lot. Chris chose a spot in the back, even though it meant I'd have to push the goods farther to get to the car. He was probably worried about security cameras in the parking lot. *Fucking coward.* I had nothing to say to him. I opened the door and started to get out.

"Wait," said Chris. "You sure you got this?" His eyes searched my face. He didn't give a shit about me. If anything went wrong, Chris wouldn't think twice about driving away and leaving me for the police.

"I'm fine."

"Give me your phone," he said, reaching out a hand.

"Why do you need it?" I demanded.

Chris rolled his eyes. "Could you stop acting paranoid?" He reached over and snatched my phone off my lap. "I'm putting in the number for my burner. It's gonna be stored as Dylan Richmond, 'cause that's your boss, right? The owner of Richmond Food Market."

I nodded.

Chris handed back my phone and pulled a burner out of his pocket. "I'm gonna call the store and tell them my employee's coming to place an order. If the manager needs to talk to me again, call me on your phone and hand it to him. I'll verify everything."

I got out of the car and slammed the door. The sun hurt my eyes. The heat was blistering, and my body was damp with sweat. My skin itched, like ants were crawling all over me. I scratched at my cheek, and when I brought my hand down, there was blood under my fingernails.

In front of the store, I saw the long-haired guy again. Was he following me? Our eyes met, and neither of us looked away. He let out a menacing smile, and I realized that he didn't have any teeth. I moved toward him but then stopped myself. I needed to do the job and get out of here. Starting a fight would ruin the whole thing.

Inside, I grabbed two carts, pushing one with each hand, and found the cigarettes. Something moved in the corner of my vision. I swung my head around and saw a dark pant leg move across the end of the aisle. Was it the long-haired guy? There was an evil force in here. I think it was in the lights. My face itched, and I could feel my eyelid start to twitch. My muscles felt jumpy, like when your body shivers in the cold. But I was burning up.

I pushed my carts over to the electronics section and pulled down several televisions. This was a flaw in the plan. What kind of market wants big-screen TVs? These guys were sloppy, and it was gonna get me busted.

I moved toward the register and got in line. When it was my turn, the clerk looked at my carts and frowned. "I'll need approval from a manager," he said.

"My boss already called," I told him.

"Who's your boss?"

Crap, I couldn't remember the name Chris had given me. If I didn't say something, he was going to ping Security. My hands shook as I pulled my phone out of my pocket. I scrolled through my contacts until I saw the new entry Chris had made. "Dylan Richmond," I said, holding up the screen. "You want me to call him?"

The clerk seemed to relax. "That's right, Richmond Food Market. I think you guys put in an order last week. Look, it's not personal; I need a manager to enter a code for orders over three grand."

He picked up the phone and called for assistance. I didn't like this. Was he really getting a manager, or was he calling Security? Sweat ran down my neck, and the creepy-crawly feeling came back. I reached behind me and clawed at my upper back. They were playing horrible soft rock from the eighties, which mingled with the sound of the buzzing lights. The duet from *Dirty Dancing* came on. Why was he taking so long? I wanted to get away from the music and the lights and the buzzing. Then I saw the long-haired guy again. He was in line at the next register, grinning at me with that creepy smile. I needed to teach him a lesson.

I took a step toward him but stopped when I heard the cashier's voice. "Don't go—my manager is right there." He pointed at a balding guy in a short-sleeved button-down shirt.

"Russ," the man said, extending a meaty hand.

I didn't want anyone to touch me, but I met his grip. His palm was warm and moist.

"Dylan Richmond sent you?" he asked. I nodded. "Yeah, he just called a few minutes ago. I've been working with Dylan for a couple weeks now." He turned to the clerk. "We're all set—these guys are legit." Russ turned and walked away. I wiped his sweat off my palm, on the front of my jeans.

The clerk rang me up, and I pushed the carts outside, back into the heat. The sunlight was blinding, and I stared out at an ocean of cars. Everything blurred together. My heartbeat pounded in my temples. I didn't feel well. I called Chris on the burner. "Dylan speaking," he said.

"Cut the crap. I'm at the front—come get me."

"Just push it back to the truck."

I pushed the carts across the parking lot. The air was thick with exhaust, and I had a weird feeling like the ground was moving. I squeezed my eyes closed. The inside of my eyelids looked crimson, and I could see a web of blood vessels. I opened them again and the dizziness became too much. I leaned over and vomited onto the pavement. A mom rushed past me, clutching her daughter's hand. "I'm fine—thanks for asking," I muttered. Once the ground stopped spinning, I made my way back to the truck.

"You stink," said Chris.

"Just help me load this stuff, and let's go."

We emptied the carts, shoving everything into the back of the truck. The motion and the heat went to my head, and the ground started spinning. A wave of nausea came over me, and I threw up against one of the tires. My stomach was empty, and nothing but greenish bile came out. Chris jumped back like he was afraid I'd splash some on him. "Man, that's disgusting!" Almost as an afterthought, he added, "You okay?"

I nodded, although I felt horrible.

"I hope so—we got two more stops before we're done."

"Are you shitting me?" I asked. He shook his head. "Two more, same procedure, then we deliver the stuff."

We drove in silence to the other stops and repeated everything. No one even seemed suspicious, although the third cashier told me I looked a little green. Once the truck was full, we went out to some warehouse in Fontana. A metal sliding door was open, and there were several more trucks parked out front.

"That's him," said Chris, pointing to two men by the sliding doors.

"What?" I asked, rubbing my temples. My head was killing me.

"That's the boss. Over there in the black shirt. We should hang back 'til he leaves."

I looked over in the direction where he was pointing, eager to lay eyes on the puppet master who was basically running my life. Then I spotted him and started laughing.

"What?" asked Chris. "Not what you pictured?"

"No," I said, stopping to catch my breath. "I know him."

19

Present—Kate

A LL I'D CONFIRMED was that Nick and Abby had shared an attraction, and there was a good chance he was her mystery lover. But as a defense investigator, I didn't have to find the actual murderer. To convince a jury to acquit, we just needed to show that the cops *might* have gotten it wrong. One way to do that is to throw shade at the investigators. Another is to propose an alternate suspect. If I could show that a married investigator had slept with the victim, I could potentially do both.

As an ex-cop, I don't like working this way. I prefer truth and facts and certainty. But Jacob was charged with a double murder-arson, and the DA was still weighing whether to seek the death penalty. I didn't have the luxury of thinking in absolutes.

I also wanted to identify the person who had called in the fire. Oddly, this fact wasn't included in any of the police reports. The Santa Ana winds had blown hard that night. All of Idlewood could have burned. According to news reports, the town was saved by an astonishingly fast response from firefighters. But the fire happened in the middle of the night. So, how did they learn about it so quickly?

If the killer lived in Idlewood, he might have tried to contain the spread by calling it in himself. I needed to know who had reported the fire, and the nature of Nick's role in putting it out. Bryce Chen, the investigator who had showed me around the crime scene, might be able to answer both of those questions. But I'd have to tread lightly. If he thought I was looking into his colleague, he'd end the conversation.

I called Bryce from the car on my drive to Escarra Hills. He answered the phone and was as friendly as before. "Thanks again for meeting me the other day," I said. "I just have a couple follow-up questions."

"Sure," he said. "What's on your mind?"

"I've read all the reports, but I didn't see anything about who called in the fire."

"Actually, it was Nick," said Bryce. My heart beat a little faster. "Nick woke up and smelled smoke. He'd left a bathroom window open, and I guess the wind blew in the odor. Most people wouldn't have thought anything of it, but Nick's a firefighter, so wildfires are always on his mind."

Or maybe he started the blaze after killing his mistress and followed up by playing hero. "So, he wasn't working that night?"

"Not at first, but everybody was on duty once it started."

"How'd he end up writing the initial report?"

"He asked to be assigned," said Bryce, a little coolly. "Like I said, this was his town, and he wanted to do everything he could to help."

"Of course." I'd pushed Bryce as far as I could on this. "Did anyone else report it?"

"Yeah, one guy called around the same time as Nick. But he didn't leave a name. We sent out the text alert pretty quickly, so most residents knew we were on top of it."

I thanked Bryce and hung up. Then I remembered my next task, and the sinking feeling in my stomach came back. I was on my way to the antique store in Escarra Hills. I wanted to talk to Victor Dupont because he'd been an adult relative of Myra and had lived in Idlewood when Lisa was killed. Intellectually, I knew he was probably just a distant cousin. But something about his picture made me feel like our genetic connection was closer than that.

He's probably not your father, I kept telling myself. But emotionally I was a wreck.

I had no idea what I was going to say to this man. I usually try to go into a potential interview with a plan, but every time I tried to game this out, my heart raced and my brain shut down.

My mouth was dry, and my throat felt tight. I unscrewed the lid of yesterday's water bottle and took a sip of warm, plasticky water. *Get it together, Kate,* I ordered myself. The last thing I needed was another panic attack.

I felt ridiculous. As a cop, I'd survived any number of dangerous situations and kept my cool. But here I was, hyperventilating over some old man I'd never met. Odds were, this guy was neither my dad nor a viable suspect. I certainly couldn't afford to get this worked up every time I met one of Adrian Dragomir's descendants. But the more I tried to talk myself off a cliff, the sicker I felt.

I drove down the mountain from Idlewood to Escarra Hills. Despite its name, the place was a flat, low-desert community with picturesque views of the San Gabriel Mountains. Seventies ranch houses were widely spaced on half-acre lots. The ground was a dusty beige marked by Joshua trees and giant succulents crowned by an explosion of white flowers that looked like something you'd use to dust your living room.

There were a number of fast-food joints and signs for gun ranges and gentlemen's clubs. I passed the Escarra Hills golf course and marveled at the amount of water needed to maintain green lawns in a place like this.

Eventually, I spotted a hand-painted sign for Vic's Antiques and Oddities. The lettering was done in a flowery Victorian scrawl. Seeing the sign made everything feel real. My muscles felt jerky and my vision blurred. I was breathing fast, like I was trying to outrun someone.

Feeling like I might throw up, I pulled over by the side of the road, leaned over, and rested my hands on my thighs. The sun beat down on my back as I breathed in the hot, syrupy air. *I won't talk to him today,* I decided. I was in no shape to interview Vic. I'd just look around and assess the situation. Observe him, take stock of his mannerisms, learn what his voice sounded like. Then I could come back another day and try to have a conversation.

But even the thought of seeing Vic was throwing me for a loop. A part of me wondered if I would just instantly know from his appearance how we were related. What if I just felt it on a cellular level?

I got back in my car and continued on my drive. After another mile, I saw the place, a large cinder-block building with few windows that looked more like a small factory than an antique store. There were more cars parked in the generous parking lot than I would have expected. I opened my door and felt the oppressive desert heat on my skin. Then I noticed the silence. You couldn't hear anything except a light rustle of wind blowing through the dirt.

Toward the back of the building, I noticed a scruffy man in his forties hanging around by an open side door. He looked almost like a bouncer at a nightclub, but why would a junky antique store need to hire security?

I walked through the front door and heard 1920s jazz blaring. Every inch of the place was filled with objects, and the walls were covered with gilded mirrors and yellowing posters. My eye immediately went to an enormous poster for a magician. In the picture, an elegant, clean-shaven man dressed in white tie held a human skull in his hands and seemed to contemplate his mortality as a series of demons and spirits flowed from its eye sockets. The poster read "The Wonder Show of the Universe." It was decorative and awesome in its creepiness. If I'd had money and weren't temporarily homeless, I might have bought it for my living room.

"Isn't that fabulous?" said a voice behind me. I spun around and saw the backgammon player from the café. Up close his resemblance to me was even more striking. He had high cheekbones and hazel eyes with bits of green, like mine. I was so overwhelmed I could barely speak. "Yeah," I managed. "It is."

He reached out and shook my hand. "Vic Dupont. Are you familiar with Howard Thurston?" I shook my head, unable to tear my eyes away from his face. "In his day he was the most famous magician in the world. He entertained royalty and three American presidents—Houdini had nothing on him. Would you like to see a video of Thurston performing the levitation of Princess Karnac?"

"What?" I asked.

"His famous levitation trick—it's amazing what you can find on YouTube. Would you like to see it?"

"Sure," I said. He must have mistaken the look of shock on my face for an interest in old-time magicians. But why not? I was already in the middle of nowhere, listening to a long-lost relative—possibly my possible birth father—talk about levitation. Things couldn't get any weirder.

I followed him over to his desk, where he pulled up a black and white video of a man in a tuxedo, waving his hands around beside a reclining woman. Slowly, her body lifted into the air, and he passed what looked like a hula hoop over her body as the crowd went wild.

As we watched, Vic talked a mile a minute about Thurston, and I started to fall for his eccentric charm. It must be some kind of sales technique. Pull customers under his spell, create a memory for them, and maybe they'd buy a trinket as a souvenir of the experience. I looked around the store, but there were no other customers. Where were all the people parked outside?

I saw another old man in the back and recognized his backgammon partner. He was fiddling with an old record player and took the jazz CD out. A minute later, Frank Sinatra's smooth voice filled the room.

"Ugh, you're killing me, Jeff," Vic called out, and dramatically covered his ears with his palms. He turned back to me. "Do you like Frank Sinatra?"

"No," I answered truthfully. "He always sounds cold and full of himself."

"Thank you!" he said. "So cheesy and false."

"His love songs never sound like he means it," I added.

"You hear that, Jeffrey? Finally someone who gets it." He turned back to me and pointed at his partner. "He's obsessed with the guy—even bought a fedora and a skinny tie and went as Sinatra for Halloween one year. I told him if I have to listen to 'Fly Me to the Moon' one more time, I'm out the door."

At that moment, I was pretty sure Victor Dupont was my father. My friend Jenny once compared my aversion to Old Blue Eyes to the way some people hate the taste of cilantro. Cilantro is delicious, but a few poor souls have a genetic quirk that makes it taste like soap. According to Jenny, everyone loves Frank except a handful of weirdos like me who must have a biological defect. I protested that he was just too slick for my taste. But one part of her assessment was undeniably true. Virtually everyone loves Sinatra. Except me. And, apparently, a weird antiquarian with a bump on his nose, and hazel eyes.

I felt dizzy. I needed a minute to breathe and process what I was experiencing. "I'll let you two duke it out," I said, and wandered over to a narrow aisle filled with vintage jewelry. I pretended to browse the shelves while listening to Vic and Jeff banter. It didn't take me long to figure out that they were a couple, with their occasionally barbed but mostly loving back-and-forth. I was fascinated. Part of me was too overwhelmed to speak. Another part wanted to sit Vic down and ask him a million questions about his quirks. *So, you hate Sinatra, but Dylan's great, right?" "Do you think peanut butter and jelly sandwiches are gross?" "Do you like whiskey, or do you think it tastes like lighter fluid?" "Can you smell ants?"*

Instead, I faded into the background and listened. I hung on everything he said. Even his choice of words fascinated me. Every now and then, I heard a quirky turn of phrase that I'd used before. Meanwhile, I kept my eyes on the vintage jewelry to avoid staring. There was a basket on a glass display case where someone had written "Five dollars each." I sifted through it, trying to find a trinket for Amelia. Then I pulled out a wooden bangle covered in little pineapples and a strand of yellow beads that looked like it was from the sixties. Yellow was her favorite color at the moment.

A door opened in the back of the store, and the scruffy forty-something walked through. I turned to look at him, and our eyes met as he passed by me. He looked a bit like Vic, but his features were more severe. And where Vic's eyes radiated warmth, this guy chilled the air around him. He walked up to Vic, leaned in, and whispered something in his ear. I couldn't make out his words, but he didn't look happy.

Vic's expression darkened. "Tell him no, Roman. We're done giving him credit. If he doesn't like it, he can get the hell out."

Roman disappeared again into the back, and I heard other male voices before the heavy door closed. There was another business back there. And given the lack of signage, possibly not a legal one.

That realization brought me back to the main reason I was out here. Seventeen-year-old Lisa Forrester had been killed by one of my extended relatives, and I was looking for suspects. I still had no actual evidence that Victor Dupont was my father, which would make him too close a genetic match to be the killer. But he was a relative of Myra's, and a public records search showed that he'd been living a few towns over when she was killed. Then there was Roman. By the looks of him, he would have been in his twenties at the time of the murder. Yes, I was grasping at straws here, but we still had no leads, and I'd have to chase a few tangents if I was going to find the killer. And if there was a sketchy, possibly criminal business in the back of the store, I wanted to know about it.

I went over to the checkout and Vic came to meet me. A modern cash register sat next to an ornate gold-plated one with Victorian flourishes. He caught me looking at it. "She's a beauty, isn't she? Someday I'll find her a home."

I paid and went out into the parking lot. The blistering desert sun reflected off the dry beige dirt and was almost blinding. I shielded my eyes and looked back at the windowless building. Most of the cars were parked near the back. I watched as a skinny guy parked a sun-bleached Honda Civic and made his way over to the back door. Roman was nowhere to be seen. I wanted to at least peek inside and see what was in there. It wouldn't be trespassing; the parking lot was open to the public, and I'd just seen a customer walk in.

As I approached, I heard the electronic beeps and hums of gaming machines. No way these guys had a license to operate a casino. I peeked inside. There were a dozen machines lining the walls of a small room and a computer on a desk, where a bored-looking young guy with gauged ears surveyed four or five gamblers.

"You going in?" asked a voice behind me. I spun around and saw Roman glaring at me. "You got the password?" he asked. He had a phone to his ear, and I wondered if he was calling Vic.

"No," I said. "I was just curious."

"Yeah, we don't need your curiosity. You should leave. Don't come back here."

I stared at him and took a second to collect my thoughts. If I left now, without saying anything, this bridge would be burned. I wasn't ready to tell them why I was here. After all, Roman or Vic or someone they knew might have killed Lisa. Vic came out of the antique store and walked over to us. The warmth was gone from his face. I wondered how much of it had been an act.

I played the only card I had left. "I came to see Vic," I said. "I need to ask him something."

"She says she wants to ask you something," said the younger guy.

Vic looked at me through narrowed eyes. I couldn't tell if he was glaring or squinting against the sun. "Fire away," he said coldly.

They were obviously worried that I was some kind of cop or state investigator. I needed to be direct enough to convey that I wasn't here about their little side hustle. *Well, here goes nothing,* I thought.

"Did you ever donate sperm in the eighties?"

20

Present—Kate

TIME STOPPED AS Vic stared at me, mouth open in shock. I became very conscious of the electronic dings coming from the gaming room and the rustling of the desert wind. Then Vic came closer and examined my face. "Holy shit," he said. "Why don't you come inside?"

I followed him back into the antique store, too stunned to say anything. I could hear my shoes squeak against the concrete. The sun beat down on my skin, and my throat felt dry. My chest was tight, like my rib cage had shrunk. Every breath of hot air felt like a struggle.

It was impossible to tell what was going on in Vic's head. I hadn't come here planning to drop a bomb on him. But I'd done it. And I desperately wanted to keep talking to him. I didn't know if he was my father. After years of investigating cases, I'd learned to be suspicious of my first instincts. But as much as I tried to be rational, a part of me was already convinced. And here I was, desperately hoping that this weird old man I didn't know—a petty criminal with an illegal casino in the back of his store—would give me the time of day.

He led me back inside and pointed to an ornate empire couch. It was dark wood with Kelly-green upholstery and curved arms. I looked over my shoulder and saw a glass case filled with presidential memorabilia. Twin Richard Nixon figurines with exaggerated noses smiled menacingly.

"You want some tea or something?" asked Vic.

"Sure," I said, although tea felt like a strange choice given the heat.

"Jeff," he called, "can you put on the kettle—and for heaven's sake turn that crap off." The Sinatra finally stopped, which was a small relief.

Vic sat down next to me on the couch, and before he could open his mouth, I heard myself spewing the whole story about finding the papers from the clinic and mapping out a family tree online. Luckily, he didn't ask a lot of questions about how exactly I conducted my research. I wasn't ready to bring up Myra and the murder investigation. But at the same time, not saying anything about it felt like a lie. A part of me wanted to get to know this person, and we were starting out from a place of dishonesty.

"I'm sorry," I said. "I really didn't mean to dump this on you. I was just curious, so I wanted to check out your store, see you in person, and see if I got a sense whether we might be related. Then I saw you, and, well, you look like me and hate Sinatra, so that was a major head trip." He laughed, which broke some of the tension. "I don't want anything from you—I was really just curious." I was rambling and sounded like an idiot.

He waved a hand, dismissing my concerns. "You said your mom went to a clinic in Pasadena?" he asked.

I nodded.

"What year were you born?"

"Nineteen eighty-five," I said.

"Let me get us some tea," he said. I watched him walk out of sight and heard him and Jeff talking in low voices. A minute later he was back, holding two absurd 1970s mugs shaped like owls.

Jeff followed behind, wearing a huge grin. "Stand up, dear," he ordered.

I did as I was told. Jeff looked back and forth between us. "Vic, she's the spitting image of you. He reached out and tapped the bump on my nose. I blinked in surprise. "Get the DNA test, but I don't know if you need it."

Vic handed me an owl mug, and I slunk back down on the ridiculous couch.

"I'm gonna give you two a minute," said Jeff. He walked toward the back of the store and found a perch where he could probably still hear everything we said.

As soon as Vic recovered from his initial shock, he reverted to his mile-a-minute conversational style. He launched into his whole life story, by way of a million tangents. Vic told me about joining the Air Force after college. Of being a hyperactive daredevil whose dream was to serve his country and fly fighter jets. But this was the early eighties—years before even the "Don't ask, don't tell" policy went into effect. One day a sergeant caught him stealing a kiss outside a bar from a local guy he'd been hooking up with. They hauled him in the next day to interrogate him. He was truthful, and it was the end of his military career.

Vic quickly discovered that no airline would hire a pilot with a dishonorable discharge. He put in applications with a half-dozen police departments, hoping that if he couldn't serve his country in the military, he could at least have a career in law enforcement. But that discharge was always a deal breaker. He was untouchable.

My eyes welled up. After spending ten years with LAPD and going out on disability, I knew what it felt like to lose a career you loved. But I couldn't imagine having everything ripped away just for being who you are.

Vic had ended up doing odd jobs and developing a drinking problem. When things got really tight, he sold his sperm for what he called "pennies on the pull." But he swore he only did it a couple times. "I didn't like the idea of having a bunch of kids running around out there. It kind of weirded me out—no offense."

I caught a whiff of alcohol on his breath, which hadn't been there when we were talking about magicians. He must have put whiskey in his tea. I couldn't really blame him for needing a drink, but he'd just described a past problem with alcohol. Maybe this was where my addictive personality came from. My mom could never understand how I'd gotten hooked on pain pills. *Vic would probably get it,* I thought.

He told me about taking a job hawking lemonade at the Rose Bowl flea market and meeting Jeff, who ran a stall selling vintage furniture. The two of them ended up bonding over their love of old things and fell in love. Then, when Vic randomly inherited a big, ugly industrial building in what he described as "the middle of nowhere," they decided to try their hand at antiquing. The work suited Vic's restless nature. He drove around San Bernardino, going from estate sale to estate sale, searching for overlooked treasures. They resold their finds, occasionally at the store, but more often at flea markets around LA, where rich Westsiders paid good money for quaint castoffs from poor people one county over. They had a blast and lived cheaply, shacking up in a back room of the store to save on rent. But in later years, Jeff had developed health problems, and the antiques revenue wasn't cutting it. That's when they started the other business.

"Aren't you worried about getting caught?" I asked.

Vic shrugged. "Gaming violations are all misdemeanors, and the sheriffs out here are too busy chasing real gangsters and trying to bring down the murder rate. They don't care about a couple of old queens with slot machines in the back. Besides, if they arrested us, they'd have to seize and store all the equipment, and the county doesn't have the resources for that. Bottom line is, they look the other way. We even have a couple of deputies who come in here on the regular." He paused. "We did get robbed a couple times. The last guy pistol-whipped me and knocked out a few of my teeth." He lifted up his lip and showed me a void on the side of his mouth. "Then we learned our lesson. We got a couple of firearms to defend the store and brought in someone younger to manage the back shop—that's what we call it."

"The guy from outside? Is he related to you too?" I had mixed motives for asking, which made me feel guilty. I was genuinely curious about these people. But for all I knew, the unfriendly guy skulking around the "back shop" had killed Lisa. Harry should really have gotten someone else to pose as me. I was an emotional wreck right now, and it was really hard to think clearly or know how to act.

"Yeah, that's Roman. He's my—I don't know what the technical term is—second cousin? First cousin once removed? Something like that. My grandfather's sister's grandson. Roman's a good kid. He hit a rough patch and needed a little help."

I heard a snort from Jeff and looked over in time to see him roll his eyes. I wondered what Vic wasn't telling me.

"What happened?" I asked.

Vic looked at me funny. I detected hesitation, which was fair. I wouldn't have asked if I was just here for a family reunion. "He was a coach at one of the high schools. Things didn't work out, and he needed a job. That's about it."

I wondered if he'd been fired for some kind of shenanigans with a student. But I was making a lot of leaps here. For all I know, the school had run out of money and eliminated his position. On the other hand, when I was a cop, a couple of the sex crimes detectives used to joke that they could start a whole pervert coach unit. It seemed like they caught a new one every other month. "How long has he been with you?" I asked. I wanted to narrow down the timeline without seeming like I was trying to pry.

"It feels like forever," said Vic. "Certainly more than a decade." That gave me something to work with at least.

My phone chimed, and I looked down to see a text from Sam: *Still on for tonight?* I'd completely forgotten about our dinner plans, and I texted him back quickly. I realized that I'd been sitting here talking to Vic for hours, mesmerized. I'd also been meaning to swing by Chris's dad's motel before it got too late.

"I should get going," I said. "But I'd love to talk again—would that be okay?"

To my surprise, he took both of my hands in his. "I would love that. I never had any children, and I'm incredibly curious to get to know you." We exchanged phone numbers and agreed to talk soon.

I really hoped he meant it.

21

Present—Kate

I COULD HAVE SAT and talked to Vic all day. I wanted to learn everything about him—what his parents were like, how he grew up,
what made him tick. Even just watching him fascinated me. I kept
staring at his face, trying to see traces of myself. He did this thing
when he got nervous where he bit his lip, and for a second, I could see
my daughter in him.

I hadn't brought up Amelia during our conversation. I didn't
know where this was going, and it was way too early to involve her.
I'd had a wonderful father who could never be replaced. And I didn't
know or trust this man yet. But at the same time, I felt a strong urge
to somehow incorporate him into my life. Maybe as a friend or a kind
of uncle figure. Of course, I still hadn't confirmed our relationship.
But he looked just like me, and what were the chances that *two* people
related to Myra with Romanian ancestry had donated sperm at the
same Pasadena clinic in 1984? At any rate, I'd know soon enough.
He'd agreed to submit his DNA to GeneExploder.

Of course, there was more to think about here than Vic's effect
on my life. There was also a real risk that I could hurt him. What
if I proved that one of Vic's relatives had killed Lisa? Would he feel
betrayed? Would he assume I'd been using him and that my interest

in getting to know him had been a ploy? He'd told me some really personal stuff, and I didn't want him to think I was exploiting his emotions in a visceral, possibly unethical way. Then again, maybe I was. The whole thing was too much. The more I tried to untangle it, the more my brain wanted to shut down.

It was about an hour drive from Vic's antique shop to Chris Taylor's motel outside of Arrowhead. I put in a CD that Vic had given me before I left, a jazz violinist called Stéphane Grappelli I'd never heard of. It was light and whimsical, and a little bit ridiculous in a good way, like Vic. I'd never really heard anything like it before, and I suddenly burst out laughing, remembering the magicians, Nixon dolls, gambling machines, and the truly insane experience I'd just had.

I let my mind drift during the rest of my drive to the Welcome Inn. After a while, I was out of the desert and back in the pine-covered mountains. I could feel my blood pressure drop as I took in the beauty of my surroundings.

The motel was on the outskirts of town and had clearly seen better days. The sign out front was dirty and faded from decades of sun bleaching. The few cars in the parking lot were old and run down, and the building itself, a mid-century strip of brick walls and single-paned windows, was in desperate need of a paint job. The peeling, pale-brown exterior clashed with the ugly orange doors and window trimming. It felt like the kind of establishment that rented rooms by the hour.

I made my way to the front office. A middle-aged woman with stringy bleached-blond hair sat at the front desk and read something on her phone. I smiled when our eyes met, but she didn't return the gesture.

"You want a room?" she asked.

"No, I'm looking for someone—Chris Taylor. I think he might live here."

She crossed her arms over her chest and sat back in her chair. "I can't tell you anything. Our customers need their privacy," she said, confirming Chris's presence at the motel, without realizing it.

"Look," I said. "I'm a private investigator working for a friend of his—Jacob Coburn. Jacob could really use his help. I just want to talk to him."

I paused to see if I was having any effect on my listener. "Can you at least take down my information and give it to him?"

She picked up a piece of scrap paper and uncapped a pen. Her movements were slightly exaggerated, like my request was a major imposition. "What's your number?" she asked.

I handed her my card, and she slipped it into the desk drawer, where it would probably stay undisturbed for years. "Can you tell him it's about Jacob?" I asked. She nodded absent-mindedly, her attention already beginning to wander. I tried another approach. "I was also hoping to speak to the owner. Do you know when Doug Taylor gets in?" Maybe Chris's father would be more inclined to help me.

Her eyes narrowed. She probably thought I wanted to complain about the service.

"I can't give out that information. Anything else?"

I smiled, concealing my frustration. "No, that's it—thanks for your help."

I walked outside and took a moment to appreciate the fresh air and the feel of the sun on my skin before driving back to Idlewood. Maybe mentioning Doug by name would convince her to say something to Chris.

Down the street, I saw a young man making his way toward the motel. He was scarecrow thin, and his mesh shorts sat low on his emaciated frame. Most of his left calf and part of the right were covered in blocky tattoos. There was something strange about his walk, and when I looked again, I realized that he was barefoot.

I watched him as he crossed the parking lot with the jerky movements of someone who'd been using for a while. He was about Jacob's age and clearly not in great shape. Could this be Chris?

The man disappeared inside a motel room. I hesitated for a moment and then decided to walk over. If he told me to get lost, I'd just head back to Idlewood, no worse for the wear.

I knocked on the door, but there was no answer. I knocked louder. "Chris?" I called. "Can I talk to you?"

The door swung open partway. I could see his face and half of his body, but the rest of him was obscured. In his left hand, he held an open gravity knife. The blade was long and scalpel sharp. With one move, he could gut me like a fish.

I kept my arms at my sides, trying to avoid any sudden gestures. "My name is Kate Myles," I said slowly and calmly. "I work with Jacob Coburn's defense lawyer. I'm trying to help him. Are you Chris Taylor?"

My eyes stayed fixed on the blade as Chris retracted it and tucked it into his waistband. Once the weapon was out of sight, my eyes fell on the dark shapes covering his legs. They weren't tattoos, but open wounds. I'd never seen anything like it. They looked like burns that had been left untreated. Some had turned black, like overcooked barbecue. Then I noticed the smell. I gagged and stepped back, away from the door.

"What happened to you?" I asked.

He shrugged. "Tranq."

"You need to go to the hospital. And what the hell is tranq?"

"They use it to cut dope," he said. "Guess I got a bad batch."

My mind traveled back to a conversation I'd had a few years ago with a police sergeant from Philadelphia. They were having a brand-new nightmare of a problem—meth and amphetamines cut with a horse tranquilizer called xylazine. It was cheap and still unregulated. Supposedly, it intensified the high. But something in the chemical caused skin to rot and deep wounds to form. My contact had been calling to warn me because they'd heard calls on a wire about a shipment of xylazine-infused dope coming to the LA market. "It's horrifying, Kate," she'd said. "The frequent fliers out here, they're losing fingers, toes, whole feet. They're just rotting."

I looked up at Chris's face. His cheeks were red and inflamed, like after a bad sunburn. I noticed him sway slightly, and he tightened his grip on the door to steady himself. My eyes drifted back down to a gaping wound on his left leg. Parts of it shined as liquid oozed down. "You need to go to the hospital," I said.

"I'm fine," he snapped. "Just ask me your questions and leave."

This guy wasn't taking the stand in anyone's trial. "Let me drive you to the hospital. We can talk on the way," I pleaded.

"I said I'm not going! Ask me your questions, and then get the fuck out of here."

"Jacob's lawyer wants to build an insanity defense," I heard myself say. "He wants me to ask if you saw Jacob showing signs of mental illness."

Chris snickered. "Seriously? Yeah, I saw it. Dude lost his freaking mind. Started hearing voices and seeing things. He thought the government was after him. That all? You want me to say that—no problem."

"When did you last see him?" I asked.

He shrugged. "Jake disappeared a week or two before he got arrested. He'd been staying with me here. It was fine for a while, but then he got real paranoid—started sleeping with a baseball bat and stuff like that. A couple times people came back to the motel late, and Jacob opened the door holding it." He shook his head and laughed darkly. "He even smashed some guy's windshield once. Then he just vanished in the middle of the night."

I wanted to show Chris the still of the man in the hoodie walking toward Abby's cabin. But he was so jumpy, I was scared to make any sudden moves that could set him off. "I'm going to show you a picture," I said. "I'm just gonna pull it out of my bag." I slowly reached into my tote and took out the folded still. Chris's eyes stayed on my bag, and one of his hands went to the pocket where he'd placed his knife. This guy wasn't all there. If Jacob had seemed crazy to Chris, things must've really gotten bad.

I held out the picture, and he snatched it from me. "Have you seen this before?" I asked. Chris shook his head. "Does this person look familiar?"

Chris shrugged. "It's some guy from the back—how am I supposed to recognize him?"

My thoughts exactly. "What about the hoodie?"

"I mean, yeah, Jacob had a black hoodie with stuff on the back. So do a lot of people." He handed me the still, and I slid it back into my bag.

I looked up at Chris's face. He was sweating profusely, and his hair was plastered to his forehead. The effort of standing there and concentrating on my questions seemed to be draining his energy. This guy needed immediate help, and I couldn't in good conscience keep interviewing him. "Chris, you need to get to a doctor," I told him.

"Mind your business, lady," he said. "I'm done with this."

The door slammed in my face, and I stood there, staring at the peeling paint, wondering what to do. Chris could have a massive blood infection. He could lose a leg. I'd spent ten years as a cop, and I couldn't just let him die in there. I could call an ambulance. But he'd probably send them away.

I banged on the door. Silence. I banged harder. "Chris, open the door," I shouted.

It swung open again, and I saw the open blade at his side. My stomach condensed into a hard knot. "Before you slam the door again, listen to me," I said in a calm, slow voice. "You think I want to stand here with a goddamn knife in my face? I used to be a cop. I've seen people in trouble before, and I'm telling you, if you don't go to the hospital right now, you could die. Your leg smells like rotting meat, and you look like you're about to pass out. You're gonna put the knife away. You're gonna get in my car, and I'm gonna drive you to the hospital."

He stared at me for several long seconds before he finally retracted the blade and followed me to my car. As he stepped into the sunlight, the full extent of his wounds became apparent. I got in the car and rolled down all of my windows. He slid into the front passenger seat, and the stench made me gag.

I searched my GPS for emergency rooms and found the Pine Mountain Community Hospital. As the car started, the wind blew away some of the stench of rotting flesh, but I still had to breathe through my mouth. I tried to force myself to ask more questions about the case, but my brain was filled with adrenaline from having a knife pulled on me, and I was working hard to keep from throwing up. We drove in silence.

I pulled up to a stop sign and had to wait for another car to cross. My gaze slid over Chris's leg, and I thought I could see exposed tendon.

His bare feet rested against the carpet of my car, where Amelia puts her feet when I pick her up. I was horrified at the thought of her sitting here after he dripped God knows what bacteria onto the upholstery. I'd have to spring for a deep cleaning. Maybe put down a towel for her to sit on. Then I felt disgusted with myself for thinking about cleanliness with a man this sick beside me.

I drove up to the main entrance of the hospital. "Do you want me to come in with you?" I asked.

Chris shook his head. "Nah. Thanks for the ride, though. Sorry about the knife." He got out of the car, closed the door, and limped into the lobby.

My phone chimed, and I looked down to see a text from Sam. *Pick you up at seven?* I burst out laughing. It was a dark, uncomfortable laugh—a release of the tension that had built over the last thirty minutes. Romance was the last thing on my mind after that horror show. But I needed something to exorcise the image of Chris' festering wounds from my brain, and I didn't want to spend the evening alone in Idlewood. I knew the image of Chris and the smell of rotting flesh would haunt me all night if I didn't have a distraction. I could end up swinging by the liquor store and quickly falling back into some bad habits.

Driving back to town now—see you soon, I texted.

CHAPTER

22

Present—Kate

WHEN I GOT back to my cabin, I threw all my clothes in the washer, turned on the shower, and climbed in. I sat down and let the hot water cover me—desperate to cleanse myself of the afternoon's horror. How could a person do that to their body? How long had his legs been in that condition? How could he keep using when it was literally making him rot?

Cupping my hands, I let the shower fill them with water and plunged my face into the warm pool. I wanted to wash away the image of Chris, which was burned onto my retinas. Thank God I had a distraction tonight. I didn't want to be alone with my demons, wondering if Chris was going to die or lose a limb.

Seeing Chris Taylor had made me feel helpless. There was nothing I could do for him. I wasn't a social worker or even a cop anymore. And as much as I wanted to distance myself from the skeletal, foul-smelling man who'd stuck a knife in my face, part of me identified with him. Before I got help, addiction had brought me lower that I could have imagined. By the end, I was conning two doctors into writing me prescriptions, and occasionally picking up extra oxy on the street. I'd taken pills and gotten behind the wheel with my daughter, endangering her life.

Hitting a parked car with Amelia beside me was the worst moment of my life. But the accident had put everything into focus and led me to seek help. What would have happened if I hadn't crashed that day? A lot of people start on oxy and end up shooting heroin. I never touched meth, but they cut opiates with tranq too. I could have ended up shoeless and rotting in a fleabag motel. I wasn't that different from Chris Taylor. Just lucky to have gotten out when I did.

A few minutes into my shower, I'd exhausted the small hot-water tank. My head was still covered with shampoo. I forced myself to rinse my hair in the weak spray of cold water before climbing out and wrapping myself in a towel. The old house had a draft, and I shivered as chilly air blew against my wet skin. With the day's commuting, I'd skipped lunch and now felt weak and vulnerable. I needed to get out of this cabin and away from myself for a night.

My thoughts turned to Sam, with his blue eyes and easy banter. *He's probably a player,* I thought. A hot bartender in a small town with a penchant for chainsaw art. He'd probably slept his way through the women in Idlewood, I told myself, and only focused on me because I was new. But maybe that's what I needed. A night out with someone fun and easy to talk to. A distraction from the thoughts swirling around in my head. It was just dinner and maybe a drink. One drink. And then back to my cabin.

I hadn't packed anything date appropriate, which was probably a good thing. I didn't want Sam to think he was in for more than conversation. Besides, people in Idlewood tend to keep it casual. I slipped on a pair of jeans and my most flattering plain-colored T-shirt and towel-dried my hair so it didn't drip on to my shoulders. I looked at myself in the mirror. A tired, washed-out face stared back. I pulled a tube of red lipstick out of my purse—the only makeup item I own—and carefully applied it. Lipstick wouldn't send the wrong message, and I wanted to feel marginally attractive.

The doorbell rang. Sam was ten minutes early. I opened the door and found him standing there. My heart sped up. I'd forgotten how handsome he was.

"You ready?" he asked. Over his shoulder, I spotted the golf cart parked on the street. He saw me looking at it. "I do have a car, for the record. Well, a truck anyway. I just figured it was a nice night, so we might as well get some air."

If by "nice," you mean freezing, I thought. But then again, as an LA girl, my tolerance for cold is nonexistent. "Let's go."

There was an awkward silence as we walked toward the cart, and I remembered that I didn't know anything about Sam. "Where are we going?" I asked. "You said you'd pick me up at seven but kept it pretty cryptic."

Sam looked embarrassed. "The only restaurant in town open on Mondays stops serving at seven. People tend to eat really early around here. I was thinking I'd make dinner at my place. But if that's weird, there's a diner one town over. The food's mediocre, which I shouldn't say since the owner's a friend. But honestly, he'd tell you the same thing."

"Your place is fine." To be honest, I felt a little iffy about going to a strange man's house. But I'd met his daughter, and he wasn't setting off my dangerous pervert alarm.

Sam climbed into the driver's seat, and I sat next to him. He turned the key in the ignition, and we were off. I stayed quiet for a minute, enjoying the feeling of wind against my skin and the fragrance of the night air. "How's the crest coming?" I asked, to make conversation.

He laughed. "I accidentally decapitated one of the lions, so now I'm making it into something different. I think I'll stick to woodland creatures for a while."

"Where's Willow tonight?"

"She's at her mom's this week," he said. I detected a bit of sadness in his voice. "My older daughter, Molly, is visiting from college. They're doing a girls' thing. I miss her when she's not there, but it is what it is."

I remembered the photograph he'd shown me at the restaurant, of him and Willow and a beautiful twenty-year-old. She must be his daughter and not a super-young girlfriend, which was reassuring. "I know how it goes," I said. "I'm counting the days until Amelia comes back up."

There was another silence, and I tried to think of a less depressing topic. A minute later, we pulled into the driveway of a charming, copper-green cabin. "Your place is adorable," I told him truthfully.

"Built in 1925, and the plumbing and electrical aren't much younger. But it works for me."

I followed him up the driveway and through the front door. Inside, I saw an old stone fireplace that looked like the one in my cabin. On the adjacent wall hung a violin, a guitar, and some figure-eight-shaped instrument I didn't recognize.

"I made shepherd's pie," said Sam. "I just need to pop it in the oven. Can I get you a glass of wine or a beer?"

I hesitated. I don't have the easiest time stopping after a glass. But I needed something to take the edge off. It had been years since I'd slept with a man or did anything more than banter. I'd been on a few dates since my divorce. With one memorable exception, none of them had progressed beyond a boring dinner or coffee. I wasn't sure how I was supposed to act. On top of my awkwardness, I was still processing my meeting with Vic and the memory of seeing Chris and his gravity knife. It had been a truly insane day. And yes, I wanted wine. Just a glass.

"Wine would be great," I said.

Sam went into the kitchen, and I sat on a couch next to the wall of instruments. I heard him uncork a bottle, and the sound made me relax a bit. A moment later he handed me a glass of red. I took a sip, and it was delicious. "This is nice," I said.

He sat down next to me, and I noticed that he smelled incredible. "We serve it at the restaurant. It's from a small winery in Temecula. I try to support the Southern California vineyards when I can."

I felt very aware of Sam's body just a few inches from mine. He had one arm spread across the top of the couch. I wanted to move closer to him but wasn't sure if that would be weird. After years of being married, you forget the norms.

Sam smiled at me, and I felt my pulse quicken. I could see the outline of his chest through his fitted sweater. I wanted to reach underneath and run my hands along his torso. "Tell me about the instruments," I said.

"Violin is my passion. I was supposed to go to school for it, but that didn't work out. Now I dabble. I'm in a folk quartet that plays at local places. You should come check it out."

Sam was full of surprises. The chainsaw thing had already caught my attention, but now I was really intrigued. "Did you end up studying something else instead?" It was none of my business, but there was a story here, and curiosity got the best of me.

His smile faded, and I immediately regretted prying. "After high school, I was supposed to go to Berklee College of Music. But then my ex found out she was pregnant with Molly, so I couldn't exactly run off to Massachusetts."

"A lot of people would have," I said. That was a major sacrifice to make at eighteen. "Amelia was an oops," I told him. "I acquired a husband out of it, which worked out about as well as any shotgun marriage."

"I used to dream about being in a city and surrounding myself with art and music," Sam told me. "I fantasized about meeting interesting people and talking late into the night. Instead, I ended up in a town with no streetlights that shuts down at eleven. And that's only because I keep my doors open at the Bighorn."

He looked a little wistful, and I felt for him. "So, now you keep busy with chainsaws and instruments?"

Sam nodded and ran a hand through his shaggy hair. "I've never been good at sitting still. The restaurant works for me because it keeps me on my feet—I'm always chatting with customers, and I don't have time to get bored. Sometimes you don't see people at their best. But they're gonna drink somewhere, and if it's at my place, I can make sure things don't get crazy, and everyone has a safe ride home."

"That's what I used to like about police work," I told him. "The busyness and the variety."

"You were a cop?" he asked, surprised. "Why'd you stop?"

I didn't feel like sharing the whole story. I was here to have a good time and forget my troubles. "Car accident. I went out on disability." It was a partial truth, at any rate.

Sam winced. "Sorry to hear that."

"It's in the past," I said, eager to move on to another topic.

"And now you're doing private investigations, right? Are you looking into that fire from last year?"

I stiffened. I hadn't told him anything about the Coburn case. In fact, I'd only mentioned my connection to Myra, which had nothing to do with the arson. "Why are you asking?"

Sam looked uncomfortable. "I'm a chatty guy and I own a bar. A few nights ago, some cops and firefighters came in, and I heard one of them mention a nosy PI. It made me think of you—not the nosy part, just the PI part."

"Was it Bryce Chen?" I asked.

He shrugged. "I didn't catch his name."

"Do you remember who else was at the table?" I pressed. "Does the name Nick Fieldstone sound familiar?"

He ran his fingers through his hair again. "There might have been a Nick—dark-haired guy with a mustache. Kind of handsome."

"Can you text me if they come back?" I asked.

Sam hesitated for a moment. "Sure, I can do that." He grabbed the bottle and refilled my glass before I could stop him. My plan had been to stop at one, but he'd already poured it.

A timer sounded, and Sam went into the kitchen to retrieve the shepherd's pie. He placed the baking dish on the table, which was set for two, and motioned for me to join him. I grabbed my glass and moved over to the dining room.

The food was delicious, and the second glass of wine tasted even better than the first. Sam was warm and easy to talk to. Conversation got easier, and the tension melted away. I sensed that I'd been wrong about him. He wasn't a player looking for a new conquest. Just a slightly hyperactive eccentric struggling to meet someone with compatible quirks in a town of four thousand people.

There was a lull in the conversation, and I heard myself say, "I think I met my biological father today." It was a ridiculous thing to share on a first date, but it had been an insane day, and he was probably wondering why I seemed a little distracted. Besides, I was alone out here, and I wanted to talk to someone about it. Sam listened with genuine interest as I told him about Vic, and Thurston and his antiques and gaming machines. As it turned out, Sam knew Vic by sight and had even bought a few decorative odds and ends for the Bighorn at his shop.

I told him about the CD that Vic had given me, and he lit up. "Jazz violin is the best," he said. "Vic has good taste—they're always playing something interesting when I've gone in there." He walked over to the stereo and put on more vintage music.

We kept talking about music, and family, and life-altering surprises. I realized that I really liked this guy. And the chemistry between us was undeniable. As I filled my belly with delicious food and sipped that second glass of wine, his charm and good looks became irresistible. He talked with his hands, occasionally touching my arm in conversation and setting my skin ablaze. It had been so long since a man had touched me with anything close to desire. Under the table, my hands fidgeted as I tried to focus on our conversation and ignore the electricity between us.

A few hours into our meal, Sam went into the kitchen to grab another glass of water. I looked down at my watch and realized that it was already eleven. I needed to get home. I had to work the next morning. I told him I should go, and he offered to drive me back—in the truck this time.

We walked over to the door, and he reached past me for a set of keys on a side table. His face was very close to mine, and our eyes locked. Then I did something I've never done before. I leaned in and kissed him. Sam took me by the hand and led me to the bedroom. I knew it wasn't a good idea, but I didn't stop him.

23

Present—Kate

I WOKE UP FEELING groggy and realized that I wasn't in my cabin. *Oh God, what did I do?* The previous night came back to me in flashes.

Where was Sam anyway? That's when I noticed the smell of bacon and the sound of grease sizzling on a stove. Was he actually making breakfast? Is that a thing that men do outside of romance novels?

I jumped out of bed and pulled on my clothes. Stumbling into the bathroom, I did my best to finger-brush my teeth. After two years of living alone, the idea of casual intimacy with a man came as a shock to my system. I was so used to privacy, to being by myself. The thought of someone seeing me unwashed, undressed, and uncaffeinated was mortifying.

I splashed cold water on my face and looked in the mirror. I looked tired, which made sense. We hadn't slept much. Sam had . . . it was like he hadn't touched a woman in years and wasn't sure he'd get another chance.

I made my way to the kitchen and found him standing over the stove in a pair of boxers, manning twin skillets of bacon and eggs. My breath caught in my throat at the sight of him.

"Good morning," said Sam, grinning.

"What's all this?"

"Just making myself some breakfast. But if you're hungry, there are several options in town."

"Well, I guess I'll be on my way," I said, playing along. He caught me by the waist and kissed me gently. *Oh,* I thought, as I felt myself soften. *I could get used to this.*

Sam guided me over to the breakfast nook and slid two plates and two cups of coffee onto the table. "Milk?" he asked. I shook my head. The eggs smelled incredible. This was a far cry from my normal routine. I usually grab a protein bar and run out the door.

"I don't think anyone's cooked me breakfast since I was a kid on Christmas morning."

"Well, that should change," said Sam. A pang of sadness came over me. I'd only be in Idlewood for a hot minute, and then all of this would just be a nice memory. "I know," said Sam, reading my thoughts, "you're here on business. But we might as well have a good time while you're in town. And frankly, LA's not that far. We can play it by ear."

I sipped my coffee and ate my eggs in silence, letting myself fantasize that this could become routine. Idlewood was only an hour and a half away. And we both had split custody. Would it be so terrible to strike up a casual thing with a handsome man in a beautiful place?

"What are you doing today?" asked Sam.

"Working," I told him. "My client is putting me up while I'm here. Hanging out after hours is one thing, but I can't take a day off."

"Got it," he said. "What about this evening? My quartet is having a little concert at the Red Barn Opry."

"The what?" I asked.

"Have you seen an outdoor stage surrounded by fake buildings that looks like the set of an old-time Western?" I nodded. I'd noticed the weird setup the other day and made a mental note to explore it with Amelia. "That's the Red Barn Opry," said Sam, "they do a festival in the summer, which is a blast, but we borrow it from time to time for smaller shows. It's just four of us—my friend Regina on guitar, Luther on mandolin, and Crispin on bass."

The name Regina stood out to me. Where had I heard it before? "What's Regina's last name? I don't know why that name sounds familiar."

He shrugged, "Miller. But she's barely ever left Idlewood. I doubt you'd know her." He scrolled through his phone and pulled up a picture of a laughing redhead.

I remembered the photograph of Regina and Lisa Forrester I'd seen at the sheriff's office. That's right—they'd been childhood besties. I needed to talk to her. Myra Davies wasn't going to be much help tracking down our long-lost killer cousin; that part of my original plan was clearly a bust. But after twenty years, Regina must remember things that never made it into an official report. Maybe some small nugget could reinvigorate the investigation. "What time is your thing?" I asked.

"Five o'clock."

"I'll be there."

I looked at my watch. It was already past seven, and I had a busy day ahead. I took a quick shower and headed out. My first stop was the Sacred Heart Academy, Lisa's high school, half an hour outside of town. Vic had hired Roman after a coaching job at a high school "didn't work out," which is usually polite speech for *he got fired*. I had no specific reason to think he'd worked at Lisa's school, or that his termination had to do with underage girls. But I'd worked in law enforcement long enough to know that when a high school teacher is fired, it's worth asking the question.

Sacred Heart was housed in a pretty, Spanish-style building with a red tile roof. The newish-looking bars on the windows told me that that the neighborhood had fallen on hard times but that the school still took pride in its mission. I parked on the street and walked past harried parents dropping off teen girls in shapeless polo shirts tucked into plaid skirts.

I introduced myself to the principal and gave her my card. She looked about fifty, possibly old enough to have worked there when Lisa was killed. But as it turned out, she'd only been with the school for about a decade. She'd heard of the grisly crime but had no personal knowledge of the events. She also had no memory of a former coach named Roman.

I asked the principal if I could check out the yearbooks from Lisa's time there. She escorted me to the library and introduced me to the librarian, Nancy Jamison. Mrs. Jamison wore a heavy-looking wool dress with a pattern of falling leaves. She led me over to the yearbooks, and I quickly located the volumes from Lisa's sophomore and junior years. Sure enough, I spotted her and Regina in the sophomore class photograph. Flipping through the pictures, I was surprised to see Grace as a freshman, posing with the debate team. I'd asked her about Lisa the first time we met. Why hadn't she mentioned that they went to the same school?

Turning to the faculty pages, I found a group portrait of the physical education teachers, including Roman Dupont. He'd set off my creep radar the first time I saw him, with his cold eyes and abrupt tone. I'd thought maybe he was just hardened by life. But even in the twenty-year-old photograph, he still gave off a sex registrant vibe. I don't know how to explain it, but any experienced cop will tell you that some sex offenders have an indefinable eerie quality to them. I remember being in court years ago when they brought a serial rapist out of custody for a preliminary hearing. I'd guessed the charge before anyone said it out loud. Roman had that energy. At this point, I still had zero evidence that he'd done anything, but I'd keep digging.

I opened the yearbook from when Lisa was a junior—the year of her murder. Lisa was missing from the class picture. She'd disappeared months before graduation. Regina was in the photograph and I was struck by how much she'd changed from the previous year. In the sophomore class photo, the girls grinned mischievously at each other, ignoring the camera. Here, Regina stood alone, half a foot from the next closest kid, with a haunted expression on her face. She'd lost about twenty pounds and looked older than her years, like a woman in her late twenties. *The poor thing.* I wondered if Lisa had been found yet when the photograph had been taken, or if Regina had still been wondering what happened to her best friend.

I turned to the faculty pages and saw that Roman was also missing. That must be the year that he got fired. *So Roman was a possible genetic match for the killer, had worked at Lisa's school, and had been terminated the same year that she went missing.*

I picked up the sophomore yearbook again, opened it to the faculty page, and walked over to Mrs. Jamison, the librarian. "Excuse me . . . by any chance, were you working here in 2003?"

She nodded. "I've been here twenty-five years."

"Do you remember a coach named Roman Dupont?" I placed the open book in front of her and pointed to his face. I could tell from looking at her that she recognized him. "Why did he leave?" I pressed.

Mrs. Jamison blushed. There was a story here. "I don't really know anything. I only heard the rumors."

"About a student?" I pressed.

"It's not my place to say."

I explained to her why I was asking. Her eyes welled up with tears at the mention of Lisa's name. "I remember her. She was a sweet girl—very smart. Spent a lot of the time in the library. So terrible what happened to her."

"Did she hang around Roman Dupont at all?"

Mrs. Jamison shrugged. "I don't remember, dear. It's been a long time. Would you like to borrow those books for a couple days? I'm not supposed to give them out, but if you promise to return them, it'll be our secret."

"Thank you," I said. I didn't tell her that I planned to go home and cross-check every faculty member with my family tree.

24

Fifteen months ago—Abby

I LAY ACROSS THE bed, exhausted—all my nerves on fire. He traced the length of my spine down to the small of my back. I shuddered. Then his fingers slowly made their way around to the front of my body. The intensity was too much, and I pulled his hand away. "I need a minute," I said.

He grinned, proud of the effect he had on me, and kissed my neck. I watched him get up and move toward the kitchen. My eyes took in the sight of his long, muscular body and taut ass. Even his mustache was hot, in a seventies-porn kind of way. He opened the fridge, pulled out the bottle of white we'd started, and poured us each a glass.

This whole thing was a mistake. The first time, I'd blamed the alcohol, but we'd been meeting like this for months now, and I couldn't stop. I knew he had a family. I knew it made me a terrible person. But the feeling I had around him was addictive. I spent most of my time going through the motions of my shitty day job or feeling like a failure after getting yet another rejection. Then I'd meet up with him, and the only thing that mattered was the flame between us.

I wished I could be like my parents. Settle down with someone, relax into a comfortable routine. I tried it for a while with a really good guy, a special education teacher. But after two years of joint trips to the grocery store and Netflix-and-takeout date nights, I felt caged. I started snapping at him over nothing. He just took it, not understanding my behavior or the growing tension between us. After a while, even his niceness grated on my nerves. I left before things got ugly.

The truth is, I'm hooked on a certain kind of emotional intensity. It's the way I feel when I have a great script and the perfect scene partner. It's that first bloom of a relationship, when you want to learn everything about a person, devour them, merge with them. But it never lasts. Passion fizzles, and I get restless.

In a sick way, I prefer the pain of ending things to the drip, drip of domestic monotony. It makes me scared for the future. I can see myself in twenty years, with a face full of Botox and fillers, trawling bars for sad old men with white chest hair poking out of Tommy Bahama shirts. I shared this with Jacob once, and he laughed. He said he'd keep me company at the bar, maybe try his luck as a gigolo.

The wineglasses clinked against each other as he set them down on the nightstand. I felt his hand on the small of my back. I'd seen him with his wife and kid today. They were heading over to the park, laughing, looking happy. It crushed me, seeing that beautiful picture of family life that I knew I wasn't wired for. For the first time, I truly felt the wrongness of what we were doing. I'd watched them for a few minutes and then slunk off into the shadows. But here I was again, hours later.

"What's wrong?" he asked.

"Nothing," I said, forcing a smile. He placed one hand on either side of me and slowly leaned in. I wrapped my legs around his back, pulling him closer.

My phone rang, and my hand shot out, feeling for it, so I could turn off the volume. But I accidently answered instead and heard Jacob's voice. He hadn't returned my calls for weeks. The last time we'd talked, he'd sounded paranoid, scary.

"I'm sorry, I have to get this," I said, leaping to my feet.

I threw my robe over my shoulders and moved onto the porch. It was chilly, and I shivered as the wind whipped through the thin material.

"I just got out of jail," said Jacob, "Can you come get me? I'm outside the courthouse."

My stomach clenched into a fist. Jail? They must have finally picked him up on that warrant. "What happened?"

"I was just walking by the side of the road, and the pigs attacked me," he said. "I wasn't doing anything. They were targeting me."

"Tell me where you are exactly."

"Corner of Third and North Arrowhead Avenue. They took all my stuff. I'm in this stupid jail uniform. It's like made out of paper, and it's already ripped. I don't have my wallet or anything. I gotta go, Abby—this lady is letting me use her phone. Can you come get me?"

"I'll be there as soon as I can." Tears burned my eyes as I went back inside. My brother was spiraling out of control. I couldn't understand what was happening to him.

"Is everything okay?" called a voice from the bedroom. I'd forgotten that he was in there. I wished he'd leave. He couldn't be here for me on this, so why have him here at all? He couldn't drive me to the courthouse to get my idiot brother. I couldn't even rely on him for emotional support; he didn't owe me that. He needed to go. I heard footsteps behind me and felt him take me in his arms and pull me close. "Abby, talk to me. What's going on?"

"It's my brother—he just got out of jail," I said. "I have to pick him up."

"I'm sorry, babe. Do you know what he did?"

I shook my head.

"Do you know what agency arrested him? I might know someone over there. I could make some calls."

The tears were really coming down now. I just wanted to be alone. I broke free, walked over to the laundry basket, and threw on a T-shirt and jeans. "I need to go," I said. I caught a flash of myself in my full-length mirror. Blotchy skin, running nose. My face, swollen and ugly. Probably not what he dreamed of in a mistress. God, what was wrong with me? How was I even thinking about that right now?

"Just let yourself out, okay?" I said. "I have to bring Jacob here, and I don't know what shape he'll be in, so I really need you to be gone."

I grabbed my purse and the keys and headed out the door.

"Abby, wait!" he called, but I ignored him. I got in my car, and sped toward Lone Pine Canyon Drive, the windy mountain road leading out of Idlewood. I called Grace. She's a prosecutor, and she understands these things. I couldn't tell my parents. My dad had suffered his second heart attack last year, and the doctor had begged him to avoid stressful situations. Telling him his son was standing outside a courthouse in a torn jail jumpsuit might trigger another one.

"What's going on?" asked Grace.

"Jacob called me. He's getting released from jail. I'm going to pick him up. Can you find out what he was in for?"

There was silence on the other end of the line. "He's such an asshole," she said finally. "This is going to kill Mom and Dad."

"That's not helpful, Grace," I snapped. "Can you forget you're a prosecutor for two seconds?"

She let out a long sigh. "I'm on the court website now. It looks like assault with great bodily injury—probably that Arrowhead incident—resisting arrest, public intoxication, and meth possession."

"So why is he out of custody? Isn't there bail we need to pay or something?"

"I doubt it," she said. "In California, bail is tied to what you can afford, and right now Jacob's homeless and unemployed."

"Okay, I'm going to bring him back to my place. I'll call you later."

Jacob wasn't outside the courthouse. I drove around, scanning the streets for my brother, and saw a half dozen other freshly released inmates wandering around in jail uniforms. One of them had tattooed the whites of his eyeballs. He looked like a giant insect. I hit the lock button on my doors.

I finally spotted my brother in a park by the courthouse, talking to a tall, scruffy guy with shoulder-length hair. Was he trying to score more drugs? The scruffy guy seemed to be lecturing Jacob about something, wagging a finger in his face. I rolled down my window and tried to listen, but I couldn't make out what he was saying. The scruffy guy caught my eye and glared. There was so much hostility in that look, it was terrifying. Was he going to come over to my car?

"Jacob!" I called. Now my brother looked up too. "Get in."

I studied him as he walked toward me. He looked terrible, thinner than the last time I'd seen him. His hair was so matted, you'd probably have to cut the tangles out. There was a bruise on his right cheekbone and a cut above his left eye.

Jacob opened the door and climbed in. He stank of old sweat. I rolled down my window. "You look terrible."

"Thanks, Abby—it's great to see you too."

"What happened to your face?"

"I told you, I was walking by the highway, and the pigs started harassing me. Looked in my bag for no reason. Then they arrested me on a warrant. I fought back, but there were too many of them."

"When's your next court date?" I asked. "We need to get you a lawyer."

He shook his head. "I'm not going back. They might kill me if I'm inside."

"What are you talking about?" I asked. "Who might kill you?"

"You got any cigarettes?" he asked, ignoring my question.

"No, Jacob. I don't have any cigarettes." He knew I didn't smoke. "I'm taking you back to my place. If you have a craving, we can get some along the way."

"I can't do that Abby. They know where you live."

"Who is *they*?" I'd never seen Jacob like this before. He sounded like a complete nutjob. "Just come back with me. I'll give you your space, and you can stay as long as you want."

He turned and stared out the window. "Drop me at the Welcome Inn outside Arrowhead." Then without missing a beat, he told me how the jailers had been controlling his brain with blinking lights and making his muscles twitch.

I started to cry. Jacob's grip on reality was gone. I thought about driving straight to a hospital and having him committed. But my brother would never forgive me. I was the person he came to when he was in trouble. If he stopped talking to me, he might disappear altogether. "I'll bring you food and whatever you need. No one will know you're there."

"Shut up about it!" he shouted. "I'm not going home with you. The pigs already busted my face. I'm tired as hell—I don't need a lecture. Can you just buy me something to eat?"

Jacob never talked to me like that. He'd yell at other people, but not me. My tears started again, and I reached up to wipe them away.

"*What,* Abby? I'm tired and hungry, okay? Can I just get a burger? I haven't eaten in a day."

"Okay, Jacob," I said, defeated. I pulled into a McDonald's drive-through and bought him a Quarter Pounder. I was too devastated to eat, and the smell of my brother made me nauseous.

I typed the Welcome Inn into my GPS, and we drove in silence. The quiet of that car ride was unbearable. Usually, Jacob and I can't stop talking. Now we had nothing to say. I pulled up to a rundown dump of a motel with small, single-pane windows. I couldn't imagine my brother burrowed inside, in some depressing room filled with garbage and rancid clothes. "It's not too late," I pleaded. "Let me take you home."

The look on his face told me he was done talking. I held up my hands in a gesture of surrender. Jacob turned away from me and opened the door. I put my hand on his shoulder to stop him. Reaching into my wallet, I pulled out all the cash inside and handed it to him. "Call me if you need anything," I said. "When you're ready, I can take you to the police station to get your things.

"Thanks," he mumbled. Then he got out of the car without saying goodbye.

25

Present—Kate

SOMETHING SKETCHY HAD clearly happened with Roman Dupont. I wondered if Grace remembered the story—she'd been a student at Sacred Heart, and teens love to gossip.

When I was in high school, a math teacher had been canned for moonlighting as a sex worker. She made the mistake of putting an ad for escort services in a local paper. Someone, probably a horny dad looking for side fun, recognized her and mailed it to the principal. Within forty-eight hours she was gone. We all gossiped about the scandal for weeks, and I could still remember it years later. The same sort of thing might have happened at Sacred Heart.

It was still early, so I decided to swing by Grace's house and try to catch her before work. As it turned out, she was working from home because of an asbestos leak in the courthouse. Hearing that brought back memories. When I was in LAPD, the crumbling courthouses always had a section of hallway cordoned off with white sheeting and warning signs.

Grace invited me to talk on her porch. When I arrived, she was seated cross-legged on a wicker couch, with a laptop in front of her.

"Beautiful day," I said as I climbed the front steps. "It's nice that you can work outside."

Grace closed her computer and smiled. "Yeah, and I'll trade a business suit for sweats and a T-shirt any day." She tore a can of fizzy water off a six-pack and handed it to me.

"So, I think I mentioned before that I was looking into Lisa Forrester's murder. I didn't realize that you went to school together."

Grace nodded. "I didn't really know her. I was shy in those days, and Lisa was a year ahead of me. I think she had a best friend who wore goth makeup." That sounded like Regina.

"I also wanted to ask you about something that happened when you were at Sacred Heart. Do you remember a coach named Roman Dupont?"

Her eyes lit up with remembered glee from the old scandal. "Mr. Dupont! Yeah, they fired him for fooling around with a student. Apparently, he got a mysterious call in the middle of practice and told the swim team, 'If I'm not back in twenty minutes, you'll never see me again.' Then he disappeared."

"How do you know he slept with a student? That call could have been about anything."

Grace shrugged. "Mostly the rumor mill. But another girl disappeared from class around the same time and never came back."

This was getting interesting. If nothing had happened between Roman and the student, that was one heck of a coincidence. I needed to find the girl. "Do you remember her name?"

"Carole Bernardi," said Grace. "Abby and Jacob went to Serrano High, and Carole ended up switching in to finish the year. According to Jacob she had a reputation for being a—" she stopped herself, probably realizing how ugly the word *slut* sounded. Especially coming out of an adult's mouth about an underage girl. "For being promiscuous. It was probably bullshit, but you remember what it was like in those days. You wore a short skirt a couple times and flirted with boys, and got branded a slut. I heard someone even graffitied a chart on the wall of how much sperm was in Carole's stomach."

I winced. Kids can be heartless. *That poor girl.* I was shy and awkward as a teen and had been spared that particular ordeal. But a couple of my friends hadn't been so lucky.

"Did you know Carole at all? You're not in touch by any chance?"

"I didn't know her well, but I heard she owns a yoga studio in West LA."

I'd pay Carole a visit and find out exactly what happened. But while I had Grace's attention, I decided to switch gears. Richard had forbidden me from asking the Coburns about the actual crime. But Grace had been forthcoming every time I talked to her, and didn't shy away from ugly truths. So far, no one in the family had described the night of Abby's murder. It was a gaping hole in my understanding of this case, and something I was eager to fix.

"Grace, while I'm here, can I ask you about the night of the fire?"

Without hesitating, she described walking the dog late at night, seeing an orange blaze on the hilltop, and watching her sister's cabin burn. One detail in her story caught my attention.

"You said the dog woke up because Ted was in the shower. If I remember right, the fire started around four AM. Did he have an early shift?"

She shook her head. "No, he was just getting back from an overnight. They were putting him on a lot of last-minute night warrants back then. Apparently, Ted said the wrong thing and pissed off a superior. And the dog—he's getting older, and his bladder isn't what it used to be, so once he was awake, he wanted out."

My Spidey sense tingled. *Something was off.* Police need special permission from a judge to execute a night warrant. They're usually reserved for situations where an early warning could endanger officers or cause a suspect to destroy evidence. Night warrants are complex operations that require planning—not something you throw together at the last minute. Ted's story sounded fishy. I wondered if he was cheating on his wife.

Did Grace suspect anything? I didn't get the sense that she was covering for him. My guess was that she believed her husband. After all, she'd worked sex crimes and family violence, not drugs or gangs. The circumstances that necessitate night warrants don't come up much in her area of practice. And a lot of DAs, even badge bunnies, don't have an interest in the mechanics of police operations.

"What is it?" asked Grace. "You look confused."

My skepticism must have shown on my face. "Nothing. I just remember those days," I said with a forced smile. "A good friend of mine at LAPD pissed off a captain's nephew and got shipped to Frauds as punishment. Law enforcement is all about retaliation. One thing I don't miss about the job."

Grace nodded slowly and seemed to relax a little. But there was worry in her eyes, like I'd just hinted at something that had been gnawing at her. "Is he still having that problem?" I asked. "With the last-minute assignments?"

"Yes," she said. "From time to time. It's slowed down a bit."

I tried to pick her brain for more information, but she seemed distracted. I got a few more details out of her about the night of the fire, but her answers were short, and she didn't volunteer a ton of information. I caught her looking at her watch, and I realized it was time to wrap things up.

I said goodbye and walked down the porch steps. From the street I turned around and glanced back at Grace. She looked unsettled. Her face was aimed in my direction, but her eyes were far away.

26

Present—Kate

B ALASANA WELLNESS CENTER wasn't like any yoga studio I'd seen
before. The place was enormous and gleaming white, with sky
lights and sparkling blond wood floors. According to a menu of services, in addition to yoga they offered New Age treatments like "cryo
facials" and "T-shock therapy," which all sounded vaguely like torture
techniques. One procedure involved using liquid nitrogen on your
face. I hoped they had good insurance.

I handed my card to the chick behind the desk and told her I
wanted to speak to Carole. She told me that Carole was currently
teaching, but invited me to wait. I browsed the small gift shop, which
was full of eighty-dollar "healing bracelets" and one-hundred-fifty-
dollar yoga pants that looked identical to the ones I'd bought at Target.

I peeked in at the class in session, through an all-glass door.
Carole was in the middle of demonstrating a complicated pose. Her
hands supported her body, and her legs stuck out to the side, one ankle
wrapped around the other. She looked like she was barely breaking a
sweat, and was actually chatting with students while wrapped up like
a pretzel.

Watching her in action made me desperately miss yoga. Before my
car accident, it had been my favorite form of exercise. Running bores

me, and the sweaty communal workout machines at the gym gross
me out. Yoga is one of the few things that could focus my ADHD
brain. But ever since a drunk driver left me with six herniated discs,
it's become too dangerous. One wrong move could further damage my
spine. At any rate, in my new life as a PI, yoga isn't the kind of expense
I can justify.

After about twenty minutes of biding my time and drinking
free mint tea in the waiting room, the class ended. Carole's students
streamed out, all young and gorgeous. I was pretty sure I recognized
one of them as a pop singer my daughter worships. Carole lingered for
a few minutes, chatting with a male acolyte with eight-pack abs. His
tiny workout uniform looked like a European men's bathing suit and
seemed to be designed to show off the goods.

Carole caught my eye, smiled, and came over to greet me. I
couldn't tell if she was a savvy businesswoman bringing a personal
touch to a potential new client, or trying to get away from the sweaty
banana hammock guy.

"Hi, I'm Carole," she said. "I don't think I know you yet. Are you
here for the eleven o'clock class?" I shook her hand and was struck by
her beauty up close. We were the same age, but she looked ten years
younger and had flawless skin and a lithe, toned figure. She wore a
white one-piece outfit that brought out her olive skin and dark eyes.

This was dicey. If I went in straight about Roman, Carole would
almost certainly tell me to get lost. If Grace's gossip was on point, then
this woman had been seduced and manipulated by a predator before
she was old enough to understand. And here I was, showing up at her
work twenty years later and inquiring about her sex life as a teen. I
decided to start with asking about Lisa. Carole probably knew about
the murder, even though it had happened after she left Sacred Heart.

I handed her my card. "Kate Myles, I'm a private detective looking
into the murder of a high school classmate of yours—Lisa Forrester.
Do you have a few minutes?"

"Poor Lisa," she said, glancing at the clock. "My next class starts
in fifteen minutes, and I have to get ready. I can give you five. But I
didn't know Lisa well. I'm not sure how I can help."

Carole ushered me into a small office and closed the door. I could smell her, a mix of essential oils and fresh perspiration. There were slight sweat stains under her arms, and her previously smooth brow was now creased with worry lines. Maybe she knew what I was really here to ask her. I needed to rip off the Band-Aid and let her get back to her day.

Straight to the point. "The police have a DNA match for Lisa's killer," I told her. "We don't know who that person is, but they've identified a couple of his relatives who are also related to a former Sacred Heart coach, Roman Dupont. I'd heard you might have had a connection to him."

"Roman?" she said. "Oh my God." Carole slapped a hand over her mouth and sat down on the desk. "I can't believe this. He's a son of a bitch, but I never thought he was a killer."

"We don't know that," I cautioned. "I'm just doing my due diligence."

"He messed me up for years," she said, her voice quivering. "The school told me to withdraw or I'd be expelled for violating their morality policy. My dad told me I'd embarrassed the family and ruined myself." She practically hissed the word *ruined*, as decades of anger bubbled to the surface. "Even after I switched schools, everyone knew what happened. Of course, all the boys harassed me, asked me for hand jobs behind the bleachers. It was horrible. And I blamed myself for all of it. I actually felt guilty that he lost his job over me." She let out a sharp puff of air through her nose. "It wasn't until college that I started understanding concepts like grooming and power differentials and realized that I'd been taken advantage of."

There was so much pain in her eyes, I hated to press further. But I still didn't know what had occurred between them. I took a breath. "I'm so sorry to ask, but what did happen exactly?"

"He was my swimming coach—and my biology teacher, by the way. Roman is a smart man. In training, he was brutally hard on me. I was good, right on the cusp of scholarship material. I guess he thought he could push me to get better. That's what he told me at any rate—that he wanted me to be great. In retrospect, it was probably all bullshit." She shook her head in disgust. "He started having me stay late and swim extra laps. Then one day he kissed me. I was too shocked to tell anyone. The next day in practice, he acted totally different. No more verbal abuse. He even complimented my form and told the other girls to watch my backstroke. Before long he had me giving him blow jobs in the girls' locker room after practice."

"Wasn't he worried about getting caught?" I asked. "The locker room seems risky."

"He should have been, but we did it after everyone else had gone home—or so we thought. And I think he liked the element of risk."

Carole paused and I gave her a minute to collect herself. I was asking a lot of her, and she didn't owe me any of this.

"Looking back, I think he targeted me from day one. He could tell things weren't great at home. My mom had passed away, and my dad was a controlling asshole. Then Roman stepped in to fill the void."

"I'm so sorry this happened to you," I said. "He should have gone to jail."

She shrugged. "Well, he didn't. Back in those days, people tended to sweep things under the rug."

"How did it end? You said the school made you leave, but how did they find out?"

"Someone saw us," she said. "We were in the locker room. He was facing the door. I was facing him and on my knees. I heard footsteps, and then what sounded like a person running away. Roman shouted something like 'nosy little bitch' and pulled up his pants."

"Do you know who it was?"

She shook her head. "I never saw them, and Roman didn't say. He just ordered me out of the locker room and told me to go home. Then, the next day at swimming practice, he got a call and told us that if he wasn't back soon, we'd probably never see him again. Everyone started gossiping about what happened. But I felt like dying because I knew. I got out of the pool and went to the bathroom and threw up. I just sat there on the floor, with my knees tucked into my chest, shivering. Then the next day, the principal summoned me, and my dad was there. They grilled me in front of him about everything I'd done with Roman. Like, explicit details. It was mortifying."

I was furious, listening to her. They should have called the police. Carole should have been interviewed by a trained forensic examiner, not interrogated by some judgmental creep in front of her father. "I'm sorry you were treated that way," I told her. "You weren't to blame, and that never should have happened."

She laughed bitterly. "Yes, I know that now, but it's taken many years of healing and therapy to make peace with it."

"Did you ever find out who saw you?" She shook her head. "Any chance that it was Lisa?" If Lisa was the one who had tattled and ruined Roman's career, maybe he'd killed her to get even.

Carole shrugged. "It's possible. Lisa wasn't on the swim team, but maybe she played a different sport. Maybe she forgot something in the locker room and came back for it? It could have been anyone, really."

CHAPTER

27

One year ago—Abby

I HAD MIXED FEELINGS about going back to school at thirty. Most of my classmates were almost a decade younger than me. A number of them had just graduated from college and still acted like coeds who'd been institutionalized since birth. Meanwhile, I'd spent my twenties living and working independently. As much as I wanted to get to know my peers, I didn't care who was hooking up with who, and I didn't have much in common with any of them.

In my first week, a girl named Winnie invited me to a party with business school students. I immediately felt bored and claustrophobic. I was the oldest person there and well past the point where I wanted to drink vodka and orange juice out of a red Solo cup or play beer pong. I tried to be a good sport. Winnie was there to meet men. And what could I say—*"I'm in love with a thirty-eight-year-old married dad, and these guys look like children to me"*?

I ended up playing wingman while she flirted with a bland Bradley Cooper look-alike and trying to make conversation with his idiot friend. The guy was an aging frat bro with a bald spot and khaki shorts with little whales on them. He was already slurring his words, and his breath and skin reeked of beer. In between swaying and sloppily touching my arm, he asked me what I'd done before going back to school. I told him I'd been an actress, and he asked me if I'd ever done porn. That's when I stopped trying to make small talk.

I didn't want to abandon Winnie, so I went over to a bookshelf, found a copy of *The White Album*, probably left over from someone's college English class, and started reading. I guess it was a touch on the passive-aggressive side, but it beat standing around by myself. When I looked up, Winnie and the Bradley Cooper type were gone. I put the book down and made my exit.

I didn't get any invitations to hang out after that, which was fine. I was here for a reason. Acting hadn't worked out. I wanted to pick up the pieces of my life and translate my interpersonal skills into a meaningful career. I'm good at talking to people, excluding drunk business students. I'm good in a crisis—I've always been a better friend for breakups than marriages. Weddings feel forced and phony, and a solid chunk of the time I secretly dislike the husband-to-be. But when things fall apart, I'm a great friend. I'm there for people when they need me. And I don't cut them off after one or two venting sessions—that's a big pet peeve of mine.

I wanted to help people like my brother. It had been months since I'd heard from him when I'd driven him to his disgusting drug motel. If I couldn't save Jacob, maybe I could work with people like him. I felt helpless just sitting on the sidelines, watching him deteriorate. Being here made me feel like I was doing something. Which is how I ended up in Dr. Miguel Figueroa's Intro to Addiction course. But I wasn't prepared for the gut-wrenching way it would affect me.

In our first week, he brought in two guest lecturers on methamphetamine, a journalist and a psychologist specializing in addiction treatment. I sat in my usual spot in the back. Winnie and a couple of her girlfriends were chatting away, probably excited for another weekend of parties. I just wanted to get home. I wanted to spend Friday night alone with a good book, a glass of white, and a pint of ice cream.

Bob Fuentes, the journalist, talked about the history of meth and how the drug had exploded in the last fifteen years. He explained how meth production switched from biker crews to sophisticated criminal organizations in Mexico. "The drug they produce is abundant, cheap, and pure," he told us. "It's cheaper than ever and way more toxic. Anyone seen *Breaking Bad*?" Half the hands in the room flew up. "Remember that whole premise where Walter White was making the purest drug?" Several people nodded. "That's standard now. It's all pure, which means it's wreaking more havoc on people's brains. And what we're seeing is that people can't always come back from that, even when they stop using."

I winced. Despite everything that had happened, I'd felt in my bones that Jacob would snap out of it someday. Was he saying that wouldn't happen? I had a clear picture in my mind of the two of us, old and wrinkled, toasting cocktails, listening to live music, and talking about life. The last time I'd seen Jacob, he was a paranoid shell of a person, but I'd assumed that the man I knew was still alive, buried inside there. *Had I been wrong?*

"I'm going to turn to our other guest, Dr. Keisha Richards," said Dr. Luna. "Dr. Richards has been on the front lines of treating some of the hardest cases and is a trail blazer in coming up with new approaches to fighting meth addiction. Dr. Richards, can you tell us what all of this means on an individual level?"

Dr. Richards cleared her throat and picked up a microphone. "Like Bob was saying, the meth we see today is a far scarier drug than the meth of ten years ago. They used to make meth from a natural substance called ephedrine. But now it's predominantly made with industrial chemicals called phenyl-2-propanone, or P2P. And it's destroying the mental health of its victims."

I tried to scribble down every word as they spoke. They were talking about Jacob and what was in store for him. And their grave tone gave me chills.

"How did individuals suffering from meth addiction present when you started practicing, and how has that changed?" asked Dr. Luna.

"It's a whole new ball game," said Dr. Richards. "Meth has always been a neurotoxin. But when I started practicing, it took people a long time before they suffered permanent brain damage. Meth made people feel good, but they retained a grip on reality. Once people detoxed, you could talk to them, reach them."

"And now?"

"This new stuff is causing serious, sometimes irrevocable damage after just a few doses. Especially in people predisposed to mental illness." My stomach clenched. That was Jacob, who was prone to anxiety and depression. As Grace likes to say, there's always been something off about him. "I've seen users go from functional to psychotic in weeks. Some of my patients end up with devastating brain damage. Don't get me wrong—many people make a full recovery, but it can take months or even years. And others can get stuck in a psychotic state that never really goes away."

My heart was breaking. What if it was already too late for Jacob? I felt tears rolling down my cheeks. I wiped them away with my sleeve, but more came. Great, I was already the older weirdo who reads Joan Didion at parties, and now here I was, openly crying in the middle of class. At least I was in the back. I brought both my hands to my face and wiped my eyes, but I couldn't stop. I looked up and saw Dr. Luna watching me with concern. Wonderful. Now the teacher had flagged me as a head case. I looked down at my notebook and tried to be as discreet as possible.

"There's no medication that can ease cravings, like methadone for opiates," said Dr. Richards. "In the most serious cases, users have wreaked so much havoc on their brains that communication can be a challenge. Sometimes it takes months for them to heal enough to have a meaningful conversation, if they get there at all. That's a problem because traditional addiction therapy is about talking, building a connection. And most court-ordered or insurance-funded programs only last a few months . . ."

I didn't hear what she said after that. My breath caught and a sob escaped. The girl in the row in front of me turned around and stared. I packed up my books as quietly as I could and made my way toward the exit. I needed to get it together if I was going to do this, to learn how to help people. But right now, all I could think about was my brother.

28

Present—Kate

CAROLE'S STORY HAD left me shaken. Roman was an aggressive, manipulative creep who preyed on young girls. The thought of our family connection made me sick. But was he a suspect in Lisa's murder?

When Lisa had gone missing, Roman had already been fired. He was raging and humiliated and may have felt he had nothing to lose. Maybe he saw another teenage girl from Sacred Heart and decided to take out his revenge and pent-up desire on her. Unfortunately, Lisa's body had been too deteriorated by the time she was found to determine if she'd been raped.

It was also possible that Lisa was the one who'd reported Roman and Carole. Whoever told the principal about them had cost Roman his career. That could be a motive to kill.

Of course, Roman might just be a predator who had nothing do to with Lisa's death. If he wasn't the killer, then I had one homicidal cousin and a second relative who bullied a minor into sex. The thought of sharing blood with multiple monsters was too much to wrap my head around. And then there was Vic, who'd employed Roman for decades. Surely, Vic had to have known what happened with Carole— or at least suspected something similar. I desperately wanted to go back in time, stop myself from snooping in my mom's garage, and unlearn everything I'd come to know about my biological family.

But that wasn't an option.

I forced myself to mentally shift gears and think about my upcoming meeting with Abby's thesis advisor. Dr. Luna was having office hours, and I wanted to swing by and talk to him. I'd sent an email a few days ago, introducing myself. But when I'd heard about Abby's married beau, I'd decided to surprise Dr. Luna instead of setting up an appointment. As an older man in a position of authority, I couldn't rule him out as Abby's lover. I wanted to catch him off guard in case he was somehow involved in her death.

I parked by the humanities building and made my way over to Dr. Luna's office. His door was already open. I peered inside and watched a young woman with a buzz cut frantically jot down notes as the professor talked.

He spotted me in the doorway and frowned in confusion.

"Hi, I'm Kate Myles. I sent you an email a couple days ago."

Dr. Luna put a hand on the young woman's arm. My eyes zeroed in on the place where his skin met hers. Were professors supposed to do that these days? I'm not a touchy person. But I also thought there was a strict keep-your-hands-to-yourself rule in academia. But maybe talking to Carole had left me paranoid.

"Raven," said Dr. Luna, "I have a meeting, but feel free to come by tomorrow, and we'll finish going over your paper." Raven shoved her notebook into a backpack covered in iron-on patches and brushed past me. Within seconds, the professor was guiding me over to a chair across from his desk. "It's good to meet you, Kate," he said. "Please forgive me if I get a bit emotional. Abby was one of my best students— and a dear friend. I'm still processing what happened to her."

Dr. Luna didn't seem annoyed by my unannounced visit. He radiated warmth, and his body language told me he was eager to help. But I never trust first impressions. "You said Abby was a friend. Did you see her socially?" I asked.

He nodded. "Yes. Abby was older than most of my students, more mature. She came to social work with life experience, not the wide-eyed idealism I see in some of her peers. Twenty-three-year-olds bent on changing the world, but who've never actually spoken to a homeless person. Honestly, I felt pretty burned out on teaching before I met her."

Dr. Luna's eyes shone as he talked about Abby. He definitely had strong feelings for her. "So, you started hanging out with her outside of class?"

He looked at me funny. "Yeah, she'd come over for dinner once a week or so. My husband loved her too. He's a mean cook and Abby had a talent for making cocktails. She'd mix us Negronis. Nathaniel would make his Bolognese. We'd really have a wonderful time."

Husband. Got it—the professor wasn't into Abby. He was just a touchy person. "How did you become Abby's advisor?" I asked. "Were you randomly assigned, or did she seek you out?"

Dr. Luna smiled patiently. "How familiar are you with my research?"

"Just what I read on your faculty bio," I admitted. "I know you do a lot of work on addiction."

He nodded and seemed please that I'd done a little homework. "I study evidence-based treatment programs for the hardest cases. There are a few programs that work and a lot of quacks who push ineffective techniques on suffering people. I use statistics to understand which is which."

I glanced down at my notebook and scribbled a few lines so the professor couldn't see the look of recognition on my face. I'd gone to a New Age rehab program before finding one that was a better fit. The deal-breaker moment involved an afternoon of coloring books and "sound therapy" in the form of a multi-pierced Gen Zer with a gong.

"I also teach Intro to Addiction, which is how I met Abby," continued Dr. Luna. "A few weeks in, I started my segment on treatment challenges for severe meth addiction. Anyway, I was explaining this to the class, and my eye landed on Abby. Tears were streaming down her cheeks, and she just sat there crying. I wanted to catch her after class, but she left early. So I looked up her email in the student directory and asked her to swing by my office. That's when she told me about her brother."

"Is that when she asked you to be her advisor?"

He shook his head. "I suggested it after she told me about her interests. Abby wanted to focus her research on treatment techniques for long-term meth addiction, with a special emphasis on dual-diagnosis individuals."

"Was she a good student?"

"Brilliant. Abby was one of the best writers I've ever taught. I tried to convince her to stay and get a PhD, but she was eager to start helping people. She'd found her calling a bit later and wanted to make up for lost time."

It made sense. Abby had watched her brother deteriorate. Social work gave her an opportunity to help others struggling with the same disease. I glanced down at my watch. Office hours were almost over, and I still hadn't asked about Abby's romantic life. I needed to change topics before the professor politely dismissed me and returned to his work. "Did Abby ever talk about her personal life?"

"She spoke about her family a lot."

"What about her love life?"

He thought for a moment and then nodded. "One night, she had one too many at dinner and ended up sleeping on our couch. We stayed up late talking, and she confided in me that she was having an affair."

"Did she tell you the guy's name?"

Dr. Luna rubbed his temples, trying to remember. "She referred to him by his first name. It was something generic and one syllable."

"Could it have been Nick?"

He shrugged. "Maybe? Honestly, it didn't register with me at the time. I was focused on the fact that my friend was in pain."

"Did she tell you anything else that could help me identify him?"

"I'm trying to remember why, but I think he worked in law enforcement." He clapped his hands together. "Oh, that's right—it was a race he was participating in."

"Baker to Vegas?" Baker to Vegas is a law enforcement relay race that hundreds—if not thousands—of cops, prosecutors, and other law enforcement personnel run in every year. My mind flashed on Bryce Chen's outfit at our first meeting. He'd been wearing a B2V T-shirt, a common abbreviation for the race. Maybe the Idlewood Fire Station sent a team. But then again, I couldn't remember if fire departments participate. Bryce could have gone to support friends in the sheriff's office or another agency. Then I remembered my conversation with Grace about her husband's supposed night warrants. Ted Vera was a cop with a generic one-syllable name who was missing on the night of Abby's death. "What did she tell you about the race?"

"Apparently, the guy convinced her to meet him in Vegas at the end of it. He'd shelled out for a suite in some five-star hotel. They just hung out and had room service. She said it was wonderful. But then, on Sunday morning, when he thought she was asleep, he called his wife from the bathroom, asked about the kid, and said he loved her. That was a very sobering moment for Abby."

"Did she tell you anything else about her lover? Maybe a description or the age of his kid?"

He shook his head. "No, she only brought it up that one time. I think she was ashamed, to be honest."

I wasn't going to get anything else out of him. It was time to wrap this up. "Can you think of anyone else who might have wanted to hurt Abby?" I asked. He looked taken aback. "I know it's a strange question. Abby sounds like a wonderful person. It's probably hard to imagine anyone wishing her ill. But somebody killed her, and I'm trying to make sure I don't miss an important lead."

He rubbed his temples and thought for a moment. "Um, maybe someone from the clinic she worked in? Abby saw clients at New Vistas in San Bernardino. Ben Friedman is the person running the clinic. I think Abby knew him before she started working there. I know she had one patient who made her nervous."

My ears perked up. "Do you remember his name?"

He shook his head. "Not off the top of my head. I'll see if I can figure it out. I can't tell you much, because of client confidentiality issues. But I can try to get you a name."

I thanked him, eager to explore the possibility of another suspect. But in the meantime, I needed to look into Nick Fieldstone and Ted Vera.

29

Present—Kate

I ARRIVED BACK AT my cabin just before the concert at the Red Barn Opry. My back hurt and my legs felt cramped after too many hours of driving, so I decided to walk over. On the way, I thought about Sam. All day long, he'd crept into my brain whenever I'd had a quiet moment. Images from the night before ran through my head like a film reel. At one point, while navigating the UC Riverside campus, I distractedly walked into a bike stand, scraping my shin on a pedal.

Every cell in my body craved more of Sam, but I wasn't going to the concert for him. I was in Idlewood to find out what happened to Lisa, and I needed to talk to Regina Miller. Somehow, I'd have to ignore the electrifying effect that Sam had on me and act like a professional. I hate mixing business with pleasure. When I'd slept with Sam, I hadn't known he was in a band with my victim's childhood friend. But there was nothing I could do about it now, and I certainly wasn't going to avoid places because of him. My plan was to quickly introduce myself to Regina and set up a time for an interview, away from Sam and her bandmates.

The Red Barn Opry stood out among the evergreens and modest wood cabins. The outdoor stage was built to look like a giant barn and painted a deep burgundy. Around the small theater, someone had constructed a kid-sized Western town, complete with a tiny jail and a saloon. The pine trees had been cleared from the front of the theater to make space for an audience. A dozen families had laid down blankets and folding chairs in preparation for an evening of free music.

Off to the side, a grizzled grandpa with a Santa-like beard was selling popcorn and Dixie cups of hot cider. I wished Amelia were here, and made a mental note to come back with her the following weekend. Even if there wasn't a concert, we could have a picnic, and she could explore the little town.

I spotted Sam and my breath caught in my throat. He was setting up the sound equipment with the other musicians. I felt tongue-tied, not sure how to act around him in public. I stuck my hands in my pockets to keep them from fidgeting, and walked over to say hello. Sharing none of my awkwardness, Sam put an arm around my waist and gave me a quick peck on the cheek. I could feel myself blush. My job required discretion, and here I was being publicly affectionate with a guy who knew everyone in town.

"This is Regina, Luther, and Crispin," he said, motioning toward his bandmates. "Guys, this is my friend Kate." I waved at the three of them. Regina offered me a knowing smile. She'd seen me getting friendly with Sam, and I could tell her curiosity was piqued.

Sam went back to setting up the sound equipment. I turned to Regina, who was sitting on a tree stump and tuning her guitar. She was pretty in a hard kind of way, with bone-straight red hair and a red leather jacket. The lashes surrounding her light blue eyes were coated in thick mascara and reminded me of tarantulas. I wondered if she and Sam had ever been an item. He seemed like the type to stay friends with his exes.

"It's nice to meet you," she said before dropping her voice. "I haven't seen Sam this happy since his wife left."

The level of intimacy surprised me. Maybe things moved faster in small towns. "When did she leave?" I asked, mentally kicking myself for indulging my curiosity. I wasn't here to pry into Sam's personal life.

Regina shrugged, "God, has it been a year now? I'm not sure. I mean, don't worry—they're not reconciling. It wasn't exactly a love fest beforehand, if you know what I mean."

Was Sam technically still married? I stifled the urge to dig further and shifted my attention back to the investigation. "Regina, I'm not sure if Sam told you why I'm in Idlewood," I said. "I'm a private investigator, and I'm looking into a murder, from twenty years ago, of a teenage girl named Lisa Forrester."

Regina turned white as a sheet and stared at me. Her whole body tensed. "Lisa? I don't understand. Did her parents hire you?"

"No, it's a long story, I'm helping out with the sheriff's cold case unit."

She shook her head in disgust, and her eyes welled up. "It certainly took them long enough. I told them who to look at, and they dismissed me like a stupid little girl." A tear that had been trapped in her clumpy lashes broke free and rolled down her cheek.

I caught Sam's eye. He shot me a worried look. Crispin, the base player, walked over, noticing the change in Regina's demeanor. "Everything okay here?" he asked.

She nodded and wiped her eyes on her leather sleeve.

"We need to get this thing started," said Crispin.

"Can we set up a time to talk?" I asked Regina. "I really need your help."

She nodded again, still collecting herself. "Sam has my number."

"Okay, so we're done here?" asked Crispin, his voice more of a command than a question.

"Yeah," I said, and wandered out into the audience to find a seat. I shouldn't have approached her before she went on stage. It had been twenty years since Lisa's death, and I hadn't expected her to react that strongly. But losing her friend had been the defining tragedy of her childhood. I should have waited and talked to her in a more private setting. The awkwardness with Sam had clouded my judgment, I thought.

I debated whether to leave before things got more awkward. But then I spotted a man who looked like the picture I'd seen of Nick

Fieldstone, lounging on a blanket with a petite woman and a toddler in pigtails. I took out my phone and googled him again. Up popped his Facebook profile picture. Sure enough, it was Nick. I wasn't going to confront him in front of his family, but I could at least observe them together. Get a sense of who he was. I sat down on a tree stump a few feet behind them.

The band opened with a spirited rendition of "Wagon Wheel." Regina sang with a clear, powerful voice. With her flaming hair, she reminded me of Bonnie Raitt. At the chorus, Nick's wife sprung to her feet, took the little girl by the hands and started dancing. The mother and daughter wore matching blue dresses with little pink flowers. I could tell she was a good mom. Probably the kind who sent her daughter to school with candy and individualized cards for every kid on Valentine's Day. My heart ached for her. I hoped I was wrong about her husband.

After a few songs, Nick got up and walked over to the popcorn vendor. This was my chance. I'd put in a request at the fire station to speak to him, and had never gotten a response. I'd have to ambush him and see if he let anything slip before shutting me out.

I followed him over to the popcorn machine. There were a couple of people in line before us, which gave me a chance to introduce myself. "Nick Fieldstone?" I asked.

He turned around and smiled politely. "I'm sorry, do I know you?"

"This is a weird question, but did you run Baker to Vegas last year?"

Nick gave me a weird look. "Um, no. Fire doesn't run. But a couple of us went up to support the sheriffs. We're pretty tight with those guys."

So he was definitely in Vegas on the weekend of the race.

I handed him my card. "Kate Myles. I'm a private investigator working for the Coburn family. Can I ask you a few questions about Abby Coburn?"

Nick's eyes registered pure animal panic for a second before he regained his composure. "She was one of the victims in the Hillside Fire. Terrible."

"But you knew her as well," I prodded.

He plastered on a smile. I looked down at his tapping foot, which was pointed away from me. Nick wanted out of here. But he'd promised his kid popcorn and wouldn't want to tell his wife why he got out of line. "It's a small town. I said hi to her a couple times in the coffee shop where she worked. That's about it."

I rolled the dice. "Nick, I've seen the text messages."

His eyes narrowed, and he grabbed my arm roughly. "Let's take a walk."

I pried away his fingers. "Good idea," I said. "But don't touch me."

We crossed the street and walked up the block, away from the concert. "I think this is far enough," I said. I could see a family a few houses down, hanging out on their porch. I wanted witnesses in case Nick got desperate and did something stupid.

"How dare you pull this in front of my family?" Nick was seething. His hands were balled into fists, and for a second I thought he was going to hit me.

I took a step back. "I tried to go through the station, but—"

He cut me off. "Look, I broke it off with Abby a month before the fire. Which you should know if you've actually seen any messages and aren't bullshitting me." He kept his voice low, but he was practically hissing at me. "I had nothing to do with what happened to her."

"Why were you awake the night she died?"

Nick looked up at the sky and shook his head. "Are you kidding me? I couldn't sleep. I'd cheated on my wife—who's amazing, by the way, not that you care—and I felt bad about it. I'd been waking up a lot and would just lie there feeling like garbage and trying to decide whether to confess."

"So, you were awake, and you smelled smoke. How'd you know someone wasn't making a fire or having a barbecue?"

"Because I'm a goddamn firefighter, that's how. And no one roasts marshmallows at four in the morning. Listen, I'm done with this. Stay away from me and my family. If you come near me again, I'll get a restraining order." He turned and jogged back to the concert, probably trying to figure out how to explain his absence and the lack of popcorn to his wife.

I didn't know if Nick was the killer, but his infidelity would definitely come in at trial. Nick had confessed to sleeping with a woman whose arson-murder he investigated. Ethically, he should have recused himself from the case. Instead, he'd volunteered to work on it. And the fact that he called in the fire was suspicious.

We didn't have to prove that Nick killed Abby—just that it was a viable alternate theory. Jacob would be on trial for his life. The death penalty was still on the table. If there was a reasonable chance that someone else committed the crime, Richard would be allowed to present evidence of it. Nick would get crucified in open court. His wife, neighbors, and colleagues would all hear about his affair and sloppy investigation. I was doing my job, but I felt like a slimeball. Part of me hoped that Nick was the killer. Because if he wasn't, we were about to blow up an innocent man's life and career.

My phone vibrated. I pulled it out and saw that it was my ex-husband. "What's up, John?" I asked. "Is Amelia okay?"

"She's fine, but can you take her to her ballet recital tomorrow?"

I bit my lip and took a deep breath before responding. "What recital?" I asked, trying to keep the anger out of my voice. "And why is this the first time I'm hearing about it?"

He let out an exasperated sigh. John can't stand it when I question him about anything. "I didn't mention it because you were against her even taking lessons." Bullshit. When he thought he could attend, he didn't want the unpleasantness of having to see me at the recital. So, he kept me in the dark until he needed my help.

"I didn't want her taking lessons because I didn't think she'd like ballet," I reminded him. "But now that she's doing it, I want to be kept in the loop. We've discussed this." When I was little, my mother had signed me up for ballet. I'd ended up skipping class, hiding in the basement, and binging on candy and comics. Amelia is like I was as a kid: clumsy, uncoordinated, and a little pudgy. I didn't think she'd enjoy prancing around in a leotard and trying to keep time with the music.

"Could you stop freaking out? I'm telling you now. There's a recital tomorrow night and I can't make it, so I'm hoping you can."

"Why is it on a Wednesday?"

He sighed again. The sound of it made me want to reach through the phone and strangle him. John tries to exchange as few words with me as possible and gets irritated if I ask too many questions. "Because her classes are on Wednesday. Anyway, we have a couple last-minute motions in limine due, and I can't take her. Can you go so she's not alone?"

"Yeah, I'll be there," I said. "Why doesn't she spend the night with me? We'll crash at my mom's house, and I'll take her to school on Thursday."

"Fine—whatever. Just don't let her stay up too late."

John can be really patronizing when he wants to. It's a good thing he couldn't see my expression. "Can you put Amelia on the phone?"

I heard his footsteps as he went into my daughter's room. "Hello," said a small voice. She sounded glum. I wondered it something had happened at school.

"Hi, sweetie. I'm going to come see you dance tomorrow, and then we're going to sleep over at Nana's. Doesn't that sound fun?" I hadn't asked my mother if we could crash at her place, but I couldn't imagine she'd have an issue with it. We hadn't talked since I'd come up to Idlewood. Truth be told, I didn't feel ready to talk to her, but I wasn't going to give up a chance to see my daughter.

"It's okay, I guess," said Amelia quietly.

"Why just okay?"

"Ballet is stupid." Well, that was predictable. I wish John would listen to me. "Cameron and Sonya called me fat and said I look gross in my leotard. But I think they'll leave me alone now."

I didn't like the last part of her statement. Amelia was developing a morbid streak. After the tooth incident, I was a little scared of what she might do next. "Why do you think they'll leave you alone?"

"'Cause I put a dead lizard in Cameron's backpack."

My heart sunk. I'd saved her from becoming Tooth Girl, but she was hell-bent on making herself a pariah. "Honey, you can't do that.

It's gross and you should never put things in people's backpacks with-out permission. Where did you even get a dead lizard?" *Please tell me she didn't kill it.* I couldn't deal with animal cruelty on top of every-thing else.

"I found it on the street. It got squashed by a car."

Gross, but at least she didn't squash it herself. I gently explained that she should not touch other people's things and that dead animals carry diseases. A small part of me was impressed by her ballsy attempt at revenge. But I knew it could only hurt her.

After my lecture, Amelia asked me to sing her a song. So I sat on the curb and croaked through two of her favorites before saying goodnight. When I hung up, I saw I had a text from Sam: *You disap-peared.* I realized that the music in the background had stopped, and I'd missed the whole concert.

CHAPTER

30

Eight months ago—Jacob

I KNEW THEY'D KILL me the minute I shut my eyes. But as long as I kept using, I didn't need sleep. Chris was passed out, snoring with his mouth open like an old man. Not me—I had to keep watch.

My body felt weird, like when you're a kid after a candy binge and your skin tries to sweat out the sugar. Everything itched—my face, my scalp, my arms, my stomach. Little sores had formed on my arms and legs. I told Chris that bed bugs were coming in from the next room. But I was starting to think they lived in my skin. One of my cuts itched like crazy. I picked at the scab and squeezed, trying to push the critter out.

There was a noise in the parking lot. I grabbed my bat and walked over to the window. A pizza box crunched under my foot. It was hard to see in the dark. My toes connected with an empty beer bottle and sent it flying across the room. Chris half woke, looked around, and then collapsed back on his pillow.

I opened the curtain enough to see out. A white Honda with a six in the license plate was parked out front. That was their code. They drive white cars with sixes in the plate—for "666," the sign of the devil. They'd finally found me. They must have put a tracker inside my body. Maybe that's why my skin felt funny—it was moving around inside me.

The driver just sat there, staring at his phone. Probably telling them where I was, so they could come kill me. Unless I got to them first. I grabbed the bat and burst out the door. The driver looked up and saw me right as I brought the bat down on his windshield. He screamed and the glass spiderwebbed into a million diamonds. I lifted the bat over my head, and the car backed away, tires screeching against the asphalt. "Yeah, fuck you!" I called as he tore out of the lot. "You can't mess with me."

"What the hell are you doing?" shouted Chris. "Have you lost your mind?" I spun around and saw him standing in the doorway in his boxers.

"They're following me," I told him. "It's the people who've been after me for months."

Chris leaned against the two sides of the doorframe. He was so skinny now, his protruding ribcage looked like bird wings. "That guy's probably calling the police," he said. "You know what'll happen if they search the room?"

"I can't worry about that now." I clutched the bat in my right hand and slowly dragged it along the ground. Bits of windshield crunched underneath.

"We don't have a choice," shouted Chris. "We gotta make a plan so we don't get arrested." His eyes dropped to the pavement, where the bat was crushing glass shards into dust. "Put that down—you're acting crazy!"

I stared at Chris in disbelief. He was trying to disarm me. Suddenly everything made sense. Chris was the one who'd gotten me into this mess. I'd been with Chris when Longhair first showed up. He was working with them. I shoved past him into the room, grabbed my phone off the nightstand, and took off running. I ran into the woods, following the road. Then my foot landed badly on a rock. My ankle buckled under me, and I came crashing to the ground. I closed my eyes right before my face met dirt and dried pine needles. I tried to stand and felt a sharp pain when I put weight on my ankle. I looked down at my feet. That was when I realized I wasn't wearing any shoes. I couldn't keep going like this.

I called Abby.

CHAPTER

31

Present—Kate

ORRY, I GOT *a call.* I texted Sam. *You still there?*

He responded with a thumbs-up. I sped toward the Red Barn Opry. When I arrived, the audience had already left, and the band was packing up their equipment. Sam spotted me and came over. He looked annoyed, and there was hurt in his eyes. "Where'd you run off to?" he asked with a forced casualness.

"I'm sorry. I got a call from my daughter." Sam looked skeptical. He thought I was lying, I realized. How was I already justifying myself to him?

"I saw you walk off with some guy, and you never came back."

I blinked. He must have meant Nick Fieldstone. "That was a work thing." I hoped Sam wasn't about to start interrogating me. I don't have much tolerance for jealous men. And after my call with John, and hearing about my daughter's lizard fiasco, I was already upset and on edge.

"And what happened with Regina? I don't understand. You came to the concert, interrogated my friend, and then wandered off with some dude. What's going on?"

"I told you, I had to talk to him for my investigation. Same thing with Regina."

He rubbed the back of his neck. "You could have said something. I invited you because I thought it'd be fun, and then you cornered her before she had to go on stage. That was messed up."

My jaw clenched and my muscles felt tense. I wanted to walk away. Sam didn't know me well enough to be proprietary over my time or give me a lecture on etiquette. I'd spent five years with a man who had nitpicked me half to death, and I wasn't about to repeat that. "I didn't corner her. I asked if I could talk to her later."

"And brought up her dead friend with no warning."

I crossed my arms over my chest. "Sam, I told you what I do for a living and why I'm here."

"Fine, but I don't like feeling used or seeing my friend break down in public."

"I think you're overreacting," I said. John had constantly accused me of being disrespectful or embarrassing him. Two years after our separation, I was finally getting to a point where I didn't second-guess myself all the time. And Sam's tone was taking me back somewhere I didn't want to be. "And I don't appreciate having my behavior dissected—particularly by someone I've known for less than a week."

Sam laughed darkly, and I realized how cold my words had sounded. "Good luck with your investigation, Kate," he said before turning away from me. He reached down and picked up a box of sound equipment. I stood there for a moment, stunned. Not understanding how something that had felt so good had turned so bad in a matter of minutes. I looked back at Sam, but he was done with this conversation. Maybe with me altogether.

I walked off, stung and annoyed by my own inability to see things clearly. But I spotted Regina, loading the last of her things into a cherry-red Camaro. "Regina," I called, jogging after her.

She gave me a weary look. "Did you just break my friend's heart? Or do I need to get my eyes checked?"

I ignored her question. "I really need to talk to you about Lisa." Regina looked hesitant. I couldn't blame her. The authorities had brushed her off the last time she'd tried to help. Why would she want to revisit that tragedy twenty years later with a stranger who didn't even wear a uniform? I jumped back in before she could tell me to pound sand. "Look, I know the police dropped the ball before. I'm trying to make up for that now. It sounds like you have important information to share, and I'd really like to hear it. Can we please set up a time to talk?"

Regina let out a long sigh and stayed quiet for several seconds. "How 'bout now?"

I scanned the empty theater grounds. The light was growing dim, and a cold wind had started to blow. Less than ideal circumstances for an interview. "You mean right here?"

She shook her head. "No. I need a drink. We'll go to my place. Get in." She motioned toward her car, and I did as I was told.

As soon as the engine started, I tried to ask about Lisa. But Regina shut me down. "Drink first. You know how many years of therapy it took me to get past what happened?" She turned and looked at me.

"I can only imagine," I said. "And I'm sorry that I'm asking you to talk about it."

She met my gaze and then turned back to the road. I noticed that at some point, an earring had been ripped from her earlobe, which had healed in sections. The two halves hung side by side like a crab claw.

"I almost flunked out of high school," she told me. "I couldn't get out of bed for a month. You know I kept a gun in my purse for years? Just in case that psycho decided to kill me too."

"Why'd you stop carrying?" I asked.

"I didn't want my son digging through my purse and finding a loaded pistol. If it was just me, I'd still have one."

"I'm sorry," I said. We lapsed into silence. She wanted to be home, in a place of comfort before talking about Lisa. I thought about asking about the band, to make conversation. But I didn't want to remind her of my connection to her friend.

Regina was clearly already thinking about it anyway. "Sam's a good person, you know." I didn't say anything. This was exactly the conversation I'd hoped to avoid. "Smart, loyal, feels things deeply. If you're looking for a quick fuck, that's not him." She looked over at me and snorted, taking obvious pleasure in my discomfort. "I know, hot bartender with a band. Then there's the chainsaw thing. You're probably expecting a short-term fun guy. But that's not his style."

That was exactly what I'd been thinking when I'd first met him: a sexy distraction. But I could already tell that Sam had a lot more to offer. It didn't matter. We'd just imploded, and I had two investigations to finish and a life to get back to.

We pulled up to a navy-blue cabin with white trim. "This is me," said Regina. She'd taken the local affinity for lawn ornaments to a new level. There were gnomes, wind chimes, and a menagerie of ceramic animals. The side of her house was covered in rustic signs with cutesy sayings like "Hippies use the back door."

Sam had clearly been out here with his chainsaw. He'd carved reliefs into two aging pine trees. One appeared to be Regina as a mermaid, with long red hair, a scaley green tail, and purple shells covering her ample bosom. The other was a Siberian husky with "RIP Franky" carved at the bottom. A rectangular outline of rocks in front of the tree told me that Franky had never left home.

I followed Regina, through the front door, into a cluttered living room. The walls were painted a deep burgundy and covered in photographs, drawings, and aging memorabilia.

"What do you want to drink?" she asked, opening a bottle of mid-shelf bourbon. "Water," I said, "or coffee if you have it."

Regina walked into the small kitchen and put a pot on to brew while I examined the pictures on her living room walls. A minute later, Regina came over to where I was standing. "This one is me and Lisa on our way to a Halloween party," she said, pointing to a photograph of tween girls, one dressed like a zombie and the other in black cat garb. Zombie Regina was making her best terrifying face, and Lisa was holding her stomach and laughing.

"You guys were adorable," I said. I turned and looked at her face. A mixture of pleasure and pain as she remembered her friend. After all these years, she still had a picture of Lisa in her living room. "I'm so sorry this happened to her. And to you." Her eyes grew watery, but she didn't say anything. "Back at the concert, you said you told the police who to look for. What did you mean by that?"

Regina poured us each a cup of coffee and added two shots of bourbon to hers. She nodded toward the bottle, inviting me to partake. I shook my head. "I told the police that Lisa had been hanging out with this sketchy senior—not in a dating way," she said. "I think he was into her, but it wasn't mutual."

"So, you think she rejected the sketchy senior and he got angry?"

Regina shook her head. "No, it wasn't like that. She knew stuff about him."

"What kind of stuff?"

"This guy—he wasn't from our school. Lisa and I went to Sacred Heart, a Catholic school for girls. Lisa met him at a chess tournament, and they were kind of drawn to each other in a nerdy, platonic way. I was smart but more interested in the arts. This guy and Lisa would talk about history and chess and science. Geeky stuff."

"Do you remember where he went to school?"

Regina sipped her coffee-whiskey. "I think he was at the public school—Serrano High."

"But you don't remember his name?"

She shook her head. "Lisa never told me. She just called him 'my chess buddy.'"

I'd read the entire case file, and this was the first time I'd heard anything about the sketchy chess player. The only documentation of Regina's interview was a three-sentence report saying that Regina hadn't seen Lisa on the night she disappeared. I wished I could travel back in time and throttle the lazy clown who had drafted it. "Did you ever meet chess guy?"

She shook her head. "No, Lisa thought we wouldn't get along. I was kind of cool in high school and could be a jerk about it. This guy was on the other end of the spectrum. Lisa thought I'd be a bitch to him if we met. She was probably right."

"He sounds like a mild-mannered nerd who had a crush on Lisa. That doesn't explain why you think he killed her," I pointed out.

Regina put her head in her hands. "I'm getting there. Don't rush me. I put this stuff in a box and closed it. Now you're asking me to think about all this again. I'll do it, but you're gonna have to bear with me."

"That's fair," I said. "Take your time." Her voice was cracking, like she was on the verge of tears. We were just getting started, and Regina was already coming apart at the seams.

"My coffee's getting cold," she said. "I'm gonna heat it up. I can nuke yours too if you want."

"Thanks," I said. I handed her my mug and followed her into the kitchen. She refilled it and put it in the microwave for thirty seconds. I noticed a picture of a smiling little boy on the fridge. I wondered where he was tonight and whether her situation was like mine.

"You hungry?" asked Regina. "I don't have much, but I can make popcorn."

She was a weird woman. In ten years as a cop, no one had ever offered to make me popcorn while I listened to them talk about their dead friend. But I was starving, so I took her up on it. When the microwave dinged, we went over to the dining room table, and I watched as she shoveled two handfuls in her mouth. "Sorry—I eat when I'm stressed. And drink, obviously." She laughed nervously.

I stayed quiet, waiting for her to collect herself and finish the story.

"Anyway, a few days before Lisa vanished, she started acting strange. We had homeroom together, and usually we'd just goof off. But this time she was super quiet, so I asked her what was wrong. She told me her chess buddy had confided in her that he had a side hustle writing college entrance essays for people. He'd even taken the SATs for two kids she knew from the chess scene."

"Quite the little businessman," I observed.

Regina grabbed another handful of popcorn, and I followed her lead. "He asked Lisa to promote his cheating business at Sacred Heart. That was a big mistake. Lisa was shocked to learn that he was basically a professional cheat."

"What did you say when she told you about the scheme?"

Regina started to cry. It seemed to come out of nowhere. I moved and sat next to her and patted her back. After a minute, she reached for the bourbon and added another healthy dose to her coffee. I walked to the kitchen, poured a glass of water, and set it in front of her, along with a box of tissues. Then I waited for her to cry it out.

"It was my fault," she said finally. "Lisa wanted to call his school principal. I was worried she was gonna ruin his life over a stupid side hustle that didn't hurt anyone. I tried to reason with her, explain that he could get expelled. His college would rescind their admission offer if the principal told them. But Lisa was convinced that she had a moral obligation to stop the cheating. She was kind of a goody two-shoes. It was something I both admired and couldn't stand about her."

I pushed the water closer to Regina. She took a sip and then wiped her eyes on the sleeve of her sweater. "So, I told her—" The tears came again, and lines of mascara traveled down her face. "I told her to talk to him first. I told her they were friends, and it wasn't right to betray him without so much as a word about it. I'd hoped he'd convince her to let it go."

"Did Lisa agree?"

Regina sniffed and dabbed at her nose with a tissue. "Yeah, she did."

"So, you think he killed her because she threatened to turn him in?" I asked.

She closed her eyes and nodded slowly. No wonder Regina was a hot mess. She'd spent twenty years thinking that her bad advice had gotten her friend killed. And frankly, she might have been right.

Chess guy was definitely a theory worth following up on, but I also wanted to get her take on Roman Dupont. "Do you remember a teacher named Roman Dupont?"

She looked up in surprise. "Yeah, the pervy swim coach. He was my biology teacher. You should have heard how he taught human reproduction."

"Did you ever see him show an interest in Lisa? Or—do you have any idea how he was caught?"

Regina shook her head. "I never saw anything between him and Lisa, no. As for getting caught, I always assumed that Carole just had enough one day and reported him, but I have no idea."

"Any idea what happened to him after he was fired."

"I heard he kind of went off the deep end, got a couple DUIs, that kind of thing. Then after a while, he disappeared. I saw him once or twice driving a van around town, but that's about it."

After a while, Regina told me she had to go pick up her kid, who was having dinner at his grandparents' house. I thanked her for her time and started the long walk back to my cabin.

The wind whipped around me, and I felt the chill in my bones. It made me long for Sam, his warmth, his touch. But I guess I'd screwed that up.

I thought back to our argument. He'd been right, I shouldn't have ambushed Regina. It was insensitive and sloppy. That was especially clear after seeing her fall to pieces and confess that she still blamed herself for Lisa's death. Sam had been protective of his friend. He wasn't attacking me, just trying to speak to me like an adult. And it was rude, I realized, to have skipped most of his concert, even if I had a good reason for it.

Talking to John had put me in a weird place, and my shit ton of baggage had prevented me from seeing it.

Maybe I should call him and apologize. The thought made me slightly nauseous. Talking things out went against all my instincts and history. I'm much better at walking away or just pretending something didn't happen. But as cavalier as I wanted to be, I felt something for Sam. I was tired of shutting down and steeling myself for disappointment. And it was cold, and Idlewood was lonely, and I didn't want to go back to my cabin. I called and held my breath while the phone rang. My heart pounded as I steeled myself for an awkward conversation.

"Hey," he said.

"I'm sorry about the concert," I said, my throat tight. "I should have told you about Regina. And you're right, I shouldn't have surprised her like that. I talked to her tonight. Pretty awful stuff. I understand why you're protective of her."

"It's okay," he said. "I shouldn't have jumped down your throat. Anyway, what are you doing now?"

"Right now?"

"Yeah, my kid's still at her mom's house, and I just ordered a pizza. You wanna come over?"

"Yeah," I said. "That would be nice." I picked up my pace as I made my way over to Sam's house. There was a light in the window, and my breath caught as I spotted him moving around in the kitchen. He saw me and smiled. The front door swung open, and then I felt his lips on mine.

32

Present—Kate

THIS TIME, I didn't have that out-of-body feeling waking up at Sam's. I knew exactly where I was. I looked over at him. A soft morning light poured in through the window, giving his skin a warm glow. He pulled me close and kissed me. Soon we were picking up where we'd left off the night before.

I glanced at the alarm clock on his nightstand. It was already seven thirty. There were a ton of things I needed to do before Amelia's recital. "Can I use your shower?" I asked.

"Of course—mind if I join you?" It was too good an offer to pass up.

Afterward, I tied up my wet hair in a ponytail and put on my clothes from the night before.

Sam went to the kitchen and put on a pot of coffee. "I'm out of eggs, but we can run over to the Bean and Grape if you want," he said.

I shook my head. "I need to get moving." Then a thought occurred to me. Sam had grown up in Idlewood and was pretty close to Lisa's age. "Hey, did you go to Serrano High by any chance?"

"Yup, class of 2003." That was the year before Lisa would have graduated.

"Do you still have your old yearbooks, by any chance?"

He laughed, "I didn't realize we'd progressed to sharing awkward high school pictures."

I felt myself blush. "I'm sure you were a very dreamy teen, but it's case related. Regina told me something last night that could be relevant. I want to check it out."

"It's been a while, but I think I have them boxed up somewhere. Let me look." Sam poured me a cup of coffee and left the room. A few minutes later, he came back holding three dusty yearbooks.

"Can I borrow these?" I asked.

He shrugged. "No problem."

I finished my coffee, kissed him goodbye, and walked back to my cabin. I was tired—we hadn't slept much. But it was a good kind of exhausted. All my senses were heightened. I closed my eyes for a second and let myself feel the cool wind on my skin and the warm sun on my face. I thought about turning around, knocking on Sam's door, and climbing right back into bed. But I had work to do, and I couldn't let this thing between us get in the way of that.

Back at my cabin, I settled down on the front porch and flipped through the yearbooks. I found Sam's graduation page and smiled. His hair was neatly combed and parted in the middle. Pretty straightlaced for a guy who owns a bar. But back then he still wanted to be a concert violinist. There was a picture of Sam playing a solo in front of the school band. He was in the zone, totally concentrated on the music. The young man in that picture had imagined a whole different life for himself—spent his childhood training for one. Then when his dreams were about to come true, life had pushed them out of reach. Eighteen was young to swallow such a bitter pill. I felt for him.

My mind traveled back to adult Sam. The excitement in his eyes when I had mentioned Stéphane Grappelli. He'd jumped up and put on another old-time jazz record. Rich, playful music unlike anything I'd ever heard. Was I falling for this guy? I shook my head and smacked each of my cheeks to bring myself back to reality. *Get it together, Kate.* You've barely known him for a week. You're just sex-and-romance starved. But in my gut, I knew it was more than that.

With effort, I put Sam out of my mind and flipped through the club pages. In the Shakespeare players photograph, a freshman-year Abby wore a Grecian-style dress and beamed at the camera. Her long hair, not yet bleached and tortured straight, hung in loose curls down her back. She looked beautiful and happy. There she was again in the drama club photo, as Sandy from *West Side Story*. She wore a faux-leather catsuit and projected a mix of sweetness and spunk. It was sad to see her alive and in her element.

I turned the pages until I found the chess club group picture, and inhaled sharply. I hadn't expected to recognize anyone. I reached for my laptop and opened up the family tree I'd been working on for Myra. None of the names in the chess club picture matched the people I'd mapped out. Of course, there were wings of Myra's family that I still hadn't fully fleshed out. And Regina's theory about Chess Guy was just that: a theory. There was no reason to think he was the killer.

I checked my email and saw that I had a new message from Dr. Luna. He'd spoken with the other volunteers at the clinic. One of them remembered Abby complaining about a walk-in client who gave her the creeps. The guy asked her weird personal questions and gave off a bad vibe. The volunteer was pretty sure his first name was Jonas, and there was only person with that name in the clinic records—Jonas Reid.

I'd been hoping for something more concrete from Dr. Luna. A guy who once made Abby nervous wasn't exactly a major lead. She was a beautiful, compassionate woman who helped a lot of troubled souls. It wasn't surprising that one of them had taken a shine to her. But they have confidentiality rules to follow.

The name "Reid" didn't ring a bell, but I wanted to make sure it wasn't buried somewhere in the case documents. I pulled the Coburn file out of my bag and reread a short supplemental file about a transient who'd identified Jacob's phone and hoodie. According to the report, the witness had used Jacob's cell a couple times and later recognized its turquoise cover. And there was his name: *Jonas Reid*.

The report stated that Reid had reached out to police after hearing about the fire on the news. The lack of detail was frustrating. Maybe

the police had released a surveillance still of the shadowy figure walking in the direction of Abby's cabin. Maybe Reid had seen that picture, recognized Abby's last name, and put two and two together. But
a more paranoid side of me wondered if the whole thing was a setup. If
Reid had killed Abby, framing her drug-addicted brother would have
been a smart move. If Reid had been down on his luck and needed
cash, he could have been susceptible to bribery.

The report identifying Jacob's fingerprints also mentioned a partial match recovered from the phone that belonged to a second man:
Jonas Reid. If Reid had used Jacob's phone, like he'd claimed, it made
sense that he'd left a print behind.

But could there be another reason that Reid's print had been on
the bloody phone found outside Abby's cabin? It seemed suspicious
that someone who knew Jacob well enough to recognize his hoodie
was also a client at Abby's clinic. On the other hand, if Reid was
hanging around Jacob, there was a decent chance that he had his own
substance abuse issues, and there weren't that many treatment centers
in this part of the county. Maybe it was a coincidence. But I wouldn't
know that for sure until I talked to Reid.

Reid's last known address, a motel, was included in the reports. I
googled the place and saw depressing pictures of a cinder-block dump,
along with one- and two-star reviews. I dialed the front desk and asked
for Reid, pretending to be his sister calling about an emergency. The
front-desk chick informed me that no one by that name was staying
there, which brought me back to square one.

I could try public search databases. But Reid sounded like someone living on the edge. He was probably at a shelter, in another drug
motel, or on the street. I wasn't going to find a searchable record of
that. Maybe Chris Taylor knew Reid and could tell me where he was
staying. They probably traveled in the same circles. I decided to pay
him a visit.

33

Present—Kate

M Y HEART RACED as I pulled up to the Welcome Inn. The memory of my first encounter with Chris took hold of me. I could almost smell his infection and hear his gravity knife open and close. My hands gripped the wheel so hard, my knuckles turned white. I inhaled deeply and let it out slow. *You don't have time to be a princess,* I told myself, and got out of the car.

No one answered when I knocked on Chris's door, so I moved to the window. The thinning beige curtain was slightly too narrow, leaving a small gap at one end of the glass. I pressed my face against the pane and peered inside. The place was deserted. Every square inch of floor space was covered in empty bottles, clothes, and old take-out containers. Dozens of cigarettes were strewn across the floor. From a distance, they looked like little white worms.

Chris was probably still at the hospital. The thought of talking to him in a medical setting was a relief. The nurses would keep him sedated and away from anything sharp.

I drove to the hospital, parked my car, and walked inside. This place brought back a different kind of bad memory. I'd spent too much time in hospitals when my dad was sick. They all have the same harsh lighting, antiseptic smell, and flickering TVs with the volume turned too low. I walked up to the front desk, which was staffed by a middle-aged woman in scrubs covered in cartoon pizza slices. "I'm here to see Chris Taylor," I said.

"Are you a relative?" she asked. "We're only letting in family right now."

"I'm his cousin," I lied.

She nodded and typed something on the computer in front of her. "I'm glad you're here. No one's visited him since the surgery."

My heart sank. "Surgery?" *Oh, my God, what had they had to do?*

A worried look crossed her face when she realized that I wasn't in the loop. "He might still be sleeping—let me look in on him real quick." I watched her walk down the hall and peer into a room. I held my breath, hoping she wouldn't mention my fake familial status to Chris. But a moment later, she was back at the desk, motioning for me to follow her.

The nurse stopped before we got in the doorway. "He's on a lot of painkillers and a sedative, so he might not be acting like himself."

A little out of it might be a good thing. I needed information, and the lower Chris's inhibitions, the better.

"Chris, your cousin's here," she said, doing her best to sound cheery.

I held my breath, waiting for him to call me out on my lie. But he just lay there, expressionless. My eyes traveled to the sheets on the bed and the shape underneath. The symmetry of his body stopped at around knee level. I could make out the shape of one calf and one foot.

The nurse walked away, and we were alone. I sat down on a hard plastic chair next to the bed. "Hi, Chris." I felt like crying, but instead I bit down on the inside of my cheek and dug my nails into my palm as hard as I could. Chris didn't need a stranger's hysteria.

"You wanna see it?" asked Chris.

"What?" He couldn't possibly be asking what I thought he was asking.

Chris pulled at the sheet, revealing a stump wrapped in gauze. His leg had been amputated at the knee. I noticed the rotten meaty smell again and breathed through my mouth, determined not to throw up.

"They might have to take the other one," he slurred. "You should have left me there to die."

"Don't say that," I said.

Chris let out a dark laugh. "I'll say what I want. It's my hospital room and my goddamn leg. If you don't like it, get the fuck out."

His syllables were jumbled together and came out like one long slur. I hated myself for thinking it, but if Chris had information to share, now was the time to get it. The painkillers and sedatives had probably loosened his lips. As a cop, I wouldn't have interviewed someone in this condition. But the ethics are different when you're working for a man charged with a death penalty-eligible murder, and you're starting to believe in his innocence.

"You're right, Chris," I said. "Say whatever you want. I'm sorry this happened to you."

"What the hell am I supposed to do now?" he demanded.

I didn't answer. What could I say? He was a young man who'd already been skating around rock bottom, who'd just lost his leg. "Can I call anyone for you?" I asked. "Is your dad at the motel? I can call him."

He shrugged. "The nurses called him. He's probably already passed out drunk for the day. He'll show up eventually."

"Is there anyone else?" I asked.

Chris shook his head and then looked away from me, toward the floating images on the muted TV screen.

I waited a few minutes in case he wanted to say anything else. When he stayed silent, I jumped in with my questions. "Chris, I'm sorry to do this now, but Jacobs's life is literally on the line, and I need to ask you a few questions. Do you know Jonas Reid?"

He shrugged. "I might. I worked with a guy I knew as Big Jonas."

That was a start. Jonas isn't the most common name. "Did Jacob know him?"

He nodded. "Yeah, we all worked together. Me, Jake, Ivan, and Big Jonas. One big happy family." He almost spit out the words. His voice dripped with bitterness.

"Did Jonas have a meth problem?" I asked.

Chris smiled darkly. "I guess it depends on what you mean by *problem*."

Was he really equivocating about meth addiction? Even now? "You said you worked together," I pressed. "Was that at the dock? Jacob's sister said you guys were doing something with waterskiing." My information was probably out of date. But I hadn't heard anything about Jacob being recently employed.

Chris shook his head. "Nah, we work for this guy," he said.

"Doing what?" Talking to him was like pulling teeth. Understandable, since his brain was swimming in morphine.

He sighed, "I'm not supposed to talk about it, but what the hell? It's not like I can work now." He made a sweeping gesture to indicate his missing leg. I started to ask another question but thought better of it. His processing speed was glacial. It was better not to rush him. "Mostly scams and drugs," he said. "The boss would think of stuff, and we'd do it."

"So, you, Jacob, Ivan, and Jonas were all involved in doing crimes for this guy?"

Chris nodded. "Yup. Selling drugs and ripping people off. He liked to mix it up. Didn't want to keep all his eggs in one basket. It wasn't just us either. He had a whole crew working for him. We only knew the people we were involved with directly. It was kind of a need-to-know operation."

"Do you know where Jonas is?"

He shook his head. "I don't keep tabs on these guys. We worked together a couple times, but we're not buddies or anything."

"What about a phone number?"

Chris pointed to his phone, which was lying on the sheet by his side. "Should be in there." I picked up the cell and it asked for a PIN. I handed it to Chris, who unlocked it and then handed it back.

I scrolled through Chris's contacts until I found "Big Jonas," and then pulled out a notebook and wrote down the digits. I kept scrolling, hoping to see something like "boss" stored in there, so I could write that down too. But no such luck.

"Chris, I need to know who you were working for." His body stiffened. The drugs in his system had loosened his tongue. But not enough. A few minutes ago, he'd expressed interest in dying. But now I saw real fear in his eyes. Chris stayed silent and stared at the door.

"I wouldn't ask if it weren't important," I pressed. "Jacob's facing murder charges, and I don't think he's guilty. I don't think you do either."

Chris shook his head. "I said too much already. He'll kill me. You want to know about the boss? Go ask Jake." With that, he pressed the "Call" button, and a pretty nurse in pink scrubs stuck her head in the door. "I'm tired," he said. "And she's leaving."

34

Eight months ago—Abby

I HADN'T HEARD FROM Jacob in weeks. Then one night he called out of the blue. That's how it was with my brother. He'd disappear and reemerge when he felt like it. But it used to be a matter of days. Now I'd go a month without hearing from him. And every time he called, he was a little crazier than the time before.

Jacob's decline mirrored what I was learning about in class. I tried to absorb what I could from Dr. Luna. I'd started volunteering at an addiction clinic. During breaks, I peppered the social workers with questions. I told myself that I was just trying to learn my new profession. That all of this wasn't a misguided quest to save my brother. My mentors explained to me over and over that you can't help someone until they're ready. But in my heart, I clung to the idea that I could learn something—a technique, a treatment, a medication—anything that could fix Jacob.

Then my phone rang. He was hiding somewhere, convinced that a secret organization was out to get him. I tried to reason with him, but he just rambled on about satanists and lights controlling his brain. He told me he'd smashed their windshield with a baseball bat. I grimaced. Did Jacob really mess up someone's car? Was he becoming dangerous? He couldn't even tell me who "they" were. I'm not sure if he knew.

I swallowed my emotions and did my best to sound calm. I tried to channel the studied patience of the senior therapists at the clinic. Somehow, I was able to coax a location out of him. Jacob was in the woods near the motel where I'd dropped him off. I didn't know how far he'd gotten. He said he'd run for about ten minutes in the direction of Idlewood before hurting his foot and stopping. I got in my car, terrified of what I might find.

There were hardly any cars on the road, and I sped to find my brother. It was a moonless night, and once I got closer to the motel, I slowed down and scanned the wayside, looking for him. But all I saw were my high beams bouncing off the pines.

My phone lit up. It was Jacob. He must have spotted my lights. I looked toward the trees but didn't see anything. "Where are you?" I asked.

"Is that you? In the car?" whispered Jacob. He sounded terrified.

"Yeah. Just come over here—let's go." A ghostly, emaciated figure emerged from the trees, carrying a baseball bat. Jacob was limping. It was a cold, windy night, but he wore nothing but a pair of shorts. The passenger door opened. He climbed inside and threw the bat into the back seat.

"What happened to you?" I asked. Despite the cold, he was sweating. Bits of dirt and dried leaves stuck to his damp skin like he'd been rolling on the ground. "You look like death." As he climbed into the car, I noticed that he was barefoot. "Jacob, where are your shoes? And your shirt?" He glanced down at his bare chest and shrugged. I studied his face, pale with hollow cheeks. His eyes were sunken but manic. "I'm taking you to the hospital."

Jacob shook his head. "They'll find me there."

"Who's gonna find you? The police?"

He nodded. "And the satanists. They're working together."

"You're high." I turned on the overhead light and grabbed his chin, pulling it toward me. At the clinic, they'd taught me some physical signs of intoxication. "I can see it in your eyes. They're bloodshot and your pupils are huge."

He grabbed my wrist and wrenched it away from his face, twisting it slightly. "Don't touch me!" shouted Jacob.

I yelped in pain and broke free, cradled my smarting wrist in my other hand. He had never laid hands on me before. I was stunned, but to my surprise, I didn't cry. I think I was all cried out. I turned the key in the ignition. "We're going to the hospital. You're out of your mind."

Jacob opened the door and stepped back outside.

I panicked. I couldn't let him leave. Anything could happen to him in this state. He could wander into the street and get hit by a car. I had to bring him somewhere clean and safe. "Get in. I won't take you to a hospital, okay? I'll take you to Idlewood. There's an extra cabin you can stay in."

"I don't want anyone to know I'm there."

"Fine," I said. "Just get in the car."

He slid back into the shotgun seat and closed the door. But he kept his body turned away, like I repulsed him. I remembered sitting on my porch together, laughing about something Grace had said. He'd had an arm around my shoulders. Where was that guy?

As we drove, my shock faded, and I started getting angry. I wanted to know who had done this to my brother, and I wanted them to pay. "Who were you staying with out here?" I asked, trying to sound casual. "Chris?"

"Yeah."

"You mentioned before that you've been working. Was that with Chris too?"

Jacob ignored me and rolled the window down. He stuck his whole head outside, like a dog. Cold air filled the car, and I shivered. "Were you working with Chris?" I asked again, practically shouting as my voice competed with the wind.

"I heard you the first time! Yes, okay? We've been working for this guy."

"Doing what?" I tried to sound calm and conversational. There had to be a connection. In thirty years, Jacob had never done anything harder than weed. Then he'd moved in with Chris and everything had fallen apart.

Jacob stayed quiet, so I waited a beat and asked again. "What were you and Chris doing?"

"God, Abby, would you give it a rest?" he shouted. "I don't know—this and that!" His jaw was set tight, and I could hear his teeth grinding together.

"Can you give me an example?" Slowly, calmly I asked questions, and eventually he started answering. He told me about some criminal who had hired them to sell drugs and do a bunch of cons, and had gotten them hooked on meth, to keep them dependent. Or maybe it was just cheaper to pay in drugs than cash. I clenched my jaw as I listened—I was going to find the son of a bitch who had done this to my brother, and destroy him.

"Who is he?" I asked. "The boss. What's his name?"

Jacob turned to look at me with his huge eyes. "That's the craziest part."

35

Present—Kate

I SAT IN MY car, staring at the wheel. My eyes welled up, and I wiped them on my sleeve. I couldn't shake the image of Chris lying in that hospital bed. Seeing a young man like that, hooked on meth, crippled and unsure if he'd keep his other leg. He'd probably sink deeper into addiction, trying to forget what had happened to him. I'd been there before. Not like Chris, but close enough to feel it.

And where was his deadbeat dad? I wondered if Chris had someone to take him home when he stabilized. As a cop, I'd seen homeless victims chucked onto the street by cost-conscious hospitals. They'd end up wandering around, delirious, with nowhere to go. Patient dumping was illegal, but an all-too-common practice. I'd come check on him in a day or two. Maybe give him a lift back to the motel. It wasn't much, but it was something.

The fear in Chris's eyes when I mentioned his boss had also shaken me. I'd been too focused on my jilted-married-lover theory. I should've been scouring Jacob's past for clues about what had happened to Abby. Either Jacob killed his sister in a fit of rage, or someone set him up. It hadn't occurred to me that a person in Jacob's circle would have a motive for killing Abby. Or the ability to pull off a sophisticated frame job. But maybe I'd been too quick to judge.

From the look on Chris's face, he and Jacob were involved with some really dangerous people. What if Abby had threatened to expose them, and they'd killed her? If Abby was going to turn her brother in, he might have murdered her to keep her silent. Or one of his associates might have taken the initiative and pinned it on him.

But was Abby the snitching type? All the social workers I knew were wary of cops and cynical about the justice system. On the other hand, Abby blamed her brother's mental health struggles on his addiction. If she thought Jacob's associates had gotten him hooked on drugs, maybe she'd wanted revenge.

I needed to talk to Jonas Reid. He'd probably blow me off, but it was worth a shot. Reid was the only link I had to Chris and Jacob's shady employer. I dialed the number Chris had given me, but it didn't work—probably an old burner. Another dead end.

Chris had told me to talk to Jacob. He was probably out of tuberculosis quarantine by now, and I was way overdue for an interview. Hopefully, he'd be lucid enough to answer my questions.

But my visit would have to wait until tomorrow. I had to pick up my mother in La Verne and drive to Amelia's recital. The timing was terrible, but I couldn't let her be the only kid without a parent in the audience.

I took a deep breath and exhaled slowly, trying to switch off the part of my mind that was focused on addiction, hospitals, and murder. Amelia is a sensitive kid and she's very perceptive. When I show up feeling anxious about a case, she can tell. My daughter was having a hard enough time right now. She didn't need to deal with my stress on top of bullies, insensitive teachers, and her parents' divorce.

I put on the jazz CD that Vic had given me. Closing my eyes, I focused on the music. It was light and joyous and free. My pulse started to drop again. I opened my eyes and turned on the engine.

I messaged my mother to let her know I was on my way. We'd arranged the visit through texts, and I hadn't actually spoken to her since leaving for Idlewood. We don't usually talk on the phone much, but right now, the silence felt loaded. I knew she was hoping that I'd just move on from what she'd told me about how I was conceived. But

I couldn't. And frankly, I didn't want to. For more than a week, I'd been walking around in a daze, spending sleepless nights staring at the ceiling, and trying to make sense of my childhood.

I was tired of burying my feelings and pretending that everything was normal. That pattern had left me a divorced emotional wreck in my late thirties. I needed to start facing things head-on if I was going to get my life back on track and become a better mother for Amelia. I didn't know how, but my mother and I would have to talk through things if we were going to find a way back to each other.

My phone rang, and I was surprised to see that it was Vic. I turned off the music and answered on Bluetooth. "Hello," I said.

"Hey," he replied, with an ex-smoker's rasp that I hadn't noticed before. There was an awkward silence, and he started laughing. "I'm sorry—this whole thing's been so weird. It's just—I've been thinking about you a lot since you came into the shop. It's pretty much all I've been thinking about, actually. Like I said, I never had any kids. Jeff has a daughter, back from when he was trying to convince himself he was straight. But she won't talk to him anymore. Sorry—I'm rambling. Anyway, I—we, actually—are very curious about you and interested in getting to know you, which is why I'm calling."

Now it was my turn to laugh. He sounded genuine, nervous even. It was such a relief. When I'd left his shop, he said he wanted to talk again. But part of me thought he was just trying to minimize the awkwardness until I was gone. We'd only met once. But I desperately wanted to learn everything I could about Vic. I even felt a need to incorporate this strange man into my life somehow.

Then I remembered his connection to Roman Dupont, and my guard went up. "Yeah, I'd really like that," I said. "I'm so curious about our whole family." I winced as the words left my mouth. I knew I'd added the part about our family in the hopes of milking him for leads on Lisa's killing. But the idea of using Vic made me sick. He was an old man with no kids, who'd had a hard life. And I'd just pranced in and upended everything. Now here I was, planning on plying him with family-related questions, in the guise of being an interested long-lost relative, when what I really wanted was to find a killer. What kind of person did that make me?

"I'm so glad to hear it. But it's your turn," he said. "I've already rambled, and I don't know anything about you. What do you even do for a living?"

I told him as much as I could about myself, about my time in the LAPD, my failed marriage, how I'd injured my back and gotten hooked on pills. I felt like I owed it to him to be honest where I could. But I left out Amelia. One of my suspects—a known abuser of young girls—worked for Vic. I wouldn't do anything to endanger my daughter.

"Those pills are garbage," said Vic. "They gave Jeff a prescription after his knee replacement. It only took a couple days before he was craving the stuff." There was a silence, and he let out a sigh. "I hate to say it, but it sounds like you might have an addictive personality. You probably got that from me." He told me that after his discharge from the Army, he'd experienced blackouts, sometimes waking up on strange couches or in strange beds. After meeting Jeff, he'd managed to get sober and stayed that way for decades. But in recent years, his demons had started to catch up with him, and alcohol had become a problem again. There wasn't much for two old men to do out in the desert, and he needed something to take the edge off.

Vic was thrilled to hear that I'd been a cop. His own father had been a police sergeant. But his father didn't take it well when Vic finally came out, and they'd fallen out of touch.

Before I knew it, I was almost in La Verne, where my mother was waiting for me. I didn't want to hang up—I felt like I could talk to him for hours. But there was something that I really needed to ask him. It was pushy and intrusive, but I owed it both to Lisa and myself. "Vic, can I ask you something?"

"Fire away," he said.

I paused, taking a second to choose my words. "I've heard the stories about Roman Dupont. I know that family is family, but I guess I don't understand how you could work with someone who could do that?"

There was silence on the other end of the line. I wondered if he was going to hang up or get angry. Finally, he spoke. "Because I'm not going to cut someone off for rumors and innuendo. I don't know what happened at the school. I know he was fired for some kind of morality clause violation, whatever the hell that means. He never told me the details, and I didn't ask. And that other thing was total nonsense."

My ears perked up. "What other thing?"

"All the rumors about that poor dead girl. People's tongues started wagging after he got fired, and when that girl turned up dead, they just assumed it was him because he was the disgraced former teacher. There was no evidence, no nothing. Roman couldn't hurt a fly, let alone do something like that. You don't turn your back on someone over malicious gossip. He needed a job, and we gave him one."

I couldn't believe what I was hearing. Roman had been a suspect in Lisa's killing? "Are you talking about Lisa Forrester? Who accused him of killing her?"

Vic let out a deep sigh. "Can we talk about something else?" He sounded impatient for the first time. I got the sense that he genuinely believed in Roman's innocence. Besides, Vic didn't know me yet and didn't owe me answers to any of these questions. And over the phone while driving wasn't the best time to be asking these sensitive questions anyway. I changed the subject, and we ended up talking about travel, something neither of us had been able to afford in quite a while. He told me about being in college and backpacking all over Europe and North Africa. I listened the best I could, but my mind was fixated on Roman Dupont.

Eventually I pulled onto my mother's street and I told him I had to go. We agreed to talk again soon. Vic proposed taking a paternity test, which would be a lot faster than waiting for GeneExploder to process his results. We made plans to go to a clinic together the following week.

I hung up the phone and looked across the street at my parents' house, feeling a million things at once. It was surreal, talking to a man who might be my biological father, an alcoholic antique dealer who ran an illegal casino, while parked across from the house of the cop who had raised me. A large part of me hoped that the paternity test would confirm what Vic and I already believed. But at the same time, he'd just heightened my suspicions about Roman, a man he clearly cared about. Vic would be devastated if Roman were arrested, particularly if it was because of me. Damn. I was confused and overwhelmed. I desperately wanted to talk to my mother about all of it, but I was afraid she'd just shut down again.

Another thought occurred to me. If Roman turned out to be guilty, the sheriffs might come for him at his workplace. They'd be forced to deal with Vic's gambling side hustle. It could literally cost him his livelihood.

I called Harry. It was time to fill him in. We didn't have any hard evidence, but there was enough to go dumpster diving for a DNA sample outside Roman's home. The police didn't need a warrant for trash that someone was throwing away. And if I leveled with Harry, maybe he could do me a solid and leave Vic out of it.

I told Harry everything I knew, and he listened with enthusiasm. "Look, this old guy—it's a long, weird story, but I think he might be my biological father. If you go through his trash, can you do me a personal favor and do it at Roman's house and not at the antique shop?"

"Jesus, Myles. Any more skeletons in your closet I need to know about?"

I laughed. "Probably. I'm finding new ones every day."

"I'll try to run down an address for him and see what I can do."

I hung up, got out of the car, and walked across the street. It had hardly been a week since I'd been here, but I felt like I was stepping back in time. So much had happened.

My mother answered the door and gave me a warm hug, which was slightly out of character. The house smelled like fresh cookies and I could tell she'd been baking. "It's good to see you, honey. It's been so quiet—I was getting used to having you around."

She was making an effort. This was her version of an olive branch. "We should get going if we're gonna make the recital."

On the way over, she told me about the latest gossip from her book club. A woman whose name sounded vaguely familiar had a new grandchild. Her friend Beverly Fincher's daughter was finishing up a PhD. I wondered what my mom said about me during these conversations. *"My daughter kicked her pill habit and lost custody of her kid."* Or maybe she didn't talk about me at all.

Eventually, we pulled in front of the ballet studio and made our way inside. I scanned the room, trying to figure out which woman was the mother of the little witch who'd been torturing Amelia. The lights dimmed over the audience, and a spotlight illuminated the stage. Classical music started playing from a small speaker, and a line of little girls emerged from the back room. They all had their long hair tied up in buns, except for Amelia. Oh my God, her hair was *gone*. A few long strands hung down on one side of her face. The rest of it was cut short, unevenly. I felt like crying, but I didn't want her to see me upset. I dug my nails into my palms, forcing myself to keep it together. I took out my phone and texted John: *What happened to her hair?*

Last night, meant to tell you. he texted back. *She cut it, looks terrible.*

Yeah, that was the understatement of the year. I couldn't believe he'd let her go to school like that. Last-minute court filings or not, he could have at least evened it out before letting her out in public.

"What happened to her hair?" asked my mother, too loudly.

"Apparently, she cut it herself," I whispered. Something had to change. Amelia had been acting out so much lately. I couldn't help but feel it might be different if I were around. If I could get custody back, maybe I could convince John to let her switch schools, give her a fresh start.

The tiny girls all formed a line in the front and bounced up and down on their heels while drawing circles in the air with their arms. Most of them were more or less in time with the music. Except Amelia. It was like she was listening to a different soundtrack. And then when the song changed and the little girls started flexing their toes and bending their knees in a faster, more complicated pattern, Amelia just hopped up and down. She simply lacked the coordination to do the fancier steps. I could barely stand to watch. Enough was enough. I would be putting my foot down. No more ballet. I don't know why she needed to be in any class at her age. But if John insisted, they could find something she liked and had an aptitude for, like drawing.

When it was over, Amelia ran over to us and hugged me tightly.

"Honey, what did you do to your hair?" I asked. She shrugged and looked down. "Is it okay if Nana fixes it tonight?" She nodded. My mother used to cut both my hair and my dad's when I was growing up, and she still cuts her own. She has a knack for that kind of thing.

"We'll do a pixie cut," said my mother. "You'll look very chic and grown up." She knew how to handle this kind of disaster. Meanwhile I was at a loss.

We went home, and my mother heated up mac and cheese and then produced some homemade cookies. Once Amelia had eaten her fill, my mom brought out the scissors, trimmed the excess strands, and made Amelia's hair look remarkably even. You'd almost believe it was a professional cut.

I wanted to understand why Amelia had done this to herself. But she looked so exhausted. I took her into my childhood bedroom, tucked her in on the air mattress, and read her thirty-year-old Berenstain Bears books until she fell asleep.

Once she'd finally dozed off, I went back into the kitchen and found my mother sitting at the table, drinking a cup of tea. I slumped down across from her and put my head in my hands.

"She's asleep?" asked my mother. I nodded. "She's acting out, Kate. She needs you around."

"Don't you think I know that?" I snapped. There was a silence. "I'm sorry. I didn't mean to get angry. I'm just really worried about her. She stole a girl's tooth and put a lizard in her backpack. I don't know what to do."

My mother got up, went over to the fridge, and pulled out a pint of butter pecan ice cream. I watched as she scooped out a generous helping, stuck a cookie on top and placed it in front of me. I broke off a piece and popped it my mouth. Oatmeal chocolate chip, my dad's favorite. Mom used to bake on the weekends, and once the cookies were in the oven, my dad and I would each grab a spoon and take turns scraping dough off the side of the mixing bowl.

But thinking of him brought me back to the tension between us. We needed to talk about it. My life was in shambles, my daughter wasn't doing well, and I needed my mother. I had to move past what happened and I couldn't do that until we addressed the lie, which had upended my world.

"Mom, we need to talk about the fertility stuff." Her brow furrowed, and she opened her mouth to protest. I cut her off. "Please, Mom, I think about it all the time. I just keep remembering things from the past and questioning them. I feel so mixed up and confused."

"Nothing's changed," she said. "Your dad was your dad, and that's all there is to it."

I sighed and put my head in my hands. "Of course, he is. But that doesn't mean this hasn't been a lot to process. I really need to talk about this. I don't have anyone else, and I'm a wreck right now."

She let out a long sigh, moved over to the stove, and put a pot of water on to boil. "Okay, I'm listening."

I hadn't actually been expecting her to agree. Now that she had, I didn't know where to start. "Why didn't you just tell me?"

"Because it didn't mean anything," she said defensively. "It didn't affect how your dad felt about you. Why burden you with a secret? And when you were little, you wouldn't have understood. You would have told all the other kids."

"So what?" I countered. "You didn't do anything wrong—why was it a secret in the first place?"

The kettle whistled. She got up and poured herself a cup of tea. "People don't think about these things the same way anymore," she explained. "Back then, people viewed it as akin to adultery. They thought it was something seedy that happened in back rooms. They didn't understand that it was a scientific process. And the church was very against it. Officially, it still is. Why would we put that on you? That your very conception was immoral? And the stigma for men— your poor father. He was a cop, for God's sake. Can you imagine if his friends knew he couldn't have a child with his own wife and needed help from another man? He would have been the butt of endless jokes. Why would I do that to him?"

Some of the anger I'd been holding in started to lessen. She'd been desperate for a child and felt like the help she needed was dirty and shameful. I couldn't imagine thinking that way. But I wasn't religious, and it wasn't 1984. Her feelings were hers, and they were very real. "Did my grandparents know?"

She shook her head. "No, but I think your dad's mother suspected something. You really didn't look anything like your father. It's strange, because we picked a donor whose description sounded a lot like him."

"You could have told me as an adult," I said. "I can't tell you how often I blamed myself for things that were part of my genetics. No one in our family has ADHD. I spent so many years thinking I was lazy, that I had some kind of character defect."

She shook her head. "You know I think that's a phony diagnosis. They're coming up with new terms and diseases all the time. It's just an excuse for a lack of self-discipline."

We'd had that discussion before. I doubted she was going to budge, even now when Amelia was showing signs of the same problem. But I'd met Vic, and judging by the way he bounced around in conversation—jumping from the military to jazz, to antique wall sconces—he had a flaming case of it. His brain was like a Ferris wheel. It was part of the reason that I liked talking to him so much. There was no pressure to stay focused, and if I suddenly busted out an anecdote about something we'd talked about ten minutes earlier, he didn't bat an eyelash.

"Mom," I said. "It is real. And I met a man who is probably my biological father. He has a screaming case of it. His brain works a lot like mine."

My mother rolled her eyes impatiently. "I don't understand why you'd go seek out some stranger. How did you even find this person? And I'm sure he doesn't have ADD or whatever. The man's a doctor, after all."

My brain froze. "What are you talking about? He's not a doctor."

"Yes, he is. I read the paperwork. They gave us a list of potential donors. The one we picked was a medical student."

I studied her face to see if this was another lie. But I could tell she believed what she was saying. "Mom," I said gently. "I met him. I can't say for sure—we're waiting on DNA results—but I know he's a relative of some kind. He looks exactly like me, and he donated sperm to the clinic in April of 1984. He's not a doctor. He's an antique dealer in San Bernardino." I felt queasy. I could be wrong about Vic, but I really didn't think so. And if I was right, then there'd either been a mix-up, or my mother had been deceived.

"If you don't have DNA yet, then you don't know. And if he's not a doctor, then it isn't him." She suddenly got up from the table and went out to the garage. I followed her and watched from the doorway as she pulled out a box and started rifling through papers. This really mattered to her, I realized. She'd just told me that none of it was important. But there she was on her hands and knees, trying to salvage the idea that her daughter had doctor genes.

When my mother found what she was looking for, she handed me a piece of yellowed paper. Donor 174, it read, along with a description. A six-foot-two, blond, blue-eyed medical student who played college football and sang a capella. I'm five four on a good day, clumsy, brunette, and tone deaf. She must have known that something was off.

"You see," she said. There was a pleading look in her eyes. It gutted me that she cared this much. On a cellular level, I wasn't the child she'd wanted and expected—had even tried to design. Where did that leave us?

"It says medical student," she said, as if I couldn't read the words in front of my face. I took the papers from her hand and flipped through them. Her procedure had taken place in April, the same month that Vic told me he had donated sperm.

I looked at her face, full of hurt and confusion. If I was right about Vic, I couldn't imagine what that meant for her. Did the fertility doctor just make up profiles of impressive men to get his clients to pay more? Vic had told me he donated sperm for "pennies on the pull" back when he was destitute and prone to drunken blackouts. Had the doctor just picked up random men who needed money and lied to his patients about where the sperm came from?

I reached past my mother and pulled out a document listing different donor options. They were all as impressive as Donor 174. Doctors, lawyers, engineers, professors, an architect. A disproportionate number of them were blond and blue-eyed. There was no way that this was a mix-up. Vic had been an unemployed drunk with no college degree. The fact that Vic had donated at all was proof that the clinic had lied to women, defrauding them in the most intimate, personal way imaginable. A sickening thought hit me. Had Vic known that this was going on? I imagined him, laughing with some sinister creep in a white lab coat about all the bourgeois ladies who thought their kids would have doctor genes. I felt sick.

"Yeah, Mom," I heard myself say after a horrible silence. "I see that. Maybe I was wrong." I'd desperately wanted to bring everything out in the open. But I couldn't bear the thought of putting this on her. What did this mean for her as a woman? To have such an intimate procedure done under false circumstances. Was it some kind of assault? I didn't know. I felt like throwing up. I needed to talk to Vic—I wanted answers.

36

Present—Kate

I SAID GOOD NIGHT to my mother and lay down next to Amelia. I was in for another sleepless night. The old air mattress slumped beneath me. There was a small leak, and it already felt partially deflated. After an hour of tossing and turning, I gave up and carried a pillow into the living room, settling down on the couch. My mom's clown figurines stared at me with their unblinking little eyes.

I pulled a crocheted afghan over my head, and the wool felt scratchy against my skin. My heart was still beating a mile a minute, and I could already tell the lumpy couch would do nothing for my aching back.

My brain was full of images—Amelia prancing around with long tendrils of uneven hair. Chris Taylor in his hospital bed. Vic, looking cold when he caught me outside by the casino. My mother's face in the garage as she held up the donor paperwork, eyes pleading with me to let it go.

I walked to the kitchen, poured myself a glass of water, and took out my computer. Had I been totally wrong about Vic? I didn't think so. But the thought that my mom had been lied to about such a huge, life-changing thing was almost too much to bear. I was the product of that deception. I wondered if it was a common fraud back in the 1980s, when fertility treatment was still newish and unregulated.

Pretty soon, I was way down the Google rabbit hole, on a website that served as a sounding board for people who found out they were something called an NPE, which stood for "not parent expected," or "non-paternity event." I learned that since the rise of genealogy sites, thousands of people had made unwelcome discoveries about their families. One poster had discovered that he was the product of a rape. Another learned that she'd been fathered by a perverted fertility doctor who only used his own sperm. She had fifty-five siblings—including her high school boyfriend. Some of the stories were truly devastating. In comparison, what I was dealing with seemed manageable.

As I read on, the isolation I'd been feeling eased a bit. It was a huge relief to see that I wasn't the only person going through this. I typed the name of my mom's clinic into the search bar and found one essay by a woman whose parents had sought help there. Her parents had selected a handsome oncologist as a donor. But when she grew up and did a DNA kit for fun, she found a half brother whose dad was serving time for a string of bank robberies. She said she'd connected with other NPEs who were conceived at that clinic. They all had similar stories.

I felt nauseous. I didn't know yet if Vic was my father. But my mother had probably been conned, since that seemed to be the clinic's standard practice. She'd been promised one child and delivered another. Did she wonder all those years why I was bad at math and got a "C" in chemistry? Growing up, I'd never seemed to live up to her expectations. Deep down, did she really think I was just lazy, or did she suspect that something wasn't right?

I shook my head hard, trying to clear it of these thoughts. I was going to drive myself crazy. Sleep wasn't going to happen, so I tried to make use of my time and do a little work. I made a list of cheap motels and homeless shelters within a fifteen-mile radius of Jonas's last known residence. There was no guarantee that he'd be at any of them, but it was worth calling, at least.

Eventually, light started coming in through the blinds. Amelia needed to get up soon for school. I winced, thinking about her day ahead getting tortured by little witches for having a weird new haircut.

I decided to make her pancakes. Let her start the day with something fun and special. I couldn't control what happened after that, but I could do something to remind her that I cared. I rifled through the pantry until I found the pancake mix. Then I reached into the fridge and pulled out a gallon of milk. In the process, I knocked over a glass butter dish, which smashed against the tile floor.

I cursed under my breath and bent to clean up the mess. I felt a sting on my pointer finger and looked down to see that I'd sliced it on a broken shard. I went over to the sink, pushed down on my fingertip until a drop of blood appeared, and ran it under the cold water.

Behind me, I heard the shuffle of my mom's slippered feet. "Kate?" she called. She came over to the sink and saw my bleeding finger.

"I'm sorry about the noise," I said. "Watch where you step—I broke the butter dish." I grabbed a broom and dustpan and then felt her take them from me.

"Leave it," she said. "Go get a Band-Aid from the hall bathroom. I'll take care of this."

I did as I was told. When I came back, she'd swept up the mess and was pouring pancake mix into a bowl. "Well, honey, you've never been much good in the kitchen." There was a silence. "What we were talking about before," she added, and sighed. "I've seen articles about other clinics that lied about things. I have the internet too, you know. And yes, I've certainly wondered over the years. You don't really fit the profile of the donor we picked. I just want you to know, I don't care and your dad didn't care."

I nodded, feeling choked up. I knew it was hard for her to talk about these things. Part of me wanted to jump in with more questions, but I felt like we'd covered enough for now.

When the pancakes were finished, I went to wake up my daughter, and the three of us had breakfast together. I watched Amelia from across the table, smiling and chatting away. But then when I told her it was time to get ready for school, her whole mood changed. She got up from the table and went off into the room to get dressed. I remembered the junk jewelry I'd bought her at Vic's antique shop, which was still in a little paper back in my purse. When she reemerged, I gave it to her and got a half smile in return. The jewelry matched the yellow dress she was wearing. She looked cute with her short hair and sunny outfit, even if the other kids weren't going to see it that way.

Amelia was silent on the car ride. I put on a Disney soundtrack to cheer her up. "I'll be back to get you tomorrow night," I said. "Maybe we can play with Willow again this weekend." That got a smile, at least.

After dropping off Amelia, I headed to a quiet coffee shop to wait out the morning traffic. I called the hotels and shelters on my list, asking about Jonas Reid. A few places brushed me off, but most confirmed that no one by that name was staying there. It occurred to me that I should check the morgues. Reid was a meth addict living on the edge, and any number of bad things could have happened to him. Besides, if he was dead, he couldn't testify against Jacob, which would weaken the prosecution's case. But neither the LA nor the San Bernardino morgue had any record of him. That didn't necessarily mean anything. A lot of transients are brought in as a John Doe. Maybe Jacob could tell me if Reid had any distinguishing features, like a scar or a tattoo, that could help narrow the search.

After a few hours of searching, I got back in my car and headed toward Idlewood. When I was almost back in town, my phone rang— Richard, Jacob's attorney. His timing was good. By now, I had a lot to share with him.

"Hi, Richard. I've been meaning to call you. I have some updates."

"Great!" he said. "I'm actually going to be in Idlewood today. I'm meeting with a client this morning. Do you have some time to get together?"

"Sure," I said. "I'll be back in town in about ten minutes."

"I'm actually just sitting down to lunch. Why don't you join me? Then maybe we can stop by the Coburns' place, and you can fill me in on the investigation."

"Sounds good," I said. "Where are you?"

"At the Bighorn Grill. Have you been? They make a great burger." I winced. It wasn't surprising; there were maybe five restaurants in Idlewood. I really didn't want to conduct business around Sam. *Suck it up,* I told myself. It'll be fine.

"I'll see you soon," I said, and hung up the phone.

I spotted Richard at one of the picnic tables outside. Sam was off to the side, chatting with another customer. My heart sped up at the side of him. I forced myself to think of the most unattractive things I could imagine, to get myself back into business mode. I got out of my car and walked over to Richard.

"Kate," he said. "Great to see you—have a seat." I sat across from him, and he passed me the menu.

Sam came by to take our order. "What can I get you?" he asked. Richard was a well-known defense attorney in the area. Sam knew I was doing criminal work and must have figured out that this was a business lunch. Other than the warmth in his eyes, you'd never have guessed that we knew each other.

I stared at the menu, to avoid his face. "A California burger with avocado." I looked at Richard. "You'll split some sweet potato fries with me, right?"

He laughed "Sure—why not?"

Sam disappeared inside the restaurant.

"Richard, I have to talk to you—"

"Later," he said. "We can talk about the case when we're at the Coburns—not when we're out in public."

We made a bit of small talk about the weather and Richard's upcoming vacation plans in Sicily. Sam brought out the sweet potato fries, and we both dug in. They were good—thick and garlicky.

Halfway through the fries, I heard a loud familiar cackle and saw Myra Davies coming up the street with one of her friends. Sam hadn't been kidding when he said she gets an early start. Our eyes met and she walked over to my table. "Hi, Miss Private Detective!"

"Hi, Myra," I said.

Then, unexpectedly, she turned to Richard. "Ricky Murphy, is that you?

"You know each other?" I asked. I couldn't imagine these two traveling in the same circles. And Richard had introduced himself to me as Richard Evans.

"Ricky is my cousin Stephanie's son. I haven't seen him since—well, it has to be since I moved up the mountain. Fifteen years?" I willed myself not to react.

"Hi, Myra," said Richard. "It's Richard Evans now," he said.

Myra literally smacked her forehead, "That's right! Your mom married that guy—you were what? Like seven? I didn't know you took his name."

"Yup, I did," said Richard, with a tight-lipped smile. I studied his face for any sign of alarm. I'd told Richard about my cold case, including the genetic angle. I'd even mentioned Myra's name, and he'd said nothing.

Myra turned to her friend. "This is the PI who came by the other day, asking about genetics." Myra started laughing. "I forgot all about you, Ricky, but you were just a kid—you must have been, like, ten years old when that girl was killed."

The years of drinking had affected her memory. Richard hadn't been ten when Lisa was killed. He was a senior in high school. And a chess enthusiast. I'd been surprised to find him in the chess club photograph in Sam's high school yearbook. But I'd cross-checked everyone on the team with the family tree I'd been building. I hadn't encountered an Evans—but of course, I'd never checked for a Murphy. Idlewood is a smallish town, so Richard's presence on the chess team hadn't seemed like anything more than a coincidence. What if I had been wrong?

If Richard was related to Myra, he might be related to me too. The thought crossed my mind: *Could he be Lisa's killer?* My blood chilled in my veins. I glanced up at Richard, who looked extremely uncomfortable. I couldn't tell if it was because he didn't feel like discussing family history in front of me or if there was something more sinister going on. My heart pounded. I concentrated on my breathing, trying to slow it, and willed my face to stay neutral.

I thought back to when I'd met Richard. When I'd told him about my cold case, he hadn't mentioned knowing Myra. And since Richard had been on the chess team, surely he'd gone to tournaments that Lisa had also attended. He must have known her at least to some extent. Why wouldn't he mention that? And there was the controlling way that he tried to maintain distance between the Coburns and me. I'd thought he was being protective of his clients, but maybe there was more to it.

"It was so good to see you, Myra," said Richard in a voice that said, *"I'm done with this conversation."* Myra and her friend moved on to a table on the other side of the restaurant just as Sam came out and placed the burgers in front of us.

"I'm just gonna run to the bathroom. I'll be right back," I told Richard. I walked into the restaurant as casually as I could, and grabbed Sam.

"Listen," I said. "I need a favor."

He must have sensed the urgency in my voice, and his face registered concern. "What's going on, Kate?" I glanced over and saw Richard through the open door. The bathrooms were down a dark hallway, out of view from the outside patio.

"I'm going to go over to the bathroom area. Can you wait, like, thirty seconds and then follow me?"

He nodded. "Okay."

I walked over by the bathroom. A moment later, Sam joined me and gently took me by the arm. "What's wrong?"

"That guy I'm seated with. I think he might have been involved in something bad, and I need his DNA."

"What do you mean 'bad'?" asked Sam.

"I'll explain later," I told him. "But whatever you're envisioning, it's worse. I'm going to leave half my burger and ask for a box. I need you to bring me a box, but don't put my food in there. Put the remnants of his food—the fries and bits of burger, anything he would have touched."

"Okay, I can do that," he said without hesitating.

"I'm supposed to meet him in private after lunch, and I need an excuse not to go. Can you call me on my cell right after the check comes? I'm gonna pretend you're someone else."

"No problem," said Sam, "but is everything okay?"

I nodded. "Yeah, but I need to get back before he suspects something." I waited until Sam was behind the bar again before rounding the corner. Sam's eyes were on me as I made my way toward the front of the restaurant. Richard was watching me too. I'd tried to be subtle, but he was anything but stupid.

"I saw you talking to the waiter," said Richard.

"Yeah, I was in here the other day, and he gave me advice about local hiking spots. I wanted to thank him."

"Ah," said Richard. "Glad you found time to hike. What trail did you go on?" Was he testing me? Thank God I'd done a little homework in preparation for Amelia's next visit.

"The Blue Ridge trail," I said. "It was really beautiful."

"That's one of my favorites," said Richard. "Especially the view of the lake."

I couldn't tell if this was a trap. I had no idea if there was a lake on that trail, it was just the first name that had popped into my head. "What are some of your favorite hikes?" I asked.

Richard started prattling about different trails, and I did my best to keep the conversation going. Sam stopped by and plopped two hamburgers in front of us, along with two little plates with oven-warmed biscuits. Richard broke off a buttery chunk and popped it in his mouth.

"How are they?" I asked.

"Amazing," he said. "You should try yours."

The thought of eating made me nauseous, but I took a bite and forced it down with a gulp of water. I noticed hints of cheddar and jalapeño. In a parallel universe when I wasn't dining with a possible killer, I would have been in heaven.

We continued bantering about things to do in Idlewood and the surrounding areas. All the while, I kept watching his mouth as he bit off hunks of hamburger, as if I could engineer a DNA transfer with my gaze.

Richard finished the food, leaving a few stray fries and a fifth of his bun. *Thank goodness.* I'd watched him put the hamburger in his mouth over and over, creating a biological record.

Sam brought the check, which Richard quickly snatched up, and I asked for a box. Sam adeptly cleared all of our dishes at once, on a large black tray.

"This one's on me," announced Richard.

"Well, thank you for a delicious and very pleasant lunch," I replied, hoping Sam would think to include the pen.

Sam brought me a box in a plastic to-go bag, and I placed it next to me. A few minutes later my phone rang, and the sound made me jump, even though I was expecting it. "Myles here . . . Are you serious? . . . I'll be there as soon as I can."

"Something wrong?" asked Richard.

"Yeah, apparently a pipe burst in my place in LA. There's water everywhere—I have to go deal with it. I'm so sorry, Richard. Can we postpone our meeting?"

"Of course," he said. "I'm sorry to hear that. Go tend to your house. We can talk by phone if you prefer."

"That sounds good," I agreed. Richard's eyes glanced over at my box. Did he suspect something? "Thank you again for lunch. I'll give you a call later when I get everything sorted."

I grabbed the bag and walked quickly up the street to my car, my heart racing. As I opened the door and climbed in, I looked back toward the restaurant and saw Richard standing on the sidewalk, watching me leave.

37

Present—Kate

I TORE DOWN LONE Pine Canyon Drive, the winding mountain road leading away from Idlewood. I was above the clouds. My eyes squinted against the sea of blinding white blocking my view of the pine trees and blue mountains. A three-foot-high guardrail separated the road from a precipitous drop, and I was going much faster than caution warranted. They probably had accidents here from time to time on dark nights.

Myra's revelation about Richard was shocking. But it made sense. Lisa's friend from the chess team had been smart and ambitious. I'd looked up Richard's credentials: Harvard and then UCLA law school. Clearly, he was someone who had no trouble acing standardized tests, and would have been smart enough to sell essays to desperate college applicants. And I knew from the yearbook picture that he was on the school chess team the year that Lisa died.

But it was important not to jump to conclusions. Roman Dupont was still a viable suspect, and there were other explanations for Richard's weird behavior. Lawyers have huge egos, and cold cases get a lot of press. He probably didn't want to be associated with a child murderer. It seemed weird that he'd never mentioned his relationship to Myra. But she had married. Maybe he knew her by her maiden name.

After all, Myra hadn't known about Richard's name change. They weren't exactly close relations. Or maybe he'd just forgotten about the distant cousin he'd only met a few times before he even hit puberty.

Still, there was enough here that Harry should be involved. I was carrying with me a sample of Richard's DNA. If there was a hit, then Harry could take it from there. At the very least, Richard was one more distant relation to the killer, and his DNA would be another data point they could use to identify him.

Using my Bluetooth, I called Harry.

"Kate, great to hear from you!" he said. "Tell me you have something for me?"

"I'm bringing you a DNA sample."

Harry laughed, "You solved it already? I knew my luck had changed when you entered the picture."

"Don't jump up and down yet," I warned him. "It's still just a theory, but there's another person you should look into. I told him about my conversation with Regina, Richard's participation in the chess club, and his distant relationship with Myra.

Harry was cautiously optimistic, but not as excited as he'd been about Dupont. "Yeah, we'll test it," he said. "But if I were a betting man, I'd go with the fired pervert over the chess nerd tuned lawyer."

"Yeah, but this particular chess nerd had a motive to kill," I pointed out. "And I gotta say, Harry, there's something a little off about this guy."

"We'll check it out. At the very least, it'll be useful to eliminate a potential suspect. I'll test the sample and cross my fingers. But Kate, whatever happens, Richard's name and DNA are going in the case file."

"I know," I said, wincing. I'd been impulsive when I'd asked Sam to get me a sample. If Richard hadn't killed Lisa but had a genetic connection to the killer, Harry would have to interview him. Harry could be careful about how he phrased his questions—and just mention that I repeated our conversation with Myra. But Richard would still know that I'd pointed them in his direction. The trust between us could really be affected. I might have to get off the Coburn case. "How much time do I have, Harry? Before you get results."

"Normally, DNA takes months," said Harry, "but the captain is eager for some good press. They might try to rush this one."

"Thanks for the heads-up."

Harry agreed to meet me at the sheriff's homicide station to pick up the sample, even though it was his day off. We said goodbye, and I hung up, feeling dejected. I should have let him handle things. Harry could have sent a rookie to go dumpster diving behind Richard's house. Instead, I'd acted rashly and jeopardized my place on the Coburn investigation.

My phone rang. It was Richard. I had to play this off as normal as possible. "Hi, Richard, I'm sorry I had to run off like that."

"No problem," he said. "I hope your house is okay. You sounded like you had something pretty urgent to tell me earlier. Can you give me a quick preview?"

I couldn't tell if he was genuinely asking about the case or trying to feel me out. Either way, I owed him an update and had to tell him something. "Abby was having an affair with Nick Fieldstone, the fire investigator."

"That's fantastic! He should have been recused from the investigation. That's probably a major breach of protocol." Richard sounded thrilled, and I felt uneasy.

"Nick's also the one who called in the fire. He claimed he couldn't sleep that night. And his initial report said the cause was undetermined, when the other experts thought it was arson. This isn't just about misdirecting the jury. I think he's a genuine suspect."

"Great work," said Richard. "I don't know if the judge will let it in as third-party culpability evidence, but we have a good shot."

"What about impeachment?" I suggested. "Attacking the investigation is always fair game. Nick should have told his boss he had a conflict."

"Good thinking!" said Richard. "Even if the judge won't let me argue that he's the killer, the jury will start to speculate. It gives us a fighting chance." There was a pause, and then he asked, "Is that it or was there anything else you wanted to tell me?"

I told him about my suspicion of Ted Vera's affair and how the timing didn't explain his absence on the night of the fire. "Ted may have been sleeping with someone when Abby died, but I have no reason to think it was Abby," I cautioned. "The Coburns have suffered a lot, and we should put a pin in this unless we learn something more."

Richard agreed, to my great relief. "And Kate," he said, "good work. We're going to make a great team."

My cheeks burned. I couldn't tell if he was bullshitting me, but his words made me feel terrible about driving to sheriff's homicide with a care package of his genetic material. "Me too," I said. "And there's more." I told him about Chris Taylor, Jonas Reid, and the secret criminal organization that united them.

"Have you talked to Reid?" he asked.

"Not yet. I'm still trying to find him. I'd like to talk to Jacob, though. Chris hinted that he knew who the boss was. Do you know if he's out of tuberculosis quarantine?"

"I'm not sure if he's still quarantined," said Richard, "but I don't know what mental state he'll be in. He hasn't been taking his meds. Last time I talked to Jacob, he thought the judge, the prosecutor, and the police were all involved in some satanic conspiracy."

"I'm not expecting much," I told him, "but maybe he can at least give me a name."

I hung up with Richard and continued my drive to the sheriff's homicide station. By the time I'd dropped off the box in Monterey Park, my back was killing me. I took a minute in the parking lot to stretch and think about my next move. Then I called the jail, gave them Jacob's inmate number, and asked about visitation. As it turned out, he was out of quarantine, and I still had time to make visiting hours.

38

Present—Kate

SAN BERNARDINO's HIGH Desert Detention Center was virtually indistinguishable from other jails I'd been to—an ugly beige building surrounded by barbed-wire fencing. The pre-visit drill was the same too. As a cop, I would just flash an ID and walk through. Now it was more of a production. I took off my shoes and placed them in a filthy plastic bin, along with my purse, and sent them through an X-ray machine. A deputy in a tan uniform ran a detection wand over my body, looking for anything I might be trying to smuggle inside.

Next, I placed my purse in a locker and took out my ID. It was the only thing I could bring with me. I sat down in the waiting area. It was empty save for an older couple a few seats over. The man didn't look healthy. His skin was yellow, and his drooping eyelids were lined with pink. He looked up, and our eyes met. I smiled, trying to send over a bit of warmth. As a cop, I'd put a lot of people in jail, usually for terrible crimes. But I'd never lost sight of how their families were affected.

After a few minutes, a guard came over and escorted me to the visitation area. It was a narrow, windowless hallway with a line of booths. A wall of plexiglass separated visitors from the inmates on the other side. I sat down in one of the booths and waited for Jacob. A few minutes later, he shuffled in and took a seat on the chair across from me. There was a wild look in his eyes. I noticed an old gash on his forehead that had started to heal and formed a scar.

"Hi, Jacob. I'm Kate," I told him. "I'm a private investigator working with your attorney."

"Then you're one of them," he said.

"One of who?"

Jacob smacked the glass, his fist coming within inches of my face. I blinked hard, and tried to slide back in my chair, but it was bolted to the floor. "Cut the bullshit!" he shouted.

"Jacob, your lawyer and I are just trying to help you," I tried to explain. "We want to put on the best defense and try to get you out of here."

He covered his ears with his hands, like he couldn't stand to hear me talk. "Bullshit, bullshit, bullshit!"

A guard came over and glared at Jacob. "Coburn, calm down or we're gonna end this right now."

"It's fine," he said. "You can go." We both stayed silent until the guard was out of sight.

"Jacob," I said as calmly as I could, "I'm not here to hurt you. I'm helping Richard. I want to ask you some questions about Jonas Reid— Big Jonas. Do you know where he might be?"

"Ask my lawyer," he said. "He's in charge of it all. Ask him." Jacob punched the glass, and my neck snapped back. He punched it again, harder. "Get away from me!" he screamed. "You're not fooling me! I know what you're doing!"

Two guards rushed in, grabbed him by the armpits, and dragged him back. I watched, horrified, until another guard tapped me by the shoulder and led me back to the waiting area.

Shaking, I collected my phone and wallet from the locker where I'd left them. After washing my hands to get rid of any jailhouse germs, I walked out into the parking lot. My knees felt weak and my back ached. I squatted down and sat on the pavement, leaning my back against the rough stone wall. My heart pounded in my chest. Being in that tiny room with Jacob had made me feel trapped, and I needed a minute outdoors, under the big sky, before I could get back in my car again.

Jacob was as far gone as anyone I'd ever seen. He was scary, but he also seemed terrified of me. The poor man thought I was part of some conspiracy to hurt him.

But as crazy as his rant had been, one comment had set off alarm bells in my brain. Jacob had said that Richard was "in charge of it all." Did he mean the imaginary conspiracy in his mind, or was he talking about something real?

Surely not—it was one thing to think that Richard had killed back in high school to keep a cheating scam from ruining his future. But could he be running a criminal operation today?

I remembered a case from years ago, where a rogue public defender had started a side hustle selling dope. He'd recruited some of his clients to work for him and used attorney-client privilege as a shield to make drug sales. As a veteran defense attorney, he'd learned what mistakes to avoid and how not to get caught. Until a coconspirator got picked up on a third strike case and started talking to reduce his sentence.

Maybe Richard was doing the same thing. In a way, it made sense. If Regina's theory was right, Lisa had been killed by a brilliant, ambitious boy running an illegal side hustle for extra cash. What if that boy had grown into a brilliant, ambitious man who continued his penchant for making money in unsavory ways? Richard had been a defense attorney for more than a decade. He'd seen it all and knew what worked. It would explain the variety of crimes that the organization was involved in. It could also explain why Richard had volunteered to take the case. What better way to control what Jacob said and who he said it to?

But wouldn't this be a crazy coincidence? That the attorney for the family who hired me to investigate was both the actual killer *and* the killer in the cold case I was working? My head was swimming.

I peeled myself off the pavement and walked over to my car. I took my tote bag out of the trunk, pulled out both case files, and climbed into the front seat. I was eager to find other parallels between the crimes.

In Lisa's case, the cops had been thrown off the killer's trail by a series of text messages from her phone, claiming that she'd run away. I pulled out the phone report from Jacob's file. There were several texts from Jacob's phone to Abby, telling her that he was on his way. But what if they were fake? I already knew that Jonas had at least touched Jacob's phone. What if he'd stolen it before the murder, and Richard had made him send those texts to cover their trail?

Jonas was the one who had identified Jacob in surveillance. But maybe the man in the footage was actually Jonas. All you could see was a broad-shouldered figure in a baggie sweater. Richard could have sent Jonas up there with Jacob's phone and a hoodie from the restaurant where Jacob had worked. If Reid was posing as Jacob, he could have worn the mask to conceal his identity.

Sending Jonas to talk to the cops seemed risky if he was the actual murderer. But Jonas's interview had taken place after Jacob's arrest and after Richard had seen the discovery. Richard would have known just how shaky the surveillance footage was. Jonas's interview created a plausible explanation for the presence of his print on Jacob's phone.

And where was Jonas? A dark thought crossed my mind. Maybe the drugs were all part of the plan. What if Richard deliberately got his minions hooked on meth to destroy their credibility, and then discarded them when they were too damaged to be productive? I'd seen Jacob and Chris. If Richard ever got caught, neither of them would be capable of testifying against him in court. And if one of them became a liability, Richard could make him disappear without raising anyone's suspicions.

I still couldn't understand why Jonas had come to Abby's social work clinic. But then again, I didn't actually know what had occurred between them, only that it made her uncomfortable. Maybe Jonas had threatened her, to keep her quiet, and she'd neglected to share the full details of that encounter with her coworkers. Or maybe he'd wanted to see what she looked like, and then followed her home. There were a million possible explanations.

Another question popped into my mind—one that I needed Harry's help with. I dialed his number, and he picked up right away.

"Kate, what's up? You got hungry and you want your doggy bag back?"

I didn't have time to joke around. "This is going to sound crazy, but I think there's a chance that Richard killed both Lisa and Abby."

There was silence on the line. "I gotta be honest, Kate. That's nuts."

"I know, and I'm not sold on the idea, but hear me out. Chris Taylor said that he and Jacob worked for some guy who's running a small drug and fraud empire. And I just talked to Jacob, who said his lawyer's in charge of everything. I realize that's probably the crazy talking. But I need to at least consider the possibility that he's telling me something real."

Harry sighed and started to protest.

"Harry, it's just a theory, okay? But I want to check a couple things. Jonas Reid is a witness in the San Bernardino case. I don't have his birthdate, but I know his fingerprints are in the state database, which means he had a felony at some point. Can you find me the case number? I want to see who represented him. Same with Chris Taylor. I don't have his date of birth either, but he's currently a patient at the Pine Mountain Community Hospital. Can you find out if he ever had a court case, so I can try to track down who his lawyer was?"

"You know how common a name like Chris Taylor is?" Harry sounded annoyed. "I could run his rap and get a thousand entries."

I let out an exasperated sigh, "That's why I'm hoping you can get it from the hospital. If I were still a cop, I'd call them myself, but they're not going to tell me anything. If it helps, the meth has added a few years, but he looks like he's in his late twenties to early thirties. And he probably put his residence down as the Welcome Inn."

"Okay, well at least you're giving me something to work with," said Harry.

"You know what? He's probably still in the hospital. I'm gonna go there now and try to talk to him again. I'll keep you posted."

I hung up the phone and headed toward the hospital. Maybe Chris would open up to me now that I had a name. He'd been too scared to tell me who was running the show. But maybe he would nod a confirmation if I had it right.

I pulled into the parking lot and jogged over to the front entrance. A male nurse was at the front desk. "Hi," I said. "I'm here to see my cousin, Chris Taylor."

"You're too late," said the nurse. "His brothers already checked him out."

"His brothers?" I asked.

"Yeah, two big guys. We told them that Mr. Taylor needed to stick around for a few days so we could monitor his condition." He shook his head in disgust. "The guy just had an amputation, and he's still on major antibiotics. It was way too early to move him. But they wouldn't listen. They said they were taking him to a different hospital to be closer to family, but didn't say where."

My chest tightened and I felt dizzy. I could hear my heart pounding in my ears. Those weren't his brothers. I'd taken Chris to the hospital closest to his dad's motel, and a quick background search had told me that Doug Taylor lived ten minutes away. Besides, no one in their right mind would try to move a man right after his leg was amputated. Chris must have been too out of it to protest. My knees felt weak, and I grabbed the counter to steady myself.

"Um, are you okay?" asked the nurse.

I ignored him and stumbled into the parking lot. Bracing myself against the outside wall, I threw up into a planter. This was my fault. I'd told Richard that Chris filled me in on the organization, and within hours two goons had checked him of the hospital and taken him God knows where.

I got back in my car and called Harry. "Guess what?" he said before I could even get a word in. "Jonas's last felony was an LA Sheriff's case. And you were right: Richard was his lawyer."

"Dammit!" I shouted, smacking the steering wheel.

"I thought you'd be happy," said Harry, puzzled. "Your harebrained theory might be checking out. I haven't found anything on Chris yet, though. Did he give you his DOB?"

"No—he's gone. Two men checked him out of the hospital, claiming to be his brothers."

"Huh," said Harry. "How do you know they weren't?"

"Because Chris just had his leg amputated, and I'm pretty sure he doesn't have brothers. He's a very sick man on massive painkillers and antibiotics. No one in their right mind would have moved that guy."

Harry went silent for a moment as my meaning sunk in. "Kate, you need to come back to LA. If your theory is right—and yeah, maybe you're starting to convince me—then you're gonna be next on this guy's list."

"My stuff is in Idlewood," I told him. "Besides, Richard doesn't know where I'm staying."

Harry snorted. "This guy is super smart and well connected. I don't think he'll have a hard time finding you. Just go back to LA, and I'll drive up with you tomorrow to get your things."

"Thanks, Harry—I appreciate it," I said. "I'll talk to you tomorrow." I didn't like the idea of needing an escort, but Harry could carry a gun. I was still on court diversion from a little trespassing snafu I had on another case. As a result, I wasn't allowed to have a weapon, and I didn't want to be unarmed in Idlewood, with Richard and Jonas out there.

I started heading to my mom's house, when I remembered Sam. What if Richard figured out that Sam had helped me collect his DNA? I'd tried to be careful, but Richard was a savvy guy. Sam could be in danger. I dialed his number, but the call went directly to voicemail. His phone was probably switched off. I could keep calling, but if he didn't pick up, I'd have to warn him in person.

I turned around and headed back to Idlewood. I tried calling Sam again but still got his voicemail. The road was deserted, and I flew down the highway. By the time I got to town, night had fallen. The narrow roads were totally dark, and I couldn't see beyond the reach of my headlights.

The lights were out at Sam's cabin, but I knocked anyway, just in case. No answer. He was probably still at work. I couldn't remember if the Bighorn Grill was open late on Thursdays. I knew Sam closed it at the beginning of the week during the off season. I googled the restaurant on my phone. It looked like it had normal hours in the tourist season. In spring and fall, it was closed on Monday and Tuesday.

On Wednesday and Thursday, he shut down early. A little unconventional, but the guy was a single father, after all.

If the restaurant was closed, Sam might still be in there cleaning up or doing the accounting or something. I got back in my car and drove to the center of town. The white Christmas lights that usually adorned the deck of the Bighorn Grill were switched off, as were the lights in the dining area. I tried the front door, which was locked. But through the window, I could see a light on in the rear of the restaurant.

I went around to the other side of the building, to try the back entrance. The screen door was slightly ajar, and the wood door behind it was open. I pulled the screen out farther and looked inside. "Sam?" I called. No answer.

I walked into the restaurant and saw a little windowless room off to the side. Sam was slumped over the desk like he was sleeping—but something wasn't right. "No, no, no, no, no," I said, running over to him. There was a dark liquid on the back of his head. Blood had leaked out, covering his neck and staining his blue T-shirt.

Tears stung my eyes as I grabbed his wrist. He still had a pulse, but he needed help. I reached into my pocket for my cell phone, when I heard a noise behind me. I spun around and caught a glimpse of something moving toward my head before everything went dark.

39

Present—Kate

WHEN I WOKE, I felt a pounding ache in the back of my head. I tried to sit up and realized that I couldn't move my arms. I was lying across a bed with my wrists bound together and fastened to a headboard. I kicked my legs, but my ankles were also bound. What the hell was this?

Pain shot through my skull as my head fell back on the dingy mattress. My vision blurred, and the naked lightbulb above me seemed to split in two as my eyes struggled to focus. I shut them tight, waiting for the spinning sensation to stop. When the ache faded to something less immediate, the image of Sam, slumped over his desk, came back to me. I felt tears start to flow. It was all my fault; I'd been reckless. I should have just told Harry what I knew about Richard and let him figure out the rest. I thought I was being so fucking stealthy, and now Sam was hurt and maybe dying, Chris Taylor was missing, and I was tied up on a disgusting mattress.

I started kicking wildly, trying to see if I could somehow get my legs up to my hands. As if I could magically untie my wrists with my bare feet. And where the hell were my shoes? Richard must have taken them off. God, I hoped he wasn't a foot guy. No, he was probably worried that I'd escape. It's harder to run without shoes. Where was I anyway?

I thought back to my yoga days—back before I messed up my back. I tried to force my body into a shoulder stand, bending my feet toward my wrists. But the sudden rush of blood to my pounding head made everything fade out. My legs came crashing down, and the headboard knocked against the wall. I winced. If he was here, Richard would definitely have heard that.

Sure enough, the door creaked open, and he walked in. He had that same weird, professional-seeming fake smile plastered on his face. "I see you're awake," said Richard. His voice was strangely pleasant, like he was about to ask if I'd like a cup of coffee.

I tried to think about how to handle him. My death was a near certainty. Richard was a cold-blooded killer who had murdered someone when he was still in his teens, and he literally specialized in getting criminals off the hook. He knew how to kill, had no qualms about doing it, and was good at covering his tracks.

But his attack on Sam felt hasty, sloppy. I had him panicked, and he was starting to make mistakes. That thought gave me a tiny bit of hope that I could find a way out of here. I would get as much information as I could about my whereabouts, try to find something I could use to escape. And I wanted to get him talking about his crimes. On the off chance that I left this filthy cabin alive, I'd be testifying against him in court. And I owed it to Abby and Lisa and Jacob to extract a confession if I could.

"What the fuck is this, Richard?"

"Let's not waste each other's time, Kate. I've worked with you enough to know you're not stupid—you make the obvious connections, and I knew that my little reunion with Myra wasn't going to slip past you. Also, you have a tell."

"Oh?" I said.

"You play with your hair when you're nervous. I'd suggest keeping your arms folded in your lap next time, to avoid giving yourself away, but I don't really think that's going to be an issue." He smiled coldly, and a wave of fear washed over me.

"Why Sam?" I demanded. "You know he has a little girl?"

Richard rolled his eyes and ran his hand along the back of his neck. "Your doggy bag—that was my food, right? For a DNA sample?"

I stayed quiet, trying to decide which answer was most likely to keep me alive.

"We can come back to that. I thought I was just being paranoid at first, because involving the waiter seemed like a weird move. But then I saw the way he looked at you when we were leaving, and I got a sense that you were pretty well acquainted. I put out some feelers and heard a few rumors. Good-looking guy, by the way. Glad you found time to have some fun while you were in town."

I willed myself not to cry. *Fucking monster.* "So, you shot him in the head because of rumors?"

"Someone saw him kiss you at a concert the other day," said Richard. I winced, remembering how Sam had pecked me on the cheek at the Red Barn Opry. "And even if I'm wrong about the doggy bag, I couldn't take a risk that you'd confided in your new boyfriend. I planned it to look like a robbery. I trust you didn't make it into the dining area and see the state of the cash register." He paused, like he was waiting for me to say something. "But then you showed up and messed up my crime scene. Your DNA, which we both know the sheriffs already have, is going to be all over the place. I'm trying to figure out how that factors in. But I can't kill you until I come up with a story that'll make all the pieces fit together."

I felt a glimmer of hope. "You're right, killing us both on the same night would look very suspicious. Especially with all those rumors floating around."

He ignored my comment. Richard's eyes darkened, and the false friendliness was suddenly gone. "I need to know what you did with the box."

I stayed quiet. My answer to that question could determine how long I had to live. Richard's need for information was the only thing I had left to bargain with.

"Why did you kill Abby?" I asked.

Richard laughed. "Kate, you might be confused about what's happening here."

"I don't think so," I countered. "Because you still need information. You have to get rid of me in a way that won't draw too much police attention. Another death on the heels of Sam and Chris's murders will look suspicious, and you want an innocent-sounding story to sell to the cops." I needed him to believe that Sam was dead. He'd seen me checking his pulse. If Richard thought Sam was alive, he'd go back and finish the job.

He blinked and looked surprised by my mention of Chris.

"I called the hospital," I said. "They told me Chris's brothers checked him out." One side of Richard's mouth curled upward into a smirk, which told me I was right. He was listening, so I kept going. "You need to find a way to kill me and make it look like an accident. And you're not an amateur," I said, switching to ego stroking. "You committed a nearly perfect murder when you were—what, seventeen? With no time to plan?"

I paused, hoping he'd say something incriminating—something to bolster the DNA evidence.

"I'm not sure where you're going with this," said Richard. He was starting to look anxious. Better reel him back in before he got bored and gagged me.

I also wanted to remind him that I was an experienced homicide investigator. Perverse as it seemed, I could even help him plan my own death. Richard was at least as smart as I was, probably smarter. But I'd been manipulating psychopaths for years, and this guy was a walking personality disorder. Maybe I could convince him to factor my advice into his plans for me. If I could keep him talking, I could buy myself a little time and maybe think of some way to get out of here.

"You killed Abby and perfectly framed someone else for it. It sounds like you thought out Sam's death in detail. Let me guess: you used a crime gun, and ballistics will trace the shell casing to another crime scene—maybe even another robbery? Something to throw the police off your trail?" I doubted that he'd gone that far. But it would have been a good idea. Richard saw people as tools that he could exploit and discard. *Let him think he could use me before throwing me away.*

He offered a cold smile that told me he hadn't thought to use a crime gun or hadn't been able to get one.

I went on: "We both know how this is going to end, but in the meantime, we both have something the other one wants. You want to plan another perfect murder, which should really look like an accident and probably shouldn't happen for at least a couple days."

"And what exactly do you want, other than for me to let you go?" he asked.

"Well, survival instinct has kicked in, and I'd like to buy myself a little time. Plus, I'm pretty invested in this case by now—well, both cases—and I'd like to find out what happened."

Richard burst out laughing. "Kate, you're an interesting woman—I'll give you that."

"So, tell me, why did you kill Abby? You knew her, right? You both went to Serrano High. You told me she was friends with your sister. So, what happened? Did she confront you about turning her brother into a meth-addicted criminal? Threaten to call the police and get you disbarred?"

The smiled disappeared from Richard's face. I'd pushed too hard and too fast. Richard might be willing to let me babble in case I said something useful. But he needed to feel in control. "I really don't have time for games," he said. "Let's try this a different way."

He walked out of the room. Blood pumped in my ears, and I started to tremble, terrified of what he was going to come back with. Was he going to shoot me now? Or torture me? I forced myself to look away from the door to see if there was anything that I could use to sever my restraints. But the place was barren. Just the gross bed and a dresser against the wall with peeling paint.

Richard came back about a minute later, holding a roll of duct tape. My heart sank. Talking was my only chance of getting out of here. If he gagged me, I'd be dead, and I'd never see my daughter again. It also occurred to me that if he hadn't gagged me yet, we were probably somewhere pretty remote. Where no one could hear me scream.

"Tell me what you did with the box," ordered Richard, "or I'll tape off your mouth and your eyes, and your last hours on earth will be silent and dark."

"I gave it to the sheriffs," I admitted—instantly wishing I could take it back. Tell him I'd left it somewhere remote, send him on a wild goose chase. "So it's over, Richard. They have your DNA. And they'll know you're responsible for whatever happens to me. You can end this right now."

"Wow, in that case, I'll just cut you loose and turn myself in," he said in a deadpan voice that sent chills down my spine. "I read your notes, Kate. If a stranger had killed Lisa, then a DNA match would be a home run. But I knew Lisa. All that DNA proves is that we hung out at some point in the days before she died. I doubt that's even enough for an arrest warrant, let alone a conviction. And if I'm wrong, I've had decades to come up with a plausible reason for a DNA match. You know what I do for a living, and I'm not sure if Grace told you this, but I'm very good at my job."

He was right. The case was thin, even with DNA. "We also have a motive," I countered. "They know you were selling essays and that Lisa wanted to expose you."

"Like I said, I read all your notes while you were passed out. You can't prove that was me, and I doubt any of my former customers are going to come forward and risk getting their college degrees revoked twenty years after the fact."

That was an admission of sorts. Although I'd probably never get to repeat it in front of a jury. "The cops will know you had a motive to get rid of me."

"Yes, I'm aware," said Richard. Of course, he was. That's why he was taking care of business himself instead of sending a goon. Jonas or some other creep could kill Abby and Chris because there was no obvious trail leading back to Richard. But Harry knew that Richard had a reason to kill me. That made planning my murder a bit trickier. And it was the only reason I was still alive.

"What else have you told the police about me?" asked Richard. I stayed quiet, trying to think about my options, until the sound of tearing duct tape grabbed my attention. "If you're not going to tell me anything else, I'd just as soon shut you up so I can think."

"Wait!" I said, panicking. "I need to use the bathroom."

Richard blinked, looking annoyed by my request. He left the room again, and I heard a screen door open, then slam shut. It didn't sound like he'd unlatched a deadbolt or anything. I realized that while Richard had gotten away with murder several times, he'd probably never kidnapped anyone. Richard called the shots and hid behind his white-collar career. From the looks of his skinny arms and puffed-out tummy, he wasn't much for hitting the gym. Whereas I'd been in more than a few street fights. If I could get my legs free, I could run outside, disappear into the woods, and maybe have a fighting chance. But a minute later, the screen door groaned open again, and Richard came back, holding a tin bucket covered in dirt stains.

"Richard, give me a break," I said. "There has to be a bathroom in here. Don't make me pee in a freaking bucket. Honestly, I'm not sure if I even could."

When he didn't move, I added, "It's going to get pretty ripe in here if you keep me tied up long enough to stage an accidental death without letting me use the bathroom."

"Fine," he said. "But if you try anything, you're going to regret it." He untied my hands from the bedpost and freed my legs, but kept my wrists lashed together. Then he lifted his sweater and pulled a gun out of a side holster. He stood and pointed it at me. "Get up and walk." I did as I was told.

Richard led me into a threadbare living room. My eyes scanned the room, trying to pick up as much information as I could. There was trash everywhere, and the walls were covered in graffiti. It looked like a million drug houses I'd seen when I was on the force.

I quickly spotted the door to the outside, which was now closed and probably locked. Richard shoved me into a tiny water closet with just a toilet and a small sink with a cabinet underneath. It was filthy, with rust stains inside the toilet bowl, dried piss polka dots on the porcelain, and ambiguous brown stains on the wall.

A lightbulb went off in my brain.

"Can you please just stand outside. I can't do this if you're watching," I pleaded, trying to sound pathetic, which wasn't hard right now. Richard let out an exasperated exhale and took two steps back. I closed the door ninety percent of the way, before he ordered me to leave it open. I scanned the floor for anything I could use as a weapon. But there was nothing.

I reached over with my bound hands and turned the faucet on. "I can't pee if you can hear me," I said. As quietly as I could, I opened the door of the tiny cabinet under the sink. If this was a drug house, maybe there'd be something I could use inside. I saw a single small needle, unused, with its cap still on. It would have to do. I picked it up and tucked it into my pants pocket, and then forced myself to pee, since Richard was still by the door, listening.

I washed my hands and then turned and noticed the porcelain rim of the toilet. If I hit him hard enough to knock him out, I could run. I grabbed the top as gently as I could, but I wasn't quiet enough. Richard heard me and threw open the door. He grabbed me by the armpits and dragged me back to the bedroom. I thrashed, desperate to get away.

Richard threw me onto the bed and straddled me, holding down my legs with his. I lunged forward and tried to headbutt him, but he shoved me down and punched me hard. I felt my lip split under the force of his knuckles, and I tasted metal as blood ran down my throat. I clawed at his arms, trying to at least secure a healthy DNA sample for whoever found me. But then Richard racked the gun and pointed it at my head. I stared at the dark little void in the center and stopped fighting.

He grabbed my bound hands and yanked them above my head with one hand. The other held the gun to my temple. He pushed my chest down with a knee and brought the gun hand up to meet the other one. Then I heard the sound of pulling duct tape as he secured my wrists to the bedpost. "Bitch," he muttered under his breath as he pulled out more duct tape and moved toward my mouth. I shook my head and recoiled, but he grabbed me by my hair, held my head in place, and wrapped the tape around my injured mouth.

Then it was done. I couldn't move. I couldn't speak. My head ached and my mouth tasted of blood. Richard stood up and examined his scratches and the flecks of red on his shirt. He was furious. I'd probably just shortened my lifespan by several hours.

He shook his head and walked out of the room, turning off the light and leaving me alone in the dark.

CHAPTER

40

Present—Kate

I MUST HAVE LAIN there for hours, metallic taste in my mouth, skull pounding, wondering if my daughter would ever know what happened to me. Would Richard leave a body, or would I simply disappear? Amelia would wonder if her mother had abandoned her—run off and relapsed, never to be seen again. I had to get out of here, for her sake. I tried to form a plan, but the blows to my head had made me groggy, and I couldn't think straight.

From outside, I heard the sound of car wheels on a dirt driveway. I tried to scream into the duct tape, but only a muffled squeak sound came out. A strong wave of nausea from the effort and the motion came over me, and I thought I might vomit. I heard the sound of two male voices and tried to scream again, but it quickly became apparent that the mystery guest was a friend of Richard's. Probably one of his flunkies coming to help finish me off. I collapsed back down against the mattress and awaited my fate.

The screen door opened again, and I heard the engine start and the car pull away, out of the driveway. I was alone again with Richard.

I heard his footsteps approaching the room. Then the light came on. My field of vision splintered into a kaleidoscope of crystal daggers.

It was like a migraine on steroids. I turned my head to the side and closed my eyes to shut out the glare.

"Okay," said Richard cheerfully. "I finally figured out what to do with you." He sat on the edge of the bed, and I saw that he was holding a handle of cheap vodka and a pill bottle. Richard put them both down on the mattress, and then ripped the tape off my mouth, taking some of my skin with it. "I did my homework before adding you to Jacob's defense team. That was my decision, by the way. The Coburns think I agreed to hire you because your friend Harry put in a good word. But I did some digging with LAPD sources. It seems you went out on disability after an accident and got hooked on oxycodone. And you're a bit of a lush. Then last year, you were arrested for trespassing? Glad to hear they gave you a diversion, but it sounds like you've had a rough couple of years."

The pills were on me—fine. But that arrest hadn't happened the way he made it seem. I'd gone into an endangered witness's house to look for him, and a nosy neighbor had called the cops. Good Samaritan caught trespassing. It wasn't my finest moment, and it made quite an impression on some of my former coworkers.

"Even your kid—you only see her what? Twice a month?"

"Leave her out of this," I snapped.

Richard smiled cruelly. "I've touched a nerve. Well, anyway, like I said, you really messed up my plan when you showed up at the Bighorn and left your prints and DNA all over the scene. But I found a way to work with what I have. By now, enough people know about your dalliance with the barkeep. The story is you went over there to see him, and found the body. Then you took comfort in old habits, started driving back to LA on Lone Pine Canyon Drive while intoxicated, lost control of the car, and careened off the mountain."

I looked down at the drugs and the booze. "And if I refuse to touch that stuff?"

Richard shrugged and moved the side of his jacket, revealing the handle of his 22-caliber pistol. "Well, I could shoot out your kneecaps. Or start slicing you until you see reason. But that's not really my style. Believe it or not, I'm not a fan of gratuitous violence. And when they find your body, it shouldn't display any signs of torture. That wouldn't be good for the narrative. So how about this—I know that Amelia lives in a nice house on Mirada Street. I know that she goes to a charter school in Sherman Oaks. And if you don't do what I say, I'm going to kill her."

Amelia. I can't even describe how I felt hearing him say my daughter's name.

I looked at the pill bottle again. Part of me wanted to reach for it. Let my fear and regret and the splitting pain in my head melt away. But it would also take away my fight. And I knew that if there was a tiny sliver of a chance that I could get out of this, touching oxy again would be my undoing. Alcohol had been a problem for me, but not the same way. I made my choice.

"I'll drink the vodka, but I'm not touching the pills." Richard raised an eyebrow and started to speak, but I cut him off. "It's a better narrative. Everyone close to me knows that I haven't used opioids in years. It'll look too convenient. And since my death will probably trigger police interest, they might try to find the dealer who sold me the pills. The booze actually simplifies things for you. It's more believable and less likely to spark too much police interest."

That son of a bitch actually smiled. "You know what? I think you're right. There's a parallel universe where we could have worked well together. Anyway, drink up," he said, unscrewing the cap from the vodka bottle. "When you've had enough, we'll go for a drive."

Richard picked up the bottle and held it up to my mouth. I grimaced as the alcohol stung my busted lip. The liquid burned as it went down. I coughed, to clear my throat, which sent a jolt of pain through my aching skull. The nauseous feeling came back. "Your sources didn't tell you I prefer wine or gin?"

He laughed. "The coroner tests for blood alcohol. Pathology doesn't cover your drink preferences."

My eyes landed on the butt of the gun in his waistband. If I could get him to untie my hands from the headboard, I might be able to reach it. I could fire with my wrists lashed together and I wouldn't hesitate before killing this psychopath.

"This would be a lot easier if I could do it myself," I told him. "I'm not going to fight you.

Richard smirked. "Nice try, but we'll do it this way. It's getting late and we don't have much time. He tipped the bottle again, and I let the alcohol run down my throat. It didn't take long for it to affect me after the blow I'd taken to the head. You're not supposed to drink when you have a concussion, and I was starting to understand why. I needed to stop before I completely lost my wits. After about four shots' worth, I shook my head. "Richard," I rasped, "I'm probably twice the legal limit already, and if I keep at it like this, I'm going to barf."

"Take a few more sips for good measure." I did as I was told, trying let as much of it dribble down my face as I could. I reeked of alcohol.

When Richard was finally satisfied, he put the bottle on the ground and then reached into his pocket and pulled out a knife. My eyes widened. "What do you need that for?" I asked. Richard ignored my question, leaned up, and cut the band holding my legs together. He took the gun out, cocked it, and placed the nozzle to my temple. I closed my eyes. "I'm going to free your arms. Don't try anything." He reached up and cut the duct tape that was securing my arms to the headboard, but he kept my hands tied together. Richard took several steps back, still pointing the gun at me. "Get up."

I struggled to a seated position, and the room started spinning. I waited until the moving stopped and then slowly rose to my feet, stumbling a bit.

"Walk," said Richard. I did as I was told. He directed me into the living room and out the screen door. The second my feet hit the dirt, I took off running. But my legs were wobbly, and I was no match for Richard. He easily tackled me and hit me over the head with the gun. I saw flickers of light and heard the sickening sound of metal on bone. Richard hoisted me to my feet and half dragged me to an old pickup truck.

"Aren't we doing this in my car?" I asked. I'd left it parked by the Bighorn. If we were going to town, there was a chance that someone would see us and help me.

"My associate is picking up your car and meeting us," said Richard. My heart sank. We rolled down the dirt road. Richard's right hand was on the wheel and his left hand stayed firmly planted on the gun.

I noticed something poking my leg, which was when I remembered the needle. If I could get him to crash the truck somewhere around witnesses, I might have a fighting chance.

Slowly, I moved my bound hands over to my right jeans pocket. My fingers found the outline of the needle and I gently forced it up toward the opening of my pocket. When it was in my hands, I removed the cap and felt the sharp side poke into my skin.

Richard glanced over at my lap, where my hands were now folded. "What are you doing?"

"What do you think I'm doing?" I could tell that I was already slurring my words. "I'm sitting here waiting for you to kill me."

The bastard actually chuckled.

I kept my eyes straight, waiting for the right moment. The dirt road turned into a paved one, but the houses were still set back from the street. I tried to figure out where we were, but everything was so dark, and between the alcohol and the throbbing in my temples, I felt totally disoriented. I saw an old, hulking RV parked in someone's front yard. A good crash might be enough to disable the car.

I knew I needed to do more than just stab the needle into his leg or arm—he'd just shove me off him. I pushed the small needle out from between my closed fingers, lunged forward and plunged it into Richard's eye. He screamed. I slammed my bound hands down on his wrist, which was holding the gun, putting all my weight on it. When I heard the gun hit the floorboard, I pulled up on the wheel. I felt the crash and heard the screech of metal against metal as the car plowed into the trailer and came to a sudden stop. The airbag smacked me in the face, pushing me back against the seat. After a few seconds I slid out from underneath it, opened my door, and started running toward the house. At first, I didn't hear anything behind me. *Maybe I stopped him.* But then came the sound of running feet. Somehow Richard had recovered enough to give chase, and was closing in. He lunged forward, our bodies colliding. I hit the cold ground, and Richard landed on top, knocking the wind out of me.

I felt the nozzle of the gun push against my cheek. "Bitch, I'm going to kill you."

But then I heard something else, the deep sound of a shotgun racking. "Drop the gun, asshole, and get off her." The homeowner must have heard the crash and come out to investigate. *Thank God.* I felt Richard roll off me, and I closed my eyes.

41

Present—Kate

I WOKE UP TO the sting of an IV in my arm. It took a minute for the hospital room to come into focus. My head felt like someone had used it for batting practice, and my back didn't feel much better. I vaguely remembered telling the nurses not to give me anything stronger than ibuprofen.

I opened my eyes and saw Harry sitting in the visitor seat. "How you feeling?" he asked.

"I've been better," I said.

He chuckled as if I'd told him a joke. "From the looks of you, I'd say that's an understatement."

I tried to smile, but it hurt to move my face muscles.

"We arrested Richard," said Harry. "Booked him for kidnapping, assault with a firearm, and two counts of attempted murder."

"Two counts?" I asked. "Sam's alive?"

Harry nodded. "He's doing better than you, actually." It turned out that Sam's band had scheduled a practice that night at Regina's house, and when he didn't show up, they all got in her car and drove over to the restaurant to look for him. That's when they found him slumped over his desk, and called the police.

"How's he doing better than me?" I asked. "Richard shot him, didn't he?"

"Apparently, the bullet hit at a weird angle and scraped his skull without piercing his brain. He got knocked out by the force of it, but they're not expecting lasting damage. They think Richard shot him from across the room and then moved over to the cash register to set the scene of a fake robbery. I suspect Richard would have gone back to make sure Sam was dead before leaving. But then you showed up, which wasn't part of the plan."

Tears of relief welled in my eyes. I'd been holding out hope that Sam would make it, but I hadn't really expected it. When I was lying there, tied up in that disgusting cabin, I kept thinking about Willow and Amelia. Two little girls, each about to lose a parent. And I would have been responsible for all of it.

"Nice guy, by the way," said Harry. "The deputy who interviewed him said he asked about you a lot."

This was more than I could have hoped for. Sam was alive; he was going to be okay, and from the sound of it, he didn't hate me. I hoped I could find a way to forgive myself for getting him mixed up in all this.

"What about Lisa's case? Richard basically admitted that he used to write essays for money. Not directly, but when I asked about it, he said he doubted any of his former clients would come forward."

Harry nodded, approvingly. "That's great evidence. Not to mention, he kidnapped you to keep you quiet, which is not gonna play well with a jury. If the DNA comes back as a match, which we're all expecting, I think we'll have enough to charge him."

"What about Jacob?" I asked. "Are they going to release him?"

"He's still in custody, but the DA's evaluating whether they can proceed to trial. His supervisors are still mulling it over, but unofficially, they're probably gonna drop the charges and release him in the next few days. With everything you brought forward about Richard, they can't possibly continue the prosecution. But I'm not sure if we have enough to charge Richard for Abby's murder, unfortunately. Not without tracking down Jonas Reid or Chris Taylor."

"I wouldn't count on that happening," I said. If they hadn't found Chris by now, they probably never would.

Harry smiled sadly. "Officially that case might remain unsolved for a while. But we have enough to put Richard away for a very long time." He paused and looked a little sheepish. "Hey, I hope I didn't mess up—I've talked to your mom a couple times, and she asked me for details on that antique dealer you think might be your father."

Now this was surprising. Last I talked to her, I was pretty sure she'd shut the door on that topic. "What did you tell her?"

"I said she'd have to ask you, but I let it slip that his shop is out in Escarra Hills. I can't imagine there are a ton of antique stores out there. She said something about going to see for herself."

I didn't know what to think. Had my mom actually driven out there to confront Vic? It was so wildly out of character. I thought of my prim and proper mother listening to Vic rant about dead magicians, with a hint of whiskey on his breath.

"Anyway," said Harry, "I'll let you rest. Just wanted to give you the updates. I'll come back tomorrow to interview you properly, after you've had another day to rest."

"Okay, but can you turn off the lights when you leave?" I asked. My head was killing me, and the glare from the fluorescent bulbs was making me nauseous.

He left and I shut my eyes again. Now that I was alone, I felt a flood of relief. I was alive. Sam was okay. Jacob would be free soon, and Richard would be behind bars. There were a lot of things to be happy about. But despite everything, I kept flashing back to Richard and that gross cabin. Remembering the smell of mold and rot and my own sweat, the taste of vodka mixed with blood and the fear of dying and never seeing Amelia again. I knew it was going to take me a while to recover from this one. Right now, I just wanted to sleep.

As I felt myself drifting off, I heard a child's footsteps running down the hall, and recognized the squeak of my daughter's sneakers. I really need to get her a less annoying pair. I opened my eyes and managed to sit up as my body screamed at me. Then she appeared in the doorway, looking adorable in a plastic tiara and her pink jean jacket.

She ran up to my hospital bed and threw her arms around me. I hugged her back with one arm, the other arm held down by the IV still stuck in my vein. I stroked the top of her hair and felt tears in my eyes. "Hi, baby," I said. "I missed you."

"Give Mommy some space," said my mother from the doorway. I glanced over at her.

"Thank you for bringing Amelia." I heard a quiver in my voice, and I wasn't sure if I could keep it together. There were a couple hours where I didn't think I'd ever see my daughter again.

"Of course," said my mother. She sat next to me and squeezed my hand. "How are you doing?"

"Tired," I said. "But I'll be okay."

"Kate, I went to the antique shop and met Vic," said my mother. "He's a charming man, and the resemblance is uncanny." She gave me a meaningful look. "You know he apologized to me. He said he'd read some things online after meeting you that made him think I wasn't fully informed. I think he meant it." That was as much as we could say right now, with Amelia in the room. But it was a lot. And I was enormously relieved to hear that Vic wasn't in on the fraud.

"And I've made a decision about something," she said. "I'm taking out a reverse mortgage on the house."

I didn't understand why she was springing this on me now, of all times. "What's going on?" I asked. "Isn't dad's pension covering everything?"

"The house is your inheritance, and I think it might be more useful to you now than later," she said. "I'm taking out a lump sum. I'll give some to you, which you can spend as you see fit, and with the rest, I'm hoping to take all three of us on a girls' trip. Then after that, I'll get a little bit extra every month and live a little more comfortably."

Amelia squealed with delight. "Where are we going?"

"I haven't figured that out yet," said my mother. "Maybe we can decide together."

"Can we go to the Galapagos and see penguins?" asked Amelia. "We learned about it at school."

My mother shrugged. "Wherever we want."

I was too choked up to say anything. She was talking about paying for a lawyer. I could reopen my custody case with a decent attorney and fight for my daughter. I could move back into my own house and stop renting it out to strangers. "Thank you," I managed, my voice almost breaking. She squeezed my hand again.

Amelia climbed onto the bed and snuggled against me. I winced under her weight but didn't push her away. "I'm gonna get a cup of tea from the cafeteria," said my mother. "You want anything?" I shook my head. She was giving me alone time with my daughter, which I appreciated.

"Can we go play with Willow?" asked Amelia.

I tried to answer, but the words caught in my throat. "Not right now, sweetie," I managed. "Maybe soon. Why don't you tell me about your day?" We stayed like that, cuddled up while Amelia prattled away about art class, where the teacher complimented her haircut and had them draw penguins and seals and giant sea turtles. I shut my eyes and listened to her voice, not wanting the moment to end.

ACKNOWLEDGMENTS

I'D LIKE TO thank:

The team at Crooked Lane for giving me the opportunity to become an author. Sara J. Henry for being brutal and for being brilliant. Liza Fleissig and the Liza Royce Agency for your help, hard work, and good advice. My husband for doing virtually all the housework when I was trying to finish this book, and for reading countless drafts. Christina for watching the toddler and spending endless hours listening to him talk about cars and planes. My parents for teaching me to appreciate art and books.

THE
MATRIX
OF YOGA

THE
MATRIX
OF YOGA

TEACHINGS, PRINCIPLES
AND QUESTIONS

Georg Feuerstein and Brenda Feuerstein

Foreword by Judith Hanson Lasater

Hohm Press
Chino Valley, Arizona

Cover Design: Adi Zuccarello

Interior Design and Layout: Accurance

Library of Congress Cataloging-in-Publication Data
Feuerstein, Georg.
The matrix of yoga : teachings, principles, and questions / Georg Feuerstein and Brenda Feuerstein.
    pages cm
Includes bibliographical references and index.
ISBN 978-1-935387-47-3 (trade pbk. : alk. paper)
1. Yoga. 2. Yoga--Miscellanea. I. Title.
B132.Y6F475 2013
181'.45--dc23

                    2013015456

Hohm Press
P.O. Box 4410
Chino Valley, AZ 86323
800-381-2700
http://www.hohmpress.com

This book was printed in the U.S.A. on recycled, acid-free paper using soy ink.

CONTENTS

FOREWORD

We are often warned to be careful about what we wish for because we just might get it, and with that "success" come inevitable, unpredictable, and unintended consequences.

I have learned this lesson over and over. When I became a student of yoga, no one who knew me, neither my family nor my friends, had any idea what I was doing. For all they knew, I was sitting on nails every morning. I used to long for everyone to understand and practice yoga so I wouldn't feel so weird.

No doubt my wishes were inconsequential in their effect, nonetheless today, decades after I began my practice, yoga practice has indeed spread everywhere in the West. Unfortunately, the results of this popularity is that apparently what has spread the most widely tends to be the most superficial aspects of yoga.

Stop anyone on the street today with the question "what is yoga?" and they likely will tell you that yoga consists of challenging exercises done in heated rooms to lose weight and get fit.

I feel despair at this truth, but now find myself happily cheered by reading *The Matrix of Yoga*. The authors remind the reader that the power of yoga is so much greater than the limited power to touch our toes. Yoga can teach each of us to touch our soul as well, and how to become free at long last from the tyranny of our mind.

I was lucky enough to meet Georg Feuerstein when we served together on the Advisory Board of *Yoga Journal Magazine* many years ago. I was equally awed by his dedication to his practice and by the depth of his knowledge about this ancient art of yoga I love so well.

The awe soon turned to admiration and friendship. We continued this friendship electronically from afar. Georg never failed to promptly answer any question I put to him about an esoteric yoga term or "what exactly did that verse from Patanjali mean again?". Brenda extended the same warm connection to me.

As mentioned before, I am cheered from my despair about the popular misunderstandings surrounding yoga in our culture in part because of the publication of *The Matrix of Yoga*. This book makes such a cogent, concise and readable argument for us all to re-dedicate ourselves to the profound truths to be found in the midst of our practice. And it is clear the authors mean us to re-dedicate equally to practice on the mat, on the meditation cushion, and in our daily lives, busily interacting with real human beings.

Georg and Brenda write with the conviction that can only be born from their personal and mature practice of yoga. They write not only from their brains with knowledge and wisdom, but also from their hearts with love and devotion. This is a very rare combination.

I take great inspiration in the fact that we can read this book, and pass it on with confidence to students of all levels knowing it will improve their practice and lives.

Simply put, I like this book. I like the book's organization that presents the vastness of yoga teachings with just enough depth to be valuable and just enough breadth to be interesting. The reader is neither talked down to nor overwhelmed.

Another thing I like about *The Matrix of Yoga* is its approachable tone. When I read it, I feel more like I am in the Feuerstein's living room having a deep but personal conversation with like-minded friends.

I am especially appreciative of the *Questions* section at the end of the book. Yoga teachers are asked these kinds of questions all the time, and I for one am thrilled to have such an excellent · guide to recommend.

Finally, I cannot pass up the opportunity to state here how much I believe the world has lost when we lost Georg Feuerstein: an outstanding scholar, a fine friend and a devoted yogi. May the example of his life and the wisdom of his books remain with us forever.

Judith Hanson Lasater, Ph.D., PT
San Francisco, California
June, 2013

Judith Lasater has taught yoga since 1971. She holds a doctorate in East-West Psychology and is a physical therapist. She is president of the California Yoga Teachers Association and the author of eight books, including Relax and Renew; Yogabody; *and* Living Your Yoga.

PREFACE

Yoga was introduced in 1893 when the illustrious Swami Vivekananda, a yogi from India, spoke to an enthusiastic crowd of Westerners at the World's Parliament of Religions in Chicago. Since then literally thousands of books on Yoga have been published. Most of them treat Yoga as a system of body improvement in one way or another. We refer to that as "Modern Postural Yoga"—a phrase coined by the British scholar Elizabeth de Michelis (2004). Especially since the 1960s, with TV programs like Richard Hittleman's, millions of people in the Western hemisphere have taken up (and have significantly benefited from) this version of Yoga. Had they not experienced Yoga's beneficial effects, they would most certainly not have stuck with it year after year.

The majority of Yoga enthusiasts, especially in North America, are unfortunately ignorant of the fact that Yoga is very much more than physical postures for flexibility, fitness, strength, or relaxation. They also do not understand that, in its original form, Yoga could do them even greater good.

Yoga stands for *spiritual discipline*, as it was developed in India over thousands of years. This is the focus of our present book. *The Matrix of Yoga* aims to be as simple an introduction to the authentic teachings of Yoga as we can make it. To be sure, Yoga traditionally included physical postures, but this was just *one* aspect of practice. Mental discipline was counted as far more important. Some approaches didn't even include any physical exercises other than the discipline of sitting still for a long time in order to meditate.

Above all, Yoga traditionally was wrapped within a *spiritual* framework. Every single discipline had the purpose of helping the practitioner to grow toward inner (or spiritual) freedom. Modern Postural Yoga, by contrast, largely excludes any spiritual (or even ethical) consideration. Thus, contemporary practitioners in the Western hemisphere are often shortchanged. They are neither made aware of the real nature of Yoga nor encouraged to explore it.

The spiritual poverty of much of Western Yoga is due to the fact that all too many Yoga teachers jump into teaching after only the most rudimentary training. We would argue that they are therefore generally ill equipped for the huge responsibility to correctly instruct others. Often this extends even to the postural practices. We do not wish to deny that many, if not most, modern practitioners of the physical postures of Yoga are significantly helped by them. Many scientific studies prove this beyond doubt. Yet, the core power of Yoga—which is in its spiritual and ethical wisdom—remains untapped.

Toward the end of this book, we have given our answers to the most commonly asked questions. They are of course given from the perspective of traditional Yoga. While some of our answers may fall into a range of "unpopular" views when assessed within the contemporary Yoga marketplace, we have attempted to remain true to tradition as we know it.

Notes about Terms: To keep things as simple as possible, throughout the book we will use only the most important technical words in the Sanskrit language that are frequently used in Western Yoga centers and schools (see Appendix A). A male practitioner will be referred to as a *yogin* (in the nominative case: *yogi*); a female practitioner as a *yogini* (with a long *i* at the end). Most modern Western practitioners know these two terms but don't always use them.

Further Reading and Study: At the end of this book, Appendix B lists and briefly describes some of Georg's other, Yoga-related books in stepwise fashion, so that anyone wanting to explore Yoga further has a useful graduated guide.

Many of Georg's other books on Yoga were not written for novices. As we have learned, even his *Path of Yoga*, republished by Shambhala in revised form in 2012, presupposes too much for some readers. This is why we wrote the present book, which, we hope, is simple in language and argument. We offer it to beginning students so that they may begin their journey into Yoga on the right foot. We wish all our readers well.

—Georg Feuerstein and Brenda Feuerstein
Traditional Yoga Studies
www.traditionalyogastudies.com

PART ONE

Exploring the Tradition of Yoga

1. Introducing Yoga

Yoga evolved on the Indian subcontinent over the course of several millennia. Its physical exercises continue to be developed today, partly in response to the physical limitations and also the mental challenges (notably the lack of concentration) of modern people. The difference between now and then is this: In the past, Yoga was developed by accomplished masters who had a *spiritual* interest first and foremost. Today, imaginative Yoga instructors invent physical postures and styles that they think will benefit or excite their students. It is fair to say that by no means would all of these new-fangled approaches have passed the critical eye and wisdom of a master from long ago. What, one wonders, would such masters have made of *Hiphop Yoga, Disco Yoga, Nude Yoga, Nude Hot Yoga, Ganja (Marijuana) Yoga*, and so on? Our brains reel.

Since we will use the word "spiritual" often in this book, let us explain what we mean by it up front. "Spiritual" suggests a quality that relates to the luminous core of our being, however you may understand it or whatever you may call it. That core goes beyond language and the mind. Yet, it is not religious as commonly understood. Yoga as a whole also ought not to be equated with religion. It developed by trial and error on the part of thousands of practitioners. Its goal is inner freedom—which is freedom from the compulsions of our limited personality; above all, freedom from the habit of self-centeredness. Yoga wants us to become as transparent as glass, or as clear as a mountain lake on a windless day, so that we can be present in the world with wisdom and compassion.

Yoga's goal does not contradict the highest aspirations that a deeply religious and mystically-inclined person has. Yet, as we said before, Yoga is not a religion. It is not merely a philosophy either. It is a *discipline*. This is not a popular word in our time, because we have become accustomed to doing "our own thing" at our own leisure. But Yoga is not someone else's discipline to which we have to conform rigidly. It is essentially *self-discipline*.

Yoga comes wrapped in certain philosophical ideas or ideals. These may have a Hindu, Buddhist, or Jain flavor. Perhaps, one day, the West will have its own form of "spiritual" Yoga, which then can be expected to have its own distinct philosophical coloring. Whatever form Yoga will take, it will most certainly not be materialistic.

Some schools of Yoga, admittedly, have a stronger religious element than others. The main point, though, is that Yoga comprises many approaches. Each approach is tailored to a particular personality type—the thinker, the man (or woman) of action, the performer of rituals, the heart-oriented person, the individual who enjoys singing or chanting, and certainly the contemplative, as well as the person who has strong monastic tendencies.

Yoga comes in three basic *forms* depending on the culture with which it is most closely associated: the Hindu, the Jain, and the Buddhist. These three are *not* religions, as often thought. All three are associated with their own distinct language, alphabet, architecture, art, scripture, and social customs. In this book, we will focus exclusively on Hindu Yoga, which is best known in the West. Increasingly, though, Buddhist Yoga—especially in the form of Tibetan Buddhism—is becoming popular. The Dalai Lama, who is commonly seen as *the* spokesman for Tibetan Buddhism, has much to do with this success. This has been especially so since he was awarded the Nobel Peace Prize in 1989—a most remarkable accomplishment for the political and spiritual leader of a remote country whose takeover and suppression by the Chinese has been all but ignored in the West. We in the Western world seem to take liberally from Tibetan Buddhism, but seldom reciprocate.

Each *form* of Yoga has many *branches,* which in turn encompass many *lineages* or *schools.* Thus, Hindu Yoga has seven major branches: Raja-Yoga (the path of contemplation), Hatha-Yoga (the path of physical transformation), Jnana-Yoga (the path of knowledge), Karma-Yoga (the path of ego-free action), Bhakti-Yoga (the path of the heart), Mantra-Yoga (the path of mantric repetition), and Tantra-Yoga (the path of ritual). Each branch is represented in the West to one degree or another by various schools. The most widespread branch in our part of the world is Hatha-Yoga, which is virtually synonymous with postural practice.

In India, this branch is far more inclusive and shares the spiritual goal with all other branches of Yoga. It also includes meditation techniques, breath control, and mantra recitation.

Jnana-Yoga is rarely practiced in our part of the world, and if it is, this path is often reduced to spiritual *talk* rather than actual practice. Even rarer is the great path of Raja-Yoga with its eight "limbs," as codified in the *Yoga-Sutra* of Patanjali, the Indian sage of about 200 A.D. Still less common is Bhakti-Yoga, and hardly anyone is familiar with the actual practice of Karma-Yoga.

The most controversial branch is Tantra-Yoga, or simply Tantra, which in the Western world (and increasingly also in India) has become almost completely and misleadingly sexualized. Originally, however, Tantra was designed and practiced as an approach utilizing the transformative power of ritual and visualization. We will talk about each of these branches—and more—in this book.

Some religious practitioners may feel nervous when they hear about Hindu Yoga, primarily when they think of multiple gods (which are, however, more like the angels of their own faith) and "pagan" rituals. It's important to note that these belong to the *culture* of Hinduism and there is no need to adopt them when we practice Yoga.

Whatever religious or non-religious framework we adopt in order to pursue Yoga, we must base our practice on the principle of reality.

> *From the unreal lead me to the real,*
> *from darkness lead me to light...*

The above declaration is a guiding ideal expressed in a very old text written in the Sanskrit language—an ideal that Yoga embraces completely.

Yogic spirituality is about reality. If you can face reality, you will find traditional Yoga—which is spiritual discipline—meaningful. You can safely read on! If you have some preferred *version* of reality in your head onto which you wish to cling, then this is the point where you ought to either close this book or bravely and open-mindedly read on anyway.

2. The Secret of Change

We are subject to change from the moment we are conceived to the moment we die. We grow physically and mentally in the span of our life. If we are fortunate and take the initiative, we also grow spiritually.

Change is inside and around us. We cannot think of life without change. Yet, many people have a problem with change. When life is good to them, they want things to stay the same. When they encounter "bad" experiences, they want time to move rapidly ahead. Sitting nervously in the waiting room of a dentist's office is a classic example. Time seems to stand still, and we want the whole experience over and done with. This attitude is, however, quite unrealistic. The minutes click by as they will. We have control only over our internal sense of time, which is forged by the mind.

We can relate *consciously* to the inevitability of change and engage change as deliberate self-transformation. This lies in fact at the heart of all spiritual disciplines, including Yoga. Self-transformation means meeting life consciously, with wide-open eyes, and seeing it as an ever available opportunity to make positive changes in ourselves—from mastering our nicotine or alcohol addiction, to overcoming constant feelings of guilt or inadequacy, to becoming friendlier and more helpful toward others. The field of possible conscious change is wide open.

As spiritual practitioners, we work on ourselves not just because others want us to, or because we want to move ahead in life, but because we see the advantage in gaining control over our mind and destiny and becoming a benign presence in the world. When we have mastered our own mind, we are inwardly balanced and not subject to the whims of the ego. We are able to take into account the needs of others.

One idea in Yoga that is seldom mentioned by contemporary practitioners is that of benefiting the world. (Many modern Yoga practitioners seem too preoccupied with their own problems.) In the *Bhagavad-Gita* (3.20), a Sanskrit text from over 2,000 years ago, this idea is called *loka-samgraha*, which means something like "pulling together the world." We pull the world together by promoting the welfare of all. This can mean elevating the world socially or spiritually.

We think here of individuals like Mother Teresa and Mahatma Gandhi in India, or Martin Luther King and, before him, Hugh Burnett in North America. Each served people in his or her own way but always bearing the larger good in mind.

Mother Teresa, who died in 1997 at the age of eighty-seven, was a Catholic nun of Albanian descent and a Nobel laureate (1979). She chose to serve the poor, sick, and dying in Calcutta tirelessly for forty-five years.

Mohandas Karamchand Gandhi, better known as "Mahatma" (great soul) was an Indian national and a lawyer, who resisted British rule in India. He was at the center of the Indian independence movement and was assassinated in 1948 for his political convictions.

Martin Luther King, an African-American, was a Baptist minister and civil rights leader. He, too, was assassinated at the young age of thirty-nine. And he, too, received the Nobel Peace Prize in 1964. Following the example of Gandhi, he employed non-violent means to achieve his political goals.

Hugh Burnett was an African-Canadian who descended from slaves and, apart from working as a carpenter, was a dedicated civil rights leader. His carpentry business was boycotted when he stood up against racial discrimination, which had been abolished by law but was observed selectively in the Canadian province of Ontario.

In the *Bhagavad-Gita*, the enlightened master Krishna promoted the ideal of *loka-samgraha*. Although he supported the war between two tribes and their allies, his yogic teaching was designed to bring the people together and instil both peace and tranquility. The *Bhagavad-Gita* is a "must-read" along with the *Yoga-Sutra*. These two Sanskrit scriptures are in fact widely studied in Western Yoga circles.

3. The Mind: Agent of Change

Our culture places a premium on the mind. At the same time, however, we don't acknowledge the degree to which the mind shapes our destiny. Yet, this fact is easy to see. The mind allows us to interpret reality correctly or wrongly. We know from psychology that perception, which tells us how things are around us, is loaded with mental assumptions. Most of the time, we don't really see things as they are. We literally make things up or distort them. Often this doesn't matter. But sometimes it has grievous consequences for us and others.

We may dismiss, suppress, or even, as was the case with the German Nazis or the followers of Saddam Hussein, seek to exterminate an entire ethnic group. Or we may, based on our interpretation of reality, go to war and kill, or see no problem with mowing down virgin forests and allowing many species of plants and animals to become extinct. In an as yet unpublished manuscript, entitled *Empower Your Change*, we wrote:

> There is also the remarkable effect of the so-called placebo ("I shall please") effect, which is involved in all medical interventions. This is the curious "mind over matter" phenomenon, which leads to health improvement that cannot be explained by the medical or pharmacological intervention itself but depend on the patient's positive mindset. Thus, a fake knee surgery can improve or completely cure a serious knee problem. Or the kind attitude and verbal encouragement of the physician can work physical and psychological wonders. The placebo effect, which works in about 35% of cases, can last for months and even years.

Everything we know is filtered through the mind. As the placebo effect shows, this can be to our advantage. Often it is not.

The mind can also slay. It can hold us back. Spiritual ignorance is likely to give us the wrong picture of the world, which then prevents us from taking the first step on the spiritual path. Instead of moving toward inner freedom, we become more enmeshed in "unfreedom," or what is called "bondage."

Thus, having the right view is crucial. And the right view can be gleaned from the teachings of the great masters, who are spiritual experts. Our faith in experts shows that we value the opinions of those we believe to be in the know. We would do well to extend the same faith to the "opinions" of spiritual adepts. In fact, we should trust them more readily than we trust technical experts. The masters have nothing at stake, whereas an expert can be governed by self-interest, and often he or she is indeed self serving. Experts can be, and have been, hired to misinform the public. Witness the fiasco over whether smoking cigarettes damages health or not. The verdict has been out for some time. Hired experts and the industry were lying for years. This would not happen with the great masters; they can be relied upon to tell the truth.

Although spiritual teachings show considerable variation, they share a common ground of growth through wisdom. We can, therefore, trust them enough to launch our spiritual pilgrimage. The more we are able to suspend our preconceptions, predispositions, and emotional partialities, we will come to know reality. To know reality "as it is" is one of the objectives of Yoga.

For growth in Yoga to happen, we must understand our mind. When we use the word "self-knowledge," we refer to the workings of the mind. *Our* mind. Self-knowledge has the quality of wisdom, which is liberating.

4. Traditional Yoga Today

Yoga was invented and developed in the rural areas of India. Its social and cultural environment was starkly different from that of our own time. How, then, can Yoga be meaningful to us today? This is an all-important question, and we will attempt to answer it as clearly as we can.

Our lifestyles have become far more hectic than that of pre-modern India. We no longer allow ourselves the "luxury" of quietude. Most people live in overcrowded and horribly noisy and polluted cities with endless distractions. Our mentality has adjusted accordingly. We are restless, agitated, ambitious, distracted, and wanting to hoard ever more consumer goods while staying as comfortable and unchallenged as possible. But despite our luxurious lifestyle, true contentment escapes us.

At the same time, however, we are more dissatisfied and unhealthy than ever, and we hunger for a meaningful life. Other than this, it's difficult to see that humanity has changed significantly since the beginning of civilization. We certainly know more in terms of science, but our mind has not changed in fundamental ways from the time the sages of India formulated the principles of a sound and wholesome way of life. We are still suffering from anger, fear, greed, envy, jealousy, and all the other negative emotions that our ancestors suffered as well. We experience joy and sadness, pleasure and displeasure, contentment and grief, and so on. We have preferences, prejudices, preconceptions, likes and dislikes, as did our forebears long ago. For the most part, we still don't know how to deal with negative as well as positive mental states in a way that leads to balance, integration, and self acceptance. To be able to do so is one of the preliminary purposes of Yoga.

The teachings of Yoga can undoubtedly help at various levels—mind, body and spirit. How we use those teachings, however, is up to us. Some people settle exclusively on postural practice to trim their posteriors, stretch their tendons, or strengthen their muscles, while others enlist mantra practice or meditation to unwind and keep fit, or restore their health. A few employ Yoga for spiritual sustenance and inner growth.

Both Georg and I have taken up the path for essentially spiritual purposes, and have been grateful that we plunged into this venture when we were enthusiastic and idealistic, but still too young to really understand the depth of the commitment and sacrifices that would be expected of us. Over the decades, Yoga has been keeping us on the right track and definitely has helped us mature on the spiritual path. For many years, Georg stumbled along in his Yoga practice and understanding, but periodically a kind-hearted teacher would show up to help him out of a dead end of his own making and point him in the right direction again. Brenda found her teacher later in life. Gradually, the path has become clearer for us, and the stumbling has become more subtle. But spiritual life is necessarily a learning experience, an uphill path. It is just that we become more capable of adjusting to the rarefied air of the higher ranges of the climb.

To engage Yoga properly, we must be willing to embrace life-positive change. Even if all you desire from Yoga is to trim and strengthen your body, this implies you want to change (change your physical body, that is). If you want to employ Yoga to settle your emotions or balance your mind, you must be willing to transform your mind. This is not easy. Self-transformation is challenging and inconvenient. It calls for attentive self-discipline 24/7 and a basic willingness to explore yourself—even the dark niches of your mind.

But anyone who values knowledge in the form of self-knowledge will not reject adherence to this difficult path. Several years ago, Georg came up with Twelve Steps to explain this side of Yoga, which we want to share in a modified version in the next chapter.

5. The Twelve Steps of Spiritual Recovery

The following Twelve Steps, rephrased for our purposes here, are modeled after the AA program, which nowadays is widely used for all sorts of addictions—from nicotine to alcohol to sex, and more.

1. *We admit* the fact that we live our ordinary life only half awake, in something of a trance state, and that we normally deny this to ourselves.

2. *We begin to look and ask for guidance* in our effort to cultivate a new attitude of wakefulness. This means seeking out supportive people (such as those at a good Yoga center) and choosing uplifting reading material.

3. *We initiate positive changes* in our behavior, which affirm that new attitude, or outlook. It is not enough to read and talk about spiritual principles. We need to make our spirituality eminently practical by committing to a daily routine and an appropriate lifestyle.

4. *We practice self-understanding;* that is, we accept conscious responsibility for noticing our automatic (trance-like) programs and where they fall short of our new understanding of life.

5. *We make a commitment to undergo the purification* necessary to change our old mental and emotional patterns and stabilize the new outlook and disposition.

6. *We learn to be flexible* and open to life, so that we can continue to learn and grow on the basis of our new outlook. Openness should never be indiscriminate but be based on proper discernment.

7. *We practice humility* in the midst of our endeavors to mature spiritually. In this way we avoid the danger of ego inflation.

8. *We assume responsibility* for what we have understood about life and the principles of spiritual recovery, applying our understanding to all our relationships, so that we can be a benign influence in the world.

9. Guided by our new outlook and with the help of Yoga, *we work on the integration* of our mind.

10. *We conscientiously cultivate self-discipline* in all matters, great and small. This can be painstaking and inconvenient at times because we will be looking at our actions more closely on a ongoing basis.

11. *We increasingly practice* spiritual communion with the luminous part of ourselves through a regular meditation practice. Through this and through continued growth in self-understanding, we become gradually transparent to ourselves.

12. *We open ourselves* to the possibility of abiding happiness whereby self-centeredness is cleared away and we recover our true spiritual essence, which had been covered over. Through this awakening, the world becomes transparent to us, and we are made whole in the context of life.

Each branch of Yoga has its own version of the path. We will explain this shortly. But first we want to turn to an existential matter with which we are all too familiar but which, generally, we like to ignore: the fact of suffering.

6. Suffering Beyond Pain

We scrape our skin falling, and there is pain. We bump hard into a corner, and there is considerable pain. We have a hole in a tooth, and awful pain wells up, and when painkillers stop working, we finally run to the dentist. We break our arm, and there is excruciating pain. And so on. We can be certain that in the course of our life, even the healthiest person will experience pain occasionally.

As long as we are unenlightened, all of us experience suffering without fail. The enlightened can experience pain but have conquered suffering. So, what is suffering? Suffering is the kind of mental distress associated with pain—anger, animosity, grief, fear, anguish, sorrow, frustration, jealousy, envy, doubt, distrust, suspicion, resentment, bitterness. To give some practical examples: Suffering is when we find a bruise somewhere on our body for which we have no immediate explanation, and our mind fearfully drifts right away to thoughts of cancer. Or we have to sit for an academic test but feel utterly unprepared and worry about the result. Or we are painfully shy and dread being in large groups. Or our dreams are filled with unpleasant imagery. Or we mull over past bad experiences or anticipate them in the future. Or we have to put up with noise in the neighborhood, icy temperatures in winter and soaring temperatures in summer. Or we are forced to work at a job we find boring or stressful. Or, perhaps, we have to be around people we don't like or are obliged to be away from those we love.

Whether we experience pain or not, our life is full of suffering. Most of us remain blind to this fact and imagine that we have a "pretty good" life. We indulge in this fantasy until, suddenly, our life is interrupted by a major tragedy that stops us in our tracks. The greatest suffering is associated with death—the actual demise of a loved person or our own approaching death, which we fear.

The cause of suffering is the sense of "I," which refers both pleasant and unpleasant life experiences to itself. Suffering does not happen in the absence of the ego. Thus, an enlightened master may have physical pain but no suffering, because he or she has transcended the ego. He or she does not mull over his fate only because the body is aching or ailing. He or she does not overinterpret, or mentalize, the painful experiences of life. Pain is simply pain—a sense experience that is of little consequence.

For a spiritual seeker, who may have become somewhat aware and therefore sensitized, life may hold more of the quality of suffering than for the ordinary person, who is vital and steamrolls through with little awareness. The same is comparatively true with other species. For example, a bin full of worms that feed on and break down compost can probably experience pain but, as far as one can tell, they don't suffer. Your dog, however, does appear to suffer when he is denied more food. He may even look quite dejected. But the moment he is offered a bone or dog cookie, his eyes may noticeably brighten in an instant. And certainly one can witness various suffering-reactions in children. On a gloomy, rainy day, many children don't want to play outdoors and may look quite miserable, but the moment you tell them that there are cookies available, they suddenly cheer up.

The problem is that even positive experiences are potentially full of suffering—ponder the fact that a good experience will not last forever or that someone has a better experience than we do, and a subtle form of suffering starts. Or consider a child overwhelmed with choosing what they would like for a birthday or Christmas gift; the gifts seem to agitate the child's mind. Or think of an adult's reaction when he or she is presented with a gift that is less than expected. Disappointment is suffering, too.

The best medicine for suffering is equanimity, or inner calm. When we cultivate an even-tempered, balanced mind, we are immunizing ourselves against the mood of suffering. We just don't add suffering on top of pain or on top of some trauma. Instead, we are able to meet things as they are. A mole on your skin is not inevitably future cancer. Present cancer is not inevitably certain death. And so on. In equanimity, we don't unnecessarily elaborate. We don't let fear dominate our thinking. We don't fantasize or even neurotically project ahead.

Entire industries get rich on our anxieties: We are too fat, too unfit, too drab, too "uncool," too ignorant, etc. So, we set out to improve ourselves. But the efforts we must make to fit some imaginary ideal are formidable. They amount to a pointless struggle. Once upon a time, for example, being fat was the norm. Think of the Venus of Willendorf from the Stone Age! Then later, the cultural norm of "beauty" was having a wasp-like waist. At another time in history long dresses were in, only to be replaced decades later by the mini. Attempting to keep up with fashion styles becomes insane, because soon the fashion industry is controlling your mind.

Yoga is not about mere self-improvement, as normally understood. It focuses on real change, or self-transformation. If you want to strive, does it not make sense to struggle for something worthwhile?

Because Indian thought considers suffering to be a fundamental fact of life, Indian philosophy has often been deemed pessimistic by those who lacked a more thorough knowledge of its principles. What could be more positive than the ideal of spiritual freedom? As we will see, this ideal is written even into the value pyramid of Hinduism, which has liberation as its apex. The thought that we *can* overcome suffering is entirely optimistic. Yoga is essentially an optimistic path that puts the controls in your hands.

7. Raja-Yoga: The Path of Contemplation

The royal (*raja*) road of Yoga is intended for advanced practitioners. We mention this branch of Hindu Yoga up front because of its connection with the postural practice.

Raja-Yoga goes back to a sage named Patanjali—a name that is often heard in Yoga centers. He wrote a Sanskrit text called the *Yoga-Sutra*. (Many people say "*Yoga-Sutras*", because this work consists of 195 aphorisms, or *sutras*, on Yoga.) As with other Yoga authorities, Patanjali`s lifetime is not known precisely, but most scholars place him in the second century C.E.

His eightfold version of the yogic path consists of:

1. Moral disciplines (*yama*)
2. Self-restraint (*niyama*)
3. Postures (*asana*)
4. Breath control (*pranayama*)
5. Withdrawal of the senses (*pratyahara*)
6. Concentration (*dharana*)
7. Meditation (*dhyana*)
8. Ecstasy (*samadhi*)

As you can see, postural practice, which is the focus of much of modern Yoga, is really only the third step, or "limb." It is preceded by two very important sets of practices, which are generally ignored by the "mainstream" of modern Yoga. Practitioners who are respectful of the Yoga tradition would argue that without the inclusion of the moral disciplines, we should not expect to grow spiritually. In other words, the *yamas* need to be observed in some form or another to engage Yoga as a spiritual discipline. While these first two limbs are part of some Yoga teacher training programs, by no means are they present in all.

The moral disciplines of Yoga are basic moral values, which are found in all major religions of the world and can be endorsed by any sane person, whether of a religious or secular bent of mind.

According to Patanjali, the moral disciplines include the following five observances, which should be heeded under any circumstance and at all times: nonharming, truthfulness, nonstealing, chastity, and freedom from greed.

How is this different from religious commandments, you might ask? There is indeed a decisive difference. Yoga does not stipulate moral norms that we must obey to avoid divine punishment or win approval. The above-cited moral values—and others mentioned in other Yoga texts—are meant to simply regulate our social behavior, so that our spiritual endeavors can bear fruit.

One of the objections to Yoga by certain religious sects is that God is left out of consideration in all this, and that Yoga masters act under their own power. We would argue that such an assertion makes two unwarranted assumptions, namely that Yoga masters are necessarily godless or God-defying, and that a sensible moral provision means nothing unless God has sanctioned it.

Yama: The Five Moral Disciplines

1. We all can accept that nonharming—often called non-violence—is a sound principle. A society that allows harming others at will—a bit like movie portrayals of the Wild West—could not really function constructively; nor could a society that glorifies or allows lying and stealing. In our contemporary culture, matters are less clear when it comes to chastity and freedom from greed.

Nonharming (*ahimsa*) is extensive. Patanjali tells us that it happens physically, mentally, and also in speech. We recommend that a beginning Yoga student spends a fair amount of time considering *how* he or she might harm others—not just fellow humans but all beings, however miniscule and seemingly insignificant.

Such a serious consideration may well have repercussions in almost every area of your life, including: your choice of foods—such as whether these will include animal products, or fruits and vegetables that have been sprayed with pesticides, etc; your treatment of animals; your choices of entertainment for yourself and your children (like TV, or circus or zoo); your use of transportation that encourages environmental pollution; your support (or non-support) of political activities or social causes—like invasion, war, poverty.

2. *Untruthfulness* has many forms. We practice it when we lie about our age or some other personal detail. Some instances may seem insignificant and some we excuse by saying that "everybody does it." We speak of "insincerity," "misrepresentation" or "making a mistake" in order to soften the implications of the word "lying." But it is still dishonest.

3. Similarly *theft* (stealing) is widespread in our society and ranges from cheating on our taxes to accepting wrong change when it is in our favor. Could over-consumption be considered theft? Do we steal from the have-nots? And on and on.

4. About *chastity*... Patanjali was obviously an ascetic and wrote for ascetics who were dedicated to full-time Yoga practice. As an ascetic, he thought that abstention from sex was the best policy, and he didn't allow any wiggle room on this. But we know that for thousands of years, Yoga has included both ascetics and lay practitioners. Lay practitioners meant people who were married and had families; therefore, individuals who also engaged in sex. Since the contemporary Yoga movement consists almost entirely of lay folk, it is important to understand what *chastity* might mean in their case. Scriptures other than Patanjali's *Yoga-Sutra*, which was composed for hardcore ascetics, help us out on this point: For lay people, chastity means *disciplined* sexual activity. While we ought not to repress our sexual drive, we should also not simply indulge it at our whim. Mature self-inquiry will help us determine the best course in such matters, which must consider biological urge, consent, emotion, the role of the mind, and the situation.

5. *Freedom from greed* is not an easy consideration either, because greed is rampant in our contemporary society, which grossly over-consumes and socializes our children to start this unfortunate habit as early as possible. Georg has written at length about this vice and many others in his hard-hitting book *Yoga Morality*, which you might want to read down the road. For a beginning Yoga student, it is enough to know—if you don't know it already—that greed is involved in many of our modern habits and the destruction of the natural environment.

Georg and I have written about the environmental devastation and the role Yoga can play in creating a saner society, with an interest in restoring the health of our ailing environment. We address Hindu Yoga in our book *Green Yoga* (2007) and Buddhist Yoga in *Green Dharma* (2008), which is available on our website as an ebook at *www.traditionalyogastudies.com*.

Niyama

The second step of Patanjali's eightfold path is self-restraint (*niyama*). He understands this as having five components: purity, contentment, asceticism, study, and dedication to the lord.

Purity includes both physical and mental purity, and various schools of Yoga offer a wide range of purification exercises. *Contentment*—a rare virtue nowadays—is feeling satisfied with what one has. *Asceticism*, which may raise hackles in today's readers, is essentially an attitude of disciplining the body and the mind. Patanjali is very clear that this practice should not be a form of self-inflicted torture but be all-round beneficial. *Study* stands for immersing oneself in the wisdom of Yoga, so that we gain understanding as well as proper motivation.

The last practice of self-restraint is *dedication to the lord*, which is often interpreted as devotion to God. But, in Yoga, "the lord" is considered one among countless spiritual Selves, and so the term "God" is not entirely applicable, although we can understand it in this way. Certainly, contemporary practitioners who already have made a religious commitment can take this virtue to mean simply dedication to a spiritual ideal.

Asana

We need not say much about *asana*: *posture*, the third step, because this practice is prominent in almost every Western Yoga center. For Patanjali, it still meant no more than the most convenient posture for meditation. He did not even mention the health benefits from postural practice that are emphasized today.

Pranayama

Breath control is conscious control over the otherwise automatic function of breathing. Yoga masters discovered early on that the breath and the mind are intimately linked and that by carefully regulating the breathing rhythm, we can effectively calm the mind.

Pratyahara

Sense-withdrawal—sometimes referred to as sensory inhibition—is control over our sensory functions, so that the senses (sight, hearing, smell, taste, and touch) do not carry our attention away at random. Sometimes we become totally absorbed in meditating upon a chosen object, that is, we are unaware of what is going on in the outside world.

Dharana

Concentration is sustained focusing of the mind in preparation of meditation.

Dhyana

Meditation is allowing the mind to dwell in a relaxed and almost effortless manner on the selected object of concentration.

Samadhi

When it occurs, *ecstasy* happens spontaneously by growing out of sustained meditation. The essence of ecstasy consists in a seamless merging with the object of meditation. If your object of meditation is, for instance, the thought of your pet dog, you experience becoming one with your dog. If your object is something more elevated, you find yourself at one with it too. This is an extraordinary experience, which is generally accompanied by an overwhelming feeling of ease and happiness. Little wonder that many people confuse ecstasy with freedom. An unexpectedly large number of people experience ecstasy or ecstasy-like states without the least preparation and without taking psychedelic drugs. Often, they benefit from such states, but sometimes they are just confused by them. It is clearly better to be prepared for this eventuality by the systematic practice of Yoga.

It is important to realize that ecstasy is *not* the end of the yogic journey. Rather, the grand goal is spiritual liberation, which is also called "enlightenment." This is not merely a temporary experience but a state of being that cannot be lost. It is who you are!

As you can appreciate, the eight steps mapped out by Patanjali do not fulfill themselves overnight. Success in Yoga comes with dedicated *lifelong* practice. Anyone promising "enlightenment" in a weekend, or even as a "sure thing," is plainly a charlatan. Save yourself the expense and settle down to practicing Yoga step by careful step.

Georg took his first baby steps in Yoga at the age of thirteen and, after fifty years of practice, he still did not claim to be enlightened. Some told him that he had become more compassionate. If true, he was happy, because for him compassion counted for a lot more than the ability to meditate, recite complicated mantras, spout Sanskrit quotations, or go into ecstasy at the drop of a hat. Brenda started with Yoga postures as a young child when she was practicing along with Kareen Zebroff on TV. Later on, she taught Yoga for many years in Saskatchewan and gradually also became aware of the spirituality of Yoga. Like Georg, she also cannot claim to have become enlightened, though people think she is a compassionate person.

What we both *could* claim, however, is that we have learned a lot about ourselves and have become clear about the path and clear about the spiritual goal. And that, in turn, deepened our commitment to continue in Yoga, transforming ourselves more and more, becoming clearer vehicles for shining forth the light at the heart of all beings.

8. Hatha-Yoga: The Path of Physical Transformation

Hatha Yoga is assumed to be the most widely practiced Yoga in the West. But, really, there is a big difference between contemporary efforts going by the name of "Hatha-Yoga" and traditional Hatha-Yoga, as it emerged in India perhaps a thousand years ago. *Hatha* means force, and Hatha-Yoga has been correctly translated as "Forceful Yoga." But, as we will explain shortly, the word *hatha* also has a hidden, or esoteric, meaning.

When we examine the medieval Sanskrit texts on Hatha-Yoga, we find that this branch of Yoga is not just about postures, as widely taught in the West. Traditional Hatha-Yoga really offers a full path all its own, which is not unlike the eightfold path of Raja-Yoga. It features ethical considerations (though they are not always listed as a separate category) and aims at the lofty ideal of spiritual freedom. Although its repertoire includes many postures, so-called "seals" and "locks," Hatha-Yoga primarily revolves around the control of the breath and the mind. "Seals" are postures that hold the energy within the body, and the three types of "locks" are maneuvers that have essentially the same purpose.

Hatha-Yoga also has a good many purification practices, including diet. These are rarely to be found in contemporary Hatha-Yoga. Yet, in any type of traditional Yoga, for instance, diet is decisive, and an organic vegetarian diet is preferred for health and ethical reasons. More and more Western physicians are telling us the same, because most beef is shot through with bovine growth hormones and antibiotics, and fish is full of mercury because of the increasing pollution of the oceans, lakes, and rivers. For a Yoga practitioner, there is also the vital issue of the well-documented brutality involved in raising livestock.

Having said this, we also acknowledge that vegetarianism is not possible for everyone. There are regions in the world where it is simply not possible to grow or obtain vegetables, and where we (the authors) must practice nonharming in the form of tolerance.

The high art of meditation, which is integral to the practice of Hatha-Yoga, is pursued as a kind of visualization; and enlightenment—the supreme goal—is understood as a matter of totally transforming the physical body into a body of light. Historically, Hatha-Yoga was closely connected with alchemy and regarded the body as an alchemical cauldron in which the *yogin* skillfully mixed the body's energies.

From Tantra, Hatha-Yoga inherited the notion that consciousness has an energetic aspect. These two interrelated realities (consciousness and energy) are in actuality undivided. In the ordinary person, however, they are polarized in the body. Consciousness is associated with the crown of the head and the energetic aspect is located in potential form at the base of the spine. This energy must be activated, or "awakened," and conducted along the body's central axis to the crown, where it merges with consciousness. This merging yields a high state of ecstasy.

This energy is known as the "coiled power," "serpent power," or *kundalini*. When the energy at the base is carefully led up to the crown mainly by means of breath control and concentration, the resulting state of ecstasy takes the *yogin* beyond the brain-dependent mind. Since the *kundalini* energy tends to sink back to a dormant state at the base of the spine, it must be activated and returned to the crown over and over again. When this is done, the whole body becomes transformed into a body of light. This is not just meant symbolically. There are many stories of *yogins* actually accomplishing this feat, the most famous being Ramalinga Swami of South India in the twentieth century. The "body of light" is known in various religio-spiritual traditions around the world, including Christianity, where it is known among mystics as the "resurrection body" or the "body of glory."

The polarity between consciousness and its energetic aspect is associated with the seven (or more) energetic centers called *cakras,* which, "like blossoms on a stem," are aligned along the spinal column and correspond (but are *not* identical with) the nerve plexuses. The most important center is located at the crown of the head, the place of consciousness, which is the focus of many meditation techniques.

The awakening of the *kundalinī* energy is brought about by the union of two energetic currents—esoterically called "sun" (represented by the syllable *ha*) and "moon" (represented by the syllable *tha*). Many people think that these two syllables *mean* "sun" and "moon," but this is incorrect. The former current is connected with the breath flowing through the right nostril and the latter with the breath flowing through the left nostril. But the combination of the two currents gives us the hidden meaning of the word *hatha* (pronounced "hut-ha"!), as indicated earlier.

9. Jnana-Yoga: The Path of Knowledge

This branch of Yoga is at the heart of a tradition called "Vedanta," which was first taught in the ancient *Upanishads* (esoteric Sanskrit texts that were originally taught by word of mouth only). Jnana-Yoga was formulated almost in opposition to the old Indian school of ritualism. It put forward knowledge (*jnana*), or wisdom, as the means to inner freedom. The knowledge in question is *not* conventional or scientific knowledge but insight into the difference between the real and the unreal (false or illusory). The real is said to lead us to inner freedom, while the unreal keeps us entrapped in all the many things that distract us from finding out who we truly are beyond the name or religious affiliation given to us at birth, the occupation by which we earn our livelihood, the political membership we have chosen, and so on.

Jnana-Yoga is based on the understanding that all the countless things we perceive are in reality one. This is a difficult concept to comprehend. People who have experimented with psychedelic drugs have an easier time to understand this, which is not to say that we recommend such drugs. There are states of consciousness in which the distinction between the experiencer (i.e., you) and the experienced world is lifted. Subject and object are merged. Now, according to Jnana-Yoga, the ultimate realization, or spiritual liberation, is *not* merely an experience; it is not a mental state that can be acquired or lost. Spiritual liberation *is* reality. And reality is forever. Normally, what we see as reality (i.e., our personality and the world) is really a product of the *un*enlightened mind. Our experience of separate things (a tree, a mountain, a lake, etc.) is illusory. The sense of "I" is also illusory. We mysteriously identify with a particular ("our") mind and a particular ("our") body. In truth, we are the Self. Everyone is the same Self. Everyone is the same essence of the world. Beyond, behind, or beneath the multitude of forms is one Supreme Identity, and we are all that One.

A classic illustration of this unity is this: An empty earthen pot (our body-mind) is surrounded by space (the Self). The same space also exists inside the pot. When the pot is shattered (i.e., when the body-mind dies), the inner and outer space continues as before.

Jnana-Yoga revolves around the recognition that our innermost essence, the Self (*atman*), is really beyond the mind. Moreover, that Self is also the essence of the world (*brahman*). Thus we get the fundamental formula: *atman = brahman*.

In some works, the path of Jnana-Yoga consisted of three aspects: (1) listening carefully to the oral instructions of one's teacher; (2) pondering the metaphysical truths received from one's teacher, and (3) meditating deeply on those truths until the Self is realized. The *yogin* of this path endeavours to be constantly mindful of the truth that there is only one reality.

In the fifteenth century, the path of Jnana-Yoga was elaborated in the *Vedanta-Sara* ("Essence of Vedanta") to comprise four principal means: (1) discernment (*viveka*) between the real and the unreal; (2) renunciation of whatever reward may derive from one's activities; (3) the "six accomplishments" consisting of tranquillity, restraint of one's senses, abstention from irrelevant activity, patience, mental concentration, and faith (which we may interpret as a positive attitude to life), and (4) the urge toward liberation, or enlightenment.

This is a demanding spiritual path, which calls for great mental clarity, integrity, and staying power. Otherwise it remains at the level of an intellectual game. It is not enough to affirm "I am That"—a common mantra or significator of non-duality used by practitioners of this way. We must also *feel this deeply* and, above all, realize or *be* this. By extension, we must live that way. Jnana-Yoga is often said to be particularly suited for intellectuals. In our experience, this is not so. Intellectuals tend to intellectualize everything, including Yoga. This, the Sanskrit sources tell us, will not get us very far; certainly not to freedom.

It may be more correct to call Jnana-Yoga the path of wisdom rather than knowledge. (The term *jnana* can mean either "knowledge" or "wisdom" and has been translated in a yogic context in both ways.) Many people today understand "knowledge," which is about information. But "wisdom" is something else. It has a living quality and can affect our life directly, in a significant way. Knowledge, on the other hand, can at times be worthless information. So, as you approach the path of Jnana-Yoga make sure you don't confuse the two but stick with life-transforming wisdom.

10. Karma-Yoga: The Path of Ego-Free Action

Raja-Yoga and Jnana-Yoga are obviously demanding approaches. Not everyone is capable of pursuing them. But the Yoga tradition also includes less challenging paths. One of them is Karma-Yoga, which was first formulated in the *Bhagavad-Gita* a little over 2,000 years ago. *Karma* (or *karman,* which is the grammatical stem) means literally "action." In the West, we generally understand this word "karma" in the sense of "destiny." The connection between action and destiny is this: All self-centered action has far-reaching consequences. That kind of action keeps us "bound," that is, it reinforces our state of "unenlightenment," or "un-wisdom."

Karma-Yoga is based on the recognition that to be alive means to be active. We cannot avoid all action. Our eyes see, our ears hear, our brain sends signals to every part of the body, and our lungs breathe. The Hindu sages realized that it is impossible to fulfill the ancient ideal of renouncing the world completely. Even when we decide to live in a remote mountain cave or a jungle, we cannot avoid all action. At the very least, we must feed our body to prevent disease and death.

The idea behind Karma-Yoga, then, is very simple: Cultivate only actions that are *not* self-centered and also are appropriate in the largest sense of the term. Self-centeredness is understood broadly as (1) acting from an unenlightened (and therefore inevitably egoic) perspective, (2) having selfish motives, and (3) hoping consciously or unconsciously for a reward or personal benefit.

What is appropriate action? Generally speaking, this is activity that maintains your or someone else's existence (eating, drinking, sleeping, keeping warm, etc.), or that fulfills one's accepted roles or tasks (such as parenting or being a responsible worker), and so on. This is not considered selfish in the sense of self-centered. The best activity focuses on your own and others' material, moral, mental, and spiritual welfare, *but* without getting the ego involved.

There are numerous people who do good in the world, who may even be called "saints." Yet, if there is the least shred of selfish motivation or expectation in their noble activity, they cannot be called *karma-yogins*. Selfish motivation is difficult to determine, because some of our seemingly blameless motivations have less respectable undercurrents. For instance, we may engage in charitable work because this gives *us* joy or because we "inherited" a humanitarian tendency from a parent, or because we want to favor a particular group with which we emotionally identify (like "our" sports team). Thus, even Karma-Yoga entails a good deal of subtle self-inspection (or discernment). It is, then, simple in theory but not necessarily in practice.

In our own era, an important aspect of Karma-Yoga concerns our natural environment. The ecosystem is at the brink of collapse—50,000 animal and plant species become extinct every year! This is uniquely different from the past, and so we also must find new ways of responding to the natural catastrophe around us. We are called to make our Karma-Yoga relevant to the world at large. We have discussed this at some length in our book *Green Yoga* (mainly for Hindu *yogins* and *yoginis*) and *Green Dharma* (primarily but not exclusively for Buddhist *yogins* and *yoginis*).

Specifically, we are challenged to come up with ways to reduce our personal impact on the environment ("our footprint"). Such challenges may include not driving so much or flying only when absolutely necessary, or not over-consuming while others are literally starving from hunger, or using up water while others have only dirty water to drink, and so on. These are undoubtedly challenging measures. But a *karma-yogin* or *-yogini* does what he or she can do to reduce the suffering of others, regardless of where these others live in the world.

Our Karma-Yoga, then, can be all-embracing and as broad as the world itself.

11. Bhakti-Yoga: The Path of the Heart

This is the most "religious" branch of Yoga, which involves belief in a personal deity, who is the one absolute reality. *Bhakti* means "devotion," which is often understood in the sense of "love." Thus the *Bhagavad-Gita*, which also gave us Karma-Yoga, taught that the devotional path is the highest. The one reality was called Vishnu ("Pervasive one"), who was thought to have had many divine incarnations (*avatara*), such as Krishna and Rama, but also incarnations as nonhuman beings. (Other "schools"—lines of transmission from teacher to student within the various branches of Yoga—place God Shiva or Goddess Shri at the head of creation as the ultimate Divine.)

Well known texts of the *bhakti* approach are the two *Bhakti-Sutras* and also a massive work called the *Bhagavata-Purana*, which focuses on Krishna. Westerners have become familiar with Krishna and Krishna devotion through the Krishna Consciousness movement, which goes back to a *bhakti* master of the late-fifteenth to early-sixteenth century.

Bhakti-Yoga involves typical religious practices, such as worship, chanting songs in praise of the Divine, prostrations in front of an image of God, telling and listening to edifying stories about God, and so on. A very common practice is recitation (*japa*) of the name of God, which is a means to bring the mind closer to God. All these practices have their relative equivalents in other faith traditions. We should, therefore, regard them with respect.

On the *bhakti* path, the devotee is encouraged to feel a growing passion for the Divine. This passion is deemed yogically legitimate, as it is free from self-centeredness. It culminates in a condition in which the *yogin* or *yogini* enters the immediate presence of the Divine. This is understood as "supreme devotion."

Many Westerners who already have a commitment to Christianity or Judaism, for example, may not be immediately attracted to Hindu Bhakti-Yoga. Many others, like those who have left behind all ritual expressions from the traditions into which they were born, may react strongly against religious beliefs and practices of any kind. Therefore, Bhakti-Yoga may be the least likely Yoga path for a Western-educated person to follow. Yet, some Yoga centers have images of Hindu deities, notably the elephant-headed Ganesha, who is understood as a remover of obstacles. We need not feel compelled to worship Ganesha or any other Hindu deity but can simply regard them as symbols of everyone's true spiritual potential.

Of course, some Westerners—who have become alienated from their early religious roots—find Bhakti-Yoga attractive even without joining a sect or traditional lineage. What is found attractive is that Bhakti-Yoga addresses the heart. This is not as outlandish as it sounds. As researchers have discovered, the heart is an important nervous center and has billions of neurons, which make it intelligent. The heart and the brain undoubtedly have to work together to produce a balanced human being. Even the most fervent Jnana-Yoga practitioner must have some quality of devotion or love to succeed on his or her path.

12. Mantra-Yoga: The Path of Potent Sound

Another technically easy path is Mantra-Yoga. This approach most often consists primarily in the more or less constant recitation of a *mantra* (a potent sound), such as *om*, or a longer phrase, such as *shivo'ham* (literally, "I am Shiva"), which actually means "I am the one reality." Alternatively, Mantra-Yoga encompasses a more complex path, comprised of sixteen "limbs." These limbs include posture, controlled breathing, concentration, meditation, ecstasy, and a range of ritual practices.

We will discuss here only the repetition of a *mantra*, which has become a very popular practice among Western students of Yoga. This Sanskrit word, *mantra*, which has entered our English dictionaries, is explained as "that which protects the mind." A *mantra* protects the mind by keeping it focused on the spiritual process, instead of allowing it to wander from thought to thought, or flit from experience to experience. Outside of meditation, it is notoriously difficult to be mindful, and we tend to get lost in automatic (unconscious) thinking, which is unproductive.

Mindful (attentive) recitation of a *mantra* can be done aloud, whispered, or even recited mentally. Beginners would do well to repeat their chosen *mantra* out loud, or at least whispered. Later on, they can switch to mental recitation. Recitation of a *mantra* so that you yourself can hear it has the advantage of giving you feedback through the ears. Then, when you stop your recitation, or find that you are mispronouncing it or saying it completely without any attention, you will become aware of this more quickly. Mental recitation does not have the same feedback, and you can get lost in thought (that is, go semi-conscious) far more readily.

The popular *mantra* "*om*" stands for the ultimate reality, however it may be conceived. You can conceive it as representing the ultimate nameless reality, the Godhead, or the Supreme Self. The main idea behind it is that there is something greater than you. The *om* (or *aum*) sound, by the way, has no *literal* meaning.

Ordinarily, a *mantra* is given by one's spiritual teacher. But, short of this, you can use whatever sound is meaningful to you. Of course, it would be undesirable to adopt a *mantra* that has spiritually negative or questionable connotations, such as "enmity" or "E = mc²," or "I will succeed in my business." A *mantra* is supposed to help in your *spiritual* unfolding.

The biggest hurdle on the mantric path is boredom and the dullness of semi-consciousness. This is also a major obstacle in the practice of meditation. The mind, especially in modern times, expects to be constantly entertained. It wants distraction. So, when boredom sets in, it is best to remind oneself why one is practicing Yoga at all. We want to master the mind so that it does not blindly follow the senses, which give us any number of sensations that we then pursue: the television program, gossip, advertising billboard, or unnecessary and distracting information.

Normally, we allow the mind to do as it will. In Yoga, we seek to enlist it for the spiritual work. As the *Amrita-Bindu-Upanishad* (2) reminds us:

> The mind alone is the cause of bondage and liberation for humans. Attached to objects, (it leads) to bondage; freed from objects, it is said (to lead) to liberation.

13. Tantra-Yoga: The Path of Continuity

Tantra is the most difficult branch of Yoga, which we also describe as "the path of ritual," because rituals play an important part in most schools of Tantra. But the essential aspect of this approach is found in the Sanskrit term *tantra* itself, which means something like "continuity." What is implied in this is that Tantra-Yoga has at its center the recognition that there is no split between the ultimate reality and our ordinary reality. These are thought to be one and the same, although we experience them as radically distinct. All depends on one's perspective or state of consciousness. An enlightened adept sees the world as the one reality, whereas an unenlightened person views the world as unenlightened and regards the one reality as a goal in some other realm or future time.

"Continuity" means that the liberation—or "heaven"—to which we aspire is *here and now*. It is just that our unenlightened mind prefers to look upon the world as made up of so many good or bad things, people, or experiences. Then we struggle to realize liberation, the Self, or God beyond this world, thereby setting up a false dualism.

Tantra emerged about 500 C.E. and culminated about five centuries later. It was widely disseminated throughout India and has thousands of primary and secondary texts of which a small percentage is still available. The primary texts also bear the name *Tantra*.

Tantra's success was partly due to the fact that it presented itself as a new revelation meant for the "dark age" of the present era of the world. According to this teaching, there are four world ages that appear in cyclic fashion: a golden age in which spiritual values are foremost; a second world age in which spirituality is somewhat dimmer; a third world age, which involves a further physical, moral, and mental deterioration, and then the dark age in which ignorance, delusion, and especially the negative emotion of greed reign supreme. The last-mentioned world age reminds one of our own era. Spiritual practice, consisting above all in the mental discipline of mindfulness is particularly difficult in the dark age (known as *kali-yuga*).

Tantra evolved to help people of the dark age. The revelation of an earlier age was deemed too challenging, and so Tantra developed simpler spiritual practices, notably *mantra* recitation. In actual fact, some of its other methods, especially rituals, are just as demanding as the ancient methods.

Tantra believed that people of the dark age, which supposedly began in 3,002 B.C.E. and will be in effect for many more millennia, would be grasping for straws. Therefore, the Tantric masters allowed any kind of spiritual means, including sexuality. Many schools of Tantra employed methods that mainstream Hindu society considered questionable and even offensive. But the existence of such schools must not blind us to the fact that Tantra has contributed much to Hindu society and culture.

Tantra is a powerful tool, but it has unfortunately been reduced by Westerners to a sexual procedure, which misleadingly goes by the name of "Tantra-Yoga." Georg has dubbed it "Neo-Tantra," as it has little to do with genuine spirituality and a lot with "New Age" thought. Regrettably, some of those who sell Neo-Tantra as a commodity have been quoting Georg's earlier positive comments about authentic Tantra out of context, to give their potential victims the impression that he is favoring their approach; he is *not*. Neither is Brenda.

Years ago, Georg thought that perhaps Neo-Tantra, under skilful guidance, could help those who wanted to sort out their sexual problems. This opinion was entirely too generous and too optimistic. People with sexual problems should see a therapist!

Anyone delving deeper into Hatha-Yoga will inevitably encounter Tantric concepts and practices, some of which we have mentioned earlier. Few people, however, will ever engage Tantra more seriously, because it is incredibly challenging and requires that one adopts many cultural forms and symbols of Hinduism. It remains an esoteric teaching and, unlike Karma-Yoga, requires the guidance and supervision from an initiated teacher.

14. The Teacher: Helper on the Threshold

There are all kinds of teachers. Some pass on useful knowledge or information that allows us to live life more skilfully or competently or that is simply interesting or fascinating. But the traditional teacher of Yoga has a different purpose: His or her goal is to awaken us from our everyday trance, or semi-conscious state, and set us free. Such a teacher is called *guru* (if male) or *gurani* (if female). This Sanskrit term means literally "weighty one." According to an esoteric explanation, the two syllables of the word *guru* suggest "dispeller" (*ru*) of "darkness" (*gu*). Thus, a *guru* is someone who, by virtue of his or her own realization, is qualified to guide us beyond spiritual ignorance, which is ignorance of our true nature and the true nature of the world.

Since realization rarely means "full realization," or "enlightenment," we must not expect every guru to be able to lead us all the way to spiritual liberation. Generally, a guru can take us only as far as he or she has travelled. Yet, he can always point us in the right direction. He *will* do so if he legitimately bears the title *guru*.

Often, a guru is part of a teaching lineage of an entire chain of gurus, and is given permission to teach by his own immediate guru. That's why it is important to have a teacher who belongs to a teaching lineage. Otherwise. anyone can call himself a "guru," which has been a problem in Eastern and Western countries.

Most Yoga centers have Yoga teachers or instructors rather than one or more gurus. The majority of them indeed act only as teachers of physical exercises and have no spiritual pretensions. But you still ought to check out their credentials or reputation. Some teachers acquire certification after a skimpy training of only 200 hours, and sometimes less. Ask around.

Things can become slightly more tricky when meditation is taught. Beginners find it naturally rather difficult to tell the level of accomplishment of a meditation teacher. So, when spiritual advice is given, they have no way of knowing how sound it is. In this case, we must rely on common sense. If something sounds phoney or pretended, it probably is.

Some Yoga teachers also want to teach or advise about spiritual matters, which is fine as long as they don't assume the mantle of a guru. By the way, if you are charged an arm and a leg for meditation instruction or spiritual counsel, we would reconsider. You may well end up with a lot of hogwash.

To learn the Yoga postures, you certainly don't need a guru. If you desire to grow spiritually, you will sooner or later need an authentic Yoga master, or guru. But don't be too quick about finding or settling for a guru. It is better to prepare by taking your Yoga practice as far as you can under your own steam. Work on your emotional and social problems conscientiously, so that when you are in the presence of a genuine guru, you can bring him—or, more rarely, her—the gift of competence.

Traditionally, the disciple was expected to have—in at least undeveloped form—all the virtues, or good qualities, which are associated with mastery in Yoga. Virtues to work on especially are caring, generosity, and patience. These will be expanded through conscious discipline. But your future guru will be grateful for any seeds planted, so that he can water them and help them grow. People with major personality problems cannot really make use of the guru. They will inevitably approach him or her as someone like themselves, which is not the case. Because they see the guru as an "ordinary guy," they will become annoyed or angry with him or her, fighting all the way and not really accepting the help offered. Discipleship should not be the kind of primitive struggle one might have with a parent, a sibling, or a peer.

Psychological resistance is bound to come up in the company of a guru, but the disciple should also be able to deal with it without temper tantrums or even peevishness. Such reactions are entirely unconstructive. The relationship to one's guru is too precious for this kind of childish attitude. Child*like* behavior, on the other hand, is fine. The guru himself might display it when he or she manifests innocent delight or frankness in interaction with others. For the enlightened masters, "others" are not really others.

They *know* that others are the same essence as everyone, and they seek to bring their disciples to the same understanding—the same state of consciousness—as they have.

15. The Disciple: Pilgrim to Reality

When a spiritual seeker stops seeking and starts practicing earnestly, he or she becomes a disciple. Usually this coincides with the appearance of one's guru. Suddenly there is more of a focus or seriousness to one's practice. All of life becomes spiritual discipline. Nor is discipline occasional or haphazard any more, but a sacred obligation. Many of us resent discipline, even the mere word. With the onset of discipleship, however, we have made peace with the basic need for it. We understand that the mind needs to be trained before we can unlock its true potential.

The student is something of a pilgrim, and he or she approaches the pilgrimage of spiritual life as one would any other pilgrimage: with sincerity and gravity. Just as a religious pilgrimage might lead one step by step to a revered shrine, so the yogic pilgrimage leads one, also in a gradual fashion, to the essence of every single being and thing. The disciple understands that this goal might lie far into the future and that the pilgrimage may not be over at the time of death. But he or she is not daunted by this prospect. The important matter is that the disciple is edging closer and closer to the goal. In fact, some Yoga traditions—notably Tantra and radically nondualist Jnana-Yoga—discourage the idea that liberation is a goal. Spiritual freedom is the case here and now, but we really need to realize this.

Indeed, we could awaken in this very moment. The South Indian sage Ramana Maharshi did just that when he was only sixteen years old. Such spontaneous awakenings are rare. Most of us have to buckle down and do the work first. For enlightenment to occur, we need to remove our mental blocks. And this, unfortunately, takes time—many lifetimes in all likelihood.

A disciple does not find prolonged inner work troublesome. He or she knows that no effort is wasted on the path, as the *Bhagavad-Gita* states. Rather, the least struggle to transform ourselves will be in our favor. Sometimes, this may not seem so. In those moments, which may well come, we must remind ourselves that many other disciples have travelled the path and become masters in the end. One's own guru was a disciple once, and no doubt he will also have gone through the struggles of a disciple.

However difficult discipleship becomes, we must not succumb to discouragement, but simply persist. The spiritual path is the way of the hero or heroine who keeps their purpose firmly in mind and does not get ruffled by adversity.

Even a great master cannot relieve a disciple of all bad life experiences, though he or she may well modify the fruit of our karma so as not to interfere with our spiritual efforts. For instance, one's guru might warn about the impending ripening of heavy-duty karma, such as a car accident or the negative consequences of accepting a particular worldly task. But we must learn to listen to the guru with wide-open ears. When adversity is in the offing, then it is up to us to prepare ourselves with as much wisdom as we can muster.

We know that for a psychiatrist or psychotherapist to be able to help a patient, the patient must first establish an emotional connection with him or her (which is known as "transference"). The same is true between a disciple and a guru. Without this link, the alchemy of discipleship cannot work. Is such an emotional link not binding us in some way, you may ask? The answer is a resounding No, because a genuine guru will always ensure that this is not the case. After all, the whole idea is for him or her to help set the disciple free. And the guru would not want to lose his or her own spiritual freedom.

The disciple proceeds on the basis of a powerful ideal, which is to duplicate the guru's spiritual realization or, if possible, surpass it. Therefore, it is vitally important that we work with a guru who embodies our highest ideal or can help us move toward it. If we want to learn quantum physics, we consult someone knowledge-able in this science. We don't rely on the local grocer or music teacher. The guru has first-hand knowledge in the higher realizations of Yoga. He or she is therefore well qualified to show us the path to the same realizations, perhaps even Self-realization.

16. The Path: The Way to Spiritual Freedom

The spiritual process, or work, is frequently portrayed as a path. It is meant to take us beyond our ego-bound state to the ego-free condition of liberation. Freedom from the ego does not necessarily mean having no sense of self, which is really impossible. While we are alive, we inevitably have a body and a mind. When sand or a gnat wants to enter our eyes, we automatically blink. When someone tries to punch us, we duck without thinking about it first. This tells us that there is a sense of self wired into the body itself. But the enlightened being is not egotistical, or ego-bound, as we tend to be. He or she identifies not with the body or mind but with the ultimate reality, the Self.

This state of inner freedom is difficult to imagine. In our un-freedom (which is traditionally called "bondage"), we find it hard to believe that one could function in the world without having this rather solid sense of identity. But we must remember that the ego emerges gradually in us. As far as we know, there is no ego associated with an unborn child, which is simply part of the mother. There is apparently no sense of "I" even in a newborn baby, whose ego is as yet not differentiated from the world. The sense of "I" gradually emerges together with language. Then, during the "terrible twos," the child's ego has crystallized sufficiently to want to assert itself against parental pressure. This development continues on until the child learns to empathize with other people's circumstance or pain.

If this developmental process remains uncompleted, we as adults turn out to be self-centered or even sociopathic. Many people in our contemporary society put their own needs or wants first, what they call "Looking out for Number One." There is no room for an egocentric attitude on the spiritual path. On the contrary, spiritual discipline has the purpose of overcoming all self-cherishing.

Upon enlightenment, the normal sense of identity vanishes, so that the enlightened being regards the body and mind with which he or she was formerly (prior to enlightenment) so closely identified as being no more significant as any other body and mind. If anything, the enlightened master sees his or her "own" body simply as an instrument for serving others. Philosophically, this realization and capacity is rooted in the idea that the ultimate Self is the same Self in everyone.

On the yogic path, then, we unlearn the ways of the ego. We unlearn the habit of wanting to come first, of being a success, or of having it our way. Instead, we are taught to be humble, modest, obliging, respectful, and self-effacing. Eventually, we stop being arrogant, brash, pushy, rough, loud-mouthed, rebellious, unruly, competitive, exaggerated, or purposefully extraordinary. We learn to engage life from a spiritual point of view—simply and without fanfare.

For egocentrics, spiritual life is rather dull and boring. But for true disciples, it is entirely engaging, sane, and whole. They know that the final reward is incomparable, but they do not even egotistically clamor for it. They simply place one foot in front of the other, moved inwardly by the desire for liberation. That desire is far deeper than any egoic desire. It is an impulse that wells up from the depths of the mind until it is fulfilled in Self-realization.

17. Predictable Obstacles

All kinds of possible obstacles exist on the spiritual path. Most of these are self inflicted. Others derive from karma. All are somehow related to the mind, which we must go beyond. In this essay we will consider a few of the most important ones.

Perhaps the most severe obstacle is doubt. We may have doubt about the validity of the spiritual process, the spiritual path, Yoga in particular, or the guru. We may also have self-doubt, that is, doubting our capacity to engage Yoga properly and realize the Self. Such doubt is destructive and a source of suffering.

Studying the wisdom of the masters can remove a certain level of doubt, but if doubt is our form of neurosis, we best seek professional psychological help. Sometimes, a master will assist even with self-doubt, but we must not expect it. The best means of countering doubt is cultivating faith (called *shraddha* in Sanskrit). Faith in oneself and in Yoga is essential. Unlike religious faith, which consists in belief in the creeds or dogmas of one's particular sect or denomination, yogic faith is maintaining a positive attitude. This is called the "mother of Yoga."

Doubt is related to entertaining the "wrong view," a further obstacle. Examples of wrong view would include a gross materialism that denies all the values of Yoga, or the idea that the ego should never be transcended but be carefully kept in place. Wrong view is eliminated by studying the wisdom teachings of Yoga. Some people may find study tedious because they don't understand its value and therefore struggle needlessly with it.

Another common obstacle is heedlessness, or carelessness. In order to succeed on the yogic path we must be constantly mindful. It is so easy to become distracted, and distraction can lead to all kinds of unwelcome entanglements and experiences. For instance, we are resolved to practice Yoga every day, but then there is a TV series that we want to watch, although we know it adds nothing to our life. Still, before we know it, we are watching another alluring program, or even make room for that series in our weekly schedule.

Thus our resolution to practice daily weakens. Many beginning students get distracted in this way. (By the way, Georg and I solved the TV-problem by giving our set away many years ago, and never really missed it.)

Another hurdle to reckon with is apathy. We are apathetic when the mind is too weak to decide on a course of action and stick with it. Other things seem easier to do. To this category of hindrance belongs procrastination: We delay a beneficial activity from one day to another, from one week to another, and so forth.

Closely related is the obstacle of laziness: We are physically too lazy to initiate action. This often happens with people who have a physical imbalance from things such as lack of sleep or a draining diet. Sometimes agreeing to a short and simple physical or study practice is all we need to get started on a different path.

Pleasure seeking, which can be quite addictive, is a formidable enemy on the yogic path. We can become attached to all kinds of pleasant experiences, which seem to be more interesting than Yoga. In a culture that enshrines pleasure and makes it easy on everyone who looks for pleasurable experiences, we find it particularly hard to do anything that does not offer immediate gratification. Self-realization, or enlightenment, is likely to be a long-term affair. Although according to various traditions there are some individuals who have made swift progress toward the achievement of enlightenment, this is the exception, and we would be foolish to expect it. Our focus should be on yogic practice, regardless of how long it will take to go beyond the ego and realize the Self. In due course, treading the spiritual path becomes a daily joy. Or at least, we no longer struggle against it by struggling with ourselves.

Depression, which is epidemic in our modern society, is considered a major obstacle on the path. Often this is a physical problem, such as a food allergy or lack of sunshine. But it can also have psychological causes, which we ought to unravel through psychotherapy or in some other way. The other way is Yoga. While depression can—but need not—slow down the spiritual process, a regular posture and breathing practice can work wonders. Yoga teacher Amy Weintraub has written an excellent book entitled *Yoga for Depression: A Compassionate Guide To Relieve Suffering*

Through Yoga. (New York: Broadway Books, 2004), which we can heartily recommend.

If we go deeper into the spiritual aspect of Yoga, we find that some forms of depression are caused simply by our inability to take the Self into account. We must learn to see our depressive tendencies in a new light. They are just mind. We are not our feelings of depression. We can, as Weintraub explained, witness our feelings and thus stand apart. This standing apart is in fact crucial in Yoga. It is the foundation of discernment without which Self-realization is unlikely to occur.

18. Self-Discipline: Necessary Restraint

The spiritual path involves self-discipline to a high degree. The ordinary person is generally averse to self-discipline and prefers a self-cherishing attitude instead. Obviously we take great pleasure in our opinions and words, or why would we engage in idle talk quite so frivolously? We could be said to revere ourselves, and we certainly prefer that others think highly of us. Some people notoriously insist on being the center of attention. They are equipped with an inflated ego that wants to, and often does, deflate everyone else. The bigger the ego, it seems, the more one likes to trumpet their merits, even when everyone has heard about them already, or is not at all interested.

But, regardless of the size of our ego, we all "throw off" energy recklessly. Our senses are constantly searching for distractions that can lead us to consuming far too much. A lot of energy is wasted this way, and our attention is constantly bound up in matters that can hardly be said to be either life-sustaining or imperative.

Self-discipline, as the word suggests, is exercising conscious control over our ego, or "little" self and the two instruments—body and mind—by which we express ourselves. Normally, we like to live as we want. This desire is restrained only by the pressure of other people's expectations, as they have their own personal preferences that may interfere with ours.

Children on a playground may cooperate amazingly, but their play may also sometimes devolve into bedlam, with each one pretty much wanting to realize his or her own desires. This self-centeredness does not work in any society, and any hint of such anarchy will be resisted by the mainstream. The idea behind this resistance is for life to flow along as smoothly and peacefully as possible. No one wants his feathers ruffled, and authorities like to be in control, which is possible only when everyone conforms.

The situation is different in Yoga. Here a practitioner is not expected to merely "conform" but to "*trans*form," that is, to consciously adopt attitudes and behaviors that are constructive on the spiritual path. True enough, there have been many "misfits" in Hindu Yoga—*yogis* who do not play by the rules, who go about naked, wear their hair in dreadlocks, are jobless, have no income, and flout any sort of polite or decent behavior. For their own reasons, they purposefully defy polite social conduct. Yet, with themselves, they may be rather strict and austere.

The main purpose of self-discipline is to train the mind, that is, to make it pliable for the higher work in meditation, and for sound living. An undisciplined mind, as we may know only too well from our own experience, is not able to meditate and is easily shaken up by life's harsher experiences. So, the Yoga practitioner is charged with bringing the mind under control, especially the many desires that pull it hither and thither.

Before we can attempt to discipline the mind, however, we must first understand that it needs disciplining. This is far from obvious to some people. They do not look deeply enough and hence don't see the storm of their desires, the ups and downs of their emotions, or the fickleness of their mind. They wrongly assume that "all's perfect" with them, so there is no need for improvement.

The sincere Yoga practitioner, however, knows that there is plenty of room for developing his or her inner potential by transforming both the mind and the personality. The good qualities a guru would be looking for in a disciple need to be deliberately cultivated. These qualities don't grow on their own like grass or thistles. A garden calls for regular and mindful care or it will not flourish. Similarly, the mind will turn to the equivalent of weeds when it is not cared for properly. If the weed metaphor does not sit well with you, then think of the uncultivated mind as a junkyard stripped of all re-useable materials.

Self-discipline requires that we consciously take the initiative and then persist, regardless of the "temptations" that life conjures up for us. These range from passively watching television hour after hour while unconsciously consuming junk food, to becoming high on drugs, or drunk on alcohol, entering into casual sexual relationships, and seeking out the company of people who have no interest in spiritual life but indulge at will in their materialist desires.

Yoga masters do not indulge their desires but stand ready to help whoever needs help, or to teach when their pupils are ready to really listen to the yogic teachings. There is no ounce of selfishness in a bona fide master. He or she really lives for the benefit of others. The genuine guru has no personal preferences, although he or she may come across otherwise when pressed to choose. The guru's true preference is to communicate his or her own realization to disciples, so that they too can one day be completely free in themselves. The guru's desireless disposition is due to having realized an extraordinary state of equanimity. Because of this, he or she radiates a tangible peace that in itself can prove transformative for disciples.

19. Community: Strength in Numbers

The life of a disciple in the midst of conventional society is not easy. Especially in our own time, the distractions are numerous and persistent. Solitude, which was recommended in the past as a major transformative tool, is hardly any longer available. Nor is our social environment of average people with conventional interests necessarily supportive. When television, football, bar hopping and other similar pursuits lose their hold on a Yoga practitioner, he or she increasingly feels the need for a support system. This comes in the form of a community of like-minded and like-hearted practitioners (called *sangha* in Sanskrit). This is not the usual coffee-and-gossip clique. Instead, the *sangha* is a group of fellow disciples who are interested in practicing together or in talking about the teachings. Some, hopefully benign, gossip is natural. But the common focus is very much on the spiritual process of self-transformation.

Not every *sangha*, of course, meets this ideal. If the shoe doesn't fit, as they say, try elsewhere. Or, if there is any openness at all, you might endeavor to introduce a different attitude as long as you do it humbly and skillfully. If you encounter resistance, kindly and politely move on. You are certainly not the only person practicing with serious intention. You may not find a fellow pilgrim on the path in your local area but you surely will in another district or a nearby town.

You may feel tempted to practice by yourself. There is no problem if you can do this without feeling superior to others or simply resentful. Even then, however, you would certainly benefit from at least occasional participation in a group of dedicated practitioners. There is definitely strength in numbers. Besides, if you have a guru and want to spend time in his or her company, you are bound to find him or her surrounded by disciples. The guru might only sit quietly or deliver an inspiring talk. At any rate, his or her presence is predictably exhilarating but also inherently demanding, because the guru's mere presence represents a challenge from within the disciple's mind. The challenge is a steady call for transformation, for waking up as the Self.

Even gurus who have not yet become enlightened can be rather demanding in this way. They call their disciples from deep within or urge them on verbally. Often they are more demanding than enlightened masters, who know that enlightenment is a game that the mind plays. The Self is always the same free being, and therefore there is absolutely no urgency. The only urgency that exists is to help those for whom suffering is still a very real experience and who, if they are spiritual pupils, struggle to realize enlightenment.

Some *yogins* pursued liberation far removed from ordinary people in the isolation of a cave, a jungle, or a remote hut. Others did their best to attain enlightenment or a lower spiritual realization in the company of others. These traditional texts and teachers normally exhorted people to seek out the company of realized masters or at least (in the yogic sense) virtuous people. The *sangha*, then, is a group of virtuous Yoga practitioners, who pursue the spiritual goal of freedom with integrity.

Aspiring Yoga practitioners are not without desires, but they seek to cultivate only those desires that do not thwart the spiritual process. As they move along on the path, their desires become ever fewer and ever more simple. They should not, of course, repress desires unless they are truly destructive. They learn to enjoy inner stillness more than boisterous external activity.

20. Ego-Transcendence: Beyond I, Me, and Mine

Transcending, or going beyond, the ego is a central undertaking in spiritual work. Yogic self-transformation basically consists in this: We are asked to, bit by bit, retire the egotism we acquired in the course of a lifetime and instead nurture an attitude of wholesome altruism. The qualifying word "wholesome" is necessary, because there is also toxic altruism. Such altruism is toxic because it is self-centered. It leads to self-poisoning. Wholesome altruism, by contrast, is free from self-centeredness and is truly in the service of others without proving damaging to oneself.

Research has proven that humans are not natural predators, nor are they by instinct aggressive rather than cooperative. We actually are by nature more inclined to cooperate with others. In Yoga, self-transcendence is a central virtue. The yogic process cannot succeed without it. Enlightenment, the goal of Yoga, is consummate self-transcendence.

How can we transcend the ego when the ego is constantly in our face until the moment we become enlightened? This question is not correctly formulated, because we are enlightened even now. We have always been enlightened and will be so into the most distant future. The Self, who we truly are, is always enlightened. At one point, we merely recognize this inescapable fact. It is true that we tend to identify not with the Self but the body and mind—thus creating the ego. But by recognizing the Self and inching closer to it, we can out-maneuver the ego. The ego cannot enlighten us. By gradually diminishing it, however, we can be our true Self, our innermost essence.

Every kind act is a form of self-transcendence. Every time we give a gift for unselfish reasons, we practice self-transcendence. Every exercise in patience is a form of self-transcendence. Every compassionate gesture is self-transcendence in action. Thus we can move, slowly but surely, toward Self-realization, or enlightenment:

We act enlightened. We think enlightened. We feel enlightened. We speak enlightened. It is this simple.

Some people feel that we must meditate in order to attain Self-realization. This is not so. Meditation is helpful in quieting the mind. But, as Jnana-Yoga teaches us, meditation adds nothing to our innate enlightenment. If it is done selfishly, it foils our recognition of enlightenment to boot. As the *Bhagavad-Gita* (12.12) tells us, meditation is higher than knowledge, but abandoning self-centered activity is higher than meditation.

There is, then, nothing mysterious about Yoga and the way to the Self. Of course, going beyond the grip of the ego is challenging. It is our normal state of existence. We even endorse and celebrate the ego when we are encouraged to build it up, strengthen, toughen, or improve it by the competitive business environment. Our civilization doesn't seem to care for the Self. By and large, it doesn't even know about its existence. We tend to honour the person who is a "successful" ego instead of seeing that as a hindrance.

From a spiritual perspective, however, the ego is little more than a cause and manifestation of suffering. This is perhaps difficult to grasp. The difficulty disappears when we think of the ego as a masquerade—a false sense of identity by which we maintain the functions of unenlightened life. The Self is our rightful or real identity. When we take all our masks off, by practicing self-transcendence, we will inevitably become who we always are.

The charade we play is entertaining only as long as we and our fellow players are engaged in the same pretence. As soon as we tire of playing the game that seems to hold everyone spellbound, we have no choice but to play the far more interesting game of self-transcendence. This game has a different set of rules, which we discover as we go along. It certainly is far more benign than the ordinary game played by virtually all those who have no inkling about the Self and take their conventional concerns with extreme seriousness. That is, they behave as if even their genuinely serious concerns are of any consequence in the larger scheme of things. From the Self's point of view, all is a charade, a make-believe game. We have dressed up and taken our self-adopted roles with humourless seriousness.

We don't realize that when we take our costume and mask off, we are free.

21. Wisdom

Wisdom is not prominent in our time, which more values knowledge and information. Only very recently, perhaps because we are beginning to recognize the shortcomings of knowledge, has wisdom become an object of scientific (psychological) curiosity and investigation. Yoga, however, is packed with wisdom. The yogic masters may be somewhat ignorant in conventional terms, but they are full of wisdom. Therefore, we can confidently turn to them for wise help on the spiritual path.

The teachings of the great Yoga masters are available to us in book form in the *Bhagavad-Gītā* and the *Yoga-Sūtra of Patañjali*. Since wisdom is ageless, it is as relevant today as it was a thousand or more years ago. But we must be open to finding and applying that significance in our own situations. The outer circumstances have undoubtedly changed in the course of time. The mind, however, has remained quite constant, and the problems of an earlier age are often the same as today.

In the state of ecstasy, which comes at the peak of the spiritual path prior to final liberation, or enlightenment, the practitioner knows everything as one. We realize that all things are interconnected. For our era, which is experiencing the first "inconvenient" consequences of a flawed attitude toward Nature, this recognition that "all is one" is important wisdom. While surprisingly large numbers of people experience ecstatic or ecstasy-like moments, presumably few of us will realize yogic ecstasy in a consciously generated manner. But we can heed the wisdom of the masters, which tells us that there are states of consciousness in which we can and do experience the unity of Nature firsthand.

Their wisdom tells us, among other things, that in order to live peacefully and healthily, we must live in harmony with Nature. This is not what we have done in the past 200 years. We are now learning in a painful way that we were mistaken in thinking that Earth's resources were inexhaustible. The few highly-industrialized countries have ransacked the world to build "civilization" to an artificial height. Our brothers and sisters in the larger underdeveloped parts of the world are paying for our inconsiderateness and greed in many ways. Wisdom tells us that this is unjust, unscrupulous, and unwise.

The spiritual path has been called a "razor's edge." A great deal of wisdom is required to tread it. Yoga gives us such wisdom. In particular, it shows us how to distinguish between the real and the unreal. At the ultimate end of the path is Self-realization, or actual enlightenment. For the sages of Yoga, unreal is everything that is not the Self, not pure awareness. This includes the mind. Even when it is steeped in wisdom, they regard the mind as falling short of the reality of the Self, which is our essential nature.

The masters of Yoga understood that the mind exists, like the Moon, on borrowed light. The Moon does not give off heat or warmth but only reflected light, which comes from the Sun. If the Self is similar to the Sun, it makes sense to want to realize it. By itself, the mind cannot sustain us. But, so the sages tell us, the Self can, since it is our true identity. We only mistakenly identify with the mind. Many people even think that they *are* the brain-mind.

Training in Yoga shows that identification with "brain-mind" alone is not the real story. It has been demonstrated scientifically that there are states of mind that clearly go beyond the brain. "Near-death experiences" are one example. They indicate that the brain can be totally disabled while mental states happily continue.

Self-realization happens *without* the mind. Certainly awareness is ever present, yet the mind can come and go. This does not imply unconsciousness, however. The sages would not have aspired to this, as their goal has always been to realize the Self, which is the identity of every living being and even of the insentient natural world.

The masters of Yoga discipline the mind in order to be able to consciously go beyond it. It is difficult to fathom their consummate skill in controlling the mind. When we sit down to meditate, the mind chatters on by itself. We cannot even imagine that the mind could stop for more than a few seconds at a time. Yet, this has been the experience of every Yoga practitioner who persists. The mind can become as docile as a puppy.

Wisdom stands at both the beginning threshold and as the lofty goal of Yoga. At first, wisdom guides us to inner freedom. In the end, upon living liberation (that is, Self-realization while still embodied), the Self mysteriously inspires the mind to spawn wisdom for the benefit of others.

Wisdom is the quality of a highly refined mind, which is replete with lucidity. For this to be the case, the mind has to be similar to the Self. That is to say, it must be as still and as luminous as possible. Even if the mind cannot produce its own light, it can reflect it. This reflected luminosity is wisdom.

22. Proper Livelihood: Integrity in All Matters

To put it bluntly: If you aspire to be a bank director, you cannot also be a bank robber. Similarly, if you aspire toward mastery in Yoga, you cannot also be a moral good-for-nothing. It is important for a Yoga practitioner to pursue a proper livelihood. That means earning one's living in a decent and respectable way that does not violate any of Yoga's many moral virtues. Another way of putting this is to say that we should cultivate integrity in all matters, including the work we do.

Would it be appropriate for a Yoga practitioner to be a hired overseas enforcer for an international corporation, a factory farmer, a casino manager, or a lobbyist for a cut-throat pharmaceutical company? We think not. All these jobs involve unsavoury practices or goals that definitely compromise a Yoga practitioner's moral integrity. We actually had a student who, attracted by a handsome salary, took on a job at a casino. Before very long, he found that the atmosphere in the casino was so disagreeable that at the end of the day he felt filthy and didn't even want to continue with his practice of Yoga. In the end, he resigned and has never regretted his decision.

We cannot practice integrity part-time, or in one corner of our life but not in all respects. Integrity cannot be compartmentalized; it is an all-or-nothing matter. We regard integrity as an aspect of truthfulness, which is considered a major virtue in Patanjali's Yoga and, of course, in other branches of Yoga as well. He tells us that when a practitioner is firmly established in truthfulness, whatever he or she affirms comes true. We personally would limit this ability to spiritual matters, because in worldly affairs a master often relies, like everyone else, primarily on information that may or may not be entirely correct. As a rule, however, a master does not indulge in chitchat or unconsidered opinions.

Regretfully, the contemporary Yoga movement in the West lacks integrity in several respects. The first is that many Yoga teachers give the wrong impression that Yoga is no more than postural practice. This is unfair to traditional Yoga, which is obviously very much more. It is also unfair to newcomers to Yoga who don't know any better but should be given an opportunity to explore the spirituality of Yoga and the full range of its practices.

Most deplorable is the absence of traditional Yoga's moral disciplines from many of the teachings offered at modern centers. This is like offering a person a chair with only three legs to sit on, which is an accident in the making. What good, one may ask, will it do for a student to know the headstand if, when he or she has a car accident, they do not know how to manage life afterward? Or, of what advantage is mastering the Warrior III pose when the mind is worrying about death?

Not only is modern Yoga by and large not grounded in the moral precepts, it is also shot through with the moral apathy and shallowness that mark our mainstream culture. It is irresponsible for a Yoga teacher to tell his or her students, as we have heard, that the moral disciplines are unimportant. In fact, without them there can be no attainment of mental health, never mind inner freedom. And it is negligent for a Yoga teacher to publicly debunk the spiritual orientation of Yoga, because this is precisely what is missing from our troubled culture. Integrity, among other things, means to present and practice Yoga as the spiritual tradition that it is. Anything less is dishonest.

23. Diet: You Are What You Eat

People certainly don't think of themselves as turkeys after eating their standard Thanksgiving dinner, or as chickens when they have consumed "white meat," or as "pigs" after eating the "red meat" known as pork.

The fact is, though, that our food substantially affects us not only physiologically but also mentally. Some people find this hard to believe. Even the best food is made up of chemicals, and when these chemicals enter our bloodstream, they inevitably impact on body and mind. Think of ice cream, potato dumplings, or the Sunday roast, which in larger amounts all make us feel physically stuffed, heavy and mentally sluggish. A light salad meal, by contrast, is likely to make us feel physically light, and possibly mentally lightheaded. Mothers know that when children consume a lot of sugar, they become giddy and unfocused.

On the yogic path, much attention is paid to the food we eat. *Yogins* want their body and mind to function optimally. What, then, is an optimal diet? This question has been answered in widely-read books like John Robbins' *Diet for a New America* and Dr. Gabriel Cousens' *Conscious Eating*. Taking into account recent research, they concluded that people will thrive on a balanced vegetarian diet consisting of vegetables, nuts, seeds, and adequate amounts of vegetable oil. They support very few dairy products, but no meat or fish.

As Karl Weber's edited volume *Food, Inc.* has documented, "industrial" or "fast" food—that is, the typical supermarket food—is making everyone sicker. The reason for this is that it has little nutritional value and also contains dangerous chemicals (such as food coloring, preservatives, growth hormones, and antibiotics). Today, the food supply is in the hands of surprisingly few large corporations, which exist to make as much profit as possible. They are not concerned about people's health. Nor are they concerned about the devastating effect which industrial agriculture has on the environment. The food industry is a major polluter of soil, water, and air. (We have written about this in our book *Green Yoga*.)

In the U.S.A., the Department of Agriculture and the Food and Drug Administration, who are supposed to exist for the benefit of the consumer, condone and endorse this industrial scam, which is outrageous and disheartening. The U.S. government also grants substantial subsidies to these corporations to keep them going, which is a self-defeating practice, because we are getting sicker and sicker and health costs are rising.

For Yoga practitioners wanting to observe the cardinal virtue of nonharming, there is the additional issue over the abusive treatment of "factory" animals. For example, a factory farm might squeeze hundreds of thousands of chickens and other poultry into a comparatively small area and never allow them to see the light of day. Because of the crowded conditions, the chickens peck each other rather than morsels on the ground, and consequently factory farmers clip their beaks. The birds are given antibiotics for faster growth, and some birds grow so heavy that their legs buckle. Painful bone deformities are common. The slaughter house experience is just as traumatic and unconscionable.

This is just a small glimpse into the meat industry. We felt compelled to say something about this, because all too many people—including Yoga practitioners—are still ignorant of these unsavory facts. It is easy to see how our chosen diet has far-reaching consequences, which are indeed inconvenient but should not be ignored if we wish to live ethically and healthily.

24. Liberation: Spiritual Freedom Now or Later

Spiritual liberation is realization of our innermost essence, the Self. This can occur after death or even before the body and mind have disintegrated. The latter form of freedom is known as "living liberation." It is qualitatively the same as the former and is often known as enlightenment.

In both cases, the mind must be fully transcended. That is to say, there must be nothing in the way of pure awareness. While we are alive, Self-realization is a paradoxical state. On one hand, there is the disembodied, eternal Self, and on the other hand, there is the finite body and an equally finite mind. This is a mind-boggling combination!

The Self-realized adept who is alive has pushed the mind to its limits, such that it barely exists at all. Certainly, the adept's mind includes no tendency toward self-centeredness. In some cases, the master may spend more time being present as the Self. In (most) other cases, he or she dips into actual Self-realization periodically, which then has a profoundly transformative effect on the mind. Put differently, in the Self-realized adept, the Self—or God—is more present than the mind.

The process of Yoga is an unveiling of the ever-present Self. We are always free, or liberated. But the blocks in our mind prevent us from recognizing our innate freedom. This is comparable to a tree branch standing in the way of the Sun. When we bend the branch a little, the sunlight strikes our eyes. When we remove the obstructions in the mind—all the negative emotions like anger, lust, greed, and so on—we can welcome the light of the Self in our heart. Even a little bit of the yogic work can give us a glimpse of the Self. In a way, every step toward the Self is liberating.

Yoga is thus excavation work, which gets rid of the dross in the psyche. At first, this requires a very muscular effort. We have to apply ourselves systematically using willpower and self-discipline. Imagine spade and pickaxe. Later on, the yogic work becomes more subtle but also more challenging, because the impediments are not always easy to see. When you are still in the process of dismantling gross self-centeredness, you will in general know what to do. More subtle forms of self-centeredness involve mental obstacles that call for great discernment. It may not always be obvious to a disciple even which functions of the mind are self-centered. This is where a guru can be supremely helpful. He or she has struggled with the same or a similar problem.

Being more skilful on the ecstatic circuit of the spiritual path, the guru can point out where we are getting sidetracked. The experience of ecstasy—either in its lower forms or by dint of artificial means (such as drugs or *mantras*)—can itself be full of traps. Not every ecstasy reveals the Self. The ecstatic state can, however, look like the real thing. Only superior discernment—like a teacher is apt to have—will settle the matter.

Whenever we are close to Self-realization, our conduct is likely to become simple and inspiring to others. The nondual Self, after all, is simple. As long as our life is overly convoluted, or complicated, we are still closer to the mind than to the Self. On the spiritual path, the mind is progressively stripped of the need for complication and extraordinariness. In fact, disciples are to all appearances ordinary people. They don't wear a special sign that proclaims: "I am a disciple." Nor do disciples engage in extraordinary feats. If they do, then we ought to question their spiritual status. To *behave* in an ordinary manner while *being* extraordinary on the inside is a sign of freedom.

The freer we are, the less likely do we feel the urge to assert ourselves or display our specific neuroses. The liberated being is non-neurotic. He or she has overcome the wiles and compulsions of the mind.

PART TWO

Questions and Answers

Prelude

The following questions are selected from among many we have responded to over the years. We trust that our answers might be helpful to you and others. At the same time, we believe that, with a little reflection, most questions can be answered by the questioners themselves, relying on their own common sense and innate wisdom.

Questions and Answers

1. I am a Christian. Can I practice Yoga without jeopardizing my faith?

With the growing popularity of Yoga, this has become a widespread issue. Quite a few people agonize over this. We realize this is an important matter, and so we want to give a carefully differentiated answer. Let's start by saying: It all depends on what yogic method or approach you wish to engage.

As Part One of this book makes clear, Yoga is not a religion, though some branches of Yoga—notably Bhakti-Yoga—have a strong religious coloring. So, despite the common ground of devotion/love, it would presumably not work for a Christian to practice Hindu Bhakti-Yoga. There is, however, no ideological reason preventing anyone from practicing a good many of the methods of Hatha-Yoga, such as postures, breath control, relaxation, diet, and so on.

Moreover, the moral disciplines of Yoga have much in common with Christian ethics, but anyone with a strong commitment to Christianity can be expected to practice these disciplines already. This aspect of Yoga is incredibly important. Actually, we would argue that the moral disciplines are the most important limb of Yoga, especially for contemporary people. Unfortunately, this limb is frequently ignored and even belittled. There is also absolutely no harm in practicing Karma-Yoga whose working principles match the ethics of Christianity.

Practicing Raja-Yoga, Jnana-Yoga, or Tantra-Yoga, or adopting a yogic meditation practice may be a different kettle of fish. Personally, we would recommend that a Christian stick with a Christian form of meditation rather than feel compromised by a Hindu type of meditation. Many people are not even aware that Christianity has evolved its own systems of meditation, such as the routines developed by St. Ignatius of Loyola in the sixteenth century, or the Heart Prayer of the Eastern Orthodox Church, and others. The closer your religious practice is to Christian mysticism—aspects of which are misunderstood or challenged by individuals or various groups within Christianity—the less likely you will be disturbed by the spirituality of Yoga.

Most Yoga centers in the West focus on the postures and, to our dismay, do not teach the other aspects of Yoga. So, Christians may not be exposed at all to the spiritual side of Yoga. However, if a Yoga teacher has a more traditional and inclusive approach, anyone is free to abstain from participating in methods or considerations that rub the wrong way, or to refrain from returning to that center or class. Some religious authorities do worry and even assert that simply by practicing the postures, a person is risking their faith by involving themselves in the forms of another religious system. Ultimately, each practitioner must make an informed decision for him- or herself.

2. I am strongly drawn to Hinduism. How can I get more involved?

Hinduism is first and foremost a culture. It has so many aspects, and the best way of proceeding is to study and then study some more. We can *immerse* ourselves into a culture but cannot *convert* to it. There are many teachers who treat Hinduism as a religion and offer to initiate applicants. This usually involves a sort of conversion to a specific Hindu tradition, such as Shaivism (revolving around Shiva) or Vaishnavism (revolving around Vishnu). It is best to proceed slowly. One way of finding "your" niche is by becoming associated with a local Hindu community or, if you have to, by spending time in India.

3. Where can I find a guru?

This is a question that is asked often and prematurely. But a better question is: *How* can I find a guru? One doesn't need a guru to perform the postures or relaxation techniques. A good Yoga instructor will do. A guru is, however, necessary for growth in the more advanced stages of yogic practice. Most people worry too early about finding a guru. In the past, we would typically share with them a piece of traditional wisdom: The guru will find you! This message would either make them disappointed or angry with us. Nevertheless, we will repeat the same message here.

It makes no sense for a toddler to ask for instruction from a university professor. Toddlers have to learn many other lessons first. The average seeker is much like a toddler—eager to explore but unprepared, with few skills.

The best way of finding one's guru is to steadfastly prepare for this eventuality by practicing the limbs of Yoga as wholeheartedly as possible. An unprepared person would not even recognize his or her guru. There is no better gift we could offer our guru than to approach with an understanding of the rudiments of the spiritual process, and with a flexible and eager personality with which the guru can work. That means we have to learn gratitude, respect, and the willingness to change.

4. Why do you write Yoga with a capital Y?

A good question. Few people write the name of a spiritual tradition—like Christianity, Judaism, Vedanta, Samkhya, Zen, or Buddhism with a lower-case initial. This looks strange to our eye. It seems to put such traditions on a par with gymnastics or acrobatics. Yoga is a fully fledged spiritual tradition and, we think, deserves an initial capital. Some people have suggested that when you write *yoga*, with a lower-case initial, you refer only to postural practice. This attitude accepts the status quo, which on a certain level we don't. We would much rather see postural practice flower into Yoga proper, and in that case an upper-case initial is definitely in order.

5. My partner has no interest in Yoga, but my own interest is deepening. This has become a problem. What should I do?

This same question was put to Georg when he was teaching yogic postures in his early twenties, having little experience with married life, and having almost as little wisdom. Wanting to be helpful, he fumbled his way through some sort of a meaningful response. Many years later he would answer: Develop your own interest, but don't expect your partner to follow. Instead, practice great tolerance and a positive attitude toward your partner. Also, find as much common ground as possible, ideally before making a marital commitment.

6. I have a very busy life. How can I accommodate Yoga properly?

This is a common question and complaint. In our Western culture, everyone is busy. We feel we have to earn as much as possible, not realizing that we pay more in taxes, suffer from ill health due to stress, have large mortgage payments, and on and on.

The real question is not how to *squeeze* Yoga into our busy schedules, but how to prioritize our values, goals, commitments, etc. Many people have concluded, wisely, that they are much too busy, and have started to simplify their life. Some have relocated; others have opted for a less demanding and less well-paying job, or have decided to reduce their consumerism. This takes guts, but, as many families have demonstrated, it can be done.

7. I like meat. Can I still practice nonharming?

If you consume meat, your practice of nonharming is inevitably compromised. You will harm indirectly by supporting the meat industry, which is known to be brutal toward animals. As long as we are alive, we cannot avoid doing harm. But we can minimize this effect, for instance, by choosing a diet that is as benign as possible. Just because we like something does not give us the right to do harm or to endorse harmful practices.

There is now sufficient scientific evidence to show that a vegetarian diet is optimal. Entire cultures have lived on such a diet for centuries, and their populations are as healthy as any other.

We invite anyone preferring a meat diet to watch one of the PETA documentaries or the documentary *Earthlings*.

Apart from health reasons, abstaining from meat eating is a crucial ethical matter.

8. When I read Yoga classics, I find them rather mythological, religious, and illogical. This prevents me from starting a Yoga practice.

Is there a bias at work here? Humans do tend to see what they expect to see.

Based in our own research, study and practice over many years, we can assure you that by no means are all Yoga texts either mythological or religious. Certainly we do encounter symbolism, spirituality, and formidable logical arguments, and we also are called to face some rather inconvenient truths that these texts put forth.

Generally, we don't start a Yoga practice because we don't want to be challenged by it.

This is just a thought we offer for your consideration.

9. I try to practice Yoga every day. Sometimes I just don't have the time, which makes me feel very guilty. What should I do?

We have answered this question in part by what we said in answer #5.

As far as guilt is concerned, it is appropriate to feel this emotion when we have done wrong. Otherwise, guilt is neurotic and an entirely unconstructive emotion that merely hinders us.

Instead of indulging in guilt, we would recommend making the most of *whatever* practice (with whatever frequency) one has been able to establish. It is better to rejoice in Yoga than to focus on the negative circumstances preventing us from engaging it as often or as intensively as we would like.

10. I want to meditate, but my mind is racing all the time. What can I do about this?

Over 2,000 years ago, Prince Arjuna asked this same question of the enlightened master Krishna in the *Bhagavad-Gita*. Krishna assured him that the mind can in fact be controlled. In our own times, while it is quite likely that the mind *is* racing faster than in previous millennia, still, in principle, the truth abides—the mind can be controlled! We may, however, have to enlist some extra help to calm the mind, such as uncluttering and simplifying our lifestyle, by delegating or not taking on quite so many tasks and obligations.

It is in the nature of the mind to produce thoughts. Even a little bit of conscious relaxation or meditation can thin out our thoughts and create mental space. In the early stages of meditation practice, it is natural for thoughts to boil on and on, leaving us with the impression that we will never gain mastery over our mind. Wrong impression! As we sit in meditation regularly (daily), we find that the mind slows down, and maybe even slows down considerably sooner than we assumed.

As neurologists have discovered in recent years, the brain is surprisingly adaptable. Contrary to previous opinion, brain cells can in fact regenerate throughout our lifespan. Regular meditation will retrain the brain, so that gradually meditation will become easier and "successful." The mind will stop racing and begin to settle down. Later, it will go beyond its assumed boundaries, and still later it will find itself in the sublime state of ecstasy.

11. I think that Yoga is self-hypnosis. What's your response?

In the 1930s, researchers thought that Yoga was based on self-hyp-nosis. This view is generally not supported today, however. While certain relaxation and meditation practices do involve aspects of this hypnotic mechanism (to the advantage of the *yogin*), such an overall categorization cannot be applied to all of Yoga. The science of Yoga is traditionally well aware of the state of hypnosis, but for the most part does not employ it in its spiritual repertoire.

Even if Yoga were mostly self-hypnosis, which it is not, what would be wrong with it if this could produce positive results in one's personal health or social interactions? If anything, Yoga enables its practitioners to engage the "real" world with eyes open, not in some state of trance, and with a healthily realistic attitude.

12. I have been practicing Yoga on and off for many years. My problem is I easily fall off the wagon. Is there a remedy for this?

Why do people suddenly drop their spiritual discipline only to resume it later on, probably with lots of guilt feelings? This usually happens when practice becomes difficult or when a worldly matter (a job, a love affair, etc.) becomes overwhelmingly attractive. That's why Yoga emphasizes the need to be attentive from moment to moment. When we ski down a steep slope, we may move too fast to look behind us, or may look up into the sky to admire a bird. In order to avoid sudden obstacles, however, it is wise to concentrate on the path opening up before us.

The spiritual path is similarly fast, and it abounds with potential hurdles. Therefore, we ought to cultivate mindfulness in every moment. Life always throws us curve balls; we must learn how to meet them properly, so that we don't get thrown off balance and lose our way.

13. There are many things I don't like about my guru, and I have been struggling with this for some time. I fear that leaving him would be very upsetting for him. What should I do?

We can only offer general advice, because each situation is unique. On the spiritual path, liking or not liking one's guru is irrelevant. It is, of course, helpful and probably even necessary to have a basically positive attitude toward one's guru.

The guru's job is to promote the spiritual process in the disciple. This is never a pleasant undertaking, because the guru has to undermine all the things that stand in the way of the disciple's realization of freedom. Most of these things have to do with the disciple's personality, wrong assumptions, false expectations, and other unpalatable issues. So, the guru is inevitably "in the disciple's face"—a most ungrateful task.

Predictably, disciples resent this sort of interference. Some confuse the guru with an ordinary teacher, who is concerned with passing on information. Ordinary teachers do not assume responsibility for their disciples' spiritual welfare. The guru's area of competence is mental and spiritual transformation. They have the right and tacit permission to intervene in a disciple's personal life.

In this connection it is also worth considering: Contrary to popular belief, most gurus are *not* enlightened. They still have to deal with their own ego. But even an enlightened guru has a personality. If we don't resonate with the guru's personality, it is best not to become his or her disciple. Once we have taken this step, however, it is best to roll with the punches unless one's guru's personality really stands in the way of our own inner growth. This should be assessed carefully, primarily through introspection and perhaps in consultation with others. We should never leave a guru just because we don't like certain things about him or her.

That's why it is okay to do some "guru shopping" before making a real commitment. The guru will similarly examine the prospective pupil. But once the guru-disciple relationship has seriously started—often by initiation—one's guru should not be casually abandoned. There are, however, serious reasons for leaving one's guru, especially in the case of obvious sexual abuse or because one has stopped growing spiritually over a period of time. Even then, we really ought to examine the matter carefully.

A fully enlightened guru simply does not engage in egoically-motivated actions. As we said, such gurus are exceedingly rare, perhaps one in 500 million (just a guess!). Many of the gurus that claim enlightenment for themselves or have others do it on their behalf are questionable. By traditional standards, some are clearly not enlightened. Brenda has a good rule: Look for those qualities in your guru which you would eventually like to realize yourself.

When we have had the extreme good fortune of having come into contact with an enlightened master, we should endeavour to make a lifelong commitment to discipleship and stick with it even when the going gets rough, and it will.

Finally, if one's guru gets upset or angry about you leaving, that is really his or her business. It means that he or she still has to go beyond the ego. The only feeling that would arise in an enlightened master is regret for the disciple. But such regret would be mixed with a bundle of genuinely good wishes for the "lost" pupil.

14. I am an atheist. Can I still practice Yoga?

Atheism is an ideology, and some atheists cling to it with as much fervor as others cling to their religion. Yet, no unenlightened person can tell for sure whether there is a God, or not. Therefore, we find agnosticism both more plausible logically and also a more humble attitude: We simply don't know. To affirm that there is no God implies all sorts of assumptions, which are usually based on materialistic science. But that kind of science has itself come under challenge of late. More and more philosophers and even scientists themselves are calling for a new paradigm, a new non-materialistic worldview, which can explain things—meaning the findings of science—more satisfactorily. Be that as it may, much of what we said in answer #1 applies also to an atheist, minus our recommendations for a Christian.

15. Do I really need a guru to attain Self-realization?

Yes, unless a person is a spiritual genius, but this very question implies otherwise. Most spiritual seekers, who are fewer than 99.99 percent of us, need significant help in order to realize the ultimate essence. But, as we explain in this book, to be able to make good use of such help, we need to prepare, prepare, and prepare again. So, there is no rush to find a guru. Most of us need a lot of preparation to undermine our self-centeredness and develop positive psychological qualities.

This universe is marvellously orchestrated. When a guru has become necessary in the course of our spiritual discipline, he or she will be found. We are never alone anyway. Help comes to us all the time from all kinds of sources, including the subtle or higher realms. Some people are desperately seeking their guru, but this is often little more than a self-centered wish. We ought to relax and live life as best we can, practice Yoga as best we can, and patiently wait for the guru to appear.

We have stopped recommending teachers, because it has been our experience that seekers want to seek rather than find. They might not even recognize their guru when they see him or her. In the past, our recommendations were typically ignored. More instructive have been those cases where contact with the guru proved somehow impossible, even though he or she may have lived conveniently close to a seeker. Usually, the seeker gives up trying to connect with the guru after a number of failed attempts, or becomes sidetracked by other attractive opportunities. One must conclude that a meeting was not meant to happen just then.

16. I find "living liberation" difficult to understand. How can I begin to wrap my mind around this idea?

"Living liberation" is for sure a challenging concept. Liberation is something that happens from the viewpoint of the mind. Our innermost essence is always liberated, or free. Think of the mind as a screen in front of a bright light. That screen can be either opaque, hardly allowing any of the light through at all, or it can be completely translucent, so that the light rays are scarcely blocked. In most cases, the screen of the mind is some shade in between these two extremes, depending on one's spiritual development. Through the steadfast practice of Yoga, we can gradually remove the darker screens and thus permit the light of ultimate Awareness into our mind and being. At one point, there occurs a radical switch in us. Instead of identifying with our mind and personality, we wake up as the unchanging essence, or Awareness, which we have always been.

Many Yoga masters maintain that while we are alive in the world, there will always be a screen between us and our true essence. But that screen is completely transparent and completely "seen through," so that it is still possible to speak of Self-realization. When a Self-realized master dies, this final screen simply drops away and full liberation is the case. Essentially, then, liberation is the same before and after death. Some teachers speak of "living liberation" also as enlightenment, while others equate enlightenment with full or post-mortem liberation. It makes no difference really.

17. Some forms of Yoga seem to accept a belief in God, while others don't. How should we understand this?

This is true. Bhakti-Yoga very much assumes the existence of God, who is understood as a superperson. Jnana-Yoga, by contrast, speaks of the ultimate Self, or essence, instead. But it also admits of a creator-deity who emerges ("is born") out of the ultimate, lives for a very long time, and then "dies." When the creator dies, the universe disintegrates. After a period of time (in human terms), the creator-deity emerges again out of the ultimate and then gives rise to a new universe. Thus, the creation and destruction of the universe is regarded as happening in cycles.

The creator is named Brahma, who is often confused with the Absolute and impersonal *brahman*, or ultimate essence of everything. In Christian mystical terms, this contrast is captured in the difference between God and Godhead. The Godhead goes beyond personhood, which is why some (but by no means all) practitioners of Jnana-Yoga address Brahma but not the impersonal *brahman* when they want to pray for help. Whether we think of Brahma as an actual deity or as a psychological device (or archetype), he is clearly a helpful threshold figure.

Yogins are not so arrogant as to dismiss help from deities. They don't have to combat the intellectual bias of atheism, which prevents the mind from experiencing the full spectrum of realities. So, positive thinking, openness, and prayer are very much part of the vocabulary of Yoga.

18. If the *yogis* are so realistic and have such great mastery over their minds, including the unconscious, why do they believe in many deities?

This question implies that the deities acknowledged in Hinduism are fictional or have only a psychological reality. Briefly, this is little more than an intellectual assumption, that is, an opinion. Since the *yogins* are indeed realists and come to know the workings of the mind in fine detail, would it not be more reasonable to assume that they speak from experience? If they claim that there are deities, just as there are many subtle (normally invisible) levels of existence, they are not merely fantasizing. They encounter certain living qualities that their mind steeped in Hindu symbolism experiences in specific ways. The *yogins* know full well that they must go far beyond these deities, or angels. They must go beyond even Brahma in order to realize the essence of everything.

The *yogins* experience the universe quite differently from the ordinary person. Because Westerners basically believe in a "flat-land" universe—consisting only of matter—they have effectively banished all paranormal realities into oblivion. To put it starkly, Westerners would tend to see aliens and flying saucers, while other more traditionally-minded people would see living qualities like deities, or angels. (That is not to deny the idea of other biological life forms in the universe, some of whom may be in contact with Earth.)

19. Is it okay to charge for Yoga instruction? Should Yoga teachers not offer classes for free?

Yoga teachers, like other teachers, are professionals, and by and large they teach to make a living in addition to communicating useful knowledge or skills. To expect that they teach for free is not realistic in our society. Like everyone else, they have to pay for the studio space, take care of their rent or mortgage, make car payments, and put food on the table. Long ago, when Georg was first offering posture classes, he decided one day not to charge, assuming that students would make a donation "from the heart." This was not at all the case, and with having to travel from one end of London to the other, he sometimes was barely able to pay for the rented room. He stopped his unreasonable practice very quickly.

There is nothing wrong with charging for Yoga instruction. We would hope, however, that all Yoga centers have regular free classes for the financially stressed, and for the elderly and debilitated people. They will be grateful beneficiaries.

Understand that the contemporary Yoga movement is still "in the making," and has much to learn. With few exceptions, Yoga teachers need better training. Better training means acquiring a sturdy background in the spiritual teachings of Yoga. This often falls under the category of "philosophy" in Yoga teacher-training programs. Often this amounts to very little. In any case, Yoga philosophy without spirituality is meaningless. Some Yoga instructors confuse New Age thought with Yoga spirituality and we feel this could be remedied by ensuring Yoga teacher training have a stronger Yoga philosophy component. To address this issue, Georg wrote a Yoga philosophy teacher training manual which is being used in several countries around the world and Brenda offers an online Yoga philosophy program for students and teachers who feel they would like to learn a bit more about this important aspect of Yoga. Don't hesitate to quiz a Yoga teacher before signing on. We recommend you asking if they studied Yoga philosophy in their teacher training; if they are continuing their Yoga philosophy studies; and how they apply that wisdom in their classes. Spirituality is the alpha and omega of Yoga!

20. Recently I participated in a Yoga class in southern California. I was shocked to see women dressed in rather skimpy and provocative outfits. No one seemed to mind. Is this normal?

This may be acceptable to some, but it is definitely not acceptable from the perspective of traditional Yoga or even common sense. We guess that Yoga teachers are reluctant to demand respectable clothing in class because this might reduce attendance. Some studios have started to introduce a dress code, and no one seems to object. We think Yoga students, even if they are only interested in postural practice, should be obliged to wear a decent outfit to class, and also show respectful behavior otherwise. Yoga teachers, again, should not be afraid to set certain standards. The ethical guidelines we have drawn up, which are available for free at www.traditionalyogastudies.com, suggest such standards at least for Yoga teacher trainees.

In any case, when we participate in a Yoga class, we should use our attendance as an occasion to altogether transform our mindset, which includes our everyday behavior. Besides, we are not in a Yoga class to catch someone's eyes or to make a fashion statement, but simply to practice.

21. The Yoga studio that I normally go to is forever marketing Yoga products. In class, teachers recommend that everyone checks out the items available in the lobby, and whenever I arrive, the woman in the lobby always points out the latest gadgets. This is quite annoying, and I am loath to go there now even though the practice space is appealing. Any comments?

Western Yoga has become thoroughly commercialized, and Yoga is sold as a commodity along with Yoga-related gadgets. Some centers market aggressively, because there is money to be made. You are quite rightly put off by this. You can either express your feelings to the owner or simply choose to not buy into the commercialization and not purchase products from the studio.

22. I find it disturbing that so many studios play music during class. Who started this trend and how can one stop it?

We have no idea how playing music in a Yoga class became fashionable—and it *is* fashionable. Maybe this habit is a carryover from fitness classes, which is what Yoga is for many people. There is the lockstep kind of music, and then there is the dreamy stuff. It is definitely all distracting and defeats the purpose of traditional Yoga practice. Unfortunately, we don't think you or we can stop it, because too many people actually like being distracted that way. We recommend talking to the instructor or studio owner and asking if there is a class that is more suited to your needs.

23. Where can I find spiritually-based Yoga classes? I am at a loss.

Sadly, such classes are not common, and we can't make any recommendations. Often classes associated with an ashram (a traditional Yoga school) have a spiritual slant. But they may also tend toward the sectarian. Your best bet is to ask around. If you don't see the word "spiritual" or "transformative" in an ad, you may be less likely to find this approach when you go to the center.

24. I used to enjoy Partner Yoga. Then, when I relocated and had to go to a different center which did not offer Partner Yoga, I came to enjoy a more quiet, inward-looking Yoga practice. I am wondering whether I am becoming more self-centered?

Partner Yoga is a modern invention. Having observed classes in Partner Yoga, we know we could never go this way. Just because you prefer a more quiet Yoga practice now doesn't mean you are becoming self involved. Not at all. When you look at Patanjali's definition of posture, you will see that it is meant to be accompanied by relaxation and what he calls "coinciding with the infinite." This last qualification implies that one should practice posture with great mindfulness. Another way of speaking about this is "looking inward" and calmly observing what is going on in the body and mind. This does not seem to be a prominent feature in Partner Yoga.

We, too, enjoy a quiet posture practice. Partner Yoga can be quite distracting. Certainly, your mental focus is not on what is going on in your *own* body and mind. And, if you don't know or don't trust your partner, you may be worrying whether he or she will accidentally let go of you and cause an injury. Or you may worry that you might do the same to your partner when it is your turn to assist. Also mixed-gender Partner Yoga is unappealing for us because it involves close physical proximity, the kind you might normally have with a spouse. This can lead to flirting and more serious, if furtive, sexual fooling around. We cannot recommend Partner Yoga for all these reasons. It is not an aspect of traditional Yoga, which favors individual practice.

The question is always: What are we ourselves trying to accomplish? If we seek to grow spiritually, which is a perfectly legitimate goal, then we should look for classes that meet our inner need for quiet and focusing. Don't settle for less.

25. Where in India should I go to learn Yoga properly?

India, we are told, has become so Westernized that many Yoga classes in the cities are now as good or as bad as in the West. Georg never had to travel to the subcontinent, because his teachers always showed up where he happened to live and remained long enough for him to benefit from their teachings. (The only Indian teacher he ever wanted to meet was the great master Ramana Maharshi. He would have followed him anywhere, but Ramana had died in 1950, many years before Georg got to know about him. We both would also journey far afield for our present teacher. Although we don't see him often, we feel he is always somehow with us, and his benign presence in our life has put the capstone on the whole adventure of Yoga.)

"Proper" Yoga is spiritual Yoga. Teachers and schools exist, but they are, we would say, few and far between even in India, and we would not want to recommend specific ones. If you have the idea of studying Yoga directly from one of the "Himalayan" masters, you might be disappointed. Many genuine gurus are loath to take on Western disciples, who tend to be self-centered, anti-authoritarian, and insubordinate. And traditional gurus teach in a traditional way, which may rub a practitioner from our part of the world the wrong way.

If you want to learn posture practice, you might be better off with a Western teacher who knows the ins and outs of our Western lifestyle and therefore also our physical limitations. Again, you need to find out for yourself which "style" suits your needs best.

Most importantly, your guru will definitely find you when the time has come!

26. You and your wife have written two books called *Green Yoga* and *Green Dharma*. Have you any additional comments about Yoga's role in creating a healthier environment?

Green Yoga, which was published in 2007, provided an uncompromising overview of the problems with the ecosystem. We felt that people had been given bits and pieces and didn't have the larger picture. How else could one explain the almost universal indifference? Some readers were very upset with us, because of our head-on approach. Subsequently, we realized that this confrontation was not helpful and edited the book to offer readers a more user-friendly approach. In addition, we wrote, *Green Dharma*, about Buddhist Yoga vis-à-vis the environment, making essentially the same arguments. As of today, Green Dharma has been downloaded over 100,000 times, which is a respectable figure.

Since only a couple of hundred dollars were donated, we have had to begin charging a minute dollar amount for this and other "free" books, which every person with a computer can afford and which will reimburse us for the time invested in producing this book.

There is no question in our mind that Yoga (in whatever form) can play a major role in transforming our mind, including our current lackadaisical attitude toward the present-day environmental emergency. Yoga practitioners have traditionally been benignly disposed toward the environment, and their sparse lifestyle has been demonstrably conservative rather than consumerist. According to Yoga, we are here on Earth to realize our essence, not to ransack the precious resources we have at our disposal to survive at the physical level. We clearly must change our ways and adopt an environment-friendly outlook. At this late hour, we must make our lifestyle sustainable, which we realize is a tall but absolutely necessary order. All of us are actively harming Nature and our fellow beings by living more or less selfishly and consuming as if there is no tomorrow. (Well, at the present rate of consumption, there will be "no tomorrow" for us and most other life forms.)

Our two books—*Green Yoga* and *Green Dharma*—were intended as passionate pleas for everyone to accept responsibility as beings who *share* the same planet with a multitude of other beings. Those beings are our neighbours and have an equal right to live here. If we allow the extinction rate (now reckoned to be roughly 150 plant and animal *species* per day) to continue, our own species will blink out. Earth, biologists warn us, will be plunged back into the Cambrian era of 600-million years ago—an unthinkable prospect.

27. I heard in a seminar that the ego must be killed before enlightenment can happen. Is this true?

Some traditional teachers talk in this way. Our own view, which is also based on tradition, is that enlightenment occurs when the ego is transcended, or gone beyond, rather than killed, or destroyed, outright. Many traditions maintain that enlightenment is possible prior to death. If that's so—and, based on the testimony of numerous adepts—we believe it is, then we must also assume that the ego has to be present. Without an ego to navigate this body-mind, we would be a sorry sight indeed. We think we couldn't live without the ego-pilot. Of course, the ego of the enlightened master is a shadow of its former self. It has not an ounce of ego-tism left in it. Thoroughly transformed, it is stripped of all the stuff that makes the ordinary person tick. What a paradoxical but marvellous condition this is! We hope we all can reach it one day.

28. Why is it that we hear a lot about ancient male Yoga teachers who have written Sanskrit books but no woman teachers who are also authors?

Female Yoga teachers were by no means rare in earlier times; they just did not write texts like intellectually-minded teachers of the ilk of Patanjali, Vyasa, or Vidyaranya. Not that females were necessarily illiterate. They just did not feel the need to express their thoughts in writing, as did Lalla in the Kashmiri language during the Middle Ages. For the longest time, women were sought after as teachers—or gurus—notably in the Tantric tradition. They knew that spiritual transmission happened rarely through the medium of books. Much better for their disciples, we'd say!

29. How can I make posture practice a *spiritual* affair?

We'd say that it all depends on the context. If the context is spiritual, so will be your posture (*asana*) practice. This includes approaching the postures mindfully (that is, with awareness) and reasonably slowly. Don't just whip out your mat and get going. Center yourself first. Relaxation, at least at the end of a session, is important, too. And don't forget to sit quietly in meditation to conclude your session. Even five minutes of meditation will work miracles over time. It really doesn't matter that the mind is racing to begin with. Focus on the breath going in and out of your nose, or use whatever concentration technique works for you.

30. I have a Buddhist meditation practice and also do Hatha-Yoga postures occasionally. Do they conflict with each other?

Only you are able to answer this question. If you don't feel a conflict mixing traditions, you are fine. Buddhism has its own postural practices. They are more vigorous than the postures of Hindu Yoga, but this is not a problem in itself. Some systems, such as the *Kum Nye* postural system, draws from the training and experience of the Buddhist teacher Tarthang Tulku, and seems to connect students with that lineage in a more subtle way.

Please, don't just *do* the postures, as so many people say, but *practice* or *cultivate* them. In other words, take them seriously—as seriously as your meditation practice. Then they will work for you! We can wholeheartedly recommend the groundbreaking book *Mindfulness Yoga* by Frank Jude Boccio (Wisdom Publications, 2004) for which Georg wrote a foreword. Frank seeks to bridge the apparent gulf between Buddhism and the postures of Hatha-Yoga.

APPENDIXES

Appendix A: Guide to Sanskrit Pronunciation

Sanskrit is a difficult language to learn and one that, at least for most Westerners, is virtually impossible to master. The pronunciation of its rich vocabulary with its strange sounds is just as difficult. Scholars devised a variety of transliteration schemes to indicate the correct sound of each letter of the alphabet. Then, at a conference of Orientalists held in Athens in 1912, the Sanskrit transliteration was standardized and has been in use since.

We have not availed ourselves of the academic or even simplified transliteration of Sanskrit terms in the present book, which is intended for the complete novice. But in Georg's other books, he has used either full academic or simplified transliteration. The latter recognizes merely the long vowel sounds: ā, ī, and ū. You might bear this in mind. So, don't be surprised when you see *yoginī* (rather than simply *yogini*) or *āsana* (rather than simply *asana*) for a physical posture in some books.

All vowels are to be pronounced open, like in Italian or Latin. Thus, *yoga* is pronounced with an *o*, as in *short*. The commonly used word *cakra*, which means "wheel," is pronounced *tshakra* rather than *shakra*. The word *mandala*, or "circle," is pronounced with short *a*-sounds, and the emphasis is on the first syllable, not like *mandahla*, with a long middle *a* that is emphasized.

A common mispronunciation concerns the word *Hatha-Yoga*. The *th*-sound is not at all like the English *th* in *this* or *that*. Rather, all consonants followed by an *h* are to be pronounced distinctly as aspirates, as in *top-heavy*. Consequently, *Hatha* is properly pronounced at *Hat-ha* (whereby the first *a* is similar to the *a*-sound in *hut*, not as in *hand*). The common word *phala*, or "fruit," is pronounced *p-hala*, not *fala*, and *kapha* ("phlegm") is pronounced *kap-ha* and not *kafa*. These explanations should help you avoid the worst blunders.

Appendix B: What to Read and Study Next?

With an assortment of Georg's books on Yoga in print, many students are wondering just how to proceed most sensibly with studying his work. This appendix aims at answering the above question.

If you are unfamiliar with the philosophical and spiritual basis of Yoga, which is our primary concern, and are mainly interested in practicing the physical techniques, we suggest that you begin with *Yoga For Dummies Second Edition,* which is coauthored with California Yoga teacher Larry Payne. First published in 1999, this book has served more than 100,000 readers thus far.

When the original publisher (IDG Books) first invited Georg to write this book, he declined without any hesitation. He had his plate full, and he also felt neither interested nor particularly qualified to produce a popular work that would focus on postures. But, to her credit, the acquisitions editor at the time persisted and approached Georg twice more. He thought that her invitation deserved at least his genuine consideration, and it occurred to him that this book would give him an opportunity to at least briefly present the spiritual aspects of Yoga to a wide readership. So, in the end, he agreed to take on this project. He was able to enlist Larry Payne, who has taught the physical techniques over many years, as his collaborator.

In 2009, Larry and Georg were asked by the new publisher (Wiley) to revise the book. Although they both felt that, apart from some minor corrections, it was not in need of revision, they complied with the request. The second edition, published two years later, is again a reliable and easily understandable guide.

If you have read *Yoga For Dummies* and find yourself drawn to the philosophical-spiritual side of Yoga, we can next recommend that you start your further exploration with *The Teachings of Yoga*—an anthology published by Shambhala in 1997 or with *Gems of Yoga,* which is a similar book published by Bantam House in 2002. Alternatively, you might want to listen to Georg's CD

Yoga Wisdom or the CD set (of six CDs) entitled *The Lost Teachings of Yoga*, both published by Sounds True.

Next, at a slightly more demanding level, there is the book *The Path of Yoga* (formerly *The Shambhala Guide to Yoga*), published in a revised edition in 2011. You might then want to turn to *The Deeper Dimension of Yoga*, also released by Shambhala in 2003. This book contains seventy-eight essays, which are reasonably simple-to-understand. Which written over many years, they address a wide range of topics. Arranged in five parts, the essays gradually take you from simple, orienting materials—such as "What is Yoga?" and "Forty Types of Yoga"—to essays on spiritual practice, to considerations about the moral foundation of Yoga, more demanding treatments of the spectrum of Yoga practice, and, finally, to essays on the higher stages of Yoga, such as meditation, prayer, ecstasy, the enigmatic serpent-power (*kundalinī-shakti*), and spiritual liberation.

Yoga: The Deeper Dimension makes an excellent platform for delving into *The Yoga Tradition*, which is a large-size, illustrated volume of well over 500 pages with a foreword by Professor Subhash Kak. It has been called the "Yoga telephone book" by some students, and we can see why. It covers a huge territory and was designed to be used as a comprehensive (though by no means exhaustive) reference work. First published in 1998, this book grew out of Georg's *Yoga: The Technology of Ecstasy*, which is no longer in print. A revised and expanded edition of *The Yoga Tradition* was published in 2008. This volume consists of eighteen chapters arranged in four parts, and it includes his translation of several major Sanskrit texts on Yoga, notably Patanjali's *Yoga-Sutra*, as well as selections from other texts.

The *Yoga-Sutra* is an important text, and in the West is the most studied of all the Sanskrit works on Yoga. Georg translated this text twice: First in his book *The Yoga-Sūtra of Patañjali*, published in 1979 and reissued in 1989 by Inner Traditions, and second in his recent book *The Yoga-Sūtra: A Nondualist Interpretation*. Both works have been released as e-books in 2011 by Traditional Yoga Studies. The latter publication includes detailed grammatical information for those wishing to study this text in the original.

Those wishing to delve yet deeper into the ocean of Yoga may want to participate in Georg's 800-hour distance-learning course accompanying *The Yoga Tradition*. The course comprises nearly 1000 pages, which together with the book represents a small library of several volumes. Thus far, several hundred students from around the world have braved this course, and many have graduated with a certificate of completion. This course represents the culmination of Georg's publications that aim to give Yoga enthusiasts a thorough overview of the philosophy, history, and literature of Yoga covering a period of 5,000 years. We are constantly trying to make the study of this work more accessible, so that students can benefit from it spiritually.

Our other distance-learning courses, all written by Georg, go into more detail on certain aspects addressed in the 800-hour course. Thus, the 250-hour, 380-page course entitled *The Foundations of Yoga* deals with the materials found in Chapters 1–8 in his book *The Yoga Tradition*. There is also a 250-hour, 380-page course entitled *Classical Yoga*, which expands on Chapters 9 and 10, and is based on his translation of Patanjali`s text. The 125-hour, 305-page course entitled *The Bhagavad-Gītā* expands on his recent translation of, and commentary on, this widely read work, published in 2011 by Shambhala. Finally, a 250-hour course on the philosophy and theory of Hatha-Yoga is in preparation.

At some point along this route of self-study, students of Georg's work might want to acquire a copy of his *Encyclopedia of Yoga and Tantra*, which is the 2011 revised and expanded edition of his *Shambhala Encyclopedia of Yoga*. The new version contains well over 2,000 entries and should meet most readers' lexicographic needs or curiosity.

Among Georg's other significant works relating to Yoga, we can point to *The Philosophy of Classical Yoga*, which is an academic monograph on Patanjali`s system published by Manchester University Press (Great Britain) in 1980 and reissued by Inner Traditions (U.S.A.) without modifications in 1996. Then there is *Holy Madness*, published in a revised and expanded edition by Hohm Press in 2006. This book, which has a foreword by psychiatrist Prof. Roger Walsh, M.D., addresses the important subject of gurus and spiritual discipleship.

Next we must mention *Yoga Morality*, which is our favorite book. It confronts the most neglected area of Yoga, which is its ethics, and applies the moral principles to modern life. Finally, there is Georg's book *Tantra: The Art of Ecstasy*, which seeks to clarify this much-misinterpreted and complex tradition.

Of coauthored works, we are glad to mention *Green Yoga* and *Green Dharma* (with Brenda) and *In Search of the Cradle of Civilization* (with Subhash Kak and David Frawley). The former two volumes address pressing environmental issues, while the last-mentioned book looks at the early history of Yoga. We feel fortunate to have been able to produce the coauthored volumes together.

SELECT BIBLIOGRAPHY

For more titles by Georg Feuerstein, see Appendix B of this book.

Andrews, Cecile. *Slow Is Beautiful: New Visions of Community, Leisure and Joie de Vivre.* Gabriola Island, Canada: New Society Publishers, 2006.

Baur, Gene. *Farm Sanctuary: Changing Hearts and Minds about Animals and Food.* New York: Touchstone, 2008.

Benson, Herbert with Miriam Z. Klipper. *The Relaxation Response.* New York: Avon Books, 1975.

Boccio, Frank Jude. *Mindfulness Yoga: The Awakened Union of Breath, Body, and Mind.* Boston, Mass.: Wisdom Publications, 2004.

Cousens, Gabriel. *Conscious Eating.* Berkeley, Calif.: North Atlantic Books, 2000.

Craig, Mary. *Kundun: A Biography of the Family of the Dalai Lama.* Washington, D.C.: Counterpoint, 1997.

Dechanet, J. M. *Christian Yoga.* London: Search Press, 1973.

De Michelis, Elizabeth. *A History of Modern Yoga.* London: Continuum, 2004.

Dobson, Charles. *The Troublemaker's Teaparty: A Manual for Effective Citizen Action.* Gabriola Island. B.C.: New Society Publishers, 2001.

Feuerstein, Brenda. *The Yoga-Sūtra from a Woman's Perspective.* Eastend, Canada: Traditional Yoga Studies, 2011. (E-book)
_____, Brenda. *Yoga Sleep (Yoga-Nidrā).* Eastend, Canada: Traditional Yoga Studies, 2011. (CD)

Feuerstein, Georg. *The Lost Teachings of Yoga*. Boulder, Colo.: Sounds True, 2002. (set of 6 CDs)

_____ and Brenda Feuerstein. *Green Dharma*. Eastend, Canada: Traditional Yoga Studies, 2009.

_____ and Brenda Feuerstein. *Green Yoga*. Eastend, Canada: Traditional Yoga Studies, 2007.

Goodall, Jane. *Harvest of Hope: A Guide to Mindful Eating*. New York: Wellness Central/Hatchette, 2006.

Iyengar, B. K. S. *The Tree of Yoga*. Boston, Mass.: Shambhala Publications, 1989.

Lasater, Judith. *Living Your Yoga: Finding the Spiritual in Everyday Life*. Berkeley, Calif.: Rodmell Press, 2000.

Lommel, Pim van. *Consciousness Beyond Life: The Science of the Near-Death Experience*. New York: HarperCollins, 2010.

Merkel, Jim. *Radical Simplicity: Small Footprints on a Finite Earth*. Gabriola Island, Canada: New Society Publishers, 2003.

Murphy, Michael. *The Future of the Body: Exploration into the Further Evolution of Human Nature*. Los Angeles: J. P. Tarcher, 1992.

Nagapriya. *Exploring Karma & Rebirth*. Birmingham, England: Windhorse Publications, 2004.

Robbins, John. *A Diet for New America*. Tiberon, Calif.: H. J. Kramer, repr. 1998.

Schweitzer, Albert. *The Teaching for Reverence for Life*. New York: Holt, Rinehart and Winston, 1965.

Sivananda, Swami. *All About Hinduism*. Shivanandanagar, India: Divine Life Society, 1965.

Suzuki, David and Holly Dressel. *Good News for a Change: How Everyday People are Helping the Planet*. Vancouver, British Columbia: Greystone Books, 2003.

Tart, Charles T. *Waking Up: Overcoming the Obstacles to Human Potential*. Boston, Mass.: Shambhala Publications, 1986.

Terhune, Lea. *Karmapa: The Politics of Reincarnation*. Boston, Mass.: Wisdom Publications, 2004.

Walsh, Roger. *Staying Alive: The Psychology of Human Survival*. Boulder, Co. and London: New Science Library/ Shambhala, 1984.

_____ and Frances Vaughan, eds. *Paths Beyond Ego.* Los Angeles: Jeremy Tarcher/Perigee, 1993.

Weber, Karl, ed. *Food, Inc.:* New York: PublicAffairs, 2009.

White, John, ed. *What Is Meditation?* Garden City, N.Y.: Doubleday/Anchor Original, 1974.

ESSENTIAL SANSKRIT GLOSSARY

Most Hindu Yoga texts are written in Sanskrit, but also in Tamil and various vernacular Indian languages, such as Bengali and Gujarati. To follow conversations at Yoga studios, you need to know some Sanskrit words. The following list probably includes more words than you will hear. For a full dictionary, please consult Georg's *Encyclopedia of Yoga and Tantra* (revised and enl. ed. 2011).

Abhyasa – lit. "repetition," practice

Acarya – preceptor

Adhyatma-Yoga – Yoga of the inner self

Advaita Vedanta – the philosophical system of radical non-dualism, usually associated with the name of the great teacher **Shankara.**

Aghori – member of an extremist Tantric sect, which was made famous by author and practitioner Robert Svoboda in his trilogy.

Aham brahmasmi – "I am the Absolute" (*aham + brahma + asmi*); a classic saying of Vedanta

Ahamkara – lit. "I-maker"; the ego

Ahimsa – non-violence, or non-harming; a cardinal virtue of Yoga practitioners; one of the first **yamas**

Akasha – space, or ether; as in "akashic record"

Amrita – nectar, also immortality

Anahata-cakra – the **cakra** of the "unstruck" (*anahata*) sound at the heart

Ananda – bliss

Anga – lit. "limb"; a category of the yogic path; thus, **Patanjali** distinguishes eight members

Anjali-mudra – the gesture of placing the palms of the hands together in front of the heart in order to salute or simply greet someone

Asamprajnata-samadhi – lit. "supraconscious ecstasy"; the highest form of ecstasy in the eightfold path of **Patanjali;** the equivalent of **nirvikalpa-samadhi**

Asana – lit. "seat"; a yogic posture, or pose; There are too many *asanas* to list them here individually.

Ashrama – often pronounced **ashram**; a hermitage or, nowadays, a school of Yoga

Ashtanga-Yoga – a modern style of Hatha-Yoga; another name of **Patanjali**'s Classical Yoga of eight limbs

Atman – the transcendental Self

AUM – another way of writing *om.*

Bandha – lit. "bondage," or "lock"; in the latter sense, the word refers to a threefold technique by which the breath is stopped within the body

Bhagavad-Gita – lit. "Lord's Song"; this is a widely read Yoga text

Bhakti – lit. "devotion," especially between Krishna and his devotees; hence Bhakti-Yoga

Bhastrika – one of the breathing techniques of Hatha-Yoga

Bija (bija) – lit. "seed"; sometimes precedes the word **mantra**

Brahmacarya – lit. "brahmic conduct"; the discipline of chastity

Brahman – the Absolute, often understood as the Divine in impersonal form; the transcendental core of the world, which is identical with the **atman**

Brahmana – a Hindu belonging to the priestly class

Buddhi – the higher, intuitive mind, as opposed to reason

Cakra – lit "wheel"; often spelled *chakra* and mispronounced *shakra;* Hindu Yoga knows of a series of seven cakras; Buddhist Yoga knows five

Candra – the moon; also the internal structure that oozes the nectar of immortality

Citta – the mind

Dana – generosity, gift; usually, an offering to the teacher in addition to whatever fee is charged

Deva – God, godling; in the latter sense, a *deva* has the function of an angel

Devi – the Mother Goddess, such as **Kali**

Dharma – virtue, righteousness; quality, also teaching

Dhyana – meditation; often mispronounced *diana*

Drishti – "view" or "gaze"; a way of gazing during meditation

Gayatri – a famous **mantra** of Hinduism

Gheranda-Samhita – lit. "Gheranda's Collection;" one of three major texts of traditional Hatha-Yoga

Goraksha – lit. "cow protector," but this name is likely to mean "someone who keeps his tongue"; the founder of Hatha-Yoga

Guna – lit. "strand" or "quality"; in Hindu Yoga and Samkhya, one of three fundamental constituents of the cosmos: *sattva*, *rajas*, and *tamas*

Guru – lit. "heavy" or "weighty"; a spiritual teacher

Hatha – lit. force; this word is frequently mispronounced with the English *th* instead of the Sanskrit aspirated sound *t-h;* esoterically, it signifies but does not literally mean "sun and moon" whereby *ha* stands for the sun and *tha* for the moon

Hatha-Yoga – the Yoga of physical transformation consisting esoterically in the union of sun and moon

Hatha-Yoga-Pradipika – lit. "Light on the Forceful Yoga"; one of three classic Sanskrit texts on Hatha-Yoga

Ida or **ida-nadi** – lit. "channel of comfort"; the conduit of the life force that proceeds through the left nasal passage; cf. **pingala**

Ishvara – lit. "the lord"; God

Jalandhara – one of the three **bandha**s

Japa – recitation of a **mantra**, often with a rosary

Jiva – psyche, or soul

Jnana – knowledge, wisdom

Kali – lit. "she who impels"; a form of the Goddess

Kali-yuga – the present dark era; the word *kali* is not related to the name of the Goddess

Karma – lit. "action"; the stem of the word is *karman;* it can stand for either "activity" or "destiny"

Kula – lit. "family"

Kirtana – lit. "chanting"; the common practice of singing songs of praise

Klesha – lit. "trouble"; according to **Patanjali,** the *kleshas* are the root of the karmic legacy deep within the mind

Krishna – lit. "puller"; one of the incarnations of the Divine in Vaishnavism

Kriya – lit. "action" or "ritual"; also an involuntary body movement in **Kundalini-Yoga**

Kumbhaka – lit. "potlike"; retention of the breath

Kundalini or **kundalini-shakti** – lit. "coiled power"; the psychospiritual energy residing in potential form in the lowest **cakra**

Kundalini-Yoga – the practice of awakening the **kundalini** and guiding it to the topmost **cakra** at the crown of the head

Lakshmi – a name of the Goddess

Linga – lit. "mark" or "sign"; phallus; the creative sign of **Shiva**

Maithuna – lit. "twinning"; sacred sexual intercourse in Tantra

Manas – the lower mind, reasoning

Mandala – lit. "circle"; a geometric design for focusing the mind

Mantra – a potent sound

Maya – lit. "she who measures"; illusion

Moksha – lit. "liberation"; spiritual freedom, or enlightenment

Mudra – lit. "seal"; a hand gesture or bodily pose similar to **asana**

Mukti – lit. "release"; the same as **moksha**

Nada – the subtle inner sound

Nadi – lit. "conduit"; a subtle channel through or along which the life force (**prana**) travels

Nauli – lit. "rolling"; a technique of **Hatha-Yoga** by which the abdominal muscles are rotated for intestinal cleansing

Neti – one of the cleansing techniques of **Hatha-Yoga** in which water is sucked up the nose, or which uses a thin thread for this purpose

Nidra – sleep; cf. **yoga-nidra**

Nirodha – the control of the mind

Nirvana – lit. "windstill"; the state of enlightenment in which all desires are gone beyond

Nirvikalpa-samadhi – the higher form of ecstasy in which there is no mental activity; cf. **samadhi**

Paramahansa or -**hamsa** – lit. "supreme swan"; the highest type of an ascetic, who has utterly renounced the world

Patanjali – the presumed author of the *Yoga-Sutra*

Pingala or **pingala-nadi** – the conduit of the life force that proceeds through the right nasal passage; cf. **ida**

Prakriti – lit. "creatrix"; in Classical Yoga and Samkhya, the entire cosmos, as opposed to Spirit (i.e., **purusha**)

Prana – the life force inside and outside the body

Pranayama – lit. "lengthening of the breath"; yogic breath control

Purusha – lit. "man"; in Classical Yoga and Samkhya, the Spirit or transcendental Self

Raja-Yoga – lit. "royal Yoga"; the eightfold path of **Patanjali**

Rishi – lit. "seer"; the title of an advanced **yogin**

Sad-Guru – a true teacher, who has attained enlightenment

Samadhi – ecstasy; the last limb of the eightfold path of **Patanjali**; cf. **asamprajnata-samadhi**

Samatva or **samata** – lit. "sameness"; equanimity

Samkalpa – lit. "intention"; the intention set at the beginning of **yoga-nidra**

Samkhya – a cousin of the Yoga tradition

Samsara – lit. "flow"; cyclic existence, the ordinary world

Samskara – lit. "activator"; an unconscious karmic imprint, which resides in the depths of the mind

Samyama – lit. "constraint"; the practice of concentration, meditation, and ecstasy in regard to the same mental object

Satya – lit. "truthfulness"; one of the moral disciplines of Yoga

Samprajnata-samadhi – lit. "conscious ecstasy"; the lower form of ecstasy; cf. **nirvikalpa-samadhi**

Seva – lit. "service"; unselfish service for the teacher or hermitage

Shakti – lit. "power"; generally, the **kundalini**

Shankara – a celebrated teacher of **Advaita Vedanta;** often called Shankaracarya (from Shankara + acarya)

Shanti – lit. "peace"

Shankara – the main preceptor of nondualism (Advaita Vedanta)

Shiva – a name of God

Shiva-Samhita – one of the three classic texts of **Hatha-Yoga**

Siddha – lit. "accomplished one"; an adept

Siddhi – lit. "power" or "accomplishment"; a paranormal ability

Surya – the sun

Surya-Namaskara – lit. "saluting the sun"; an exercise series apparently invented in modern times

Sutra – lit. "aphorism"; a concise statement, as in the *Yoga-Sutra*

Svamin – lit. "ruler" or "lord"; the spiritual title *swami*

Tantra – lit. "loom"; a particular spiritual tradition or the main texts used by it

Trataka – a technique in **Hatha-Yoga** by which one relaxedly gazes at a flame of light

Upanishads – lit. "sitting near"; category of works teaching **Vedanta**

Vedanta – lit. "Veda's end; the teaching of the *Upanishads*

Viveka – lit. "discernment"; a central practice of Yoga, which seeks to distinguish between the real (i.e. the Self) and the unreal (i.e. the cosmos)

Vritti – lit. "whirl"; one of the main activities of the mind, according to **Patanjali**

Yama – moral discipline, according to **Patanjali**

Yantra – lit. "device"; a geometric design similar to the **mandala,** which is used for concentration

Yoga-nidra – lit. "Yoga sleep," a deep relaxation technique involving auto-suggestion

There are too many *asanas* to list them here individually.

INDEX

A
Absolute, 77. *See also brahman*
adepts, 9, 84
ahimsa, 19
alchemy: Yoga as, 25
Amrita-Bindu-Upanishad, 35
asana,18, 21, 85, 89. *See also* postures
asceticism, 21
atheism, 75
atman, 28
attention, 22, 34, 48, 61
aum. See om
awakening: of *kundalini* 26, 42

B
Bhagavad-Gita, 7, 30, 32, 41, 54, 56, 72, 92, 115
Bhagavata-Purana, 32
bhakti, 32
Bhakti-Sutras, 32
Bhakti-Yoga, 4-5, 32, 33, 67, 77
Boccio, Frank Jude, 85
body: discipline, 21, 43; and upon enlightenment, 43, 44; and food, 61; and Hatha-Yoga, 24, 25; improvement, xiii, 3, 8; and in Karma-Yoga, 30; and liberation, 63; and mindfulness, 81; and in religio-spiritual traditions, 25; and Self, 53; and suffering, 15, 16
bondage, 9, 35, 43

Brahma, 28, 77-78
brahman, 28, 77
branches: of Yoga, 4-5, 14
breath, breathing, 21, 26, 34, 46, 85
breath control: *See pranayama*
Buddhism, 4, 21, 31, 69, 85

C
cakras, 25, 89
chastity, 19-20
Christianity, 25, 32, 67-69
Classical-Yoga, 92. *See also* Raja-Yoga
concentration, 22, 25, 28, 34, 85; *See also dharana*
consciousness, 25, 27, 32, 35, 36, 40, 56
contentment, 10, 21
Cousens, Dr. Gabriel, 61

D
death, 15, 30, 41, 63, 77, 84
deity, 32-33, 77-78
de Michelis, Elizabeth, xiii
depression, 46-47
desire, 11, 44, 48, 49, 52
devotion, 21, 32-33, 67
dharana, 18, 22
dhyana, 18, 22; *See also* meditation.
diet, 24, 46, 61-62, 67, 71
discernment, 13, 28, 31, 47, 64
disciple, 39-42, 44, 49-52, 64, 74-75, 82, 92
discipline: moral, 18-20. *See also yama*
Divine, 32
doubt, 15, 45
dualism, 36

E
eating, 30, 61, 71. *See also* diet.
ecstasy, 22-23, 25, 34, 56, 64, 72, 91. *See also samadhi.*

K

L

M

N

O

P

pain, 15-18, 43
Patanjali, 18-23, 59, 81, 84. *See also Yoga-Sutra*
Payne, Larry, 90
perception, 8
pleasure, 10,46
postures, xiii, xiv, 3, 18, 23-24, 39, 67-70, 85, 90
pranayama, 18, 21
prayer, 77, 91
purification, 12, 21, 24
purity, 21

R

Raja-Yoga, 4-5, 18-24
Rama, 32
Ramana Maharshi, 41, 82
Ramalinga, Swami, 25
reality, 5, 8,9 , 27, 32, 34, 36, 41, 43, 78
recitation, 5, 32, 34, 37
relaxation, xiii, 67, 69, 72, 81, 85
religion, 3, 4, 18, 67-68, 75
renunciation, 28
ritual, 4, 5, 34, 36
Robbins, John, 61

S

samadhi, 18, 22
sangha, 51-52
seals, 24
Self, 27, 28, 36, 45-47, 52-54, 57-58, 63, 64
Self-realization, 42, 44, 46, 47, 53-54, 57-58, 63, 75, 77. *See also*
        enlightenment; liberation
self-restraint, 21
self-transcendence, 53-54
sense withdrawal, 22
sexuality, 37
Shaivism, 68

Shiva, 32, 34, 68
shraddha, 45
sound, 34-35
spirituality: defined, 3; and Yoga, 5, 12, 60, 68, 71, 79
suffering, 10, 14-17, 31, 45-46, 54
study, 68, 71, 82, 90-92

T
tamas, 102
Tantra-Yoga, 4-5, 36-37, 68
Tarthang Tulku, 85
teachers, 38-39, 52, 59, 74, 78-80, 84. *See also guru*
theft, 20
transference, 42
Transmission: spiritual, 32, 84
truthfulness, 19-20, 59

U
unconscious, 34, 57, 78

V
Vaishnavism, 68
Vedanta, 27-28, 69
Vedanta-Sara, 28
vegetarianism, 24, 61, 71
Vidyaranya, 84
Vishnu, 32, 68
visualization, 5, 25
Vivekananda, Swami, xiii
Vyasa, 84

W
Walsh, M.D., Roger, 92
Weber, Karl, 61
Weintraub, Amy, 46
wisdom, xiv, 9, 27-29, 42, 45, 56-58

Y

yama, 18-20

Yoga: as alchemy, 27; and defined, xiii-xiv, 3-6; and Buddhism, 4, 5; eightfold,18-21, 24; and Hinduism, 4, 37, 68; and Jainism, 4; and modern, xiv, 6, 18, 59-60; and religion, 3-4, 18, 67; and Shaivism, 68; and spirituality, 5, 12, 60, 71, 79; and Vaishnavism, 68

Yoga-Sutra, 5, 7, 18-20, 91

yogin, definition, xiv

yogini, definition, xiv

ABOUT THE AUTHORS

Georg Feuerstein, Ph.D. is a leading voice in the dialogue between East and West and has authored over fifty books, many on Yoga. Among his more important works are *The Yoga Tradition, Encyclopedia of Yoga and Tantra, Tantra: The Path of Ecstasy, The Deeper Dimension of Yoga, The Yoga-Sūtra: A New Translation,* and *Yoga For Dummies* (with Larry Payne).

Georg lived a profoundly productive life of humble service and made a peaceful, conscious exit from this world on Saturday, August 25, 2012 near his home in Southern Saskatchewan. His final transition occurred after a nine-day journey of loving resolution in which he was surrounded and supported by his wife Brenda and many spiritual friends.

His legacy of scholarly contribution to the global Yoga community is vast and awe inspiring, to which we all owe a huge debt of gratitude. His work will be lovingly continued and directed by his spiritual partner, lover, friend and wife, Brenda Feuerstein.

If you wish to express your gratitude with a financial contribution, a scholarship fund to support incarcerated practitioners is being created in Georg's honor. **Please visit our website for more details: www.traditionalyogastudies.com**

Brenda Feuerstein has taught Yoga from a spiritual perspective for many years. She is a former music teacher, and health and fitness consultant. She is the author of *The Yoga-Sūtra from a Woman's Perspective* and has coauthored with her husband Georg: *Green Yoga, Green Dharma, The Bhagavad-Gītā: A New Translation.* She is the Director of Traditional Yoga Studies and maintains the position of distance learning course tutor, mentor and teaches workshops, trainings and lectures worldwide.

ABOUT HOHM PRESS

HOHM PRESS is committed to publishing books that provide readers with alternatives to the materialistic values of the current culture, and promote self-awareness, the recognition of interdependence, and compassion. Our subject areas include parenting, transpersonal psychology, religious studies, women's studies, the arts and poetry.

Contact Information: Hohm Press, PO Box 4410, Chino Valley, Arizona, 86323; USA; 800-381-2700, or 928-636-3331; email: hppublisher@cableone.net

Visit our website at www.hohmpress.com